"Mickey, what is it?" Daniel shouted. "I can hardly hear you. Take who? Are you all right?" Jesus Christ, of *course* she wasn't all right! Germany had invaded France.

The telephone stabilized, and he heard Mickey's remembered voice clearly. "You must get Philippe safely to his father."

Daniel's eyes grew wild when he realized the line had gone dead. Desperately he jiggled the hook and tried dialing the operator. But it was no use. He stomped around the room trying to make sense of the phone call. Mickey, after all these years. Memories flooded his brain. She needed him; she wanted him in France. Him and not Reuben. Why? And who the hell was Philippe? "Take Philippe to his father," she'd said. Great. But who was Philippe's father?

Praise for Fern Michaels
and
SINS OF OMISSION

"An in-depth study of relationships with well-drawn characters...A beautifully executed work from the bold pen of Fern Michaels!"

Affairs de Coeur

D0038062

Also by Fern Michaels
Published by Ballantine Books:

ALL SHE CAN BE
CINDERS TO SATIN
FREE SPIRIT
TENDER WARRIOR
TO TASTE THE WINE
VIXEN IN VELVET
VALENTINA

THE CAPTIVE SERIES

CAPTIVE EMBRACES
CAPTIVE INNOCENCE
CAPTIVE PASSIONS
CAPTIVE SPLENDORS

THE TEXAS TRILOGY

TEXAS HEAT
TEXAS RICH
TEXAS FURY

THE ''SINS'' SERIES

SINS OF OMISSION

SINS
OF
THE FLESH

Fern Michaels

BALLANTINE BOOKS • NEW YORK

Library of Congress Catalog Card Number: 90-92912

ISBN 0-345-34122-8

Manufactured in the United States of America

First Edition: June 1990

Pearls on the cover are courtesy of H. Stern, Jewelers, Inc.

This book is dedicated to the many wonderful people who have touched and enriched my life.

F.M.

Prologue

Paris, France 1941

MARCHIONESS MICHELENE FONSARD SLIPPED HER DUSTY OLD spectacles over the bridge of her nose. She rarely wore the wire-rimmed glasses because she felt they made her look like an owl. Now she wished that she'd kept them clean and polished, for if ever there was a time for good eyesight, this was it. But at least they would serve her immediate purpose of hiding her fear from her son, Philippe, and her best friend, Yvette.

Philippe watched as his mother swiped at her glasses as she peered through the lacy curtains of the Paris town house. He knew what lay beyond the window: the German Gestapo marching up and down the street, tacking occupancy notices on all the doors. His eyes slid to the thick packet of papers and the worn knapsacks in the center of the foyer table. He hated the sounds of the stomping boots, but what he hated even more was the sight of his mother's political friends licking those same stomping boots. Thank God she'd had the good sense to secure their travel warrants before the Germans showed their true colors.

The lace curtain slipped back into place. "Now," she whispered, "wait for me by the back door. I must try one more time to reach . . . stay with him, Yvette." Mickey sprinted up the long flight of stairs and snatched the phone from its cradle. Winded, she cleared her throat and dialed the number, preparing herself to speak calmly. The sounds that emerged a moment later from her quivering lips were harsh, guttural—the German words she'd been practicing all day: *Herr Kommandant*. These were magic words, she realized within seconds. She wished she'd thought of using the title on her last six unsuccessful tries at reaching Daniel Bishop in America.

Wait, wait, wait. . . . That's all they'd been doing for weeks now, hoping against hope that some miracle would remove the hateful Germans from their beloved Paris. She knew it was too late, had known it weeks before, but Philippe wanted to stay, and against her better judgment she'd agreed. If only she'd listened to her own instincts instead of giving in to her son, Henri would still be alive. Now she swayed dizzily as she heard the French operator speak to the American operator. A familiar voice—a voice from her past—came on the line, and Mickey thought she would die when she heard it. She spoke rapidly in English, knowing the line would be cut as soon as the French operator realized that she'd been tricked into putting the call through. Seconds later Mickey stared at the buzzing receiver in her hands. It looked obscene, deadly. She slammed it down and raced from the room, arriving in the kitchen breathless.

"I got through this time," she whispered to Yvette. "We were cut off. Thirty minutes and there will be more Gestapo here when they realize this is where the call came from. Go, go!" She turned to her son and waved him out of the room. "We have only minutes. Hurry, Philippe."

Silently, like thieves in the night, the trio traveled the back alleys of Paris until just before dawn, at which point they scuttled like rats into drainage ditches to sleep for a few hours.

Their destination was the Fonsard château in Marseilles, where they would wait for the American, Daniel Bishop.

Before she reached out to sleep, Mickey crossed herself and offered up a small prayer. "Please, dear Lord, grant this miracle I ask of You, not for myself, but for Philippe. Daniel must reach here safely so he can take Philippe to America, to his . . . to his mother and father."

Chapter One

THE NIGHT WAS WOMBLIKE WITH A DENSE, CLOUDY SKY hanging overhead as if suspended. Threatening, low-rolling thunder grumbled from its midst, setting Daniel Bishop's teeth on edge. All day he'd been jittery as he ambled aimlessly around his luxurious Fire Island summer home. He knew the condition of his nerves had nothing to do with the impending summer storm. His less than happy marriage was part of it, but not the only reason for his restlessness. There was something more, something lurking just out of reach, something intangible—his sixth sense issuing a dull warning. For as far back as he could remember, he'd had these feelings of foreboding, the inexplicable conviction that something was going to happen. These were free-floating, anxious feelings, ominous and hungry, as though wanting to be fed. Fed with . . . what was it this time?

Daniel opened the sliding doors impatiently. Although he could hear the ocean slapping rhythmically just a few yards away, the heat of the night was oppressive. His shirt clung to him, and everything he touched was damp. Maybe the heat had something to do with his feelings. He watched as if in a trance as lightning skittered across the sky. An appropriate end to a boring Fourth of July, he thought morosely. He was so keyed up right now, he was capable of creating his own fire-works. Rajean had cajoled him into coming to their summer place, insisting they both needed to get away from the bustle of Washington, D.C.

"Everyone leaves the city, darling," she'd repeated at least a hundred times. "It will be good for Cornelia. We can spend time together and not even plan out our holiday. Sort of leave it all open, maybe even picnic."

Daniel laughed to himself with disgust. *Picnic* was an alluring term—but *forage* was about as close as he could get to the reality. The only thing left in the kitchen remotely resembling food was a stale, damp bag of pretzels.

He peeled his shirt away from his chest. When he let go, it restuck itself to his skin with perverse tenacity. Maybe he should go for a swim. Out of the corner of his eye he caught sight of another split-second bolt of lightning racing down into the Atlantic. No, swimming is not an option, he told himself. A drink, then. Alcohol was the one thing they always had plenty of. He'd never been more than a social drinker, preferring to keep his wits about him. He supposed it was the lawyer in him. They were so different, he and Rajean. Like night and day, Reuben would say, and Reuben should know. Not only had they been best friends forever, but Reuben was married to someone just like Rajean. Reuben . . . Always the voice of authority and experience. Perhaps he should have paid more attention when Reuben had advised against his marrying Rajean—but then, Reuben had ignored *him* when he'd issued the same advice about Bebe Rosen. A pity neither of them had corrected their mistakes early. A divorce didn't make one a pariah anymore, and he should know; in his day he'd handled plenty of top-drawer divorces, some full of scandal and all full of bullshit.

He'd seen his wife exactly twice during the past four days. Once she'd waltzed through the beach house to change her clothes for an afternoon cocktail party. The next time she'd put in an appearance, it was to replenish someone's dwindling liquor supply. He hadn't seen much of Cornelia, either, but at least his stepdaughter called and breezed through every few hours. A smile tugged at the corners of his mouth at the thought of her . . . sweet Nellie with the sunstreaked golden hair and bottle green eyes.

In his thoughts Nellie was always the young innocent, shy and ever so considerate. He loved her as though she were his own, and the moment he'd signed the adoption papers she truly had become his own. She was eighteen now and in September would head for California and UCLA. He was going to miss her terribly. She was as pretty as a picture, he mused, and the one thing he could never understand was why she didn't have more friends. Every so often a horde of young people would descend upon the household for a few weeks, and then they would disappear, to be replaced months later with new faces. Once he'd asked her why she didn't seem to have any one-on-one friendships. She'd responded blithely that she didn't need them; she was her own best friend, she said, and would never disappoint herself the way friends did. She dated, and boys called, but he never saw the same one more than three times. After a while he didn't mention it. If Nellie was happy, that was all that mattered.

Nellie was late getting started in college because of an emergency appendectomy that had kept her out of school the better part of a semester. The nuns at Holy Cross felt it would be better if she stayed back a year, and he'd agreed. Now he frowned, trying to remember something one of the nuns had said about Nellie, something so totally out of character, he'd dismissed it—out of character for Nellie, that is. Nuns didn't always know as much as they pretended to. Whatever it had been, it was so ridiculous that he'd shelved it, and now it wouldn't surface.

Daniel raked unsteady fingers through his sandy hair, his deep brown eyes narrowing behind his horn-rimmed glasses. Jesus, he hated humidity. He'd been thinking about Rajean before Nellie popped into his thoughts, or was it after? Christ, he couldn't get a clear thought in his head these days no matter what he did. When Nellie left for college he was going to have to decide what to do about his empty marriage.

He leaned on the terrace railing and gazed out toward the sea. He could hear it, but it was shrouded by the night. The slight breeze was hot and stifling. Thunder growled. In the orphanage where he'd spent his youth, the nuns had called it God's wrath. At an age when they were still convinced the world revolved around them, he and his friend Jake would always run and hide, certain they'd done something wrong for God to create such a tempest. He'd been fourteen before he realized, along with Jake, that it was all a trick by the nuns to get them to behave. He smiled, wondering where Jake could be now. Someday he'd run into him, he was sure of it. Hell, he had enough money to hire a detective to track him down if he wanted to. Someday . . .

The usual evening sounds silenced suddenly, as though they'd scrambled into hiding. It was an eerie feeling, one Daniel didn't like. The sky, which seemed to be hovering just beyond his reach, grew as dark as his thoughts. Within a few steps he was at the door, sliding it surely on its track and stepping safely inside. From there he watched his own reflection in the glass as the first drops of rain splattered onto the flagstone terrace.

Daniel threw himself onto the sofa and tried to relax. It didn't take him long to realize that the drumming rain wouldn't lull him into the peace of mind he so desperately sought. Instead he felt even more tense, ready to burst. Somewhere, someplace, something was wrong. Reuben . . . he should call Reuben and see if all was well with Hollywood's biggest mogul. And he should make the call now, before the telephone lines went down the way they usually did during a storm.

Daniel groped for the telephone and was relieved to hear the dial tone buzz in his ears. He could almost picture a little old lady crawling out of bed and cursing as she shuffled in bare feet to her switchboard. He rattled off Reuben's number when the operator came on, then waited. Would Reuben be home at nine o'clock on the Fourth of July? It didn't matter; he knew Reuben's haunts and habits as well as his own. One way or another he'd find him.

"Reuben, is that you?" Daniel spoke rapidly into the phone as soon as he heard his friend's voice. "I was hoping I'd catch you home. How's it going, old buddy?"

Reuben's voice boomed over the wire. "It's going, but that's about it. How are you?"

"Great," Daniel said lightly.

"I was sort of hoping you'd make it out here in April. I know, I know, law and order and all that shit. Read about you in *The Wall Street Journal*. Big man in Washington," Reuben teased. Then his voice turned serious. "I heard about the offer to serve on the White House legal staff. Why'd you turn it down?"

"Crooked politicians aren't my cup of tea, Reuben. You know that. And I use the word *crooked* loosely. It's all a game, anyhow. It's called *Cover Your Ass*, and by that I mean if I took the position, that's all I would be doing, covering someone else's ass. That's not why I went to law school, and I'll cover my own ass, thank you." Both men laughed. "I'm doing just fine," Daniel continued, "two full partners, three junior partners, and six associates. We're turning business away. But enough of that. How's Bebe?"

"Off on a toot somewhere. She hasn't been home in three weeks."

Daniel digested his friend's statement. Even though it was said with no real emotion, he wasn't going to touch it. "And the boys?"

"Simon's up at Big Sur working for the summer. Dillon's in camp." Daniel couldn't help but hear the pride in Reuben's voice.

"Jesus, I miss you, Dan'l."

"You know, Reuben," Daniel admonished gently, "planes travel both ways. You could come east to see me. If I remember correctly, I made the last trip."

"I know. I've been thinking about it and halfway promised myself I'd make the trip in August. How's Nellie?" he asked fondly.

"All grown up. Starting college in September. She always tells me to send her regards when I speak to you. I'm going to hold you to it, Reuben."

Reuben laughed. Christ, he loved Daniel! He loved him and knew him so well that he was aware something was wrong— something Daniel wasn't telling him. "Why don't you let me know the real reason for your call now, and let's see if we can fix it together." He heard Daniel's sigh of relief. "Is it Rajean?" he asked.

"It's a lot of things, Reuben. Today was . . . is . . . I have this feeling. This . . . I don't know what it is, but something is wrong somewhere . . . you know how I get . . ."

Instantly Reuben became more attentive. Over the years Daniel's hunches and gut feelings had been beacons of light, highlighting problems before they erupted fully. The Depression had been one of them. Without Daniel's insight, Reuben and his close associates would have been wiped out like countless others during the crash of 1929.

"Jesus. Maybe it's the war . . . I can't put my finger on it." Daniel heaved another sigh. "Anyway, I had to call to see if everything was all right with *you*."

Reuben's voice softened. "I appreciate that, buddy, but I'm okay and so is the family. The war is hanging over all of us. . . ."

Daniel understood what Reuben meant without having to

hear the words. Although they had talked about the war and how it was affecting France, they had never mentioned their time there, never spoken *her* name aloud—she was always synonymous with their worries about the war raging its way through Europe.

"I hear a storm in the background, maybe that's what it is," Reuben offered gently. "You always hated storms." He couldn't think of anything else to say. "Daniel, if there's anything I can do . . . if you need me, I can be on the first plane tomorrow."

"I know that, and it's not necessary. I'm sure it's a combination of a lot of things. As long as you're all right, I'll turn in now. It was good talking to you, Reuben. Let's do it more often."

"Daniel," Reuben said simply, "I talk to you every day in my thoughts. Sleep well."

"You, too. Take care, Reuben."

When Daniel replaced the phone, the sound of the rain beating across the roof in windy spurts enclosed him. He made a mental note to get together with Reuben as soon as possible. It had been too long.

As he climbed the stairs to his bedroom, Daniel went over their conversation and acknowledged a certain amount of relief. He peeked into Nellie's room and found her sleeping soundly. It wasn't until he settled himself in bed that it occurred to him to wonder if his wife was all right. For all his nervousness and worry, he'd not once considered her as the possible cause of his uneasiness. Carefully he rearranged the pillow behind his head and turned on his side, toward his wife's side of the bed. The sight of the tidy, unused space didn't elicit any feeling at all in Daniel. Rajean could take care of herself, as she was fond of informing him.

Forty-five minutes later Daniel was still awake, the sheets and pillow damp with his perspiration. He couldn't imagine staring at the shadowy ceiling much longer. Maybe if he got up and took a shower, he'd feel better. The storm was still battering the summer house, which meant Rajean would be out all night. Not that it mattered.

Daniel had one foot in the shower when the phone jangled. Perhaps it was Reuben, he thought, calling back to see if he had settled down. He picked up the phone, a snappy retort ready, then frowned when he heard the operator's sleepy voice tell him there was an overseas call for Daniel Bishop. What the hell? No one knew where he was except his answering service and Reuben. "This is Daniel Bishop speaking. . . ."

"Very good, sir, hold for the French operator. . . ."

"Jesus Christ! Yes, hello . . . hello? Speak louder, I can barely hear you. There's a storm here. Who's calling, Operator?" A spurt of crackly French came over the wire. "Mickey! My God, Mickey, is that you?"

"Daniel, please, we may be cut off momentarily . . . Daniel, please, you must come . . . I need . . ." Daniel strained to distinguish Mickey's desperate words from the relentless crackle of overseas static. "Urgent . . . please . . . I beg you . . . we . . . we need you . . . not for myself . . . for . . . Daniel . . . you have to get him out . . . not safe for him . . . Daniel . . . speak to me . . ."

"Mickey, what is it?" Daniel shouted. "I can hardly hear you. Take who? Are you all right?" Jesus Christ, of *course* she wasn't all right! Germany had invaded France.

The telephone stabilized, and he heard Mickey's remembered voice clearly. "You must get Philippe safely to his father. . . ."

Daniel's eyes grew wild when he realized the line he held in his hand had gone dead. Desperately he jiggled the hook and tried dialing the operator. But it was no use. "Son of a *bitch*!" he roared. He stomped around the room trying to make sense of the phone call. Mickey, after all these years . . . Memories flooded his brain—all the reasons this woman could still hold a special rock-steady place in his heart. She needed him; she wanted him to go to France. "Jesus Christ!" he exploded. "How in hell am I going to get to Europe with a war going on?" Why had Mickey called him and not Reuben? The love they had shared had been remarkable. Reuben would move heaven and earth for Mickey, and she had to know that, but she'd called him instead. Why? And who the hell was Philippe? "Take Philippe to his father," she'd said. Great. But who was Philippe's father?

Philippe . . . He'd heard the name, and not that long ago. Something to do with Fairmont Studios . . . Of course! He owned fifty-one percent of Fairmont's stock, and Reuben owned the other forty-nine. Bouchet! Philippe Bouchet! That was the name. No one had ever met Bouchet, not even Sol Rosen, Reuben's father-in-law and the former head of Fairmont Studios. Morgan Guaranty Trust in New York handled all Bouchet's business. Philippe Bouchet wasn't safe in France,

and Mickey wanted him to get him out. But why not ask Reuben
to help? Because . . . because . . . Daniel's memory strained.
Get him to his father. . . . Mickey had sounded . . . as if he,
Daniel, should know who Philippe's father was.

Suddenly Daniel stopped in his tracks. Oh, Jesus, Jesus . . .
of course! Reuben was . . . Philippe was . . . had to be. All these
years . . . it would explain so much. Bebe, Reuben, Mickey,
himself. That magic time . . . France. He must be, how old
now? Twenty, twenty-one, Reuben's age when he . . .

Reuben didn't know . . . had no idea . . . That's why she
called me, Daniel thought dizzily. Bebe must have given birth,
and . . . Mickey kept the child. Yes, it made sense. Mickey
would keep the child because he was Reuben's son. She
wouldn't have allowed Bebe to abort or give away the child
for adoption. That's why she never answered. . . . All these
years and we never knew!

Daniel wept then for his friend Reuben who had never known
his son, and for the faceless Philippe who had never known
his father.

Nellie stood in the doorway of the sunroom, watching her
stepfather. She'd never seen a man cry before. Surely he wasn't
crying over her mother. When was he going to realize she
wasn't worth tears, or even consideration, for that matter? It
was a pity he'd never learned how to play the game. How often
she'd been tempted to tell him the rules, but for some reason
she'd always changed her mind. She didn't love her mother.
Actually, she detested her. But she was fond of her stepfather
because he genuinely seemed to care about her. Yet she didn't
love him, either. If she loved anything, it was money. Money.
Jewels. Power. They all went together. When she was ten she'd
wanted different colored bicycles. When she was twelve she'd
wanted a stable of horses, all jumpers. When she was fourteen
she'd wanted clothes and cosmetics and a magnificent bedroom
and a swimming pool. When she was sixteen she'd wanted her
own car, a fancy roadster that would turn heads. At seventeen
she'd still wanted all those things *and* to be beautiful. Now
that she was eighteen she wanted more; she wanted to be filthy
rich and to be powerful at a very young age. She had two of
the three ingredients she thought would make her happy—she
had beauty and brains—but she didn't have the money.

Sensing her presence, Daniel turned. He did his best to smile.

"Here," Nellie said, handing him a tissue. "Blow your
nose, that's what you always tell me." She smiled.

Daniel accepted the tissue. Lord, this stepdaughter of his was a vision of loveliness. The long golden braid hanging down her back and the wispy curls around her face made her look fifteen and so vulnerable. Lashes, thick and dark, complemented her soft gray-green eyes, eyes that were now full of concern for him.

She was nibbling on her full lower lip, her perfectly aligned teeth, thanks to an excellent orthodontist, reminding him suddenly of Rajean, whose sharp teeth were so white that they were suspect.

The long braid swished against her silk pajamas as she perched herself on her father's knee and nuzzled his cheek. "Daddy, don't worry about Mother, she's like a pigeon, she always comes home. If you're upset about her, or if there's something you know . . . I wish you'd tell me."

"I had an urgent call, and then the lines went down. I feel helpless. I should be making several calls right now, and I can't." Long, thin fingers raked at his sandy hair in a frenzy.

"For heaven's sake, Daddy, if it's that important, go down to the boat and use the ship-to-shore phone. Is it serious?" she asked.

Daniel slapped at his forehead. "Now, why didn't I think of that? Yes, honey, it's serious, but not for us, so don't start worrying about things. It's late, go back to bed, and I'll go down to the boat."

Nellie bent to kiss the top of her father's head. "Wear your slicker," she admonished him.

"Yes, ma'am," Daniel drawled. How nice it was to know she cared about him. He took an extra moment to hug his daughter and tell her he loved her. He beamed his pleasure when she echoed his response.

Daniel slogged his way through the driving rain to the pier and climbed aboard his cabin cruiser, the *Sugar Baby*. When he had his thoughts under control and a cigarette in hand, he began to wonder if he was wrong about the identity of Philippe Bouchet. Should he call Reuben? No, why upset his friend's world with wild assumptions? First he had to deal with Mickey's request.

There was no doubt in his mind that he would do all in his power to help Mickey. He owed everything he had in life to two people: Reuben and Mickey. Without their help and encouragement, their love and support, he shuddered to think what might have happened to him. How he was going to fulfill

Mickey's request was another question. He had a certain amount of clout in D.C., but not enough to wangle transportation to war-torn Europe. And Reuben couldn't help him with this one. Max, Reuben's underworld friend, probably couldn't help him, either. That left only his own influential friends from Harvard days. If there was any way at all to get to Europe, Rocky Rockefeller would find it and Jerry Vanderbilt would ease the path. They wouldn't ask questions, either, which was all to the good.

The ship-to-shore operator took down both numbers Daniel gave her and said she would place the calls back to back. When Rocky's groggy voice came over the static-filled wire, Daniel identified himself immediately. Rocky became alert instantly at the sound of his friend's troubled voice. After he'd listened to the problem Daniel outlined to him, he didn't hesitate. "Jesus, Daniel, right now your chances of getting to the moon are better than France. I'll see what I can do, but I can't promise— I'll do my best. You okay, buddy?"

"Pretty much so. I wouldn't ask if this wasn't . . . Hey, I didn't mention that transportation back includes someone else . . . a friend." Daniel let that sink in. "I'm heading home first thing in the morning. You can reach me at the office if you need to."

"Hell, I wasn't in the mood for sleep anyway," Rocky groused good-naturedly. "Did you get to Jerry yet?"

"No, I've got a call in to him, though."

"I'll call him for you. Sit tight and one of us will get back to you."

"Rocky—thanks," Daniel said.

Rocky laughed. "I always wondered how you were going to call in your favor."

"What favor?"

"You told me I owed you my life for all the clean underwear I used to borrow from you. Remember?"

"Yeah! And I also remember the pile of *dirty* underwear. . . . Listen, seriously now, I'll owe you *my* life if you pull this off."

"I'll talk to you in the morning. Try to get some sleep."

Daniel canceled his call to Jerry and made himself a stiff drink. The rain had stopped, and a low fog hung over the ocean. The sound of a far-off foghorn nuzzled itself into the surrounding air while the lighthouse searchlight swooped overhead at regular intervals, brazenly passing through the swirling mists.

Daniel sat in his spacious cabin and allowed the swaying of the boat to calm his nerves. There was no way in hell he would sleep, so why pretend.

Paybacks always rolled around, and they could be a bitch. Had he ever given any thought to his and Reuben's payback? Yes, hundreds of times, but that's all they were—thoughts. He wasn't even thinking of financial payback; that one was easy, that one was over and done with. This one, as they said, was the real McCoy. He was piss-assed scared. Not for himself, but for Reuben. And for Mickey, too. Dear, wonderful Mickey.

It was all so long ago. Maybe he should just sit here and go over everything, clear the air, clear his mind. Get everything in order. What really went on in France after the Great War? He realized now that he might not have all the answers, but he was determined to try to search for them. Reuben and Mickey, Mickey and Reuben. Mickey and Reuben and himself. She'd dubbed them the Three Musketeers . . . He was getting ahead of himself. He drained his drink and made another. What came first? Reuben and himself . . .

The war. He remembered the long lines of recruits, and himself on one of them, finally reaching the desk and getting his equipment for boot camp. The long journey overseas, wide-eyed and full of adventure and shaking in his new army-issued shoes and leg wraps. And then the trenches and the bitter realities of war—death and death. There didn't seem to be anything else but a thousand ways to die. He'd been reduced to a trembling mass of raw, exposed nerves until Reuben Tarz had entered his life and taken him under his citified, knowing wing like a big, kindly, loving brother. The brother he'd never had. They'd shared rations and fears, the pain of an emotional past and then almost identical physical pain—gassed and blinded in the same overwhelming moment. Recovery at Soissons; the makeshift hospital was like a double-edged sword. *Will I be blind forever, and if I recover, will that mean that I'll be sent back to the front again? To die this time*? Reuben had been just as green, just as scared as he'd been underneath that swaggering, city-boy arrogance. He remembered one night in particular when he and Reuben, both scared out of their wits, sat through an unusually fearful blitz. Daniel almost laughed now at the memory. How could you distinguish one night from another? Then he remembered how the body of a young boy had been thrown at him, bleeding open and steaming at the same time, the mingled stench of gunpowder and burning flesh.

When Reuben had extricated him from the mutilated corpse, they had stared at each other and voiced the same overpowering fear—that they would die on strange soil with no one but the other to care. They'd shared their youth, their dreams, and their innocence over the next few hours, looking deeply into each other's souls. When the sun came up they shook hands in open acknowledgement of their friendship. Who could ever forget the unbreakable bond they'd formed that fearful night? It was Reuben who put his ass on the line—or was it his body?—to get them out of the tail end of the war.

Michelene Fonsard was benefactress to half the United States Army, or so they said. It didn't take Daniel long to discover that the insinuations concerning her sexual prowess were half-truths. Yes, she was generous; and yes, she was vital; but he could never think of her as promiscuous. That simply was not the way he knew her. Beautiful, kind, wonderful Mickey had taken a shine to Reuben and worked her special brand of magic to get both of them mustered out before the Armistice was signed. They would never have to face the dreaded front again with its death and destruction. She'd taken them to her château and nursed them back to health. She'd royally fed and clothed them as they had never been fed and clothed before. She'd educated them, turned them into gentlemen, and shared her life with them, and she never asked for anything in return except Reuben's love—and that he had given freely. Daniel knew now, as he had known then, that Reuben had insisted on a package deal before accepting Mickey's offer. She had told him early on that Reuben had refused to go anywhere without his best friend.

Daniel loved Mickey, but not the way Reuben loved her. She'd provided them with everything they could have dreamed of needing in those days and months after the war. Incredibly wealthy thanks to her husband's lucrative wine business, she shared and gave as though money were no object. She had provided a tutor . . . an old man with a mind so sharp that by the time they'd been well enough to travel to Mickey's Paris town house, Daniel had learned enough to study at the Sorbonne, which Mickey and Reuben insisted he do. Orphan that he was, the knowledge that two such wonderful people cared about *him*, about his future and his well-being, was over-whelming. He'd have done anything they'd asked, but of course they'd asked nothing in return, except his love. That was the true friendship that existed between them.

Things changed when Bebe Rosen arrived on the scene. Daniel's eyes clouded at the thought. He almost didn't want to continue his musings. Get another drink, he urged himself. While he fixed it, he realized it took all the pieces to finish the puzzle. He decided he had to go on.

Sixteen years old, beautiful, spoiled, and hot to trot, Bebe Rosen set her cap for Reuben the minute she laid eyes on him. But she was just a precocious adolescent! Daniel laughed at the realization that he still tried to defend Bebe, some twenty years later. From what he could remember Mickey felt the same way, but she also felt maternal and jealous at the same time. But he remembered Reuben handling Bebe roughly, refusing to dance to her whims and outrageous demands. Instead he'd paddled her and made her toe the line. After finding himself manipulated by her on several occasions, Daniel had grown to have mixed feelings about Bebe. But, above all, it was Bebe's determination to have Reuben at all costs that shadowed the end of their days with Mickey.

Daniel strained his memory to figure out what had actually happened. Before Bebe had arrived, the relationship between Reuben and Mickey had seemed to nourish them heart and soul. Daniel was sure Reuben had asked her not once but several times to marry him, but Mickey had refused. In the hope of changing her mind, Reuben had begun to learn the wine business while he, Daniel, studied at the Sorbonne. According to Reuben, she had refused his offer of marriage to secure his freedom; his whole life loomed ahead of him, she'd explained, and she wanted him to return to America to make something of himself. But never would Daniel forget the joy-filled delight they took in each other, their secret overflowing glances, the way their hands always seemed to meet, and how their eyes always seemed to dance when they were together.

They'd stayed for two full years, two wonderful years Daniel wouldn't have traded for anything on earth. Besides molding lifelong friendships out of sincere caring, the time he'd spent in France had formed the bedrock that enabled him to build a life for himself—solid, secure, enduring. But whenever things are too perfect, something is bound to go wrong, and that something was Bebe Rosen.

Daniel frowned. Maybe he wasn't being fair to Bebe; it was, after all, Reuben who had raped her. This was where it always got sticky in his mind, and to this day he'd never pressed

Reuben for details. He supposed when he got to France, if he got there at all, Mickey would tell him the rest of the story.

Philippe must be the child born of that rape; nothing else made sense, and even that didn't make sense to Daniel. Maybe Mickey had had a child after he and Reuben returned to America. He groaned aloud. That was preposterous. He knew Mickey too well; she'd never do such an insane thing. It made more sense that she would take in Reuben's flesh and blood. But why remain silent? And now, after all these years . . .

"Goddamit to hell!" Daniel barked. His lawyer's mind ground to a halt. How can you come to a concrete conclusion without concrete facts? Impossible. Especially when you haven't slept for an eternity. Daniel looked at his watch—an hour until dawn. He hunkered down, but his muddled thoughts gave him no peace.

The moment the first gray streaks appeared on the galley steps, he was off the bunk and up on deck. He leapt onto the pier and sprinted for the house, tearing at the yellow slicker as he ran. In the hallway he dropped the thick oilskin on the floor and raced for the steps leading to the second floor. He stopped short when he saw his wife at her dressing table, marveling, as he always did, at her appearance. She'd been out all night and most of the day before and still looked as perky as fresh mint. Not a hair was out of place; her makeup was superb, her lips glossy and perfect. Gold winked at her ears and on her neck. The sea-green sheath with the slender straps was sleek and unwrinkled. Even the matching shoes were dry. As always, Daniel wondered how this was possible. For the life of him he couldn't remember if she'd been wearing the same dress yesterday when she'd left the house. He nodded curtly as he headed for the bathroom.

"What were you doing out so early this morning, darling?" Rajean asked with idle unconcern.

"I spent the night on the boat," he answered. He knew she wasn't really interested; this was an old game between them.

"Oh . . . Darling, I think Cornelia and I will stay on a few extra days if you don't mind. The city is so beastly hot right now, and everyone, but everyone, is gone. Maybe we should think about staying on here for the summer and you could come on weekends. . . . Daniel? Answer me. . . ."

Daniel turned on the shower and walked naked into the bedroom, ignoring the look of distaste on his wife's face. They were married, for Christ's sake. "I think you should discuss it with Nellie. Do what you like, Rajean. I'll leave the car at the ferry. I really don't have time to talk now. Look . . . there's every chance I'll be . . . I might have to go out of town . . . it's not definite. . . . I'll call you."

"You do that, Daniel," Rajean said coolly. "Then there's no rush for Cornelia and me to go back, is there?"

Daniel stared into his wife's glittering eyes. They emanated ice-cold nothingness. He tried to remember the last time they'd been in bed together. "No rush and no reason," he said just as coolly. God. Had he really loved this woman once, this cold, chiseled beauty who could easily pose in the wax museum? "I've said this before, and I'm going to say it again, it's not good for Nellie to see you coming in at dawn. Do you know what she said to me last night? She said you always come home, like a pigeon. *Your* daughter said that! Jesus, Rajean, can't you at least be discreet?"

"Don't preach, darling, unless you're above reproach. But you are above reproach, aren't you?" she said contemptuously. "Faithful and loyal to this ancient marriage. Yes, Daniel, you are a paragon of virtue. You think I'm an alley cat, don't you, darling?"

"Stop with the darling bit, Rajean," he said, trying to dead-end the conversation. They'd had it too often, and it only bored him now.

"You are just too damn stuffy, my love. All you think about is your clients and those goddamn law books of yours." Rajean kicked off one of her shoes and sent it flying across the room. The other followed. "We really should think about divorce," she said sourly.

"Yes, *we* should. I know *I'm* thinking about it very seriously." Daniel had already turned to step into the shower.

Rajean's eyes widened. She'd made references to a divorce hundreds of times before, but this was the first time Daniel had had a ready comeback. Her fingers trembled as she pulled at the gold globes at her ears. He would fight for Nellie, not that she really cared. A teenager whose eyes were always full of questions irritated her. But she knew it was out of the question anyway. She would never be able to get as much money as she'd need if she didn't have custody, even if it was just for three years. And she knew how it would look if she gave in. Women weren't supposed to give up their children without a struggle.

Damn! Daniel was so respectable. . . . It always brought her to the same conclusion—she needed that respectability and his stability. And since her own trust fund was depleted, she needed his money, too. There was no way she could dip into Nellie's. Daniel had seen to that. Damn her parents for their double suicide during the stock market crash! Her lips curled into a sneer. A paltry fifty thousand dollars they'd left her, plus an apartment on Park Avenue and a place on the social register. Big deal. Four good seasonal parties, a little redecorating, and it was all gone. She did thank God, in her own way, every day, for not having brothers and sisters she'd have had to share it with.

Daniel had come along when she was down to her last two thousand dollars. He'd shared so much with her on their wedding night, but his bank balance was the only thing she remembered in any detail. She'd never really loved him the way a woman is supposed to love her husband. Daniel was so naive; he thought passion was something you uncorked from a bottle between the hours of midnight and one in the morning. Sex was something you did between the sheets with the lights out and your eyes closed—which suited her just fine. He'd been happy as a pig in clover when she'd agreed to his adopting Nellie, and that's when he'd started the damned trust fund. Motherhood was not among her strong points. Sometimes she didn't think she had *any* strong points except perhaps throwing a hell of a party and socializing. But that was enough for her hair: she'd gone to the best schools and been introduced into society in the most accepted of ways, and she took the privilege of being a DAR very seriously. It was something she was very proud of.

As Daniel stepped out of the shower and into their bedroom, Rajean watched her husband surreptitiously. He was handsome, she had to give him that. And in his characteristic white shirt and striped tie, with those horn-rimmed glasses as the classic accent, he was every inch the successful businessman. Her friends were fond of pointing out Daniel's good looks and understated conservatism. To herself she admitted that she didn't really want him, but she'd fight to the death to make sure no one else took him away from her. Besides, he needed her, too. How would he be able to function in Washington without a wife?

His wife *was* beautiful. Everyone said so, and he agreed. Beautiful in a hard, glinting kind of way. Her hair was always perfectly coiffed in the latest upswept fashion with little tendrils curling about her ears. Her eyebrows were a fine, thin line above her lustrous green eyes, which she filled with drops twice a day to make them sparkle and glow. And those high cheek-bones! Haunting, irresistible . . . and always emphasized with coral rouge and matching lipstick. He remembered the way she used to flutter her eyelashes at him, a coy little signal he thought endearing for years until he saw her remove them one night. Rajean did turn heads, but she no longer turned his.

Daniel shrugged into his jacket. His words were so low, Rajean had to strain to hear them. "One of these days I'm going to ask you point-blank where you spend your nights. Or," he said slowly, "I'm simply going to have you followed. I'm giving you fair warning. And I meant what I said about Nellie."

"Daniel, Daniel, what's gotten into you?" Rajean pursed her lips into a pout as she sauntered over to him. "You know I was just teasing you. For heaven's sake, we've been married for so many years, I've lost count. Why, we're like two old shoes growing old together. You know," she gushed while straightening his tie, "we were meant for each other. I know we haven't exactly been bed buddies these past months, but that was out of concern for you, sweetheart. You come home so tired and fretful, I can't bear to tire you out still more. Come now, give me a big kiss before you leave."

Daniel listened to the empty words slipping smoothly from her lips. They didn't affect him one way or the other. Whatever feelings he'd had for Rajean were gone now. Love was what he wanted, the kind of feeling Reuben and Mickey had, and he was smart enough to know he and Rajean had never even come close. Without a word he lifted her hands from his neck and turned his back on her. After stuffing his billfold and car keys into his pocket, he looked back at his wife and said, "I meant what I said, Rajean. I've learned to do without your kisses, you've seen to that. Enjoy your stay here on the island. Tell Nellie I'll call her."

And then he was gone. Just like that. Rajean stared at the open bedroom door, her eyes glittering speculatively. She had to call Teddie, right now. "The hell with you, Daniel!" she muttered as she snatched the phone and dialed a New York City number.

Rajean felt herself glow all over when she heard the an-swering click at the other end of the line. She listened to the contented, sleep-filled voice mumble a response. "It's Rajean, Teddie. I'm sorry I woke you, but I have the most marvelous news. I think—now understand, this is just my opinion—I think Daniel wants a divorce! Can you believe that!''

Rajean caught sight of her reflection in the mirror, and she smiled. It was always like this when she talked to Teddie—a warm feeling stole through every part of her being, and she could barely contain her joy. When she was with Teddie she was a simpering, whimpering mass of gelatin, and she would do anything her lover wanted. Now she waited for what she hoped would be Teddie's enthusiastic response. And after a moment she heard it: the unmistakable gargle of her lover's light snoring. ''Damn you, Teddie!'' she yelled into the phone before slamming it back on its receiver. ''Damn everyone!''

The day was just as miserable as the evening before, but at least there was no thunder and lightning. Daniel particularly hated driving over bridges in storms, and driving now onto the Robert Moses Bridge in the beating rain, he felt enveloped by his squeamishness. Such times always made him feel helpless, as if he were dangling in a cloth bag he could just barely see through. Why he'd ever allowed Rajean to talk him into buying a place way out in the middle of nowhere was beyond him. In those early days he'd tried to please her whenever he could, thinking that if he gave in to her, he'd get back at least a token of affection. But it hadn't worked that way. The realization that Rajean just didn't know how to give had really undone him. For ages he'd felt defeated and sad, until at last he'd resigned himself to the reality: he gave and Rajean took. Cut and dried—that's how the relationship worked.

As the wipers swept across the rain-whipped windshield, Daniel thought he could hear the words—*get out, get out, get out.* His stomach began to knot up, and he shook his head at the thought. Get out of the marriage? Now was not a good time to be contemplating divorce. No, he had to stop thinking about Rajean now and concentrate on what he was going to do to help Mickey. The inadequacies of his marriage would simply have to be endured for the time being. Nervously he wiped the sweat from his forehead. The storm wasn't doing much to alleviate the oppressive heat and early morning humidity.

The rain began to pound down around him; the wiper blades worked harder and harder, barely clearing the windshield. Beyond his headlights, visibility was so poor that he found himself holding tight to the wheel and leaning into the glass to see his way. To take his mind off the storm, he began to ruminate about Mickey's circumstances but found he couldn't even begin to imagine what was going on with her in France. He knew the newspapers reported only what they wanted to. Terrible thoughts began to surface in Daniel's mind. . . . War . . . the rumblings had become louder and louder until—his own memories, which had lain dormant for so many years, flashed before his eyes. No matter what, he would help Mickey in any way he could—she had done exactly the same for him twenty years before.

Suddenly the rain stopped, as though he'd personally commanded it to cease. One last splatter ricocheted across the windshield, and then as if by magic all was silent. Steam spiraled upward from the bridge like the gray fog that had rolled in from the ocean the night before.

Daniel started to sweat when he caught sight of the Fire Island ferry and heard the blast of its warning horn. It was about ready to leave the slip. He pressed his foot on the gas and roared into the parking area. Without bothering to lock the car, he sprinted toward the ferry, briefcase in hand, his trousers sticking to his legs, his collar and tie askew. He made it on board without a second to spare, then checked his watch as he tried to pull himself together. By the time he got back to Washington he'd look like something the cat dragged in.

An hour later Daniel boarded the train that would take him to Union Station in downtown Washington just blocks away from his office on K Street. Now his rushing was over, and he had a four-and-a-half-hour ride ahead with nothing to do but think. He deliberately ignored the pressing legal work packed neatly away in his bulging briefcase. The two corporate mergers he had been working on could wait. If the corporation heads themselves were to issue him an ultimatum to get to work, he'd hand over the briefcase and thank them for their consideration. But that wouldn't happen, of course, because they'd waited patiently until his calendar was free. Apparently he was in demand.

Daniel settled back in the scratchy seat and closed his eyes, but his questioning thoughts still tripped over one another in his head. God, what if Rocky couldn't help? What if he couldn't get to France? Mickey was depending on him, counting on him to come through for her. And the faceless Philippe, he was waiting, too. A white knight, a savior . . . What if . . . what if . . . Think positive, Daniel, he told himself. If anyone can get you to Europe, it's Rocky and Jerry.

He took a moment to savor his long-standing friendship with two of the finest men he'd ever met. Of course their friendship was nothing like the one he had with Reuben, but it was damn close. Eventually his thoughts drifted and he slept, an uneasy, restless sleep, but one that would allow for a clear head on his arrival.

Some instinct, or maybe it was the shuffle of the passengers gathering their belongings together, woke him as the train slowed and pulled into Union Station. With only his briefcase to worry about, he elbowed his way off the train and headed for the row of phone booths on the concourse. With dismay he stared at the line of weary travelers waiting to use the phones, and then he ran, tie flapping and coattails *swoosh*ing, leaving behind him the stale, urine-smelling air.

Swinging through the revolving door of the office building he owned, Daniel raced up to the fourth floor, for once preferring not to wait for the elevator. Breathing heavily, he opened the plate-glass door with his firm's name emblazoned in gold lettering and dashed to his mahogany-paneled office, calling over his shoulder to his wide-eyed secretary, "Get Rocky on the phone and bring me an ice-cold soda."

His chair, a deep burgundy Morris and a gift from Jerry Vanderbilt, welcomed him with a resounding, comforting *swoosh*, like a well-worn slipper. He drained the Coca-Cola when it was brought to him and set the green bottle to dancing on his desk. Then he bellowed to Irene, his secretary, to bring him two more from the small compact kitchen. He was working on the second bottle when Irene buzzed him. "Mr. Rockefeller is on the line, Mr. Bishop."

Daniel gagged on a mouthful of soda, the fizz bubbling in his nose. He cleared his throat before reaching for the phone. "Daniel here, Rocky."

The voice on the other end was low and filled with subdued excitement. "We did it! Don't ask any questions, but if you can be at Dulles Airport at five-thirty, we have a Red Cross plane that will take you in. Actually, it's one of Jerry's planes, his grandfather's. Vintage, to say the least, but in tiptop shape. It will set down at Heathrow in London, and the Red Cross insignia will see you through. My daddy called F.D.R. and got clearance."

Daniel had put all his faith in his friends, and they had come through again. He couldn't speak.

"Say something, you son of a bitch!" Rocky urged with a hearty laugh. "A small show of excitement will do."

"I . . . I honestly didn't think you'd be able to . . ." Daniel sat up and tried to pull his thoughts together. "Listen, Rocky, I have to talk to you. Where the hell are you?"

"You called me and you don't know where I am? . . . Some lawyer you are. I'm at Dulles. Your secretary called my office, and they told her where to reach me. Jerry's here now seeing to the outfitting of the plane. You know, goodies and that sort of thing. Oh, and don't worry about clothes, we've got that covered, too."

Rocky paused to temper his natural exuberance with the gravity generally reserved for his courtroom monologues. "We want to help, Daniel, and if you need us to go with you—and Jerry is hoping you do, you should see him scrambling around this plane—we can say good-bye to jurisprudence at the drop of a hat. Whatever you need, you know it's yours."

Daniel's eyes misted. "There are a couple of things I've got to handle first. I shouldn't be too long. We'll talk when I get there, okay?"

"You bet." The exuberance was back. Daniel smiled and shook his head. Rocky and Jerry were doing for him what he was trying to do for Mickey. Friends . . . that said it all. Somehow he'd find a way to thank these two men, but for now he'd have to push ahead.

Richard Rockefeller, Rocky to his intimate friends, was a tall, imposing man with crisp golden-brown hair that curled about his ears and forehead. Shrewd gray-green eyes gazed benevolently from beneath thick, fringed lashes that women would have killed for. A chiseled jaw, complete with cleft, and strong, even white teeth completed the saintly look Rocky strived for. He had worked on "the look" for years to get it just right. But Daniel knew Rocky's boyish, innocent look was a facade. His friend was the toughest, meanest, nastiest courtroom lawyer on the East Coast, and proud of the fact that he'd never lost a case. Oh, he'd settled out of court at the eleventh hour, but he'd never let any arbitration be construed as an admission of guilt on the part of his client. Daniel knew that if he was ever in legal trouble, Rocky would be the man he'd turn to.

As he hurried across the busy airfield, Daniel tried to hide his smile when he caught his first glimpse of Rocky. His friend was standing just outside the plane's open hatch dressed in what he called clam diggers and deck shoes, absorbed in arguing about something to one of the crew. When Rocky turned to him and Daniel saw the noticeable hole gaping near the armpit of his friend's stretched-out T-shirt, he lost the battle. Grinning openly, he climbed the steps to join Rocky and slapped him on the back as they shook hands.

"Where's Jerry?" Daniel yelled over the noise of the hubbub surrounding the plane.

Rocky cocked a thumb over his shoulder toward the inside of the waiting plane. "Believe it or not, he's outfitting a bed for you back there—complete with satin quilt," he joked. "It's a long flight." Daniel couldn't help thinking Rocky was the one who really wanted to get on that plane with him.

"Come on, I have a bottle of the best waiting for us inside," Rocky said with a wink, "and I think we're all in need of a stiff drink."

Daniel held back. "Rock, I don't know how I can . . ."

The two friends looked into each other's eyes as the wind began to whip across the tarmac. "What?" said Rocky, grinning. "Thank me? Forget it. If it wasn't for you, I'd never have gotten through law school, and I don't mean just your tutoring. You're a damn good friend, Daniel, and I hope you consider me one. Hey, Jerry," he bellowed, sauntering off, "Crusader Bishop is here."

Daniel followed him into the cool, damp belly of the plane, his eyes quickly adjusting to the dimness. When they found Jerry, the men shook hands all around again, vigorously thumping one another on the back the way they'd done in college. With smirks and self-conscious grins, the three of them hunkered down together, hands jammed into their pockets. The display of emotion and friendship was over, now it was time for business.

Jerry was the shortest of the three, but what he lacked in height he made up in pure, hard muscle. He had bright, inquisitive eyes and curly red hair that stood out like a fire bush around his ears. Daniel always thought he looked like a precocious squirrel. But he was a good buddy, the kind of guy you wanted on your side no matter what. Well, they were on his side now and hadn't asked why.

"Okay, fella, let's hear it," Rocky said, uncorking a bottle of Jack Daniel's. He offered it to Jerry, who took a swig and then passed it on to Daniel. Daniel took a good pull, wiped his mouth with the back of his hand, and passed it on to Rocky.

Thirty minutes later two pairs of eyes stared back at Daniel in wonder. "This has the makings of an Academy Award film," Jerry said quietly, trying to wring one last drop from the now-empty bottle. "Daniel, this could be . . . hell, it's . . ." Jerry turned to Rocky. "I think we should go along, Rock. This turkey could get caught by the Germans and he'd try and talk his way out of it." He sounded worried, which surprised Daniel. When he replied, Rocky sounded just as worried.

"So you're intending to pull off something much bigger than a reconnaissance tour to size up the situation," Rocky said flatly. He took in and let out a great breath before continuing. "You could get stuck there, Daniel. Just because we get you in doesn't mean you're going to get out."

Daniel placed a hand on each of his friends' shoulders. "I know. And that's why you two are staying here. If there's one thing you two are good at, it's covering your asses. Now I need you to cover mine. I'm simply out of town on business, emergency business. Check with my secretary, she'll be expecting you. Return whatever calls look like trouble. Especially from Reuben. I wouldn't put it past him to fly east if he gets an urge to. I think I rattled him last night. He'll be able to get through on the phone to the island now, and Rajean will have him call the office. Reuben has this . . . this sixth sense when it comes to me, and he'll act on it. He's not to know, and neither is my secretary."

"Dan, what if something goes wrong?" asked Rocky. "What if you do get stuck; what do you want us to do?"

"Whatever you have to. The Red Cross will be our go-between, right, Jerry?"

"That's the ticket," Jerry said, patting the curving wall of the Red Cross transport plane.

The men talked then of details, coming up with solutions to potential problems. When they had finished their conversation, Daniel spoke. "Then I guess I'm in the hands of the angels, as the saying goes. You know, you guys are the greatest—Jesus, there's a war going on; France is full of Germans; my world is upside down, and you . . . I didn't know where to turn . . . and I know this is probably the craziest thing I've ever done, but I have to do it. You have to understand, I am what I am because of Mickey and Reuben. I can't turn my back; I just can't. If you hadn't come through, I'd probably . . ."

"Be swimming your way over," Rocky said, finishing Daniel's sentence. "We thought of that," he continued cheerfully. "Look, Daniel, we understand, and both of us feel you're doing the right thing. We're worried, and that's natural and normal. We're here for you for whatever that means, and don't give another thought to things here. We'll handle that."

When the last round of backslapping and handshakes was over, the three men walked to the plane's open door.

"Anytime you're ready, this bird is cleared for takeoff. Top priority and all that shit." Jerry grinned. "Here," he said, holding out a small velvet sack.

"What's this?" Daniel asked, feeling the weight of the bag in his hands.

"It's a bag full of goddamned diamonds. In case you have to pay for . . . you know . . . anything . . ." Jerry said, and cleared his throat.

Daniel's eyebrows shot up. "I hope these aren't the family jewels," he said lightly. His throat was so constricted, he thought he would cry.

Rocky was next, dangling a money belt in front of him stuffed full of French francs. "You never know," he said, shrugging. "I had my father tap a line of credit for you at the Paris bank. I don't know if it will do you any good, but it's there. The franc is . . . by the time you need it, it might be worthless. All of this is just a precaution, Daniel."

There was nothing for Daniel to say, and he didn't try. Jerry's and Rocky's eyes were as misty as his own as the three men stood and walked to the yawning opening of the transport. "I guess I'll be seeing you . . . whenever," Daniel said, his voice faltering.

"You better have some good French wine with you when you get back," Rocky called as he and Jerry climbed down the stairs.

"I'll take a real French maid, one with . . ." Jerry put his hands in front of his chest and drew them out as far as they would go, his eyes twinkling.

"You wouldn't know what the hell to do with her, who are you kidding?" Daniel shouted back. He could hear both men whooping as the plane's engines began to sputter. With a last wave Daniel turned to settle himself safely for the long journey.

Jerry and Rocky watched as the huge big-bellied plane taxied down the runway. As the wind swirled about them, they stood and waited until the plane was a speck in the now-clearing sky.

"If he's who he is because of this Mickey and Reuben, then we're who we are because of him. Do you agree, Jerry?"

"All the way."

They walked back to Rocky's waiting car in silence, both of them fighting the urge to cross their fingers and pray.

"Do you think it'll be okay?" Jerry asked. "I don't know if I could do what he's about to do. That loyalty, where the fuck does he get it? We have it all, Rock—the money, the power, the mainline families . . . You know what he comes from. . . ."

"Daniel's special. And we're doing what we have to do just the way Daniel is. He rubbed off on us, and I'm glad. Look, there's nothing else we can do for now. Should we camp out at his office, or what?"

They clambered into Rocky's gleaming roadster, the last of the day's raindrops beaded on its highly polished surface. "I closed my office," Jerry said sheepishly. "I gave everyone a month's vacation. My old man is probably drawing up my commitment papers as we speak."

Rocky grinned. "You're bonkers, but you aren't the only one. I did the same thing."

Both men looked longingly toward the western horizon. If Daniel had given the word, they would have leapt into what they were now considering an adventure.

At last Jerry reached over and patted the steering wheel. "Start this baby up," he said resignedly. "I think we should head for the nearest bar and tie one on. We'll be more than sober by the time Daniel gets to France."

"In that outfit?" Jerry said, pointing to Rocky's hairy calves. "There isn't a place in town that'll let you in."

Rocky shrugged. "Then I'll buy the fucking place! And you can hold the mortgage."

"I know this tailor on Fourteenth Street . . ."

Chapter Two

IT WAS A WARM, GOLDEN DAY, THE KIND CALIFORNIA WAS known for, the kind pictured on glossy travel brochures inviting you to accomplish something wondrous with the brilliant sun at your back. But Reuben Tarz admitted there was very little left in his life to accomplish. The pictorial reviews and trade papers and magazines continued to report that he had it all, still touting him as a wonder boy even though he was over forty. Wonder Boy . . . If any of them could have heard him chuckling cynically over the image, they would have been puzzled to say the least.

He looked around at his quiet, manicured garden and wondered, not for the first time, if his Japanese groundsman had a drawn plan of the terrain. His prime Beverly Hills acre of color almost blinded him with its brilliance. Nests of sweet peas, beds of begonias and cyclamen, huge healthy clumps of daisies, and intensely fragrant bougainvillea and gardenias all bloomed in pampered profusion. When he died he hoped some kind soul would drape his casket with daisies; they were his favorite flowers. The morbid image brought him up short, and he quickly banished it from his thoughts. Death was years ahead of him; he wouldn't even consider it. Why, he hadn't even reached the halfway mark yet! His career came first; then, when he was ready to retire he would do something about the things he wanted to do and the places he wanted to see.

Reuben turned and started toward his horseshoe-shaped rose garden, shears and gloves in hand. He'd come out to the garden for a reason, not to stand and gawk. Almost completely surrounded by the five-foot rosebushes, he began to cut away dead stems and dried leaves. They were hardy, these roses, and he'd taken over their care despite Osawa's protests. Of course he wasn't proficient by any means, but the need to tend something, to watch it grow and thrive through sheer persistence, was important to him.

Intent on his occupation, he examined each new bud and marveled over every full bloom still shining with early morning dewdrops. The deep emerald leaves looked as though they were sprinkled with diamonds, and the earthy fragrance of the new day filled his lungs.

Out of the corner of his eye, he noticed the maid bringing out the *Examiner* and a pot of coffee and placing it on the terrace table a short distance from where he stood. Soon she'd return with a frosty pitcher of orange juice and a crystal glass. The benefits of wealth: a maid, breakfast on the terrace, and a newspaper just waiting for him to pick up. Reuben sighed.

There were days when he liked his solitary coffee and juice, but today wasn't one of them. Today he felt his aloneness acutely, like a swift, unexpected pain. The children were busy with their lives, and his wife was off God knew where, while he was swallowed up in a huge mansion with four servants.

He'd spent the entire Fourth of July weekend alone, puttering about even though Jane Perkins had asked him weeks earlier to attend her annual barbecue and Max had called and suggested he stop by the club if he wasn't doing anything. But he couldn't face the warmth of Jane's homey get-together, even though she was a trusted friend and he loved her dearly, and Max's invitation had only made him burrow deeper into his solitude.

Thinking over the next few business days at the studio, he realized that with the exception of one meeting, things were so under control he didn't even have to show up. If he wanted to, he could take off for days at a time at this point and not worry about what was going on. But he did worry. After all, someone might come out of the blue and snap at his heels the way he'd snapped at Sol Rosen's heels some twenty-odd years ago. And he hadn't stopped snapping, either; he'd taken a good-size bite and then gobbled up the whole shooting match. Well, almost the whole shooting match. Forty-nine percent of Fairmont stock was his free and clear—stock ol' Sol had cannily gifted in trust to his grandsons in a clever twist on an agreement he and Reuben had made together. The same stock that Bebe had later turned over to him the night he'd been awarded an Oscar for his accomplishments in the film industry—to help put their troubled marriage back on an even keel, she'd said at the time. But that had not happened. If anything, he and Bebe were further apart now than they'd ever been. It wasn't even a marriage of convenience anymore. It was just a mutual, miserable existence.

Reuben stared down at the garden flagstones, littered now with dead twigs bearing sharp, treacherous thorns. After meticulously piling them to the side, he moved on to the salmon-colored roses and continued to snip. If only he could cut an armful of the lush, fragrant blooms and present them to someone, someone special who would know that he and he alone was responsible for their beauty. But there was no one he cared to share his roses with, no one who meant enough to him. His heart felt heavy.

How in the name of God had he become such an emotional cripple? Why couldn't he feel love? Why had it been ruthlessly snatched from his grasp? Would he ever again feel that pulse-quickening, heart-thumping magical excitement that made him want to rip open his heart to bare his love? Jesus, where had it all gone?

His mind raced as he kept snipping away, his thoughts circling around another topic of concern. For the last few days he had been experiencing a second gut-churning emotion, one that tied his stomach in knots and made him want to look over his shoulder like an escaping criminal, as if hounds were at his heels. Fear. Fear that something was going to happen to upset his world. It had started the night of Daniel's phone call, this intangible feeling that was setting his hands to tremble and his heart to pound.

Reuben pulled off the gardening gloves and tossed them and the clippers onto the mound of cuttings. Turning his back on the garden, he walked to the white glass-topped table on the patio. Marcy had poured his juice but not his coffee. He gulped the freshly squeezed juice, savoring the pulpy thickness, then poured himself a cup of the dark and spicy coffee—made just the way he liked it. It had barely hit bottom when he looked down at the paper nestled beside the cup. His gut began to churn faster. Maybe something was in the paper. . . . Either it was that or . . . Daniel.

There was nothing new in the paper, just a rehash of the previous day's news. As he refolded the paper, a picture of Roosevelt standing at Hyde Park stared back at him. The article reported the president's Fourth of July speech, a wealth of platitudes about the greatness of America, about dying for one's country in order to preserve the human freedom established by the Founding Fathers 165 years ago today. Reuben pushed the paper from him. Daniel knew something, had heard something, was privy to some information . . . and his call was to . . . see if he heard it, too!

"Marcy!" he roared. When the startled maid appeared at the French doors, he demanded a phone. He didn't give a shit what time it was back east.

The phone rang twenty-five times at Daniel's Georgetown house before Reuben hung up. The phone at the house on Fire Island was picked up on the seventh ring. In a sleepy voice Nellie told Reuben her father was back in Washington. Reuben hung up again and then tried Daniel's answering service. This time a receptionist told him that Mr. Bishop was out of town but someone would be in the office by nine if it was an emergency. At that Reuben lost his patience.

"I'm Reuben Tarz, miss. Mr. Bishop *always* leaves word where *I* can reach him, and, yes, this is an emergency."

"I'm sorry, sir," the operator answered contritely, "Mr. Bishop left no messages other than what I've just told you. All I can suggest is that you call the office at nine o'clock."

"Out of town, my ass!" Reuben seethed at the sound of the dial tone. Hell, he'd talked to Daniel a little over twenty-four hours ago, and nothing had been said about going out of town. Not that he told Reuben each time he made a business trip, but he'd always left a number where he could be reached, or his secretary would track him down if Reuben needed him, and he'd be on the phone within the hour.

Reuben looked at his watch. Five minutes to six—five minutes to nine in Washington. Five minutes to wait.

Promptly at six Reuben placed a call to Daniel's private office number. His nasal-voiced secretary answered on the second ring. "Daniel Bishop's office, how may I help you?"

"Reuben Tarz here, Irene. I need to get in touch with Daniel."

Irene's voice became attentive and expectant. Besides know-

ing about him through her love of the movies, Irene was well
aware that Reuben Tarz was Mr. Bishop's best friend, and in
all the years she'd worked for Mr. Bishop he had always left
a number where Reuben Tarz could reach him. This was the
first time that she would have to tell him Mr. Bishop simply
couldn't be reached. "I'm sorry, Mr. Tarz, but Mr. Bishop
left the office early today, and as yet I have no number for
him. If this is an emergency . . ." Her voice trailed off lamely.

"What about his appointments? Check his calendar," Reuben ordered. His voice was so authoritative, Irene began to
rise from her seat even though the appointment book was right
in front of her. But she knew it contained no further clues.

"Mr. Rockefeller and Mr. Vanderbilt are seeing to Mr. Bishop's clients. I'm sorry I can't be of more help. I can have Mr.
Rockefeller return your call when he gets in if you like. . . ."

"I want him to call me as soon as you hear from him or he
sets foot in that office. More important, I want to be in touch
with Mr. Bishop. Do you understand me, Irene?" Reuben said
coldly, and rang off.

He immediately dialed the house on Fire Island for the second
time. This time Rajean answered the phone. "This is Reuben,
Rajean. I'm trying to reach Daniel. Do you know where he
is?"

"Oh, hello there, Reuben, how are you?" Rajean drawled.

Reuben fought to keep his calm, sensing Daniel's ice-maiden
wife was only trying to get a rise out of him. She knew he
didn't want to chat. "I'm fine, thanks. Do you know where
Daniel is?"

"No, Reuben, I don't, as a matter of fact. His secretary
called yesterday afternoon and . . ." Rajean took a drag from
a cigarette and blew it out leisurely.

She was toying with him. Reuben took a deep breath, waited
a beat, and then said, "Yes?" drawing out the syllable as if
coaxing a child.

"She said he was going out of town for, as she put it, 'an
indefinite period of time.' She said that when Daniel got back
to her with a number she'd call me." Rajean sounded peeved
as she offered this information, as if she didn't appreciate being
kept in the dark—even about matters that didn't interest her
in the least. "Why, Reuben, is there something wrong?"

Reuben deliberately kept his voice light. "Nothing earth-
shattering. I just need to talk to him about something. It can
wait." It wouldn't do to stir up a hornet's nest—at least until

he knew what was going on. He continued to speak in a friendly, less urgent manner. "How are you, Rajean, and when are you and Nellie coming to the land of sunshine?"

"Daniel said something about October, but it isn't definite. How is everyone?" she responded politely. One never knew when the services of a Hollywood mogul might come in handy.

"Just fine. When Daniel phones, will you tell him to give me a call?"

"Of course. Take care of yourself, Reuben, and give my regards to . . . your wife and boys."

"You bet."

His forehead deeply furrowed, Reuben stared at the shiny black telephone for a long time. Now he had a new set of worries. Where the hell was Daniel?

The next call he made was to his own office. His secretary assured him Daniel had not called, and his third meeting with the union men had been canceled, but everything else was fine.

When he hung up, Reuben looked around and realized the day was rapidly picking up speed. The dew of morning was gone, the debris of his gardening labors had already been cleaned up, and his coffee was dead cold. In that moment he made up his mind to fly east.

It was more than a whim, he told himself as he stood beneath the stinging spray of his bathroom shower. Something was wrong, he could feel it, sense it in every pore of his body. Daniel was in trouble of some kind and hadn't asked for his help. Instead he'd obviously turned to his two Harvard friends. Why? Was he in some kind of political legal trouble? When Daniel had called him, his voice had sounded strained, that much he remembered, and the call itself had triggered his own jittery feelings.

As he dressed, Reuben's mind whirled. Some kind of political intrigue, something top secret. That was the only situation that would account for the fact that Daniel couldn't be reached. "Ah, shit!" Reuben exploded. An indefinite period of time could mean anything from a few hours to a few years. He knew Daniel to be an honest man, but politics was dirty business, and no one had to be a Harvard graduate to figure *that* out.

Reuben had one foot on the running board of his car when his maid called to him that a Mr. Rockefeller was on the phone long distance. He walked back to the house, his thoughts churning at this turn of events. An inner voice cautioned him to tread easy, but after he'd identified himself, he threw discretion to the winds. "I need to get in touch with Daniel, and I need to do it immediately. Where is he?" he demanded coldly.

There was a sigh on the other end of the line. "I wish I could help you, Mr. Tarz, but I don't have a number for Daniel. He said he'd get back to me with one, but so far he hasn't done that. Jerry and I are manning the office, taking turns until Daniel gets back. . . . I'll be more than happy to give him your message as soon as he calls."

Reuben instantly sensed in Rockefeller's voice the same strain he'd heard in Daniel on his Fourth of July call. "Look, Mr. Rockefeller, in all the years Daniel and I have known each other, we have never, I repeat, never, neglected to leave at least a phone number. The simple fact is I'm not buying your story, or his secretary's story. Now, what kind of trouble does Daniel *think* he's in? Is it something to do with the government work he does?"

Rocky's agile brain sifted and collated as he paused for just the right amount of time. "Daniel said you were smart and wouldn't buy our story," he said sotto voce. "The Justice Department is . . . how can I say . . . Secrecy is the name of the game over there. It's the best I can do, Mr. Tarz. For now."

"I'm coming to Washington," Reuben said flatly.

The alarm Rocky felt at Reuben's words communicated itself in his voice. "I wouldn't do that if I were you. At least not right away. Look, let's make a pact right now. I'll call you the moment I hear something, day or night. If Jerry or I think you should be here, I'll have one of our planes pick you up personally." Then he threw in the lug wrench, the one he knew would hit Tarz between the eyes. He hated to do it, but he had no other choice. "Daniel wants it this way, Mr. Tarz. That's why Jerry and I are here manning the office. It's what Daniel wants. If you're the friend Daniel says you are, then you'll respect his wishes."

Reuben swallowed past the lump in his throat. He had to agree; he had no other choice. "All right, I'll stay here for now. But when the time comes, never mind sending the old family plane, I have one of my own. And I'll keep my end of the pact, but this is yours: You call me every three hours and I don't mean every three and a half hours. Every *three* hours."

"Sealed, Mr. Tarz."

Reuben slammed down the receiver so hard, he thought he heard it break. Rockefeller's words didn't sit well with him.

He'd been too glib, too . . . He hadn't actually said Daniel was off on government work. What he'd done was pick up on Reuben's hunch and ride with it. The only thing that halfway reassured him was the fact that Rocky and Jerry had always proven themselves good friends to Daniel. And he'd seen enough of the good ol' boy Harvard-Princeton crap to know they stuck together like glue. That's why he had made sure Daniel became one of them twenty-odd years ago. They would obey Daniel's instructions to the letter, just as he himself would.

He would simply have to wait, something he didn't like to do and wasn't very good at. The realization riled Reuben so, he lashed out at the leather sofa in his study. Cursing with the pain that shot up his leg, he jerked his foot away and stomped out of the room. There was no point in going to the studio, he decided, he'd just vent his anger and frustration on anyone who came near him. The servants were already off hiding somewhere. No, he'd change his clothes and go back to the garden, finish working on his roses. Or he could go through the *Examiner* and torture himself wondering about Mickey's safety— He shrugged out of his suit jacket and ripped off his tie. The hell with changing his clothes. Who said you couldn't prune roses in suit pants and business shoes? These days he did whatever he damned well pleased, and it pleased him to work on his roses exactly as he was. So why did he feel that he had to defend his actions, even to himself?

Muttering a frustrated oath, he attacked the roses, all six feet three of him towering over the huge thorny stems and hacking away without a qualm. Once he'd made love to Mickey on a bed of rose petals. They'd gathered them in secret and arranged them with conspiratorial giggles. Then he'd undressed her ceremonially and placed her among them. The combination of the look in her eyes, her pliant body, and the heady scent of the petals had been so overwhelming, he'd thought his desire would drive him insane. Afterward the fragile petals had been bruised and crushed, but Mickey had gathered them up tenderly and placed them one by one in a jar. At the time he'd thought it the most wonderful thing in the world.

Suddenly a thorn penetrated his glove and pierced his finger, but he barely felt it. Absently he removed the glove and sucked at the blood trickling from the minute wound. Was that jar still on the bedroom mantel in the château, he wondered. And Mickey—where was she? Was she safe? Did she get out in time? Jesus, he'd give anything to know.

How many times he'd wanted to go back, actually booked passage, only to cancel at the last minute. She didn't want him, and he couldn't force himself on her. Maybe he should have gone. Maybe he should have listened to her tell him coldly, finally, that she didn't want him. Perhaps that would have freed him. Pride, the deadliest sin of all. And fear of rejection, the second deadly sin.

Reuben brushed the sweat from his brow. Guilty on both counts! Almost desperately he hacked at a bush full of delicate, almond-colored blooms, stepping on buds that would have bloomed in another day, crushing them to a messy pulp. It must be something in him that destroyed the things he loved and things he didn't care to love. Like Bebe, his wife. He should have divorced her years before, but something in him wouldn't allow that final action. On more than one occasion Daniel had told him Bebe was his link to Mickey in a sick kind of way. He hadn't listened, or he'd pretended not to. Now . . . now he had to make a decision, not this second, but in the coming weeks. His need to be free was strangling him. None of them needed him, and he doubted seriously that either his wife or his children loved him. Simon and Dillon were his, flesh of his flesh. He'd tried to love them, but in his heart he knew that if he never saw any of them again, he wouldn't care. Christ! What kind of a man was he? It was Mickey, her rejection of him, that had killed his capacity to love. It always came back to Mickey.

How in the hell had he gotten this far into his life without feeling love again, the kind of love he'd had for Mickey? Was it true that some people were capable of loving only once?

Reuben tossed the cutting shears onto the glass-topped patio table and frowned when he saw a crack spread out from where they landed. Who the hell cared? He certainly didn't. It would simply be replaced, like magic. He removed the gloves and placed them over the shears.

Right now, this second, he could walk out the door and never come back. He provided for his family—provided handsomely. Daniel handled the trusts and the accounts. His family would never want for a thing. Why not sell his forty-nine percent of Fairmont Studio stock to Philippe Bouchet? For a price . . . a price that would set him up somewhere far away from this place.

Hands in his pockets, Reuben tramped through his manicured grounds. He listened a moment to a chorus of sounds overhead.

When was the last time he'd actually stopped to appreciate the music of the birds? He couldn't remember. Could he give it up, the studio and his family, and walk away? Why not? After all, what exactly was he giving up? If Bebe and the children no longer needed him, why was he still here? *Because you want to be here wallowing in self-pity. If you wanted out, you would have gotten out a long time ago*, an inner voice replied.

Reuben rubbed his temples wearily. It was true: the guilt . . . the pity . . . I had to make amends. . . . Oh, God, how was I to know the years would fly and I'd never feel anything again? How was I to know I couldn't make up for what had happened?

Walk away, you've given enough—and you've taken enough. It's all been evened out somewhere along the way. Leave it all behind . . . make the decision.

"And what will I do?" Reuben's own voice startled him.

Take a trip around the world, suggested the inner voice. *Something will come to you once you make the decision.*

Reuben sat down on a stone bench nestled in bougainvillea. When he looked up he could see his house shimmering in the golden California sunlight. "That's just it. I can't make up my mind. I don't even know where Bebe is. I can't divorce her if I don't know where she is."

Private detectives and lawyers will find her; that's not your problem. Your problem is finding you. Get a divorce!

That means I failed.

Your marriage was a failure from the first day, and you knew it then just as you know it now. You're a coward, Reuben Tarz, a bloody coward.

Reuben stood up abruptly. He'd had enough of this arguing with himself. "As soon as the problem with Daniel is resolved, I'll act on my own life decisions. That's how I'll proceed."

He felt exhausted. The sun was warm, and a nap in the shade on one of the terrace chaises was a welcome thought. As soon as he walked back to the terrace and realized he didn't have to think another thought, he closed his eyes and slept. But his sleep was plagued with vague and clouded glimpses of Daniel.

A week passed, an angry, belligerent week. Rockefeller and Vanderbilt were as good as their word—they called every three hours to inform Reuben that there had been no word from Daniel. On the morning of the eighth day, Reuben calmly arranged to fly to Washington, D.C. He'd had enough of Daniel's friends and knew without a doubt that they were both lying through their upper-crust teeth.

As he issued orders to the staff to prepare for his departure, his mind was on his upcoming confrontation with Daniel's friends. He'd see how good they were at lying to his face. Daniel was in trouble, and he was sorry now that he'd allowed these two sharks to bullshit him the way they had. He'd gone along with it for Daniel's sake, but now it was his turn. One way or the other he'd get answers.

Just one more day, he told himself as his car arrived at the site of the waiting plane. As he walked up the steps, the crew members welcomed him aboard. The steward closed the hatch, and the plane immediately began to taxi down the runway.

His personal life was on hold. Daniel came first.

Chapter Three

HUDDLED IN THE CORNER, BEBE SAT ON THE ROOMY SEAT of the cab as it lumbered along. It was late and she couldn't wait to get into a hot shower and wash the grime of travel from her weary body before climbing into bed. For time out of mind she'd been away visiting a round of rich and racy friends on the East Coast, rubbing elbows with that part of society that had no need to catch the 8:05 to work. From Newport, Rhode Island, old-money homesteads, to Palm Beach estates and cozy ten-stateroom yachts, to elegant Park Avenue penthouses she was known as Bebe, never-miss-a-trick Rosen. When she left to go home for a while, they felt it was just to rest and rev up for the next go-round. It had been that way for the past ten years, ever since she'd realized once and for all that her marriage was not going to get any better. She felt nauseated, the same self-revulsion she felt every time she remembered how unequivocally stupid she had been to give up her children's stock in Fairmont to Reuben, hoping to sweeten their reconciliation. How could she have been the one to give the great Reuben Tarz the means to be even more autonomous and selfish? Bebe shuddered and shook her head to banish the thoughts from her mind. Her hand automatically searched for the personally engraved silver flask that was never far from her grasp.

With a trembling hand she took a good long desperate swallow, then stared idly out her window.

The journey down Sepulveda was a familiar route from the Los Angeles County Airport. How many hundreds of times had she made it, she wondered dully. And always at the end of it, the house of her empty marriage. Only once, she realized, had she considered it home, and that was on her wedding day. On that day she had felt new and triumphant and full all at once. The disastrous past she and Reuben had shared together in France—when she had been forced to watch this man of her dreams in love with another woman—was behind her. On that new day there was no need to dwell on the nightmare rape that had resulted from her misfired attempt at seducing him, no need to brood upon the abandoned child of that crazed union. France and everything connected with it had faded in her memory as she'd walked down the aisle with her father and seen Reuben standing there, waiting to claim her as his own. But only a few hours later—from the time they arrived at 5633 Laurel Canyon—she was forced to recognize that all her hopes and dreams were hideously false—a realization borne out by the utterly pathetic eyes of her inebriated and impotent new husband. From that day on, their home had become Reuben Tarz's house.

Bebe's eyes focused on the flask in her hand. She drained it dry and cursed under her breath.

The estate at 5633 Laurel Canyon was choice and prestigious. It was filled with priceless objets d'art, paintings, and fine furnishings—so beautifully embellished that it had been photographed and written up numerous times in posh decorating magazines. The kitchen was a marvel of modern convenience, and the gardens were lush; their game room and private screening room were elaborate and unique. Reuben and Bebe Tarz had entertained and lived there and two children had grown up in it, at least part of the time, but it had never been a home.

"Did you say 5633, lady?" The driver's voice startled her.

"Yes, 5633 Laurel," she managed to say. Impatiently she checked her watch. Two-fifteen A.M. Bebe looked up and saw that the driver was half slumped onto the front seat. "Could you please use the gas pedal with some authority?" she whined. "I'd really like to get home as soon as possible."

"Yes, ma'am," he said, and sullenly pressed his foot down on the gas. His passenger's furtive swigs from the silver flask had not passed unnoticed. Snippy, boozin', society dame, he said to himself.

Less than five minutes later the cab driver turned onto the long driveway and brought the car to a grinding halt in front of the large, stately mansion. "Fifty-six thirty-three Laurel, lady. It doesn't look like anyone is awake," he said matter-of-factly, and shifted on his seat to stare at her. "That'll be fifteen dollars."

Bebe handed him a twenty-dollar bill. "Keep the change," she said magnanimously.

The driver glanced at the twenty, then at her, and sniffed his displeasure. "If you want your bags carried inside, that's an extra five dollars," he said boldly.

"All right," Bebe said wearily as she fished around in her purse for another bill. All she found was a wad of twenties crunched in a ball. When she handed him one and was rewarded with a smile, she decided not to ask for her change.

It was no surprise to her that the house was still the same even though she'd been gone for three months. It was always the same. Only *she* changed; each time she returned she was different in one little way or another. It took some effort, but she straightened her back as she climbed the steps.

"Just leave the bags by the door," she said to the driver.

"My pleasure, lady," he said tartly, setting down the six suitcases in relief. Tipping his hat politely, he clambered into his cab and slowly drove down the long driveway. When he looked into his rearview mirror at the still, dark house, the woman was gone.

The door closed behind Bebe with a loud click. It would be nice to have a dog or a cat to welcome her home, she thought, at least something warm and alive. The servants would be asleep, of course, and the children were elsewhere; and certainly her husband didn't care when and if she ever came home.

Some of the other arrivals she had made to this house flashed through her mind. The day she'd arrived with her infant son Simon, for example, under Reuben's armed guard—body-guards he had hired to dog her every step after he was informed that she was drinking and smoking dope in her last weeks of pregnancy. It didn't matter to Reuben that she'd begun to abuse her body because of him—because she'd realized that he really didn't care about her health, only the baby's.

Or the morning she had come back to plead with him to help

her after she had witnessed her lover kill his wife. Reuben had tried to make her feel guilty for her infidelity—had even asked her if it had all been worth it. At the time, anything was worth not feeling as dead inside as she felt with him.

God! What's the use of thinking about all this, she asked herself wearily. It's all water under the bridge.

Drunk and weepy, Bebe crept into the house like a thief in the night. It wouldn't do to wake the master and have him see her like this again and so soon. Not in the house he'd mag-nanimously allowed her to live in after they had both realized that their marriage was a total and unsalvageable disaster.

Bebe looked down at her travel bags, beautiful calf leather, battered and scuffed now, mute testimony to her wanderlust. Reuben had told her once that the household was happiest when she was away. And she believed him. Lately she always be-lieved Reuben. It was easier that way. Picking up her makeup case, she made her way up the stairs to the bedroom she'd taken for herself. It was a pretty room, decorated in periwinkle blue and white. The double bed welcomed her. The blue-and-white satin spread was the same, the shams artfully arranged against the white headboard. The crisp organdy curtains looked as though they'd been freshly laundered, and the flowers, bright red roses, Reuben's roses, were fresh, too.

Had Reuben placed them on her night table, she wondered. Instantly she realized that the thought was too silly for words. Reuben didn't care if she lived or died, so he certainly wouldn't place his precious roses on her nightstand.

Bebe was dressed in the latest fashion; everything about her shrieked of elegance and wealth, thanks to her husband's gen-erosity. She'd been beautiful once, with clear green eyes and a lovely heartwarming smile. But the clear eyes were dull now and coated with garish makeup; the heartwarming smile was forced and oddly cold. Her hair was bleached these days, the ends dry and frizzled, the roots a dirty blond streaked with gray. Somehow, though, she'd managed to maintain her figure, which was soft and womanly. She dieted constantly, nibbling on things like toast, celery, and tiny bits of chicken, preferring to drink her calories in the form of liquor. Of course she smoked too much, both tobacco and marijuana, and her fingers were stained yellow with nicotine. The physical abuse she'd sub-jected her body to over the years had finally taken its toll. The fine lines around her eyes were deeper now, the slight droop at her mouth more noticeable with her thinness. She'd even noticed wrinkles on her earlobes.

Bebe Rosen was no longer the beautiful woman she'd once been.

Tired as she was, Bebe knew she wouldn't be able to sleep, so she began to search the old hiding places for a bottle. It took her four tries before she found what she was looking for. Holding her prize aloft in mock victory, she walked out onto the tiny wrought-iron balcony. The half moon was still brilliant, and the sprinkling of stars overhead winked down upon her. Welcoming me home, Bebe thought inanely.

She kicked off her shoes and peeled down to her slip and stockings, throwing her blouse and skirt over her shoulder into the room. The cool breeze offered comfort to her body—but not to her mind.

There'd been times in the past when she'd felt alone and lonely, but never like this. The end of the road. So why did she stay? Why did she go off on what Reuben referred to as her toots? Surely she didn't still love him. The children were seldom home and never needed her anyway, so she couldn't use them as an excuse. Reuben didn't want her, and she didn't think she wanted him any longer.

For so long now she'd been trying to come up with a name or a term to describe her relationship with Reuben. Now she knew what it was. It had come to her as she was paying the cab driver downstairs. *Parasitic*—Reuben fed off her, and she fed off him in many ugly ways. Her whole life was ugly. She was forty years old, and all she had to show for it was a guest bedroom in a house owned by a husband who didn't love her, two children who didn't need her, and a host of rich and worthless acquaintances. Not a true friend in the bunch. Bebe drank from the bottle in her hand.

So many unanswered questions . . . Why did she drink so much? Why did she take drugs? Why wasn't she a better mother? Why couldn't she find peace and love? Why?

She wanted to sleep—she needed sleep. But the only way she could do that when she got like this was to smoke marijuana. She lurched into the bedroom, her hands groping hungrily through her makeup case. She pulled from it all the items needed to roll a fat one, then did so with trembling fingers. The first drag was always the best. As she felt it spread through her body and rush to her brain, she sat on the floor of the room and pulled a pillow from the bed to hold against her chest, her eyes heavy, a smile playing about her lips. She imagined the face of her mother and then began to cry when she realized it was not her mother's face at all, but the face of her aunt Mickey.

"I hate you, Michelene Fonsard!" she spat out, crying now in earnest. "I hate you with a passion that knows no equal!"

There it was, out in the open for her to examine. The war news . . . that's what had started this whole thing. Reuben would be remembering France, the war, and the time they'd spent at Mickey's château. Reuben and Daniel would reminisce about the good times and the life they had shared with Mickey . . . until she'd come along and changed everything . . . for all of them. She was the catalyst that had destroyed their little idyll . . . and Reuben had never let her forget it. He'd made her pay and pay. Even on the night they had decided to patch things up, when Reuben had garnered the Academy Award, he had insulted her by referring to Mickey—calling her the most important person in his life. In front of the whole world.

"I hope those dirty Germans destroyed your precious château and confiscated all your money," Bebe muttered, reaching again for the bottle. "I hope they kill you! Then Reuben will be free of you once and for all. Damn you, Mickey!"

This time she'd come home for one reason: to watch her husband pore avidly over the newspapers, hoping for any news of the war in France. Masochist that she was, she'd come home to torture herself by watching her husband torture himself over his lost love. Almost immediately she had begun to pack after she had read in *The New York Times* that France had been occupied by the Germans.

And when she'd had enough of that, she'd ask Reuben for a divorce—get herself a good lawyer and take him to the cleaners. Bitter resentment rose like bile in her throat; *revenge is sweet*, kept running through her head. What a perfect way to exit. What a perfect note to exit on. Finally she would see him turned inside out, and then she'd step on him.

Maybe if *she* were free, she could start a new life someplace other than perennially sunny California. All the other times she'd been coerced by Reuben to dry out. This time she'd try it on her own. If she failed, she would have no one to blame but herself.

Bebe looked at the rolled cigarette in her hand. She tried puffing on it, but it had gone out. She lit it again and resumed smoking.

Canada! She'd go to Canada. That was far enough away. If

she wanted to, she could even change her name. A clean start, a clean identity. No one would know about her tarnished past. Such good intentions, but she never followed through because it meant she couldn't drink, and besides, making plans was too much trouble.

John Paul, that was the name she'd given her firstborn. The baby in the cradle who'd clutched her finger with such wondrous strength. The tawdriest part of her past. The single thing that unerringly made her cringe at herself. Was he a loyal Frenchman now fighting for his country? A country that he thought of as his own? He would be old enough. She thought about John Paul every day of her life. Whom had Yvette given him to? Was he as handsome as his father? Maybe John Paul was behind all her misery. The thought of her son lying dead on some battlefield, never knowing he had an American mother and father, shattered Bebe's heart. She said a prayer then for her faceless son, asking that his life be spared if he was among the French soldiers fighting the Germans.

Bebe slept on the floor that night just as she was—the pillow on her chest, the bottle clutched in one hand, and the half-smoked cigarette dangling from her limp fingers.

Chapter Four

THE SLEEPY FRENCH COUNTRYSIDE APPEARED PEACEFUL AND calm in the evening twilight, but to those inhabitants who lived in the tiny villages off the narrow dirt road it was anything but peaceful or calm. Every man, woman, and child in the villages knew that in every church, in every clump of gorse, in every cluster of trees, German soldiers lurked with guns cocked waiting for straggling partisans loyal to France and in need of temporary sanctuary. They also knew that when the loyalists emerged to forage for food and shelter in the darkest part of the night, they would be gunned down like wild animals. Then, within minutes of a shooting, hostages would be dragged from the villages and a second round of machine-gun bullets would rain down upon the peaceful countryside.

There were many who were not afraid—small numbers, to be sure—who would willingly give their lives to help those who might be able to thwart the hateful Germans. What these simple country farmers lacked in weapons they made up for with fierce loyalty and an intense desire to help their mother country drive the Boche back to their own land. Cries of "*Vive la France!*" were mouthed as often as daily prayers, as a toast with the first glass of wine at dinner, when tucking children into bed, as salutations in the street to friends and neighbors.

It was to one of these small villages that Michelene Fonsard, her son Philippe, and her friend Yvette were headed—on foot now since bicycles had proven dangerous at night on roads deeply rutted by the constant German concourse of armored cars and tanks. They were weary and hungry; their small supply of food had been exhausted days before. Now they were resting, something they had learned to do more often toward the end of the day, in a field of tall grasses that afforded them a suitable hiding place. When they spoke, if they spoke at all, it was in whispers. Quietness and stealth meant survival. So much could be said with one's eyes or with the flick of a finger or wrist.

But tonight Yvette could hold back no longer. Although at the onset she had agreed to come along with her lifelong friend, her doubts were beginning to overcome her commitment. When she had determined that the young man traveling with them was out of earshot, she spoke. "This is a foolhardy thing we're doing, Michelene," she hissed into her friend's ear. "You yourself said you don't even know if Daniel heard all of your message when the wireless went out. In your frenzy to protect Philippe you may be taking him to his death. The Germans are everywhere, like lice. How, Michelene . . . how will your American friend get here? You are dreaming . . ." Yvette hesitated, then continued in a softer tone, "But I cannot fault you for wanting that dream to come true for your son."

Michelene had never known motherhood, yet in all her years Yvette had never seen a better example of a good mother than this woman lying beside her in the reeds. And the boy she had mothered, sleeping just a few feet away, wasn't even her son.

For some reason, Yvette thought grumpily, Mickey looked the same to her tired eyes as she'd always looked. Certainly she was old enough to be the boy's real mother, but her beauty had a timelessness to it, as though God had created her full blown and forbidden her to age. Her hair was the same dark chestnut, still thick and lustrous, adorning her head like a sable crown. Finely arched natural brows and incredibly dark lashes emphasized her warm, dark eyes—bedroom eyes, Yvette called them. There were no lines on her fair skin, a fact Yvette bemoaned whenever she compared herself with her friend. She truly believed God had created perfection in Michelene Fonsard, whose curvaceous figure was the envy of many a younger woman in Paris.

Once she herself had been beautiful, at least men had thought so, for she'd had her pick many times. During her youth she'd

been fashionably thin, but now she was round in all the wrong
places, which often caused her to grumble good-naturedly that
she was "one size from the neck down." True, she still possessed a certain sultriness, perhaps because of her rich auburn
hair that when she released it from its pins tumbled luxuriantly
to her waist. But even though she was skillful with makeup
and knew how best to complement and enhance the titian beauty
of her hair, her hands gave her away—her hands and the depth
of suffering in her eyes, which no amount of makeup could
obscure.

Thus she considered herself and Mickey old, perhaps not in
appearance but in years. However, age was supposed to bring
wisdom and peace, and here they were with neither. Running
from the Germans out of fear, never knowing if the day that
followed would be their last. Hatred kept them alive, so Yvette
nurtured their hatred as she would a fragile seedling. Whatever
it took to stay alive she would do. Whatever she had to do for
the boy she would do because Mickey was the only person in
the world left to her, and whatever Mickey loved was beloved
to her as well.

"Daniel will come," Mickey said now with more confidence
than she felt. "He knows about war, remember? He will not
let me down, I know this, Yvette, in here." She thumped her
breast.

Yvette snorted. "Then he is as stupid as we are. We, at
least, know our own country. What does he know of traveling
as we have for the past five days? And if he does come, he
could be shot for his efforts. Then how will you feel, knowing
you brought an old friend here to have him killed?" she said
sourly. "You should have called the boy's father instead of
Daniel. Daniel has nothing at stake here. Reuben would move
heaven and earth to reach his son—if you had only told him
he had a son. Bah!"

Mickey Fonsard felt only love for the woman by her side.
Her crankiness, she knew, was merely the way she chose to
express her frustration at their situation. There was no better
friend on earth than Yvette. Mickey smiled and embraced her
tenderly. "He will come, Yvette. He will come. He will head
to the château, not Paris. Daniel is a powerful man in Washington," she said proudly.

"And that is going to do us a lot of good here. . . . *Chérie*,
you are dreaming. No one can help us but ourselves and other
loyal Frenchmen. Forget Daniel," she said wearily.

"No. You must believe with me, Yvette. You must. In any case," Mickey continued in a firm whisper, holding Yvettte's reluctant gaze, "you pledged to help me get Philippe to America, and part of that pledge is believing that Daniel will come."

Yvette let out a frustrated sigh. "Old friend, I want to believe, but this is my concern. If he does manage to get here, his chances are not what ours are. What will we do about Philippe if something happens to Daniel?"

Mickey had thought of nothing else over the past three days. She was as worried as Yvette but by sheer will had managed to hide her fear. "Then we will head south and try to cross into Spain."

Mickey's heart beat furiously in anticipation as she awaited her friend's response to her proposal. Yvette's next words were a surprise.

"You should have told him your intentions when we started out. It will be such a shock." Both women looked over at the sleeping young man.

Yvette overrode Mickey before she could protest. "I know, I know. In your heart you were not sure Daniel would come. Why stir things up, eh? You are so much a mother, *chérie*. It matters not if that young man is of your flesh or not. You *are* his mother, and I for one applaud you. I am proud you chose me for his godmother." Tears burned Mickey's eyes as she kissed Yvette on both cheeks.

Across the meadow and to their left, a long, low whistle echoed across the fields. Instantly they were alert. In the next few moments they waited, hushed and expectant, but nothing further happened to alarm them. The night became quiet again with only the familiar sounds of summer filling the warm evening. Soon it would be totally dark and they would move from their hiding place. Mickey looked up at the sky, hoping for the clouds to move in from the west, but they did not. The light of the quarter moon was bright and silvery, ribboning through the tall grasses like brilliant threads.

The boy had been watching the women without their knowledge. They thought he was asleep, and he allowed them to think so, hoping to catch a few of their whispered words. But they spoke too softly for him to hear. Although he wanted to view himself as his mother and godmother's protector, in reality he knew they were protecting him. He should be in the army fighting the damn Germans. Someday his heart would burst at the knowledge that he was a disloyal Frenchman.

Every day for the past year, from the moment France fell to the Germans, he had grieved for his old life. It had made him want to lash out at something, anything, to rid himself of the anger that was flooding through him—anger that had been simmering within him from the moment Paris was confiscated by the Germans. Never would he forget the sound of the hammer securing the filthy sign to their neighbors' doors. When the Germans were two doors away, they'd slipped out the back door, and with the help of friends his mother had secured forged travel warrants to aid them in traveling south to the château where he was born.

It happened so quickly, there'd been virtually no warning, and suddenly Paris was overrun—a conquered city. Overnight hundreds of huge swastikas blazed from buildings. Food disappeared from the markets to feed the German army, and gasoline vanished as if by magic, commandeered for the German war machine. His mother had looked so helpless at first, and then anger had set in, and for weeks now he hadn't seen the shadow of a smile on her face. Thank God for the timely visit a few months before of Yvette and Henri. . . . He would not, could not, think about the last time he had seen Henri . . . not now . . . perhaps not ever.

Thoughtfully he fingered his student enrollment card in his pocket. It was the only document his mother allowed him to carry. It said he was French, Philippe Bouchet. When he'd told her he wanted to stay and fight the filthy Boche as any good Frenchman, she had refused even to discuss it. "That is the very last thing you will ever do," she had said with staunch determination. But he was sure it was not because she was being overprotective—she had told him too many stories with pride of the bravery of his father and uncle Daniel and how they had fought in the Great War and been injured. They hadn't balked or turned tail and run; they'd been boys much like himself when they went to war, and they had survived. And Yvette was not the only one to tell him of his mother's seemingly boundless generosity and energy during that war. No, it was something else. Perhaps his mother had some plan other than the agreed-upon one that they would head for Spain via Marseilles.

Now Tante Yvette and his mother were always whispering together, sharing secrets that left him feeling cheated. Why wouldn't they take him into their confidence? He was twenty years old, for God's sake! He couldn't understand his mother's relentless determination to return to Marseilles, but when he had insisted upon knowing, she had answered him in a voice she'd used only in times of crisis—a voice that warned and convinced at the same time. "It is for your own safety, Philippe," she had stated. "Soon enough you will be told, and now not another word!"

His thoughts grew dark and angry. Why wasn't his father here helping them to safety? Because he was in America making films and money, so much money that it made Philippe sick. Recently he'd learned that except for their American holdings, they were virtually paupers. The Banque de Paris, where his mother had been doing business since before he was born, had informed them that the Germans had helped themselves thoroughly. And now most of his mother's jewelry was gone, used for bribes, food, and shelter.

Slowly his anger intensified, overpowering whatever tender feelings he felt for the American father he had never seen. His mother, his aunt, and he were running for their lives like hunted criminals while his father was free and safe and unconcerned. Such diabolical unfairness almost stopped his breathing. Now he was beginning to see things in a light other than the rosy ideal his mother had consistently offered throughout his life. Lifelong promises that when he finished his education he would go to America vanished from his mind. Surviving was more important at the moment—surviving and preserving a particular way of life, hanging on to the things that he was familiar with, things that made him feel as though he belonged. The loss of his personal possessions, his education, his home. The possibility that he would never walk down the Champs-Élysées nor see the Étoile. That they might become only bittersweet memories—as had the Sorbonne and the sidewalk cafés he'd frequented with his school chums—was too painful to contemplate. Avenue Foch was now home to the Gestapo and the SS. The clatter and specter of goose-stepping troops and armored tanks rattled ominously through his brain. All information pointed to one distinct, terrifying reality: The Germans had the upper hand. Filthy Boches! They would rot in hell if he had anything to do with it. Tears of frustration gathered in Philippe's eyes, and he wiped at them with the sleeve of his cotton shirt. His life as he knew it was over. What lay in store for him? All he knew was that he was terrified—not for himself so much as for his mother and his aunt Yvette. But if a decision had to be made, he would die for his mother. Of that he was sure.

Philippe jerked to sudden awareness as the cloud cover his mother prayed for suddenly slid across the bright quarter moon. As one they surged to their feet, moving silently through the tall grass toward the edge of the road. Another kilometer or two and they would be in the village where, hopefully, there would be food and water. His stomach growled rebelliously, a reminder that he had had no food for three days except for what they'd been able to forage in the woods.

An hour later the weary travelers arrived at the village and were stunned to find it deserted, the occupants undoubtedly having moved south.

"We should keep on going," Yvette said fretfully. "If everyone is gone, that means the Germans are close. I want to go on. I don't care how hungry I am. I'd rather starve than be caught by those bastards." She spat on the ground as she cursed the murderers of her husband.

Mickey shivered. Yvette was correct in her assumptions, she knew, yet she wanted to stop, to gather food for . . . Philippe. When she looked toward him in the darkness, he nodded his head to show he agreed with Yvette. With a sigh Mickey moved forward, keeping to the shadows of the village street. "We'll find food tomorrow, perhaps something left behind in someone's abandoned root cellar. Perhaps a fat frog or two as we get closer to the water."

"How much farther to the château, *Maman*?" Philippe whispered.

"Another day and a half if we haven't lost our way," Mickey whispered back. "Possibly sooner if we can travel by daylight. It is difficult to see familiar landmarks in the darkness. Are you tiring, Philippe?"

"No, of course not. It is you and Tante Yvette I am worried about. She showed me her blisters last evening. I don't know how she can walk."

"She's walking because she has to. One does what one must do, Philippe. Always remember that. Neither I nor Yvette have any desire to be sliced to pieces by some dirty German's cursed bayonet. Nor do I want to see you marched off to some camp. We walk," she said briskly.

They moved on steadily after that, so Mickey did not see the expression on Philippe's face at her last statement. At last he had a clue to his mother's innermost fears for him, he mused—she didn't want him to be marched off to some camp. There had been rumors, ugly, disquieting rumors, of some types of labor camps believed to be located inside Germany, established for the imprisonment of enemies to their country's ideals.

Suddenly, from nowhere, a thought surfaced that made his skin crawl. It was no secret that the Germans considered Jews a threat to their basic ideals—and he was a Jew. He stumbled and almost fell, then reassured Yvette with a wave of his hand as she looked back at him. In that instant he understood his mother's concern, if not her actions. He hoped she knew what she was doing.

They continued on for the next two days, stopping to rest, greedily picking at the sparse berries that lined the roadside. When they reached the crest of their village, Mickey held her hand up to slow Philippe and Yvette.

The town was strangely quiet, the streets empty of people. From her position at the top of the hill Mickey could see no sign of activity, French or German. Where were the people, the neighbors she knew by name and had shared meals with, sat next to in the village church? Had they left or were they hiding? The church—she looked to the end of the small town square where the old white church loomed, alone and solemn, its spire stretching upward as though in supplication. Where was the curé? Where were the children, the laughter, the dogs and cats that roamed? The silence was eerie and so total that she felt as though she could reach out to it. Philippe and Yvette joined her, looking down at the village.

"We're home, but I fear our friends and neighbors are gone. Listen to the stillness. Even the birds are quiet today."

"A bad omen," Yvette said tartly. "When the birds and small animals leave, it is a bad omen. Pay attention, Michelene."

"I am, old friend. We have seen no Germans for three days. I think we are safe for the moment. Come," she said, "we are going home."

Mickey looked neither to the right nor to the left as she led her son and friend through the small main street. The sight of the boarded-up shops made her want to weep. She could smell the fear, probably because it was her own. Suddenly she turned, startled, when she heard her name called. She backed up a few steps to the *boulangerie* when she saw Monsieur LeForge waving to her. She walked over and embraced him. "It is good to see you again, old friend," she said warmly. "Tell me, what has happened here? Where is everyone?"

"The men and the boys . . . most of them are gone. I was too old to . . . join the fight with them. . . . The others, they stay in their houses waiting for the sound of boots to come marching in. They said the soldiers will be here in another week or ten days. How did you get here, madame?"

"With the help of our countrymen. Thank you for being brave enough to greet us. You remember my friend Yvette and my son, Philippe?"

LeForge tipped his cap and smiled at Yvette. He looked long and silently at Philippe. "The boy is a man now."

And he should be fighting with his countrymen, Mickey added silently, reading the old man's thoughts. Philippe began to speak, but Mickey stopped him. "We will wait . . . for word. . . . He will do what he can, as I will," she said sharply. "We are patriots the same as every Frenchman."

"Not all are patriots," the old man snarled. "There are those among us who . . . Never mind, go. Go to your château and don't talk to anyone, that is the best advice I can give you."

"And I will take it, old friend. *Au revoir.*"

It was less than a mile to the château. No word had been spoken as they approached their destination. Mickey felt the tension emanating from her son and was torn between the wonderful sight of her beloved estate, nestled in its ancient foliage and welcoming her home, and Philippe's obvious torment.

At the door Philippe uttered his first words through clenched teeth. "How long will we stay, *Maman*?"

"We shall see," Mickey whispered.

The heavy doors creaked as Philippe shouldered them open. To Mickey's ears it was the loveliest sound in the world. She was home, safe at last to wait for Daniel. Surely God was on her side now, making sure they all stayed alive until her American friend came. And he would come. He had to come. Then and only then could she deal with Philippe.

Everything in the château was miraculously intact. Obviously no German had crossed this threshold.

"Philippe, see to the beds for us while Yvette and I find out if we have anything to eat. Come and join us in the kitchen as soon as you have done so."

In the root cellar Mickey and Yvette gathered turnips and

potatoes and boiled them with a large bunch of onions into a hearty, nourishing soup. As the fire warmed the kitchen, the two women bustled about chatting amiably. Ten minutes later Philippe joined them, carrying a second armful of fresh wood for the fire. There was no bread, but a vintage wine from the wine cellar accompanied the hasty meal and brought a sigh of contentment to their lips.

Mickey reached across the table and enclosed her son's hand with her own. "Philippe, you look exhausted, why don't you try to get some rest now. We can all think more clearly with food and rest. Go."

"All right, *Maman*. Do you need anything else?"

"No. Yvette and I will be fine."

"*Bonsoir, Maman, Tante*." Philippe rose heavily to his feet. The two women watched as he left the warmth of the kitchen. They looked at each other, eyes full of unspoken words when he was gone.

They sat side by side, soaking their blistered feet in a smelly concoction of water, oil, and herbs. An equally vile-smelling ointment would be applied once their feet were dried. "I don't know which is worse, the pain or the remedy," Mickey said flatly.

Yvette grimaced. "What will we do if Philippe refuses to leave with Daniel? You must decide what will be said at that time, my friend."

Yvette's words bolstered Mickey momentarily. Her friend was speaking positively about Daniel's arrival. "We'll deal with that if and when it happens," she said quietly.

Yvette watched her friend's eyes fill with tears. "Do you see how he looks like his father?" Mickey murmured. "We've not been here for two years, and in just that amount of time the resemblance has settled onto him as if carved in granite."

Yvette knew exactly what Mickey was saying. When they had all filed into the great room dominated by the portrait that had hung over the mantel for so many years, the fact was unmistakable. Philippe had stood in front of the painting, presented to his mother by his father and Uncle Daniel on Christmas Day 1918, and the likeness was uncanny.

"Yes, but did you see the way he turned his back on it? He won't leave you now. He believes you are his mother. That boy will never . . . Mickey, you will have to tell him the truth.

Only then will he go." Yvette's voice broke. "Then we will have only each other."

Mickey swallowed past the lump in her throat. "It will be enough. What more can I ask than a loyal, lifelong friend? Together you and I will see France free again. I believe this, and so must you.

"Have you noticed something, Yvette?" Mickey continued thoughtfully. "Philippe has not been questioning us. I find that strange. He's always been obedient, but he does have a mind of his own. Do you suppose in some way he knows what is happening?"

"No, I don't think so. I think it was seeing Henri killed that made him so withdrawn. He's never seen death—and to witness his godfather slaughtered . . ." Yvette could barely speak as the tears flowed from her eyes. "Oh, Mickey, I saw his knees begin to give way under him. They . . . just kept shooting and shooting . . . for no reason. He was already gone."

Mickey comforted her friend. "He walked in front of the commandant . . . he didn't know . . . they smashed his glasses and he couldn't see without them . . . He's in heaven, Yvette. He is watching over us with God. I think you're right about Philippe. I wanted to hide his eyes, to take him to my bosom, but he had to see what these animals are capable of.

"Yvette, I must make a confession. I know I said we would head south and try to cross the border to Spain, but once Philippe is gone . . . I cannot. I will head north again and join the underground. I'll go as far as the border with you and then I will go back. *Chérie* . . . tell me you understand."

Yvette's eyes shone through her tears. "What I understand is that you are not going without me. How could you think, after what happened to Henri . . . and did you think for one moment that I believed your sorry story! I will fight as you fight. France will rise again and so will we. *Vive la France!*" she cried passionately, embracing Mickey.

"It's settled, then," Mickey said. "As soon as . . . as soon as Philippe leaves . . . we'll go north. I have a map with a number of safe houses marked which contain wireless equipment."

"How soon do you . . . when do you expect Daniel?"

"If he can get here, any day now. I had hoped he would be here waiting for us. He won't go to Paris, he'll find his way here . . . I know he will. I feel this in my heart."

"We will wait for your friend."

"Yes. It is all we can do."

Chapter Five

REUBEN STEPPED OFF THE PLANE AT DULLES AIRPORT, HIS EYES behind dark glasses, searching out a redcap. When he spotted one some twenty feet away, his long-legged stride picked up momentum. Two young men, bent on securing the same porter, came to a grinding halt when they noticed the grim set of Reuben's jaw as he peeled off two twenty-dollar bills and handed them to the redcap along with his baggage ticket. "See that my bags are taken to the Ambassador. The name is Tarz." Without a second look at the porter or the hapless young men, he turned on his heel and commandeered a taxi, shouldering a businessman and a middle-aged woman out of the way as he did so. On most occasions Reuben was courteous, but today wasn't a normal occasion; today was the day he was going to find out where Daniel was and what was going on. He barked out Daniel's address on K Street to the driver before settling back against the worn seat cushions.

During the long trip from California Reuben had rehearsed what he would say when he opened the door to Daniel's offices. Each introduction had been rejected as he sought for just the right words to say in front of Daniel's two friends. When they were over the Carolinas he'd decided to say whatever he damn well felt like saying; Daniel's snooty friends could either take it or lump it. If he had to, he would camp in the goddamn office until word came from Daniel. He was angry, angrier than he'd ever been in his life, and most of the anger, he knew was misdirected. Instead of venting his frustration on Daniel's friends, he should be taking it out on Daniel.

Reuben felt a wave of self-pity wash over him. Daniel wouldn't be where he was today if it weren't for him, and who did his friend turn to when he found himself in trouble? His rich Harvard buddies, that's who. *He'd* made sure Daniel got to Harvard, footed the bills, saved his life during the war, made sure he recovered at the château. Daniel had studied at the Sorbonne because of him, regained his health and eyesight because of him, lived off *his* bounty, and by God, the first time he stepped his foot into something sticky he called on other friends!

It was these "other friends," the ones keeping Daniel's affairs a secret, that rankled more than anything. He hadn't much liked Rocky and Jerry, but he would have cut out his tongue before he admitted it to Daniel. Upper crust, born with a silver spoon in their mouths, money handed to them on gold platters. Rich spoiled brats who had turned into rich arrogant businessmen who traded on their families' golden social-register names. The only thing the three of them had in common was business, their professions, whereas he and Daniel were brothers, joined at the hip through the experiences of a lifetime. There was a world of difference.

Reuben knew he was jealous; it was a fact he accepted and hated at the same time.

"This is it, mister," the driver said, sliding his cab to the curb.

Reuben stood on the sidewalk, looking up at the building that housed Daniel's offices, a building Daniel owned, thanks again to Mickey. The deed had been presented to him the day he'd graduated from Harvard Law School by a pompous attorney from the Morgan Guaranty Bank, Mickey's American bankers in New York.

Reuben had been here only once, for the guided tour, as Daniel put it. The suite of offices that belonged to Daniel's firm suited him as no other could. The wainscoted walls; the polished oak floors; the smell of rich leather; soft, comfortable furnishings; assorted academic certificates on the walls—all were indicative of Daniel Bishop. It was a lucrative building that housed other professionals: doctors, accountants, other lawyers, and several consulting firms, all paying rent to Daniel.

Reuben thrashed his way to the second floor and marched into Daniel's outer office, stormed past Irene, and barreled on through to Daniel's private offices. Irene gave a startled gasp and was half on and half off her chair about to protest until she got a good look at who was doing the storming.

Rocky was on his feet the moment Reuben entered the room. Both men eyeballed each other for a full five seconds. Then Reuben extended his hand; Rocky reached for it. Perspiration beaded Rocky's brow, but he would have died before he relaxed the bone-crushing grip Reuben was forcing on him. He wished he was wearing dark glasses like Reuben's. The man was intimidating as hell; he hadn't remembered that. Maybe it was the dark glasses that were giving him an alien, predatory look. When Reuben finally removed the dark glasses, Rocky realized he was still intimidated. This guy didn't like him, and never had. Obviously he didn't approve of his heritage and all the crap that went with blue-blood families. "I still haven't heard anything. Sit down, Mr. Tarz," he said evenly.

"I decided California was too far away to wait for news. News that I know you have and aren't sharing with me," Reuben said icily. "I'll just camp out here and . . . wait."

Rocky swallowed as he tried to clear his throat. "Suit yourself, but it's boring as hell sitting around a lawyer's office. If you want, I can give you a book on torts that's kind of lively." He jammed his hands into his trouser pockets as Reuben put the dark glasses back on. Suddenly Rocky couldn't help himself: "Do . . . ah . . . do you wear those"—he pointed to the glasses—"all the time?"

"Only when I don't like what I'm forced to look at," Reuben snapped.

"Why don't we just cut all this crap and get to the heart of the matter," Rocky said, finally exploding with indignation. "You don't like it and I don't like it. I'm here because Daniel asked me. You're here because you and Daniel go way back. That's good, I understand that. What *you* don't understand is I can't tell you anything. Jesus Christ, if I could, I would. I closed my own office to come here; Jerry did the same. We're waiting just like you."

"For what?" Reuben bellowed.

"For Daniel to call," Rocky bellowed back. "Look, if you want me to come up with some cockamamie story, I can do that; us lawyers are real good at cockamamie stories because we get them from clients all the time."

"I'll settle for the truth; try that on for size," Reuben grated.

"Why don't we try this on for size," Rocky said. "You don't like me and you don't like what I come from; ditto for Jerry. You and Daniel came up the hard way, and anyone who isn't cut from the same bolt of cloth is no damn good. Well, let me tell you something, Mr. Fairmont. Jerry and I graduated in the top three percent of our class right along with Daniel. Believe it or not, we do have brains and we use them from time to time. I consider Daniel a friend, as you do. I know, I accepted a long time ago that you're first with Daniel. Jerry and I are poor seconds compared to you. All through law school all Daniel did was talk about you and what a great guy you were. He would have died for you, did you know that? He would have goddamned died for you if you asked it of him. Do you remember all that money you used to send him; did he ever tell you what he did with it? No, I bet he didn't. He loaned it to us, me and Jerry. Of course we always paid it back, but the bulk of it was given to other students who had piss to live on. He used to say he felt guilty taking so much from you. I'll bet you five hundred dollars you didn't know he waited on tables for his own spending money. Did you ever see the . . . the fucking ledger he kept for you? Ah, even behind those dark shades I see you don't know about it. Well, here, Mr. Hollywood, take a look at this!" Rocky said, pulling an accountant's ledger from one of the desk drawers. "All the money you sent him, the spending money, the tuition, the gifts; they're all recorded, and do you see the next column? Those numbers represent what he paid out to, let's say, lesser fortunates because he knew you wouldn't take a penny in paybacks. That third column is the money he earned waiting tables. That big red zero at the bottom of the third page means the debt is paid in full. Here's the book on torts. Sit on it, read it, chew it up, I don't give a shit, but I gave my word to Daniel I would handle this office, and I can't do it with you sitting here glaring at me from behind those damn glasses. The waiting room is all yours!"

"That was a wonderful testimonial, and I thank you for it. Now tell me where the hell Daniel is or I'm going to punch your fucking lights out right now!" Reuben said, standing up, towering over Rocky.

"Try it," Rocky almost shouted, "and I'll have your ass in jail in five minutes."

"Is that any way to talk to a client?" Reuben drawled, trying to keep his temper in check.

"You aren't my client!"

"Sure I am. Irene," he bellowed, "come in here! Take this hundred dollars and enter it in the books. I've just hired Mr. Rockefeller to handle some business for me. And when you record it, mark down the time." Reuben looked at his watch. "I gave it to him twenty minutes ago. I want a receipt, too." Three minutes later Reuben pocketed his receipt.

"Where were we? Oh, yes, I was going to punch your lights out and you were going to land my ass in jail. Now, where's Daniel?"

"Okay, okay, but you damn well better tell Daniel you beat it out of me. Get comfortable, because you aren't going to like any of it. And before you start threatening me, just remember that this is the way Daniel wanted it. . . . You want a drink or something?"

"No, I don't want a drink. I want to know where Daniel is."

"Daniel's in France. At least we hope he is. That woman you both knew in Paris, Mickey, she called Daniel on the Fourth of July and asked him to go over there and help her bring someone here to the States. Jerry and I tried to talk him out of it, but you know Daniel. He said he owed her part of his life and he had to go. We told him to call you, but he said this . . . this trip had something to do with you and he couldn't tell you. We got him over there on one of our planes, at least as far as England, and from there he was taking a Red Cross plane to someplace close; hell, I don't know where, it was sort of a momentary thing, whatever would be best when he set down. We haven't heard a word since. We gave him all the cash we could scrape up, and Jerry gave him a bag of diamonds. Look, you would have done the same thing we did if he'd asked you. We offered to go along, but he said it was something he had to do himself. Now, that's all I know."

Reuben digested the information, his heart thundering in his chest. "There's a war going on. How could you let him go?" he asked in a sick voice.

"Mr. Tarz," Rocky said, sounding equally disturbed, "a team of Clydesdales couldn't have prevented him from going. We tried to talk him out of it, begged him to call you, but he was determined. If we hadn't helped him, he would have found someone else. For the first time in our lives, Jerry and I took advantage of our families and got him the plane and made the connections for him. At least we had a little control. I wish to God he hadn't gone. We should have heard something by now," he finished uneasily.

"I don't believe he . . . what if . . ." Reuben's voice trembled with shock at Daniel's behavior and the possible ramifications. God!

"Is it Mickey he's bringing back?" he asked in a whisper. It would make sense for Daniel to go to Mickey's aid; anything else was sheer folly on his part.

"I don't think so. Jerry and I tried to figure it out after Daniel left, but we couldn't come up with anything. None of us knows who he's supposed to be bringing here. Someone this Mickey wants kept safe and someone you obviously know."

Rocky rose from his position behind the desk. "Tarz, I know the sun isn't over the yardarm yet, but I feel like a drink, and you look like you could use one. What say we bury the hatchet, at least for now, and drink our lunch. There's a pub three doors away."

"I'll buy," Reuben said, getting to his feet.

Rocky knew it was the closest he would get to an apology, and he accepted the offer good-naturedly. "Irene, we'll be at the pub," he called out. "You come running if there's word from England or Daniel. Call Jerry and tell him to join us. The hell with business. By the way, Tarz, do you want your hundred dollars back?"

Reuben shook his head. "Hell no. I still might decide to flatten your keister, and if I do, it'll look better if I'm your client."

"Then you're paying for *all* the drinks," Rocky grumbled.

"Yeah, yeah, yeah," Reuben mumbled as they made their way out of the office.

It was 11:35 when they walked into Stella's Pub. Jerry joined them at 12:05. By one o'clock the three men had finished off their third pitcher of beer, to Stella's dismay, at which point Jerry opened his briefcase, took out a quart flask, and set it on the table. "This, gentlemen, is the finest of fine liquors. It's in this flask because it eats through glass. My daddy got it from a grateful client moons ago. Kentucky moonshine with the kick of a mule. Two hundred proof, maybe more. Stella, we need some ice water over here!"

Their first toast was to Daniel, their second to the Kentucky moonshiner, their third to Stella, and the fourth and fifth were for the Washington Monument and the White House.

"If anyone lights a match, the three of them will blow up," Stella hissed to the bartender.

"It's empty," Jerry said, peering into the flask.

"You're rich, buy another one." Reuben guffawed.

"Champagne, Stella, your finest!" Rocky demanded.

"Two bottles," Jerry echoed.

"Three!" Reuben yelled, not to be outdone by the Harvard boys.

Rocky hiccoughed. "What we need are three virgins. Stella, we—"

"We don't have any," Stella shot back. Reuben snorted drunkenly. It sounded like a good way to end an afternoon.

"On the count of three, gentlemen, uncork your bottles, and the first drink is for Daniel Bishop, a hell of a guy!" Jerry yelled, jumping up on the table, his shirt half out of his trousers and his tie askew.

At two o'clock they toasted Daniel's imminent arrival. At 2:15 they toasted his belated arrival. At 2:30 they uncorked fresh bottles of champagne and toasted the Three Musketeers, at which point Reuben upended the table, along with Rocky and Jerry. "Don't make that toast again." He hiccoughed drunkenly. By 3:15 they had Daniel dead and ready to be buried, and all three were blubbering into their champagne as each offered his own version of a eulogy.

By this time Stella had had enough and sent the bartender to fetch Irene, who took one look at the drunken men and turned to leave.

"Wait a minute, you can't leave them here!" Stella screeched. "They're giving my place a bad name. Six parties left because of them, and who's paying for all this?"

Reuben raised his hand. "I have that honor. These . . . fine gentlemen have graciously . . . graciously . . . I said that . . . they said I can pay. How much?" He leered at the voluptuous Stella. "And don't charge us for the virgins. I didn't get one."

"Neither did I," Rocky said, his voice wafting up from the floor. "Jerry had two, didn't you, old buddy?"

"Yep, I had two," Jerry said, latching on to Irene. "Just point me in the right direction. I wanna go home and see . . . I wanna go home and . . ."

"Take your virgins with you." Reuben laughed uproariously. "I paid for them, so you can take them, isn't that right, Rocky?"

"Yessireee," Rocky said from under the chair.

"I'll be back for the other two," Irene said through clenched teeth. "Wait till Mr. Bishop hears about this!"

"Mr. Bishop! We just gave his eulogy." Reuben sniffed. "A fine man, a gentleman of much renown. My friend and . . . my friend . . . and I love him."

"I love him, too. Where are the virgins you paid for, Tarz?" Rocky squeaked.

"Jerry, the sneaky bastard, took them home," Reuben grumbled.

"Then, by God, let's go after him. Help me up. How did I get down here?" Rocky asked, bleary-eyed.

"You fell when you were giving your eulogy. You were looking for dust. Dust to dust, you said. You should clean this place better," Reuben said virtuously to Stella as he peeled a series of bills from his money clip.

Rocky and Reuben, their arms around each other, lurched to the door and stumbled outside.

"Quick, lock the door before they decide to come back," Stella called to the bartender.

"Here, here, and here," Irene said sternly to the three men, motioning for them to sit together on the leather sofa in Daniel's waiting room. Properly chastised, they sat like errant schoolboys as Irene laced into them.

"You are a disgrace! This is shameful! You and you," she said, pointing to Jerry and Rocky, "are members of the bar! People saw you! People actually saw you!"

"Did we have the virgins with us?" Jerry demanded, sliding next to Reuben.

"Virgins!" Irene squeaked.

"Those lasses that still have their cherries." Reuben roared with laughter. Rocky chose to slide off the leather sofa and rolled about on the floor. Irene quickly locked the door, then thought better of it and grabbed her purse, locking the door behind her.

"There goes one virgin," Jerry bellowed loudly enough to be heard all over the building.

"Shame on you! Shame on you! Shame on you!" Irene called from her position of safety behind the locked door. "Go to sleep, all of you, and I'll be back in the morning."

"She sounds like my mother," Rocky grumbled.

"Nah, *my* mother sounds like that," Jerry said, joining Rocky on the floor.

"What are you doing up there, Mr. Hollywood?" asked Rocky. "You too good for us?"

Reuben peered over his knees to stare at Daniel's two friends. "I wish I had a dog."

"I had a cat once," Rocky volunteered, "but it died."

"I had goldfish. I called them Frick and Frack. They died." Jerry wept.

"What'd you have, Tarz?" they asked together.

"I never had a dog or cat or even goldfish," Reuben blubbered.

"Jesus, that's terrible. Let's go get him a dog, Rock. A man needs a dog. Goddamn," Jerry moaned, tears streaming down his cheeks.

"We'll have to get it tomorrow, that virgin of yours locked us in here," Rocky slurred.

"What would you call the dog? A boy dog, right?"

"Yeah," Reuben mumbled. "Maybe . . . maybe . . . wha'd you call your cat, so I don't name my dog the same thing?" he demanded of Rocky.

"Maizie. May-zee, May-zee," Rocky crooned. "So what's the name of the dog we're buying you?"

"Dog. Just Dog," Reuben said sorrowfully. "Maybe Jake, maybe not." He stretched out on the leather couch. "G'night," he mumbled.

Within minutes three sets of lusty snores permeated the room.

At 7:30 the following morning, before the building came to life, Irene unlocked the office door and shook the three men awake.

Reuben sat up, instantly aware of where he was and what had transpired during the previous hours. His stomach felt sour, and the pounding in his head was equal to that of a thousand drums. He struggled to a standing position, then wished he hadn't. His shoulders shaking with exertion, he looked down at the floor where Rocky and Jerry were cursing to each other. He stretched one long arm toward Rocky, who reached for it after a moment's debate. Jerry was next, his eyes holding a mixture of respect and suspicion.

"Now what?" he grumbled.

"I don't know what you two Harvard boys are going to do, but I'm going back to the Ambassador and clean up."

"Hold on, Tarz, I thought we left all that crap at the crossroads last night. I thought we were friends waiting for news of a mutual friend. What the hell kind of a son of a bitch are you that you can turn your emotions on and off at a second's notice?"

Reuben wished he could squeeze the pain out of his head. Although he deserved what Rocky said, it didn't make things better in his mind. Daniel, loyal, wonderful Daniel, had gone to them for help instead of him when the chips were down. But it wasn't their fault. "I was out of line, sorry."

"We'll be in touch the minute we hear anything. You can stop by, camp out here, whatever you want. Do you need a car?"

Gingerly he shook his head. "No, I think I'll take on the city by foot; I can use the exercise. But thanks for the offer." He hesitated a fraction of a second before he held out his hand. The surprise on the faces of both men was worth the effort. Before the door closed behind him, Reuben heard Jerry mumbling about paying for two virgins and getting only one. He would have laughed, but his head hurt too much.

The only thing to do now, the only thing he could do, was wait.

Chapter Six

BEBE WOKE IN SLOW DEGREES. FIRST HER EYES OPENED AND then closed. It always took a good five minutes before she realized that she felt terrible, sick really. After another five minutes she'd succeeded in forcing the bile back to her stomach. Her second conscious thought was that she needed a drink to start the day more than she needed to brush her teeth and take a shower. Her third thought, always realistic, was how lucky she was that there was no one around to see how she looked and felt.

The diamond-studded watch on her wrist told her it was seven A.M. Usually she was just getting in at this hour, and here she was getting up with the roosters. Why, she asked herself, her foggy brain whirling. Oh, yes . . . she had something to do today that was important, something she'd promised herself she would do—early. Searching the pretty bedroom for the answer, she happened to glance at the little silver picture frame. Lily, sweet little Lily, Reuben's daughter by his mistress, Rosemary. Rosemary with the big red bow. Rosemary had died in childbirth, and . . . she had agreed to take the baby when Reuben said they would make a fresh start in their marriage. Lily was a robust baby with fat pink cheeks that gobbled up bottle after bottle, never crying unless she was hungry. And then . . . and then . . . one morning she had stopped breathing. What was it the doctors said? Something about infant deaths with no reason. Unexplained. The casket had been small and white, the top covered with yellow-and-white daisies. She'd mourned—God, how she'd mourned!—not just for Lily, but for what she recognized as the final failure of her marriage. Lily had been her last chance to make Reuben love her, and . . . she was filing for divorce today. *That* was the important thing she couldn't remember.

It was almost noon before Bebe had herself sufficiently together to leave the house. In the full light of day, her appearance had shocked her witless, so much so that she'd almost canceled her appointment with her attorney. Living the party life generally meant that she slept all day and partied all night. Lamplight and twilight were always kind to her ravished features, and makeup hid a multitude of flaws. Today, the harsh reality slammed her full in the face. She wanted to cry, to blubber, to wail and stamp her feet at what she'd become, but she didn't. She'd done it to herself . . . with Reuben's help. From somewhere deep inside her a warning bell sounded. It was the end of the road for her; either she straightened out her life, or she would be joining Lily in that never-never place everyone feared. Initiating divorce proceedings was to be her first step in her personal survival. From there she would take it one day at a time.

The lawyer's name was Chester Rogal. He was considered small-time by most Hollywood standards, but he was successful by his own standards and that was all that counted. When he closed his office at night, he often bragged to himself that he'd never short-changed a client or lost a case. He'd settled cases out of court, but always to his client's advantage. He was short and rotund, with a beak for a nose and an Abraham Lincoln beard that he constantly massaged while he was thinking. And he was thinking now as he listened to Bebe Tarz. Of course he'd heard all the stories before, everyone had, and he was smart enough to know that there were two sides to everything and then there was the truth. But Chester never passed judgment. Ever. Now he was listening with what he called his third ear for some telltale sign that Bebe was going to prove less than profitable.

"It's very simple, Mr. Rogal. The settlement can be one or the other. I see it as cut and dried. I want my father's half of the studio returned to me and my brother, or else I want half of everything Reuben owns. Either way, I want his resignation from the studio. If we settle for half and he fights for his seat on the board, I'll give that up if I have to, but I want him out of there. What I really want is the studio; it belongs to my family. He robbed my father, and I don't care what the media says about him *being* Fairmont Studios. Do you foresee a problem with any of this?'' Bebe asked.

"Well, I'd be lying to you if I said the man won't put up a fight. He's given his life to the studio, and you want to yank it out from under him. Of course he's going to put up a fight. But we'll work something out,'' Chester said confidently.

"Mr. Rogal, I want you to cut him off at the knees. And I want to take back my maiden name after the divorce.'' Bebe scribbled out a check for an outrageous sum of money and placed it on the desk with a trembling hand. "You will earn every cent of this, and if things go the way I want them to go, there will be a bonus in it for you. I'll be in touch, Mr. Rogal.''

Chester buzzed his secretary after Bebe had left. When he heard her voice he smiled. "Helen, I want you to get me every word that's ever been printed about Hollywood's golden boy, Reuben Tarz.'' He continued to smile as he stared at the check in his hand. Four lovely zeros, all in a row.

The moment Bebe swung the powerful car into the driveway leading to the house, she knew something was wrong. Her brother Eli and Clovis Ames, Fairmont's leading lady of silent films and Sol Rosen's second wife, were talking together on the front steps. Bebe felt her throat constrict. Something had happened to her father.

"We've been waiting, sis. Sit down. It's Pop, he's had a stroke. He . . . didn't make it. Clovis was with him in the ambulance.''

"He didn't suffer, Bebe,'' Clovis said gently. "It was quick and . . . merciful, if you can say that about death. I . . . I want to do the right thing. . . . I'm not Jewish . . . Eli said he would handle things, so perhaps you two should talk about this. I can go back to the house or . . . I can stay, it's up to you.''

In shock, Bebe could only nod. Her father gone. How was it possible? Just a little while ago she'd asked for the studio, had told the lawyer it belonged to her and Eli. But she hadn't mentioned her father. Was it possible that even then she'd had a premonition? No, her father and Clovis were happy, traveling and doing things together. More than once he'd told her that he didn't want anything to do with the studio, that Reuben Tarz deserved all the misery that went with it.

"I think you should call Reuben," Eli said.

"That's funny, Eli. I don't have the foggiest idea of where Reuben is. I just got back yesterday myself," Bebe cried, dabbing at her eyes.

"The housekeeper told me he's in Washington. With Daniel Bishop, I assume. The studio told me he's staying at the Ambassador. We can delay the funeral until he gets back. Do you want me to call him?"

"No, I'll do it. What about Simon and Dillon?"

"I'll take care of it."

"Clovis, did Daddy say anything, at the end, I mean?"

As if on cue, Clovis drew herself up dramatically. "Yes, he said to tell both of you he loved you very much. I was holding his hand and he squeezed mine. I said I would tell you." Eli's eyes thanked her for the lie.

"Oh, Clovis!" Bebe threw herself into her stepmother's arms. "I'm going to miss him. I wish I'd been a better daughter, kissed him more often, visited him more, said kinder things to him."

Clovis patted her comfortingly. "Shhh, that's not important. Your father knew you loved him and he loved you. He wouldn't want you crying like this. I want you to pull yourself together, Bebe. Things have to be done; you have to call Reuben. The whole town will turn out to pay tribute to Sol. We have to make some plans."

Bebe nodded. "What will you do?"

Clovis smiled wanly. "I think I'll go back to Texas and stay with my sister. I've had enough of this town to last me the rest of my life. Who knows, I might strike oil. The house is yours, Bebe. When your husband deeded it back to Sol, he in turn deeded it to you and Eli. Eli says he wants no part of it, so I guess it's yours. I certainly don't want it, and Sol never wanted me to have it. We had our own arrangements, and they aren't important. Come along and call Reuben."

"I filed for divorce today, Clovis," Bebe said, trailing alongside her father's widow.

"It's about time. Now maybe you'll make a life for yourself. I'm proud of you, Bebe, really proud. If you need me or if there's anything I can do, let me know."

"I always wanted to be like you, Clovis. I used to playact

and say and do things I thought you would do in a scene. I think I've been acting all my life,'' Bebe said pitifully.

"I'm flattered, honey, but what I did wasn't reality. That was all make-believe for money. Money was the thing; everything, no matter what it was, was for box office. I'm really glad I didn't make it when sound came. I got a chance to be myself, and I like who I am. That's why I have to leave this place. Enough talk now. You have to call Reuben.''

The moment Reuben answered the phone Bebe started to cry. Between sobs she told him of her father's death. "Eli said we can postpone things till you arrive. Can you give me some indication of when—''

"Bebe, listen to me,'' Reuben said, his voice full of shock. People like Sol Rosen lived forever. "I can't make it back right now. Go ahead with the funeral. I'll pay my respects when I get there. You know how I feel about funerals. They're barbaric.''

Bebe shook her head to clear her thoughts. Reuben—her own husband—was not interested in attending her father's funeral? She took a deep breath. "I heard what you said, Reuben, and I think you are the lowest form of life on this earth. Daddy practically gave you the studio, and you can't be bothered to attend his funeral. How dare you! How *dare* you, Reuben! Better yet, go to hell! Oh, I get it,'' Bebe screamed, "it finally got to you; you're afraid to show your face to the industry because they'll all start talking about the way you aced Daddy out of the studio. Well, you crud, they'll talk more now because I'm going to remind them in case they've forgotten. Go to hell, Reuben!''

Eli felt his eyes pop at Bebe's angry words. Clovis reached out to take Bebe in her arms. "He's not coming,'' she blubbered. "He's not coming to Daddy's funeral.''

Sol Rosen's funeral wasn't just a funeral, it was an event. Everyone in Hollywood, down to the last cameraman and script girl, attended the graveside service. Bebe found herself listening to the rabbi's eulogy, wondering where he'd come by his information and all the kind words and outright lies he was saying. From beneath her veil she could see others wondering the same thing. "Your father wrote his own eulogy himself several years ago,'' Clovis blurted out suddenly as if reading her mind.

Bebe, Clovis, and Eli were the last to leave the cemetery.

"I feel as if I should say something, do something," Bebe said softly.

Eli shook his head. "I wish he'd loved me. I loved him."

"I wish I'd loved him more," Bebe said.

"I loved him enough for all of us," Clovis muttered. "It's true," she said defiantly as they looked at her. "He loved you, Eli, he just couldn't show it. He thought it wasn't masculine to show his feelings for a son. You have to believe me. It's the truth."

God would forgive her this little lie, and so would Sol.

Chapter Seven

DANIEL BISHOP STEPPED FOOT ONTO ENGLISH SOIL, HIS HEART
thrumming wildly about in his chest. This, the first leg of his
journey, was over, and he was still alive, but he was far from
his final objective and had no way of knowing how much longer
it would take to reach that final objective. Someone had said
they were in Plymouth, but the Brits were a secretive lot, and
when he'd questioned the man who seemed to be his guide,
he'd just shook his head and said, "Later," then called him a
bloody fool for leaving the safety of America to come on a
wild goose chase. In the end Daniel had followed the man
blindly through the driving rain to the metal airplane hangar
where he was now sitting, waiting for someone in authority to
tell him what his next move would be.

Daniel closed his eyes and did his best to focus on a map
of England and France. Plymouth, he thought, was at the southern tip of England on the English Channel and directly across
from Cherbourg, and directly south of Cherbourg was Brest,
a true deep-water harbor that was mined by the Germans.

Angry sounds of dissension bounced off the tin walls of the
hangar. Obviously the men weren't happy with his presence
and didn't want the responsibility of crossing him over to
French soil. And he didn't blame them. What the hell was he

doing here? Patience, he told himself. An hour later he was still telling himself to be patient when the discussion became more heated. The group's words carried clearly to him.

"The old man gave the order himself, so we can't ignore it. Bear in mind, all of you, it's an order and not a request. When the prime minister says jump, lads, we jump. The best thing as I see it," announced the speaker with the loud voice, "is to draw lots. Short stick takes him over."

Daniel listened for what he was sure would be more muttered curses, but the little group grew strangely silent. His stomach heaved when a short, stocky man with a thick growth of beard approached him. "We'll go now."

"Now! But it's storming outside," Daniel protested.

"Exactly. Put this slicker on, follow me, and try not to open your mouth again until I dump you into the hands of the French Resistance."

Daniel did as instructed. "How are we going to cross the Channel if it's mined?"

The bearded man turned to him. "We aren't crossing the Channel because it's too dangerous. I have a wife and three children to think of, so we're going out to the ocean and head due south. Those important friends of yours that know the prime minister said you wanted to go to Marseilles, so I'm going to drop you off at Bayonne; if we're lucky, someone will meet you at Saint-Jean-de-Luz and take you the rest of the way. It won't do to ask me any more questions because that's all I know."

It was a garbage scow, Daniel was sure of it. Minutes later his suspicion was confirmed when the howling wind drove the stench of rotting garbage past his nose. He could see the wisdom of using the storm as a cover; if they were stopped the scow's captain could say he was blown off course. But the chances of that would be dim, he thought. Even Germans liked their comfort.

The scow, sturdy as it was, was no match for the storm they were sailing into. Rain sluiced downward, streaming over Daniel and the captain as waves strained upward to meet the onslaught from above. It seemed to Daniel that he was immersed in water from head to toe. Desperately he fought for toeholds that didn't exist, used his hands that were now raw and bleeding from hanging on to the rope the captain tossed him.

Twenty minutes into the trip found Daniel violently ill, the contents of his stomach spewing onto the slippery deck. He tried to think of pleasant things, safe things, to keep his sanity as the scow pitched forward, then sideways, always ending with what seemed like tons of water pouring over him. What time was it in Washington or California? His brain refused to function when he tried to calculate. No sane person would go through what he was going through, regardless of who owed who what. There was every possibility that he wouldn't even find Mickey.

Reuben . . . What was Reuben doing now? Most likely on his way to Washington to find out where he was. Of his two friends Rocky and Jerry, Rocky would be the one to give in to Reuben and tell all he knew. Reuben would gnash his teeth, stomp his feet, curse, bellow, and then calm down. Then it would all flood back to him, and the reason behind this trip would be clear.

Daniel found himself wondering if he would die trying to help Mickey. Probably not, since he still had a good many things to do in his life. God always seemed to listen to him when he begged for something. He hoped He was listening now.

Night crawled into day and then into night again with no letup from the storm. Daniel craved dry land and sleep, both of which were impossible. "Tie the rope around your waist, it will free your hands," the captain called. It seemed a simple order until Daniel tried to knot the rope with his raw, bleeding hands. Finally he gave up and resumed holding the rope as he'd been doing.

"You Yanks are a prissy lot, and the prime minister thinks you're going to be our salvation. Bull turds!" the captain bellowed.

"We'll save your asses because you Brits don't have the sense to do it yourself," Daniel shouted. "Go ahead, tell me to shut up, see if I listen."

"Feisty, aren't we. Who's saving your ass now, Yank?" the captain bellowed a second time. "I haven't met a Yank yet who didn't cry in his beer."

"I don't drink beer, and I don't know any American who cries in his beer. We're on your side, you asshole!"

"What are you, some kind of crusader?" the captain said, giving the wheel a vicious tug.

Daniel gasped and sputtered and almost lost his hold on the ropes when a ten-foot-high wave slapped him full in the face. "I'm a lawyer," he groaned.

"A blimey solicitor getting fat off other people's misery," the captain snarled. Daniel refused to be baited or to dignify the man's remarks with one of his own. He was a damn good lawyer, and no one was going to take that away from him.

"Won't be long now," the captain called cheerily.

Stuff it, Daniel thought nastily.

"It won't be long now" turned into four hours more of the same torture. Daniel decided he wanted to die and be buried at sea. He'd have voiced the thought aloud but didn't want to give the captain the satisfaction of knowing how miserable he was.

"Hang on, mister, I'm heading into the cove. We're going to be doing a full turn, so hang on."

Full turn, half turn, three-quarter turn, what the hell difference did it make? Daniel realized the difference the moment the scow turned and he found himself free of his ropes, sliding down past the captain, his body ricocheting from one garbage bin to the other . . . finally slamming into the last bin, which upended, burying him beneath its contents.

"Hold on, Yank, I'll have you out in a minute, we're in calm water now." Free of the rotten garbage, Daniel wished for a return of the heavy rain that seemed to have faded. "If I were you, I'd give myself a good dunking or the Germans will smell you a mile away. Come on, Yank," the captain said, holding out his hand. "Look, all those things I was saying back there was just to get your dander up. Not too many men could have held up the way you did. I wanted to make you mad. I'll drink with you any day, Yank, and good luck with whatever the hell it is you're here for. There's a copse of trees over there, you wait it out and someone will find you. Don't wander."

"You're not staying?" Daniel groaned.

"My country awaits," the captain said gallantly. "Good luck."

Daniel crawled to the copse and flung himself down. He wanted to sleep, needed to sleep, but he knew he couldn't. It was as if he were a straw doll with no nerves, joints, or spine. His head rolled crazily about on his neck, and for the first time in his life he felt totally out of control. He had no strength to marshal to the surface, no inner untapped reserve. Over and over he asked himself what the hell he was doing here. The answer was always the same: He was here to repay a long-overdue debt. An emotional debt, to be sure, but a debt none-theless.

The fine rain misting downward felt cool and refreshing on his face and body. Unfortunately it would also cover the sound of footsteps as it splattered on the leaves of the trees overhead. And he was too tired, too worn out, to strain his ears for alien sounds in this quiet, temporary shelter. If the storm worked its way inland, he was in deep trouble, he thought.

Daniel struggled to lift his arm so he could see the time, then remembered he'd been stripped of everything back in the metal hangar—his billfold, watch, and passport were all in a canvas bag awaiting his return, along with the labels that had been severed from his clothes. He knew he was inappropriately dressed for his trek to Marseilles. His shoes were the softest calf with thin leather soles, his shirt and trousers cotton seer-sucker. To his mind they screamed America.

Within minutes he was dozing, his eyelids full of weights he couldn't dislodge. He had no idea how long he had slept when a sound reached his ears, a sound other than the dripping rain. Instantly he was alert, his eyes closed, his ears straining to pick up the sound again. Concentrating deeply, he began to count backward from a hundred and was on eighty-six when he opened his eyes to see four men, their bayonets fixed and pointing at him. In the gray drizzle of the copse he was unable to discern their features. Weakly he raised his right arm, the palm of his hand facing the men as though to say, Hold it, I'm an American. Then he quickly withdrew his hand. Jesus, what if they were Germans?

The tallest of the four stepped forward, the bayonet pointed at Daniel's throat. "You have something to say?" he said in French.

Hell, yes, he had a lot to say in both French and English, but he knew what the man meant. "I'll huff and I'll puff and I'll blow your house down," he responded shakily.

Daniel's relief was overwhelming when the man reached down to pull him to his feet. For the barest second he thought his knees would buckle, but they didn't. His mobility had returned with the short nap he'd taken.

"I want to go to—"

The tallest of the men shook his head. Obviously they knew where he wanted to go, or they wouldn't be walking so pur-posefully as he trailed along behind.

"Voices carry, especially in weather like this," the man

whispered to Daniel as he fell in beside him. Daniel had thought the rain would muffle voices and movement. But he nodded to show he understood.

"This is good weather to travel, the sky is dark and swollen, there's fog near the ground, and the rain lowers visibility. Normally we travel only in darkness unless we have a day like this. We have many kilometers to cover and we must do it on foot." The man looked down at his hiking boots and then at Daniel's elegantly shod feet. Wearily he shook his head.

"How long?" Daniel whispered.

The man shrugged. "Days, nights, weeks. It depends on where the German patrols are. For the moment they are concentrating their strength to the north. They're like locusts; they are everywhere. But the heaviest concentration is in Paris. So far we've been lucky."

Lucky, my foot, Daniel thought eight days later. Never in his life could he remember being so tired, so heartsick, and so very hungry. The soles of his feet were raw and bleeding; the soles of his calfskin shoes were long gone, replaced by ripping the sleeves from his shirt to tie around the instep of his foot. If he lived to be a hundred, he would never do anything as foolhardy or as brave as he was doing now.

Daniel almost burst into song when the tall man said, "Five hours at the most and we'll have you at your village. It's a little past midnight now. I'd say you'll be creeping into the church at, say four-thirty. Someone will meet you and take you to the château. Can you make it, monsieur?"

"I can make it," Daniel said grimly.

As he trudged along behind his guide, his steps lagging more and more, Daniel marveled at the French underground network. Every stop was anticipated. The inhabitants of the safe houses, as he thought of them, seemed to know when they were to arrive, yet no signals had been sent that he was aware of; no man had gone ahead of the small parade to alert those ahead of them, and he knew when he reached the village church the curé would be waiting for him.

They were on time, he calculated by the smile on his guide's face. On their stomachs, they peered over the rise to the small village nestled quietly among sturdy, leafy trees. How many times he'd bicycled into this village, how many times he'd prayed in the village church. A moment later his guide handed him the binoculars. Nothing had changed. There was the *boulangerie* with its life-size loaf of iron bread outside the door, the *pharmacie* next door with its shaded awning, the *épicier* where he'd shopped for Mickey, the *docteur* where he'd gone with Reuben at the close of their stay. . . . How was it possible that the village hadn't changed in all these years, Daniel wondered as he handed the binoculars back to the man on his right. By God, he was here, he'd made it!

"*Adieu, monsieur*," the tallest of the men said quietly. "*Bonne chance.*"

Daniel stretched out his hand, but the men were already on their way back to wherever they'd come from.

The curé must have been watching from the bowels of the church, for the door to the sanctuary was thrust open as soon as Daniel approached. It was dark in this quiet place the priests used before Mass. And peaceful. If they walked into the church proper, there would be candlelight, he knew. How many he'd lighted for Reuben's recovery years earlier. How many prayers he and Mickey had said. So many rosaries, so many novenas. And when Reuben was finally well, he'd come back to this church one last time and had sat for hours, saying rosary after rosary in thanks. It still smelled the same. Even in this tiny closet of a room he could smell the beeswax and the faint odor of turpentine mixed with the smoky smell of the burning candles.

The curé paced nervously about the room. "It will be but a few minutes. You will travel to the château on my bicycle. Your . . . escort will have one of his own. Ah, I hear him now," he said in relief. Daniel hadn't heard a thing. *How did they do it?* "Go now, he waits for you at the main entrance. *Bonne chance, monsieur.*"

"Thank you, Father," Daniel whispered, and made his way outside.

Instinctively, he knew that he was staring at Reuben's son. Even in the dark he could see the same body build, the same chiseled features, the same unruly dark hair. The boy was straddling his bicycle as though readying for a race, and in a way it was a race. A race to reach the château before dawn. He nodded curtly and mounted the bicycle. At first he started off uncertainly, but as confidence returned he picked up speed and pedaled after Philippe until they were traveling side by side.

Reuben's son. The knowledge was so astounding, Daniel still couldn't quite believe it. But he had to believe it since the boy was right alongside him. At that moment he'd have given anything to know what Reuben's replica was thinking and feeling. How much did he know? What had Mickey told him all these years? Obviously not very much, or the boy would at least have written to his father. Daniel sighed wearily. Soon enough he would have all the answers.

Now he recognized it all—the beautiful château where he'd been so happy after the war. The road was the same, the deep ruts, the straggly dry grass along the sides and ditches, perhaps a little more overgrown, but still the same.

The boy was pedaling furiously now toward the huge barn where Mickey always kept the Citroën. With dismay he saw one of the huge swinging doors hanging by a single hinge. He remembered his dog, Jake, a gift from Bebe. How they'd romped through the meadows behind the château! The field had been full of bluebells and yellow flowers. Tears burned his eyes. Memories were a wonderful thing, happy or sad, but he had no time now to dwell on them.

The boy was waiting for him as he pulled up by the barn and dismounted. Daniel hesitated a moment, then extended his hand. "I'm Daniel Bishop," he said.

"I know who you are," the boy said in Reuben's voice, his English perfect and unstilted. He ignored Daniel's hand and started walking to the château.

It was strange, Daniel thought that the boy wasn't going to enter the château by way of the kitchen door; but a moment later he understood why when Philippe opened the front door, held it aside for him, and then walked into the library. Daniel watched as Philippe glanced at the portrait over the mantel. Jesus, it was the same. Had he ever been that young? How beautiful Mickey was, and Reuben . . . Reuben looked . . . Reuben looked just the way the boy looked now except Reuben's eyes were happy and smiling. The boy's eyes were filled with anger and hatred. Why, Daniel wondered.

Philippe towered over the mantel, one long arm reaching up to lift the heavy painting from the wall. The boy's movements were so sure, so defined, Daniel knew he'd had a lot of practice removing the picture from the wall. When he spoke his voice was cold and furious.

"I know why you're here. It was a mistake for you to come. This is what I think of you and your Three Musketeers."

Daniel watched in horror as the boy brought up his knee to puncture the aged canvas. The canvas didn't rip, but it tore loose from the tacks and frame. Philippe tossed it aside like a toy he was tired of playing with. Daniel felt like crying.

The boy and his angry deed were forgotten as Mickey rushed to him, her arms outstretched. "Daniel! *Mon Dieu!* I told you he would come, Yvette! Daniel, I can hardly believe my eyes!" Tears streamed down her cheeks, but she made no move to wipe them away. "The same, *chéri*, you look the same. I would know you anywhere. How I've missed you, my friend. I'm so sorry that I've called upon you like this, but I had . . . Forgive me, Daniel, my manners are atrocious. Daniel, this is Philippe, my son, and of course you remember Yvette." The boy nodded curtly and turned his back to his mother. Mickey looked at Daniel and shrugged helplessly.

Her arm around Daniel's shoulders, Mickey led him to the table, where she offered him food. Yvette was already setting a place for him. "It's not much," Mickey said apologetically.

"The last thing I had to eat was a raw potato, skin and all, several days ago." He did his best to ignore Philippe's stormy eyes as he wolfed down the food.

"A good, soapy bath," Yvette said, her eyes on Philippe. "You, young man, find some clean clothes for Daniel and some strong boots."

The moment Daniel finished the last bite on his plate, Mickey leaned across the table. Her eyes were swimming with tears. "I wouldn't trade this moment for anything in the world, Daniel. I thought I would never see you again. He does answer our prayers, I know He does. You are the proof. A day didn't go by that I didn't think of you and Reuben. Ah, the tears I shed, they would fill a river. Tell me, what do you think of my son?" she asked in a trembling voice.

"He looks to be a fine young man, Mickey, so like Reuben it's spooky. Why didn't you tell us? You never wrote, you . . . My graduation, how do I thank you for that?"

Mickey dismissed the statement with a wave of her hand. "No thanks are required, my friend. When one gives, one gives from the heart, out of love. I couldn't tell you or Reuben. He was all I had after you left. He's a fine young man. Right now he's angry because he suspects why you are here. He wants to stay here and join the French Army and fight Germans. He believes he is French, at least half French. I've told him Reuben is his father, but he believes, I . . . could never tell him I'm not his mother. He . . . he doesn't know about Bebe. He does know that Reuben is married to her, but not . . . I couldn't,

Daniel, it would have been like ripping the heart out of my chest. Tell me you understand, tell me you forgive me."

"Mickey, I can forgive you anything," Daniel said sincerely.

"The years have been kind to you, old friend."

"And to you. You're as beautiful as ever. Reuben . . ."

"You must tell me—how is he? I can't stand it another minute, *chéri*, how is my darling?"

"Right this minute I'd say he is one very angry man." Daniel quickly told her how he'd managed to make the trip with the help he received from his friends. "I know Reuben is sitting in my office right now waiting for news. He has never forgotten you, Mickey, and I think I can truthfully say he loves you now as much as he loved you when he left here. I don't think he's done a single thing over the past years without first wondering if you would approve. Everything was for you, to prove himself. Always for you. He's told me he booked passage here a dozen or more times, but he was so afraid of your rejection, he canceled his plans. He had no wish to cause you . . . what, Mickey, I don't know . . ."

"And Bebe?"

"Bebe was . . . Bebe was a result of Reuben's anger at you, I think. You see, he'd written this letter to you, and in his mind he gave you a certain amount of time to answer it. It was his last letter to you, if I'm not mistaken, other than the note about my graduation. He told me he poured out his heart to you and knew if you didn't answer the letter that you wanted nothing to do with him. He told me so many times that he could understand if you were angry with him, but he couldn't understand why you ceased communication with me. At least I understand now. But he was so tortured, so unhappy. When you didn't respond to his letter he married Bebe. Out of defiance, never out of love. They have no marriage; they never had a marriage."

"They have two children," Mickey said brokenly.

"Bebe leads her life and Reuben leads his. They don't see each other for months at a time. Bebe was away for a whole year not too long ago. Reuben has been talking about a divorce, and this time I think he means it. Do you still love him, Mickey?"

"With all my heart. That will never change."

"What fools you both are," Daniel said sadly. "So many years of aching and longing, of this one thinking this, and that one thinking that, and all because of pride. Do you recall once telling me that pride is the deadliest sin of all? You both could have had a wonderful life if you'd just settled things between you. So many years . . ." he repeated.

Mickey sighed. "Yes, I did say that, and yes, I am guilty. At the time . . ."

"At the time it seemed like the thing to do, and you had the baby, and then you grew fearful that either Reuben or Bebe would come and take him from you. Is that what happened?" Daniel asked gently.

"Yes," Mickey whispered, her eyes brimming with tears. "I can't change the past; we must speak now of the future, my friend."

"Philippe said he knew why I was here. He's been told, of course."

Mickey shook her head. "I . . . he suspects, I can see it in his eyes, but so far he's said nothing. Over the years I've explained about Reuben and told Philippe he was half Jewish. He accepted that. He doesn't know that both his father *and* mother are Jewish, and that's the reason you must take him to America. The stories, Daniel, the atrocities! Who knows if they are true . . . but true or not, I can't take that chance for my son. He was becoming politically involved at the Sorbonne, poring over the newspapers, making plans. Some of his friends from school have disappeared, those who spoke the loudest. I don't want my son to disappear or to be marched off to some labor camp. He wants to join the French Army, can you believe that?"

"Yes, I can believe it. You raised him too well, gave him the best education money could buy. What kind of person would sit still watching his countrymen killed, his country raped and plundered? Do you want a son who is a coward?"

"No, but . . . I'm a mother, Daniel, I want him safe—safe, do you hear me? Somewhere, someplace, there is a record of his birth. They will find it, believe me when I tell you this. The old doctor in the village helped me when Philippe was born. I have two copies of all the papers, French and American. I guess you could say he has a dual citizenship, but the Germans won't look at it that way. You must take him away to his father. It's all I can do."

"The boy looks . . . he seems to me . . . what I'm trying to say is, I don't think he's going to go with me. He's not a child,

Mickey, we can't force him. I thought . . . when you called, I assumed it was all settled.''

"It is settled. He's going. He won't defy me. Oh, he'll be angry and he'll carry on, but in the end he will leave with you. He'll be very angry with me for a little while, and hopefully that will pass.''

"And Bebe?'' Daniel asked.

Mickey swallowed past the lump in her throat. "I must leave the telling of . . . he will . . . Reuben will have to explain things. Hopefully, Reuben will tell him I . . . I kept him safe for a little while. He'll know what to say.''

Daniel wasn't so sure. The shock alone was going to rock Reuben back on his heels. Explanations were going to be difficult. He told her then of Philippe's actions in the library.

Tears spilled from Mickey's eyes. "I lost count of the times he's taken that picture down. He gets so angry. All those wonderful stories he made up about his father. They broke my heart, Daniel. Right now he's stewing and fretting because you're here instead of his father. He is so angry. My . . . my sins of omission are catching up with me.''

Daniel felt Mickey's pain. "If you think it will do any good, I can try and talk to him. You and I both know that if Reuben had known, he would have moved heaven and earth to get here.''

"No, Daniel, it is I who will have to explain, and I will. Philippe thinks of you and Reuben as his enemies. Somehow things got turned around, and it was too much effort to stop his hatred. He simply would not listen. He made up his mind when he was twelve or so, and he has not changed it one little bit. That painting is the last thing holding him back. He wants to destroy it, but he can't. He knows that if he does, there will be nothing left of his father to either love or hate.''

"He did a damn good job a short while ago,'' Daniel snorted. "He tried to put his knee through the canvas. It didn't tear, but he'd hoped it would, Mickey, I saw his eyes.''

"All the more reason for him to leave. It's time for him to meet his father,'' Mickey said in an agonized voice.

"When do we leave here?'' Daniel asked anxiously.

"Tonight after dark. The curé will come for his bicycle and tell me where you will be met. Probably the rise above the village, but I can't be sure. After your bath you will rest. Going back will be no easier, possibly worse than coming here. The

Germans are closer now. If you put your ear to the ground, you can hear the rumble of their trucks and tanks."

"And you and Yvette?"

"We'll try to get to Spain. Yvette is . . . she saw the Germans gun Henri down in Paris. It was so unbelievable, Daniel, I still cannot cope with it. We'll be fine, you mustn't worry about us."

But he was worried, and the fact that Mickey wouldn't meet his eyes told him she had no intention of going to Spain. In his gut he knew she was going to join the Resistance. And how in the hell was he going to tell *that* to Reuben?

"Is that what you're going to tell Philippe?" Daniel asked uneasily.

"Yes, but he won't believe me. Still, he can't very well call his mother a liar, now, can he?"

"Your bath is ready, Daniel, and your bed is turned down," Yvette said in an emotionless voice. "Leave your clothes and shoes outside the door, and we'll bury them out by the barn."

"This is for you, Mickey," Daniel said, handing over the sack of diamonds Jerry had given him.

Tears welled in Mickey's eyes. She wiped at them with the back of her hand. "It seems all I do is cry; what must you think of me? Daniel, this is too much. There must be a fortune here," she said, sprinkling the diamonds on the tablecloth. "How can I ever repay . . . they . . . those hateful bastards confiscated everything. Just last year I transferred the major part of my holdings to America. They're held in trust for Philippe. I have a packet for you when you're ready to leave. There is a letter for you, too, one for Reuben, and please, don't read or study any of the . . . don't . . . wait till you are home safe. Promise me, Daniel."

"Of course, Mickey, whatever you want. As for the diamonds, fortune or not, you will need them before this is all over. Now, m'lady, I think I'll have that bath," Daniel said, striving for a light tone.

"Like old times, eh?" Mickey said, smiling. "Oh, Daniel, I prayed you would come. I almost wore out my rosary. Seeing you like this has wiped the years away. If only the circumstances were . . . Daniel, I . . ."

"Shhh." Daniel took her in his arms. "Everything is going to be fine." On this end, anyway, he thought. As he cradled her dark head, he crooned softly, rocking sideways on his heels. "When we first got back to America I would play a game with myself if I couldn't fall asleep. I'd picture this château and try to imagine where everything was. I had it down so pat, I knew every nook and cranny. It was so wonderful walking in here and seeing that memory come alive again. We were all so happy here. I never wanted it to end. I've never felt that same kind of happiness since then."

"Until Bebe came," Mickey said sadly.

"Until Bebe came," Daniel agreed. "Come with me and talk while I have my bath, for once I'm asleep I will be dead and then it will be time to leave. I want to hear everything, every little detail of what went on since I left here. Jake, I have to know what happened to Jake. God, so many times . . ."

While Daniel soaped himself over and over, Mickey sat on a stool, her eyes averted discreetly. She talked nonstop until she was hoarse, leaving her story of Jake till last. "Our little Jake was a hero, Daniel. He saved Philippe's life, what do you think of that!"

"The hell, you say! Everything, don't leave out one piddle, one paw print," Daniel cried excitedly.

"In the beginning he missed you terribly when I sent him to Yvette's farm. There were many girl dogs that he made happy, and he finally settled into a blissful routine. Philippe was almost a year old when he came down with pneumonia. We sat up around the clock, taking turns, Yvette, Henri, and myself, and, of course, the doctor. The doctor had just about given up hope. It was my turn to sit up with Philippe, and I'd gone almost a week without sleep. Several days before, Yvette had brought Jake over for company. He stayed by the door, never venturing anywhere near my chair or the baby's bed. I guess I dozed off and Philippe started to choke. I didn't hear him. Jake jumped all over me, woke me up, and, as they say in America, I got to Philippe in the nick of time. Jake was a hero. He'd sat so long, guarding us both that no one thought to let the poor thing out to do his business. Once he saw the baby was safe, he peed on the rocking chair. We gave him some sugar cookies for his bravery beyond the call of duty. He and Philippe were inseparable after that. He was fourteen when he died and Yvette, Henri, and myself gave him a warrior's funeral. Henri said a blessing. No human's passing was more grieved. Philippe wasn't himself for months afterward, none of us were. He did leave a legacy, however, a pup named Dolly, but she died having her first litter. Philippe wouldn't take one, though. Even now I cry when I think about it. He

... he ... Jake, I mean ... used to go to your room and ...
and sniff about, picking up your scent. When he did he would
... he would just lay there ... his eyes so big and sad ... I'd
talk to him about you ... but I don't know if he understood,
and then one day I was cleaning the room you had while you
stayed here and I found a sweater that you left behind. I made
a bed for Jake and put it in as a blanket. It ... it's still in the
closet...." Mickey howled her grief then, and Daniel joined
her.

Alone in his old room, Daniel shed his towel and dressed
in the clothes Yvette had placed on his bed, his eyes centered
on the closet door all the while he dressed. Unable to bear it
another second, he pulled open the door and stared down at
the wicker basket that held his old gray wool sweater. He
dropped to his knees. He reached for the sweater, bringing it
to his cheeks. His touch was reverent as he plucked several
dog hairs from the collar. "Oh, Jake, Jesus ... Oh, God, Jake,
I didn't want to leave you ... Oh, Jesus," he blubbered, hunk-
ering down ... the sweater a lifeline to his past. He slept then,
on the floor, his sweater with Jake's scent, after all these years,
against his cheek.

"It's time to wake Daniel," Yvette said quietly. "It's almost
dark, Mickey. Do you have everything ready?" Mickey nodded. "This is wrong, Michelene," Yvette continued. She used
Mickey's Christian name only when she wanted to make a
point. "You should have told Philippe before.... This is ...
it's wrong. Now there's no time for fancy words. You'll have
to blurt it all out and send him away in an eye's wink. This is
not going to be pleasant," she said ominously.

"Philippe knows he's going. He's pretending he doesn't
know...." Mickey called him then and he came to her, his
face cold and frightening. "It's time to ... Do you have everything ready?"

"I'm not leaving," the boy said defiantly, tears shimmering
in his eyes.

"We've been through this a hundred times. You must leave.
I am not giving you a choice; I'm telling you you must go with
Daniel. I don't wish an argument, Philippe, this is hard enough
as it is. I don't want to carry your angry face with me to Spain.
I must know you are safe and sound in America with your
father."

"You seem to forget, *Maman*, that I am no longer a child.

You may ask me to leave, but you cannot order me to do so. I'm an adult now, and I don't want to see my father. I begged you not to call Daniel Bishop. I'm too big to spank, so what will you do?"

For the first time since leaving Paris, Mickey felt the cold prickle of true fear. "So, this is what I raised you for, to defy me to my face. Is this the son I raised? You are not of age, Philippe, and you will do as I say when I say it, and I say you are going with Daniel. Not one more word!" she shrilled.

"I mean no disrespect," Philippe blurted out. "But I can't leave you. Who will look after you and Yvette?"

"We've been looking after ourselves for a very long time, and we can continue to do so. I love you more than life, and I wouldn't send you away like this if I . . . It's for your own good. It's time I turned you over to your father."

"I'm not going, and I hate him. Why isn't he here instead of that man upstairs?" Philippe said.

Yvette stepped forward purposefully. "Enough, Michelene, it grows late. Tell him now and be done with it!"

"Tell me what?" the boy blustered, his eyes fearful.

"The truth," Yvette answered for Mickey. "You should have been told years ago, but your mother loved you too much. Too much, eh, Michelene? Now either you tell him or I will. We have no time for this!"

Philippe sat down. "Somebody better tell me or it will take what's left of the French Army to move me from this room," he said belligerently.

"Why don't I tell him," Daniel said quietly from the doorway.

"No, I will," Mickey replied. She held her son's eyes with her own and spoke softly, haltingly. "I'm not your mother, Philippe, your real mother . . . I . . . it's true that I raised you from birth and I . . . loved you from the moment I laid eyes on you. For reasons . . ."

"Bah, tell him! He's a man, he says; he can stand to hear the truth," Yvette stormed. "Your mother . . . Bebe Rosen was young when she gave birth to you. She told us to throw you out with the garbage; she wanted no part of you. She gave birth to you and walked away. Mickey took you and raised you. Your real mother is married to your father, and as far as we know, he knows nothing of your existence. That's the beginning and end of it. There is no place for you here; you're Jewish and you belong in America with your parents."

Mickey looked helplessly from her friend to Philippe and back again. "Yvette, surely there was a better way of . . . Philippe, I am so sorry; I've wanted to tell you so many times. As Yvette says, this is the beginning and the end of it. There's no place here for you now. You must leave. Your parents will see to you once you reach America."

Seeing Philippe struggling for words to lash out at his mother, Yvette stepped into the foray again. "There is no time for recriminations. Daniel must leave in fifteen minutes. They won't wait for you. Kiss your mother, Philippe, and bite your tongue if you are thinking harsh thoughts."

Philippe struggled with his emotions. He'd heard all the words, had watched his mother's face, felt her pain on top of his own. And it was true: he had no choice; he had to go with the American. A sob caught in his throat when he took his mother in his arms. "I'll be back," he whispered. She clung to him, and it was Philippe who gently removed her arms.

He embraced Yvette and again whispered, "Take care of her. And that tongue of yours is the devil's own."

Then he was at the door, watching as Daniel wrapped both Yvette and Mickey in his arms. Mickey handed him a thick packet, which he stuffed inside his shirt. "How will we know if you are safe?" she asked.

"Your Red Cross. If we can, we'll get word to them."

"Take care of my son, Daniel, he's all I have left. Tell Reuben I entrust him to his good care. *Au revoir*, my friend."

"There is no more time, Mr. Bishop," Philippe called from the doorway.

When the door closed behind them, Mickey fell into Yvette's arms. "Why can't I cry?" she asked brokenly.

"Because you did the right thing, and Philippe knows it, too. He was never yours to keep, Mickey. You had him . . . on loan. Come, we must get ready ourselves."

"Yvette, I . . . I will go with you to the . . . But I'm not going to cross over. I'm staying here. I spoke to the curé yesterday, and there are people waiting for me two kilometers south of here. I'm—"

"Joining the Resistance. Yes, I know. I said I would join you. What would I do in Spain by myself? I'm too old to fight bulls. They will take us, these Resistance leaders? What can we do? We're old women."

"*Chérie*, we're not *that* old," Mickey said with a touch of her old sparkle. "We made it here on our own from Paris; that says a lot about our stamina and our will to live. We'll be an asset to the Resistance. Come, my friend, we must start our new life so that someday we can come back here in peace.''

Yvette's eyes darkened. In her heart she knew she'd never see this château again or the farm where she'd been so happy. ''Yes, peace. I'm ready if you are, Michelene.''

Mickey smiled. Together they walked away from the château into the waiting arms of the Resistance.

Chapter Eight

REUBEN SAT ALONE IN HIS EMPTY HOTEL SUITE, A POT OF coffee at his elbow and the morning newspaper, compliments of the hotel, spread out before him. The news from Europe was horrifying, and it wasn't getting better; if anything, the war was accelerating. Who in the goddamn hell was this paperhanger marching all over Europe? And because of this son of a bitch Mickey's life was in danger; he could sense it in every pore of his body. Reading the paper first thing in the morning rendered him helpless, and if there was one thing Reuben detested, it was being locked in a situation over which he had no control.

Angrily he spread the paper across the small round table, searching for the comics. But today even Li'l Abner and Dick Tracy couldn't make him smile. So he finished the coffee in the pot and chain-smoked until his cigarettes were gone, which meant he had to leave the suite and walk about Washington as he'd been doing for the past three weeks. By now he loathed the city. At one point, when his anger was at its peak, he'd stood outside the White House shaking his fist at the massive white building. That was when he'd decided that the country was being run by a bunch of ineffectual assholes. He'd also made the mental commitment to produce a film depicting Washington politics.

Now, as he walked along the streets of Washington, Reuben tested the anger he was holding in check by forcing himself to nod or smile at total strangers. Christ, he felt so goddamn useless! Like a tourist, he'd seen everything the city had to offer, some parts of it twice. And he hated it all—the floodlit Jefferson Memorial, the Washington Monument, and the Lincoln Memorial with all its stone steps.

Colonial America, only six miles from Washington on the west bank of the Potomac in Alexandria, had taken up another few hours. He'd had no interest in the town's history; the trek was simply a way to kill time, as was the tour of the White House.

It was cool here in the park, but he was too jittery to appreciate it. There should be news of Daniel by now. Abruptly he rose and ran out of the park, rounding the corner onto Kilbourne Place and on up to Mt. Pleasant Avenue, where he hoped on the trolley that would take him downtown to Daniel's office.

Rocky's face showed the same signs of stress as his own. Without a word he shook his head wearily. Reuben turned on his heel and left the office, Irene's sniffling loud in his ears.

Ten more days passed before the phone rang in Reuben's suite of rooms. Daniel, Rocky said, was back safe and sound, and, no, he himself hadn't seen him, but he was at his house in Georgetown and Reuben was to go there at nine o'clock.

It was twenty minutes to five when Reuben replaced the phone in its cradle. Daniel was safe and sound. Closing his eyes, he offered up a prayer that Mickey was with him. After all these years . . . What would she think of him? Would she be as beautiful? Of course she would; hers was a timeless beauty. Daniel, you son of a gun, you made it there and back in the middle of a war. It had to be Mickey. Who else could it be?

Reuben stepped into the shower, whistling as he soaped himself from top to bottom. Mickey, Mickey, Mickey . . . The new Brooks Brothers suit he'd purchased several days earlier would be perfect for this first meeting. The crisp white shirt and new tie made him look distinguished. The light suntan he affected complemented the whole of him, as did his favorite after-shave. He was ready.

Daniel was bone weary and in need of a bath and shave when he escorted Philippe into his Georgetown house. It was cool indoors; the front rooms were shaded by a mighty elm outside the front door.

It was an unattractive house, long and narrow with thin windows, an impossible house to decorate, but Rajean had wanted it, insisted they buy it because so many of the "right people" lived in the area. There was nothing comfortable about it, but then, that could be Rajean's fault as well. The drapes, the carpeting, the furniture, all were in various shades of Wedgwood blue, a color he found depressing. Long ago he'd given up hope of finding sun, comfort, and warmth in this house. He'd also given up on his marriage.

His wife and daughter were back from Fire Island. Always sensitive to sounds and smells, he knew Nellie was outside in the small walled courtyard and he knew Rajean was probably upstairs in their crazy-shaped bedroom. He turned to look at Philippe, who was staring at a painting of Nellie over the mantel. "That's my stepdaughter, Nellie," Daniel said in a tired voice. "She was only thirteen when it was done."

"She's very beautiful," Philippe said carefully.

"Yes, she is, and she's beautiful inside as well, much like *your* mother. In fact, she reminds me of Mickey in a lot of ways. Come along, she's probably in the garden; it's her favorite spot."

Philippe followed Daniel, wondering how it was possible to live in such finite rooms. The echo their footsteps created startled him. Later he would have to figure out what caused the echo.

"Nellie, are you out there?" Daniel called.

"Oh, Daddy, you're home. How wonderful! We just got here today ourselves." Noticing Philippe for the first time, Nellie smiled what Daniel always called her holiday smile. "You've been gone so long I was going to send the state troopers out to look for you." She nudged her father, which meant he should hurry and introduce her to the handsome young man standing next to him. "Nellie, this is Philippe Bouchet. Philippe, my daughter, Nellie."

"I'm pleased to meet you," Philippe said in his perfect English, his eyes never leaving her face.

"I'm just as pleased. Daddy never brings home anyone but stuffy lawyers," Nellie said, giggling. She winked at her father.

"Do me a favor, honey, show Philippe to his room; he's going to be staying with us a day or so. I have some things to take care of in my office. Is your mother home?" he asked.

"She was, but she went back to the station; the car wouldn't start so she's having it towed, and she said she wanted to stop by the market since there's nothing to eat in the house. She should be home soon."

Nellie led the way up to the second floor, the staircase as skinny and narrow as the rest of the house. Philippe liked the flash of her long, tanned legs and the skimpy pink playsuit she wore. She had to be around his age, he decided. Pretty. No, he corrected himself, she was beautiful, with eyes the color of a spring meadow and ripe golden hair, the kind he'd like to run his hands through. He forgot then about the girl he'd kissed so often at the Sorbonne.

"This is your room, and you can share the bath with me, it's next door. It has a lock," she added hastily. "Towels are on a shelf and soap is under the sink. Where are you from, Philippe?"

"France," Philippe replied, looking around the cramped room. Surely even a prison cell was bigger.

"If you're as tired as Daddy looks, I guess you want a bath and a nap. I'm sure we're going to have dinner, but knowing Mother, it might just be sandwiches or something. We've been on Fire Island for the past few weeks. The larder is bare."

"I'm not hungry, but yes, I would like a bath and . . . A bath would be fine."

Nellie prided herself on correctly reading people's emotions, a trait she'd picked up at an early age, mainly due to her mother. "You look tired, but you also look . . . angry. Is something wrong?"

Philippe smiled and Nellie blinked. She stepped backward. "Sorry, you . . . you reminded me of someone just now when you smiled."

"And here I thought I was an individual in my own right. Whom do I remind you of?" Philippe asked lightly.

"My uncle Reuben. He's not my uncle, but he and Daddy have been friends all their lives, or almost. I call him 'uncle' out of respect. It's uncanny how much you look like him. You have a nice smile," she said coolly.

Philippe Bouchet, alias Philip Tarz, felt his heart melt and knew he was going to fall in love with the green-eyed, golden-haired girl. "Reuben Tarz is my father," he said quietly, so quietly Nellie had to step forward to hear him.

"Oh, how wonderful!" No, it wasn't wonderful at all, she decided when she saw the scowl on Philippe's face. "Uncle

Reuben is giving me a job in the production offices at the studio in Hollywood. My parents agreed to let me put off college for a year to see if this is something I really am suited for. Will you be working there, too?"

The scowl left Philippe's face and he laughed, a deep, rich sound that sent goose bumps up and down Nellie's arms. "I guess so, I own half the studio."

"How nice . . . what I mean is . . . we might . . . work together. I don't know a thing about producing films, but I'm eager to learn. I . . . I'll see you . . . later."

"Yes, later." Philippe smiled.

At the top of the narrow staircase Nellie smacked her hands gleefully. They would be working at the same studio, which meant they would see each other . . . often, if she had anything to say about it. Lord, he was a handsome devil . . . rich . . . and nice . . . rich . . . and charming . . . and . . . rich . . . Uncle Reuben's son . . . richer still. She decided she wasn't even going to speculate on what *that* meant.

Nellie headed for the kitchen. It would be up to her to fix something for dinner if they were going to eat. Her mother was absolutely worthless when it came to cooking, not that she was much better, but at least she knew how to make tuna and egg salad.

The cupboards were bare of the essentials she needed to whip something together. There was a can of tuna fish, but there was no mayonnaise, celery, onions, or bread, and no vegetables for a salad. Even though her mother was stopping by the market, she knew none of those ingredients would be on her list. Her mother bought things like canned artichokes, plums in brandy sauce, and jarred wieners in some kind of brine.

Five minutes later Nellie was on her old bicycle, pedaling her way to the market. In thirty minutes she returned to find Philippe sitting in the kitchen sipping Coca-Cola from a bottle. Her cheeks grew warm as she set about removing the groceries from the bag.

Philippe watched her quick, sure movements. "You have no servants here?" he asked. Surely Daniel Bishop earned enough money as an attorney to provide at least a cook, and the mother, why wasn't she in the kitchen instead of this young girl?

"Not really," Nellie replied. "We used to have a day person, but my mother . . . I don't know, they come and go. My mother is . . . she doesn't . . ."

"She doesn't cook." Philippe smiled.

"Not very well," Nellie said truthfully.

While they talked then of everything and nothing, Daniel sat in the library and pored over the packet of papers Mickey had entrusted to his care. The papers smelled musty and old, and of course some of them were old, like Philippe's two birth certificates, his two passports, and the stock certificate from Fairmont Studios. Bemused, he moved them aside to concentrate on the letter addressed to him in Mickey's neat handwriting. The letter to Reuben he placed well out of reach. Inside his envelope were two pieces of paper. When he realized what he held in his hand, he felt lightheaded. Quickly he read the short note.

My dearest Daniel,

I'm writing this to you as I sit here waiting for your arrival, and I know in my heart you will come to take my son to his father. You, of all people, must understand why I did what I did. Now I ask one more favor of you, my dear friend. Enclosed are two shares of stock in Fairmont Studios. Reuben holds 49 percent and Philippe holds 49 percent, so they are equal. At some point in time they will lock horns, as you say, and you must be the one to make the final decision based on what is best for the studio. I ask that you do not allow your friendship with Reuben or your feelings toward Philippe to interfere. I know I can trust you to be fair.

Forgive me, Daniel, for my years of silence. I remain your loving friend,

Mickey

"Son of a bitch!" Daniel exploded, then turned at the sound of heels on the terra-cotta floor. "Oh, Rajean. I didn't hear you come in." he said. "We have a guest. Do you think you could stir yourself sufficiently to make something for dinner?"

"I believe Nellie has it under control," Rajean replied indifferently. "She's making tuna salad. I'm not hungry, so, if you don't mind, I won't be joining you."

"I don't mind at all," Daniel snapped. "I can't remember the last time you cooked or sat down at the table with your family." This wasn't the time to argue, Daniel reminded himself, not with the boy downstairs and Reuben due to arrive in a few hours. Confrontations with Rajean always unnerved him, so much so that he had difficulty concentrating. And today he was just too damn tired to put up with her crap.

"Is it my fault I can't find competent help?" Rajean countered plaintively. "Surely you don't expect me to clean and cook. I didn't get married to be a slave to you, Daniel. And for God's sake, where did you get those clothes you're wearing? You are smelling up this bedroom." She held her nose with two long, painted nails to make her point.

"Then leave," Daniel said succinctly. "The only reason you can't find competent help is because you steal half their wages. I personally called Alice, and do you know what the woman's daughter told me? That her mother couldn't work for 'coolie wages.' Coolie wages, Rajean! You didn't fire her, she quit. And where is the money? Half, you stole half of Alice's money. You helped yourself to Nellie's bank account, and still it wasn't enough. Tomorrow your charge accounts are getting cut off. I will hire a housekeeper and I will pay her. You will get an allowance, and that is all you will get. I'm having an accountant go over the house bills, and when I have the totals, you damn well better have some answers, so if anyone is moving out of this room because of my smelly clothes, it will be you."

"You can't do that!" Rajean snapped. "How will that look? I have to keep up appearances."

"For whom? *I* never see you in anything but your slippers and robe. Who are all those fancy clothes for? I'm warning you, I'm going over the bills with a fine-tooth comb, and you damn well better have answers." With that he stalked into the adjoining bathroom, slamming the door behind him.

Oh, she had answers all right, but he wasn't going to like them, Rajean thought nervously. It was true, she'd spent a fortune since her affair with Teddie, and she had robbed Nellie's account, and yes, she'd filched from the cleaning lady. God, now what was going to happen? With Nellie going to California, there would be just the two of them in the house. Like two spitting cats. How was she going to get to New York to see Teddie if Daniel cut off her funds? And he would make good on his promise, too. Daniel never made idle threats. A little humble pie with a side helping of crow might do the trick, she decided.

"Darling," Rajean called through the bathroom door in a voice she hardly recognized as her own. "If Reuben is going to be in town, why don't we wine and dine him? It's been so long since I've seen him, we should make it memorable. What do you think?"

"You hate Reuben, or did you forget?" Daniel replied bitterly. "I'm not interested, Rajean. I told you before I'm seriously considering a divorce and I meant it about Nellie. You're a rotten mother and a worse wife. Let's just drop the subject."

Once again she tried, a slightly desperate note in her voice. "I think you're overtired. Your face is full of tension. I'll give you one of my delicious massages with that sweet-smelling oil, and later we can . . . Daniel, are you listening to me?"

He wasn't answering her which meant her offer was not going to be accepted. A frisson of fear curled inside her stomach before working its way up to her chest and throat. My God, a divorce! No money! No charge accounts! A prisoner in her own house!

When Daniel saw the lighted dome on the taxi creeping down the cobbled street, he broke into a cold sweat. This was Reuben, he reminded himself, not an executioner coming to call. All he was going to do was deliver . . . a long-lost son. Adjusting his glasses over the bridge of his nose, he reached out and grasped Reuben's hand as his friend emerged from the cab.

"Where is she, Daniel?" Reuben asked without preamble. "Jesus, I could hardly wait to get here. I still can't believe it! She called you! At first I was mad, and then when I thought about it rationally, I realized why Mickey would call you. Does she still look the same? Did she tell you why she didn't stay in touch? Where is she, Daniel? Sleeping? For Christ's sake, say something!"

"Hello, Reuben," Daniel said quietly. "We can sit out here where it's cool or we can go inside to the office. Mickey isn't here. I didn't bring her with me, although I begged her to come. I'm sorry." Lord, was this flat-sounding voice his?

"Mickey's not here, but you went to France?" Reuben asked, puzzled. "Rocky said you were fetching someone back. Of course I thought it would be Mickey. Nothing else made any sense. But I'm glad you made it over and back safely. Well, what was so important you had to drop everything and rush off to a war-torn country, and just who in the hell did you bring over to our shores?''

This was it, the moment he'd been dreading. Daniel looked up at Reuben in the yellowish glow of the streetlight. He cleared his throat and said, "Sit down, Reuben. . . . I brought your son back with me. The son Bebe delivered that none of us knew about. Mickey raised him all these years. That's why she wasn't in touch with us. She was afraid you'd go over and claim him. Bebe didn't want the baby. He . . . he was born right before we left France to come back here. I'm sorry to blurt it out like this, but there's no other way. The boy's in the garden with Nellie. He doesn't like you very much, and he doesn't like me, and of course it's all understandable. Until the moment we left, Mickey had not told him Bebe was his real mother. She did, however, tell him all about you. He's grown up knowing you were here in America. When he was twelve or so he decided you were a fairy tale and started to dislike you. He thought you knew about him. He's had a rough time these past weeks. He's a fine lad, Reuben. Mickey did a tremendous job in raising him. Spittin' image of you, too. Looks like you, walks like you, has your mannerisms, and he sounds like you with a French accent. . . . Say something, Reuben, I'm babbling here," Daniel pleaded.

Stunned, Reuben sat in silence for a moment.

"A son! My God. . . . What's his name?"

"Philippe Bouchet," Daniel said quietly.

"Well, that certainly explains everything, doesn't it?" Reuben said, his face white with shock. "I must be slipping. I never figured it; did you?"

"No."

"All these years Bebe never said a word. How could she do that? How could she keep something like that from me?"

"I don't know. She didn't . . . she doesn't know that Mickey kept the boy; she thought they gave him out for adoption. Maybe she wanted to forget it, I don't know. I thought you would be upset. I've been agonizing over how to tell you."

"I guess I'm . . . numb. So he doesn't like me, eh?"

Daniel nodded. "He thinks you deserted him and his mother. His face when he found out . . . I could see it ripped his world apart. Mickey told him she was going to try to make her way to Spain with Yvette; Henri's dead, gunned down by Germans in Paris, but he knows she was going to join the Resistance. It broke my heart, Reuben, each of them trying to say the thing that would give the other the most comfort. She said I was to tell you she was entrusting him to your care now. She sent a letter to you; it's in the house.''

"How is she?" Reuben asked gruffly.

"Older, but the same. Worried about her son like any other mother would be. She cried when she saw me, but then, so did I. We talked for a long time. She's never stopped loving you, if that's what you need to hear.''

Wearily Daniel stood up and turned to his friend. "It's getting dark and the bugs are starting to come out. Let's go in the house and have a cold beer. When you're ready to meet Philippe, I'll introduce you. I imagine you'll want to read your letter first. I'll fetch the beer, so make yourself comfortable.''

It was warm in Daniel's office, or maybe it was him, Reuben thought. Nervously he loosened his shirt and jerked at his tie. He was certainly well turned out to meet his son. Jesus, a son! A son about whom he'd known nothing until minutes before. How was it possible he'd gone through the last twenty years without even suspecting?

Daniel returned and handed him Mickey's letter along with a frosty bottle of uncapped beer. Then he withdrew discreetly to the downstairs bathroom, where he sat on a stool waiting for Reuben to finish the letter.

Reuben was a basket case of nerves as he ripped at the envelope. After all these years, finally, he was going to read a letter from Mickey. He found himself gripping the arms of the chair, the letter lying in his lap. When he'd calmed down, he picked it up, took a deep breath, and started the letter.

My dearest darling,

I know, darling Reuben, what you must be going through this very moment. Please forgive me for my years of silence. When you left here with Daniel, I thought my world had come to an end. I knew it was best for you, and that's all I ever wanted. Philippe was your son, and he needed me as much as I needed him. He's been my life all these years. I worried that Bebe would have told you, but I knew if she had, you would have come to claim your son.

And now I am turning him over to you. It's no longer safe for him here with these hateful Germans. I wish there were something I could say that will make it easy because I know Philippe will not be cooperative. He thinks he hates you and Bebe, but he doesn't. He will realize this with patience on your part. He's a fine young man, Reuben, a son you can be proud of. I wish circumstances were different, but they aren't and there is nothing more I can do.

Every day of my life you have been in my heart. Time has never healed the wound of our parting.

Yvette and I are joining the Resistance movement. When we can, we will check with the Red Cross.

Love your son as I have loved him.

Au revoir and *bonne chance*.

I will love you forever,
Mickey

Reuben's head dropped into his hands. After all these years . . .

The comforting hand on his shoulder brought his head up, and he stared into the worried eyes of his friend. "Bring him in, Daniel," Reuben said hoarsely.

"Are you sure you're ready?"

"No, but it has to be now or I'll walk out of here."

Five minutes later as Reuben was standing by the open window, the picture of nonchalance, Philippe Bouchet walked into the room. Reuben turned to stare at a replica of himself. There was no smile on the young man's face, no sign at all that he was glad at last to meet his father. "Welcome to America," Reuben said coolly. The boy inclined his head slightly.

"I don't suppose this is easy for you; I know it isn't for me," Reuben continued after a moment's hesitation. "I want you to know that if I had known about you, I would have done something about it."

As Philippe began to speak, Reuben heard his own voice, laced with a delicate French accent. It was so chilling, he shuddered. "My mother waited for you all these years. I waited. I made up wonderful stories about you, and I had fistfights with some of my friends when they said you didn't exist. There is no excuse that I can accept from you, Mr. Tarz. If you loved my mother, as she said you did, you would have come for us. I don't need you, I don't want you or your wife. I will be going with you to California to take my place at the studio. My mother would expect me to say I'm pleased to meet you, but of course we both realize I'm not pleased at all. As a matter of fact, I resent it. You are not at all what I expected."

"Well, you're one up on me there, Philippe. I haven't had

time to form an opinion about you. I suppose in your place I would feel exactly as you do. I can only repeat that if I had known about you, I would have done something. If you choose not to believe me, there's nothing I can do about it. You're dismissed.''

Philippe blinked. ''Dismissed?''

''Yes, you're free to go. You don't want to be here, so leave. Go back to Nellie, go to bed, go outside, do whatever you want to do. You're dismissed.''

Philippe's eyes spewed sparks, and his voice was brittle with the hint of a sob. ''I'm not a child, Mr. Tarz, for you to dismiss. I'm your equal even though I'm your son.''

Reuben removed one of his hands from his pocket and wagged a finger in the still air of the room. ''No, you have to earn that right. And I think your mother is wrong. I don't think you're a fine young man at all. I think you are a close-minded, coldhearted young man without a compassionate bone in your body. Good night, *Mister* Tarz.''

A moment later Daniel whirled into the room. ''Jesus Christ, Reuben, what did you say to him? He was taking the steps three at a time, cursing in French, saying words I never heard before.''

Reuben shrugged. ''Not a whole hell of a lot; there wasn't time. If you don't mind, I think I'll go back to the hotel and try to absorb all of this. And, Daniel, it was a brave, wonderful thing you did going to France and bringing the boy here. Foolhardy, but brave. I know there is a story behind it all, and we'll talk about it when I'm not so . . . well, raw.''

''Are you going to be all right?'' Daniel asked, concerned.

Reuben forced himself to grin. ''I've survived worse than this, pal. Don't worry about me. Good night, Daniel.''

Outside in the cool evening air, Reuben decided to walk back to his hotel. A son . . . he had a son raised by Mickey, the woman he'd loved all these years. A son who hated his guts.

''Now what do I do?'' he groaned.

Chapter Nine

THE HUGE WHITE HOUSE BEHIND THE MONSTROUS IRON gates at 1600 Pennsylvania Avenue looked so majestic in the summer sunlight, Philippe drew in his breath. Watching him, Nellie smiled. Visitors were always overwhelmed at their first sight of the impressive estate. If only there were time for a tour . . . . She didn't know how it happened that her hand was in Philippe's, but it didn't matter. Somehow, she'd moved a little closer to him and he'd taken a step in her direction, and then their bodies had touched.

"My father often visits the White House," Nellie said proudly. "The President's top advisers offered him a job on the White House staff, but he turned it down. He tries to avoid . . . politics. Philippe, what will you do when you get to California?"

The boy shrugged. "Meet my . . . biological mother, find a place to live, work at the studio, I guess. I know quite a bit about movies, my mother made sure of that. I've met and spoken with some of the most famous French filmmakers. They have wonderful, innovative ideas. Perhaps I'll put some of them into use. I've been thinking about making a film concerning the war. After all, I do have firsthand knowledge of what Paris was like when the Germans came. Do you think the American people would go to see a picture like that? Would it be too serious?" Philippe asked anxiously.

"Not if you had a love interest in it," Nellie said emphatically. "There always has to be love. That's what makes the world go around. If you depicted it right, all those boys' parents would flock to see what was happening to their sons. What's in the papers, that isn't real to them or to me, and I read the paper from cover to cover. Daddy says the news is old the moment it's printed. War moves very fast, but then, I don't have to tell you that."

"I brought my journals with me," Philippe said quietly as he gazed down at Nellie. "I have many ideas and thoughts on . . . on the subject."

Nellie listened to the young man's voice, the flawless English with just the faintest hint of a French accent. She thought it endearing and squeezed his hand slightly, beaming her pleasure when Philippe returned the pressure on her hand.

"I think it's a wonderful idea," she said warmly. "The public will go crazy about it. Have you spoken to your father about it? Uncle Reuben knows everything there is about making movies. He's received so many honors, Daddy can't keep track of them anymore." When Philippe's only response was to narrow his eyes and tighten his jaw, she squeezed his hand again to show her support. "You plan to do it yourself, is that it?"

"Don't you think I'm capable?" Philippe asked carefully.

"I really don't know," she said just as carefully. "I only just met you. I know a lot goes into making a movie. I do think you or I can do whatever we set our minds to. One must think positively."

Philippe straightened his shoulders. "I plan to write the script myself."

Nellie didn't have the heart to tell him about the unions and their writers. His father would have to get him his card and settle things. It simply wasn't her place, now, to shatter what few hopes he had. "I know it will be wonderful! Will you allow me to read it? You know, a female point of view. I'll be out there. Will we see each other?"

Philippe threw back his head and laughed. The sound pleased Nellie; it told her he was interested. Yes, she would be his rock, his fortitude . . . and his love if she had anything to say about it. "Every day," he replied, smiling down at her.

"I like you, Philippe," Nellie said wistfully. "I like you a lot. I . . . I just want you to know that."

Philippe wondered if he would ever get used to the American bluntness of the Bishop family. The girls in France would have winked or flirted outrageously but never uttered a word. A small jitter of fear rippled through him at Nellie's words, or was it a reaction to his own feelings? "I like you a lot, too, Nellie. Your father is going to be . . . at least I think he will be a little upset."

Nellie laughed. "My father has this uncanny ability to know what I'm thinking and feeling before I say anything. I've always gone to him when I'm sad or happy, and he talks to me. I've always shared everything with him. He knows about this because I saw him looking at me strangely last evening."

"I'm glad you have such a wonderful relationship with your father. I had a wonderful sharing relationship with my . . . my mother, too. I can't . . . even begin to imagine what it will be like when I meet my real mother." Suddenly Philippe placed both of his hands on Nellie's shoulders. Unintentionally, he had allowed this young girl to see his vulnerability, and in that same instant he decided he had fallen in love, completely and totally, with Nellie Bishop.

It was Nellie who broke the moment by glancing at her watch. "We have to hurry before our fathers send out a search party for us. I didn't mean for us to be gone so long." Inside she was smirking in triumph. All she had to do was crook her finger and he was as good as hers.

Hand in hand they crossed the street to return to the house in Georgetown.

Reuben and Daniel stood on the stoop of Daniel's narrow house bathed in dappled sunshine from the mighty elm. Both men watched the young couple advance down the street. Reuben strained to see his son better in the lacy sunshine. Beside him he could feel Daniel stiffen. "Are you opposed to this . . . whatever it is?" Reuben asked.

"No. I'm feeling my loss, I guess," Daniel said ruefully. "It happened the minute Nellie met Philippe. He needs someone desperately right now. I'm glad it's Nellie. I hate to say this, old friend, but you're going to be taking a backseat to my daughter."

Reuben struggled for a smile. "He doesn't like me at all, Daniel. He's not going to like Bebe, either. Jesus, I don't know what to say to him. I have this feeling he'll listen to me and then turn away and thumb his nose at me. His anger is so alive, I can feel it.''

"Completely understandable,'' Daniel said quietly.

"Daniel . . . listen to me. All my thoughts . . . all I think about is Mickey and her safety. I'm trying to feel something for this boy, but it isn't there. He looks like me, he's built like me, and for God's sake, he even walks like me. If he didn't have the French accent, he would sound exactly like me, too. I want to feel something. . . . Daniel, what am I to do?'' Reuben asked desperately. "I need to know about Mickey. Your friends . . . can they find out?''

"They're doing their best. They know how important it is. As soon as I hear anything I'll let you know. Try on a smile now, if not for your son then for my daughter. She adores you, you know.''

"I won't pretend with him, Daniel. To do so would be a lie, even more treacherous than the truth. There's only one person in this world I can love unconditionally.''

"You just need more time,'' Daniel said soothingly.

Reuben laughed, a harsh, unpleasant sound. "Time!'' he snorted. "I've had twenty years. I can't make up twenty years. No matter what I do or how I do it, I can never make that up to him. I can't even begin to think about Bebe at this point.''

Conversation ceased as the young couple approached the steps. "We're not late, Daddy, we're right on time.'' Nellie smiled. "Hello, Uncle Reuben. You get handsomer each time I see you. You should be a leading man in your own films.'' It was something she always said to Reuben, and it always brought a smile to his lips. But not today. Even when she pecked him on the cheek and tweaked his ear playfully, there was no answering smile. At last she turned her attention to her father. "Is Mother in the house, Daddy?''

"She went marketing. We'll be leaving now, so say good-bye to our guests. I'm going on to the office. If I decide to work late, I'll phone.''

Nellie planted a kiss on her father's cheek, hugged Reuben, and smiled shyly at Philippe. Reuben watched his son's eyes follow the slim girl into the house. When he turned away, Philippe met his father's gaze defiantly.

The battle lines were drawn and stayed that way all the way to California, with little being said between father and son. Reuben slept most of the way while Philippe pretended to sleep, his agile mind sifting through the past few days and planning the future. As soon as he was installed in an office, he was going to get a calendar so he could check off the days until Nellie's arrival.

The crisp California air was warm and dry, unlike Washington's semitropical humidity. Palm trees whispered and rustled as Reuben and Philippe made their way to Reuben's parked car, a large four-door silver-gray Cadillac. Before Reuben backed the car out of the parking space, he turned to his son. "What's your first impression of California, Philip?" he asked in a neutral voice. Damnit to hell, why wasn't he feeling something?

Philippe thought about the question for a moment before he answered. "It is not unlike the French Riviera. However, I much prefer the Riviera. . . . And I would appreciate it if you would call me Philippe rather than Philip."

It was Reuben's turn to ponder his son's request. "Philippe is a French name. You aren't French, you're an American Jew. The sooner you get used to the idea, the better off we'll both be. This is your country now." He hadn't meant to sound so irritated. Surreptitiously he glanced at his son before he shifted the car's gears. *Angry* was hardly the word to describe the way the boy looked.

"This will never be my country," Philippe said coldly. "You can call me a Jew from now till the end of time, and I will renounce it till the end of time. I am a practicing Catholic. My country is France! Don't ever tell me that again!"

Was this the time to wade in and say what had to be said? Reuben couldn't decide. "You can't change the truth, Philip. If you want to wish your life away or delude yourself, then go ahead. I'm sorry to say this, but that's what your natural mother has done with her life. I think I would be greatly disturbed to find out that you're like her in that respect."

Philippe's voice dripped ice. "Is that another way of saying you want me to be like you? God Almighty, I hope not!"

Reuben swallowed past the lump in his throat. "No, I don't want you to be anyone but yourself," he responded curtly.

Philippe slouched back against the comfortable seat and closed his eyes. As far as he was concerned, he'd said all he was going to say.

An hour later Philippe was settled in his bedroom on the second floor of his father's house. The lavish mansion had been somewhat overpowering, but he thought he'd covered his reaction rather well. Obviously, he thought sourly, the motion picture business generated huge sums of money.

The room he'd been assigned was warm and comfortable and decorated in earth tones. A bounce on the bed satisfied him that it would provide a good night's sleep. How quiet and silent the house was. Did all the servants walk around on tiptoe? Or weren't there any! No one had come to the door to welcome them. And where was his mother? Not that he cared. . . .

Laurel Canyon. He rolled the words around on his tongue and decided he liked the way they sounded. Home of rich Americans. Rich American Jews. He didn't like the sound of *that* at all. He sneered at himself in the mirror. In a pig's eye he was Jewish. He didn't give a damn what his birth certificate said.

What the hell was he supposed to do now? There was no unpacking to do. It was too late to make business phone calls, but first thing tomorrow he was going to phone the New York bankers and make some monetary arrangements, and after that he was going to find a place to live on his own. In between he had to shop for clothes, call Nellie, and visit the local Red Cross offices to see if he could get a message to his mother.

He was just kicking off his shoes when a soft knock sounded at his door. One shoe on and one off, he walked over to the door and opened it. His father stood in the doorway holding up a tray with two sandwiches and a glass of milk. "I thought you might be hungry. Don't worry about sleeping in tomorrow and missing breakfast. The cook will make it for you even if it's past noon. I'll leave the office early and take you shopping. You'll need an entire wardrobe, and I know an excellent tailor." He watched his son's face for any reaction, but there was none. So, it's going to be like this, is it, he thought angrily.

"I haven't drunk milk since I was ten years old," Philippe replied, turning away, "but then, I guess you wouldn't know about that. I prefer wine with my food. And as for shopping, well, I have other plans tomorrow. I'll get the wardrobe myself. Thank you for the offer, though," he added hastily.

"You're welcome to stay here as long as you like," Reuben said coolly. Why in the name of God had he thought the boy would *want* to stay here with him? Reuben shifted his weight, deliberately not stepping over the threshold. He was at arm's length, the way Philippe wanted it.

"Is there anything else?" Philippe asked, glancing at him. "I'm pretty tired and would like to turn in if you don't mind."

For one long moment Reuben just stared at him. At last he gave a tired sigh and turned away. "No, there's nothing else. I'll just say good night." He didn't expect a response, so he wasn't disappointed when Philippe closed the door. When he heard the lock snick in place, he turned back. Was the boy afraid of him? The thought disturbed him, but not enough to make him confront his son.

Reuben leaned against the polished railing on the second floor with the tray balanced in his upraised palm. Unsettled, he looked down into the entrance foyer, which was lighted from the monstrous chandelier with its teardrop crystals, hundreds of them winking in the light. In all the years he'd lived in this house he'd never taken the time to admire the chandelier or the imported black-and-white tile floor. For the first time he became aware of the silence in the house. True, it was late, but even so there were always sounds of subdued activity after dark, lights under doors, low scuffling sounds. Now he strained to hear something, anything that would prove him wrong.

Jaw clenched, he set the tray down on the polished surface of a hall table and began to walk, turning on lights as he went along. Simon's room was as empty as Dillon's. The only thing he found that attested to the fact that his children had indeed lived in the house was a colorful toy soldier that had belonged to Dillon. He clenched it fiercely in his fist. Bebe's room was silent, too. Whatever life there might once have been was gone from the house.

In his room with the door closed, Reuben paced. Bebe had moved out, probably to her father's house—her house now—in Benedict Canyon. And she was making good on her threat to file for divorce. The blinding tempest of a rage began to build inside him, not at his children or even at Bebe, but at himself. His steps grew heavier and louder, like the sounds of the Gestapo marching all over Europe. At last he stopped and lighted a cigarette, drawing the smoke deeply into his lungs and expelling it with a loud *whoosh*.

His life was coming apart at the seams. All the things he should have done, could have done, over the years . . . If blame was to be placed, it would have to be on his shoulders.

Michelene Fonsard had said one day he would make her proud of him. Perhaps professionally, he conceded, but never personally. What good was wealth, power, and glory if there was no one to share it with, that one special person who cared if you lived or died?

Reuben didn't sleep at all that night, and when dawn broke he showered, shaved, and dressed. After two cups of coffee he tortured himself by reading the latest accounts of the war in Europe and by 7:20 he was on his way to the house in Benedict Canyon to see Bebe.

Sol's old housekeeper opened the door to Reuben after he rang the bell four times. Eyes bleary, she stared at him, her sparse hair standing on end around her ears. For the life of him he couldn't remember her name. "I'm here to see Mrs. Tarz," he said in an authoritative voice. "Don't bother to announce me. I know the way." He shouldered past her.

When he saw Bebe stretched out in her old bed in her old room, Reuben felt a small surge of guilt. In sleep she looked so defenseless. Curious, he took a step closer; he'd never really studied his wife as he was doing now. What was it he was hoping to see? The lavender shadows under her eyes? The once-creamy skin, now speckled with red from a lifetime of drink and drugs? At least her hair was the same, soft and silky.

Reuben drew a small chair closer to the bed, careful not to make any sound. His gaze was intent, tortured, as he continued to watch his wife. Slowly he began a one-sided conversation in his mind.

I'm sorry I can't love you. I tried; perhaps I didn't try hard enough. Maybe it was my guilt, my impotence, for so many years. Maybe I'm capable of loving only once. Rosemary was . . . Rosemary was someone who filled a space in my life for a little while. She gave us a daughter. I tried to give you everything the way your father did. Everything but my love. I couldn't give you that because I'd already given it to Mickey. I'm sorry, Bebe, so very sorry. You allowed me to ruin your life. Why didn't you fight back instead of destroying yourself? Why? Surely you can't still love me. You should have divorced me years ago. I should have gone back to France and Mickey instead of being such a coward. The best years of our lives are gone now, yours as well as mine. Here we are at the end of the road. And today, when you wake, I'm going to break your heart all over again when I tell you about Philippe.

A vision of Bebe in a brilliant flowered dress in Paris years earlier swam before his eyes. She'd been so pretty, so innocent then. She'd also been calculating and manipulative, but that he hadn't realized until much later.

Reuben rubbed at his burning eyes. Christ, he really should have tried to sleep last evening. Now he would pay for it with smarting, burning eyes, a condition left over from being gassed during the Great War. Sighing, he leaned back in the barrel chair, his upper torso towering well above the caned back. The time had come to think about everything, to come to terms with his life and Bebe's. The fierce pounding in Reuben's chest told him his personal nightmare was over. His chest heaved, and he struggled for air.

Bebe stirred restlessly, one arm flailing at the pillow. Reuben tensed, willing her to wake on her own, and when she cracked open one eye he spoke quickly so she wouldn't drift back into sleep. "Bebe, wake up, I have to talk to you. Please, it's important."

Bebe struggled to a sitting position, staring foggily at her husband. "What are you doing here, Reuben? What time is it?" Any other time she would have worried about her appearance. Now she didn't have to care what he thought of her.

"It's early. . . . Look, get dressed, Bebe, and meet me downstairs. You're going to need some coffee with what I have to tell you."

Bebe bristled. Surely her attorney hadn't served Reuben his papers so quickly. "I'm tired of doing what you think I should do, Reuben. According to you, I have never done a single thing right in my life. Well, that's all over. I've filed for divorce, and now there's nothing for you to say and nothing for me to say. From here on in, our lawyers will do the talking. I'd appreciate it if you would get your ass the hell out of my house. Now!"

Reuben sighed. "Bebe, listen to me. I understand about the divorce. I'm willing to take the blame for everything. Whatever you want, you can have. I won't fight you. I would like to see the children, though. But that's not why I'm here."

Tears gathered in Bebe's eyes. Even now, after all was said and done, she realized she still loved this cold man she called a husband. He was like a cancer in her body that wouldn't heal or kill. Oh, God, maybe he was finally going to tell her he was sorry and that he loved her. The thought made her feel light-headed. All right, she decided, she'd stick her neck out one more time, just once more. "Why are you here, then?" she asked, her voice a whispery croak.

Reuben shook his head. "I'd really like us to talk downstairs. Outside in the sunshine. It's very important. Please, just slip into a robe and meet me on the terrace. I'm sure the housekeeper has coffee on by now. Trust me when I tell you you're going to need it. Please, Bebe.''

"How prettily you beg, Reuben.'' She laughed then, a harsh sound in the quiet bedroom. Reuben flinched. "All right, get out of here while I dress, and this better be important.''

When the door closed behind Reuben, Bebe leaned into her pillows, feeling weak all over. She didn't know whether to laugh or cry. In her heart she knew that Reuben hadn't come out of love for her, so there was nothing to laugh about. Tears rolled down her cheeks, and she made no move to wipe them away. So much of her life was over now that her father was dead. "Damn you, Reuben!'' she cried. He should have been with her at the funeral. She should have had his arm to lean on. After all, her father was responsible for his success. "Oh, damn you, Reuben, damn you to hell!''

Angry now, she stalked to the closet for her robe. With feverish hands she pulled it from the hanger and tied the belt so tightly that she gasped. Then she marched out of the room in her bare feet, down the long hallway, and on down the sixty-four steps that led to the foyer. From there she stomped her way through the kitchen and out to the terrace with its wrought-iron furniture. The sun almost blinded her with its brilliance, so she turned on her heel and walked back into the house for her sunglasses. A few more days of rising early and she'd be almost used to the bright light of day. The glasses secure on the bridge of her nose, she stalked her way back to the terrace.

"All right, Reuben, I'm here,'' Bebe snarled, "and this had better be good. Say what you have to say and get out of here.''

Reuben licked at his dry lips. How to say it, how to get the words past his thick tongue? "I'm here about Philippe, Philippe Bouchet.''

Bebe stared at him. "You came all the way over here to talk to me about someone who owns part of the studio? You must be crazier than I am. What does that have to do with me? Are you planning on selling out? If so, I hope you get a good price because I want it all.''

Reuben cleared his throat. "Bebe, Philippe Bouchet is our son—the son you left with Yvette and Mickey. Mickey kept him, raised him as her own. She called Daniel over the Fourth of July weekend and asked him to come to France and bring him here so he would be safe. Daniel's friends arranged the trip, and Daniel brought him back to Washington. That's where

I was when you called about your father. I was waiting for
Daniel to get back. Philippe . . . Philippe is at my house. He
was sleeping when I left.''

Reuben watched his wife's face turn white, saw her eyes
roll back in her head, and knew she was going to faint. In a
second he was off his chair and gripping her arms. "It's all
right, we'll handle it. Get hold of yourself, Bebe," he said,
shaking her. "You at least knew about Philippe. Daniel slapped
me in the face with it. I think the boy hates me, and he seems
to have no love for you, either. Yvette insisted on telling him
the truth because he refused to come to America. He . . . he
knows you didn't want him. Bebe, how could you have done
something like that? He was our flesh and blood. You just . . .
you just tossed him away. And all these years you never told
me. My God, Bebe, how could you do that to me?" Reuben
said brokenly.

"I called him John Paul," Bebe murmured, eyes glazed and
her voice expressionless, almost as though she'd been hyp-
notized. "I don't know why I picked those names. Yes, I did
say I didn't want him, but I didn't mean it. I held him once,
in the middle of the night. He felt so warm and he smelled so
nice. All pink and white. But I couldn't keep him, Reuben. I
was only seventeen, a child myself. They told me a family in
the village would take him and raise him. I sent money, lots
of money. Once I sent a birthday present. To Yvette. She never
wrote or said . . . He wasn't a child created out of love.''

She paused, then looked down at Reuben as though he were
a stranger. "I thought he was . . . was lost to me. You don't
know how many times I wanted to seek him out. I never forgot
him. I don't care what you think of me as a wife or mother. I
did care, but there was nothing I could do. I drank more, used
more drugs, hated you more, and gradually it got easier.''

She was shivering now, shaking under the chenille robe.
Reuben pried her hands loose from the arms of the chair and
pulled her close. He held her as though he cared about her,
stroking her matted hair and crooning words she couldn't hear.
Her body shook with hard, racking sobs, and Reuben held her
tighter, thinking her grief had something to do with her father's
death along with the shock of hearing about Philippe. It never
occurred to him that his wife might still be in love with him.
A violent surge of protectiveness rushed through him, and he
tightened his arms around her until her sobs quieted.

"When would you like to meet Philippe?" he asked gruffly.

Bebe shook her head. "Don't arrange a meeting, Reuben. He will have to forgive me first." She pulled away from her husband. "This isn't going to change my plans about the divorce. I can't let you upset my life anymore. I'm past that stage. We'll break clean; you'll give me what I want, and you'll be free to do whatever you want. This has been a shock, but then, you've always been able to shock me and then walk away."

Bebe gathered herself together and squared her shoulders. She cinched the belt of her robe tighter and felt better with something in her hands to stop the trembling. Her voice was soft and gentle, almost reverent, when she spoke again. "As much as I've loved you over the years, Reuben, that's how much I hate you now. I have to hate you to get through this divorce. You can see yourself out."

Reuben stood by helplessly as Bebe walked away from him, her head high and her shoulders straight. He was so light-headed, his vision blurred. This was a new Bebe, a Bebe he'd never known. Christ, he'd just shocked the living hell out of her, and she'd bounced back and given him what-for. He felt the crazy urge to cheer her on. Instead he sat down and finished the pot of coffee.

It wasn't until Bebe was inside her bathroom with the door locked that she gave way to her emotions. Her son, her first-born, here, just miles away! That tiny bundle she'd held in her arms and christened John Paul in the middle of the night was here, and she could see him, talk to him if she wanted to. Her tears flowed and her shoulders shook with grief. It was all too much—her divorce, her father's death, and now the boy. How was she ever going to deal with her personal problems while all this was going on? Guts. She needed guts and determination. Her willpower had long ago deserted her because it was easier to give in to her cravings for drugs and alcohol, but not this time.

Sol's death had shaken her to the very core. One minute he was alive and the next minute he was gone. Now, for the first time, she was aware of her own mortality, and the realization scared her out of her wits. Death loomed over her like some dark, forbidding shadow. Her only salvation lay in changing her life—in growing strong, getting clean, and staying that way *for herself*. Oh, she'd kicked it all before, but always at Reuben's insistence and for her husband, not for herself. And that's what was going to make a difference. This time it would be for her and her alone. God, she didn't want to die, not yet.

Maybe Eli would help her; after all, he was the one who'd gotten her hooked in the first place. Pep talks, that's all she'd ask of him. He'd gone through his own personal hell in the past few years and managed to come out on top. Now he was a serious painter and had private showings on both coasts. These days he painted by commission, and he had a list of clients that would take him into next year. Everyone wanted a seascape by Eli Rosen. Once, he'd been a two-bit, gun-packing hoodlum who'd run illegal whiskey all over the county. He, too, had used drugs and alcohol, but he'd kicked it all and straightened out his life. Well, she could, too. And by God, she would— even if it killed her!

She cried heartbrokenly then for Bebe Rosen Tarz and her lost youth. And when she dried her eyes and stepped into the shower, she offered up the only prayer she could remember for her firstborn.

An hour later Bebe Tarz was dressed in a yellow sundress and soft white sandals. She pulled her long blond hair back into a knot and twirled it on top of her head. For a moment she stared at the wire-rimmed glasses on her dressing table, then picked them up and put them on. Suddenly the bedroom came into focus, and she could see clearly the shabbiness of it as well as the dirt and dust. On her way to the kitchen she stopped to look into several rooms. Everything was dusty and grimy. If she stamped her foot, the dust would spiral upward from the thick carpets.

Mattie, the old housekeeper, was cleaning lettuce at the sink. Bebe called her name several times before she turned. With her glasses on, Bebe could see that Mattie was much older than she'd thought. "Mattie, how old are you?" she asked gently.

The wrinkled face puckered. "I'll be eighty-three on my next birthday, Miss Bebe," she said proudly.

"I know this is a silly question, but what happened to the rest of the help? You shouldn't be climbing up and down the steps at your age."

"Your father said he had to cut back. He kept me on because I've been here since you and Eli were born. He needed someone to look after him. I told him I couldn't keep after this big house, and he said not to worry about it. He said he'd make sure I was well taken care of."

There'd been no provision for Mattie in her father's will

simply because there was nothing to leave her. "Did . . . what I mean is, where will you go, do you have a place to live?"

Mattie nodded. "With my sister in Santa Barbara. But I don't think your father . . . no one has said anything, so I assumed that . . ."

"These things take time, Mattie. I want you to call your sister and make arrangements. I'll have Daddy's lawyers speed things up. I'm sure it won't take long. A check the first of every month . . . does that sound all right to you?"

"Bless you, Miss Bebe, it's more than fine." Mattie beamed. "I thought your daddy forgot, and it wasn't my place to ask. Who's going to run this big house? It's going to take a mite of doing to get it back to its old splendor."

"Don't worry about a thing, Mattie," Bebe said warmly. "I'll find someone, and if I don't, I guess I'll tackle it myself. I'm . . . I'm getting a divorce from Mr. Tarz, so I'll be living here from now on. I don't want you worrying about me. You go to your sister's and sit in the sun. You've earned your retirement."

"What about lunch?" the old housekeeper asked anxiously.

"I think I can handle lunch. Call your sister and start to pack your bags. You can be on the afternoon bus if you want. I'll take you to the depot myself."

Bebe smiled as Mattie bustled out of the kitchen. Now all she had to do was come up with the money for a pension. Although she had very little cash, she did have enough for Mattie's bus ticket and first month's wages. Then perhaps sell her car and get a cheaper one, and of course some of her jewelry would have to be sold, too. She'd do that this afternoon after she dropped Mattie at the depot. And she wouldn't take a damn thing from Reuben until the divorce lawyers told her what was what. "I was never Bebe Tarz except on paper," she muttered. Imbued with the pious unselfishness of her new intentions, Bebe literally danced around the kitchen. This would be her first step toward personal independence.

It took Bebe exactly one week to sell her expensive Cadillac and purchase a ten-year-old DeSoto with 75,000 miles on it. Next she sold all her jewelry with the exception of a strand of pearls that Mickey Fonsard had given her years before and a pair of pearl earrings that had been a gift from Reuben that same Christmas. Her own personal bank account now held $46,000, $5,434 of which was deposited in an account for Mattie. The minute she returned from the bank she tore through the house, searching for liquor bottles and drugs to pour down the drain.

Over the next thirty days Bebe fought with her mind and body to conquer her life. Several times she lost touch with reality, and when she surfaced from her pit of agony she was stronger—until the next bout. Every afternoon she forced herself to swim laps in the pool for stamina. Grimly determined, she consumed milk by the gallon and stuffed her face with oranges, peaches, and ripe grapefruits, often throwing up in the process. In the morning and early evening she walked around the estate until her feet were full of blisters.

By the fifteenth day of her fitness regimen, Bebe knew she was over the worst of her addictions. Never again would she subject her body to such torture.

On the morning of the sixteenth day, Bebe dressed and left the estate in her secondhand car. At the market she bought thick red meat, bags and bags of fresh fruits and vegetables, and eggs. On her return to the mansion she now lived in, she made up a full week of menus.

In the whole of her life she'd never done more than blow the dust off her dressing table, and now she set herself the task of cleaning the entire house, from top to bottom, one room at a time. The cleaning supplies in the pantry confused her, but she learned by trial and error—what cleaned, what streaked, what polished, what left a film, and what didn't. The glasses she forced herself to wear showed each smudge, each speck of dirt. Her fingernails chipped, and the cuticles were ragged and torn. Each night she rubbed lotion into her red, rough hands.

By the end of the third week the blisters on her feet healed, her backstroke had improved, and she could swim fifty laps in the pool and be barely winded. She ate three meals a day and was so exhausted by eight o'clock at night that she slept deeply and dreamlessly. She felt better than she had in years. Her future, whatever it held for her, would be of her own making.

On the last Monday in August Bebe stood in front of her mirror, admiring her now-trim body. She was tanned and fit, with no need of makeup. The hateful red splotches hadn't disappeared, even with all the milk she'd consumed, but the tan she had covered them effectively. Dressed fashionably in a conservative sky-blue dress that complemented her coloring, she set out for town. First she stopped at Temple Emanuel and registered. From there she went to the Red Cross and offered her services as a volunteer. At both places she signed her name Barbara Rosen.

Bebe was on a roll and had her life in check. "Bravo!" she whispered to herself as she drove the battered car back to Benedict Canyon.

Tomorrow she would go to Carmel and see Eli. He would be the judge of her transformation.

"I don't *need* you, Reuben Tarz. I may have *wanted* you, but I don't *need* you!" She laughed then, a glorious sound that tickled her ears. "By God, Bebe, you did it! You really did it!"

Chapter Ten

THE GUARD IN HIS CREASED, NATTY GRAY UNIFORM watched the sleek Cadillac approach. Mr. Tarz always drove slowly, savoring the minute the guard stepped up to the car and jokingly asked to see his pass. He'd tip his hat and say, "Good morning, Mr. Tarz, beautiful day to be making pictures," and Mr. Tarz would joke back and say, "If you have any ideas, Eddie, I'd like to hear them." Of course he never did. What would he, a guard, know about making motion pictures?

Eddie Savery stepped up to the car and leaned in. "Do you have a pass, sir?" At Reuben's nod Eddie went into his spiel. "Good morning, Mr. Tarz, beautiful day for making pictures."

"Yes, it is. Lift the gate, Eddie, I'm in a bit of a hurry," Reuben said quietly.

Eddie hastened to do his bidding. Shaking his bushy head, he removed his cap to scratch at his springy curls. Today there was a passenger, one he couldn't see clearly but for a hasty impression of youthful handsomeness. He shrugged; who could be expected to keep up with the comings and goings of studio bosses?

Reuben felt as though he had a two-hundred-pound weight on his shoulders as he drove through the lot to his office. The boy wasn't giving him an inch. He answered when he was spoken to, but that was it. Only days before, Philippe had purchased a house down the road from his own, a beautiful furnished house complete with swimming pool. The boy hadn't batted an eye at the price, nor had he bothered about price tags when he'd bought out a haberdashery store earlier in the week. Today was his first visit to the studio, and already Philippe had made a point of telling Reuben he wanted an office of his own, a secretary, and carte blanche. They were two polite adversaries each waiting for the other to say or do the wrong thing.

"Well, what do you think of our studio?" Reuben asked.

Philippe cast a critical eye at the clean-looking white buildings and manicured patches of lawn that surrounded the different studio lots. "Well maintained," he commented.

Reuben made a strange noise in his throat. "You should have seen it when I first came here. It was so run-down, it looked like a hovel."

"But you fixed all that," Philippe said slyly.

"Yes, I fixed all that, and I wasn't too proud to wield a paintbrush," Reuben drawled. "Is it your intention to start at the top or at the bottom?"

"At the top . . . Father, where else? I do own forty-nine percent of this company. I'm overqualified to be an errand boy. I think I'll step into the vice presidency and hold that position until you're ready to step down." He locked his gaze with Reuben's.

"We already have a vice president," Reuben said tightly. "No one man makes decisions here. In the old days yes, but not now. If you wish to be called a second vice president, I can arrange it. That forty-nine percent does not give you total voting power here now. Is there anything else you'd like me to help you with?"

"No. Where's my office?"

"Down the hall from mine on the second floor. I suppose you want your name on the door."

"I'll take care of it . . . Father. You're wrong about the forty-nine percent, though. My bankers have sent on a portfolio. I have as much power as you. I expect we'll, how do you Americans say, lock horns. I am a stubborn man, just as stubborn as you. We're going to make some changes in the next few weeks."

Reuben eyed his son for a moment before he got out of the

car. The boy's attitude reminded him of his own cockiness the day he'd come to Fairmont the first time to ask Sol Rosen for a job. He'd been fearful, but he hadn't let the old man see him sweat. And he wasn't going to sweat now, either. There was no fear in this young man, just pure, unadulterated hatred. He walked around the car, taking a stance just inches from the boy. When he spoke, his voice was cold but level. "Listen to me now, Philippe, because I am going to say this only once. I don't much care what you do here as long as it doesn't interfere with what's best for this studio. I did not bust my ass all these years for you to come storming in here full of hatred thinking you can run things. It won't work. While you were sitting on your ass in France enjoying the good life, I was here working twenty hours a day to make sure you got your half of my labors. The way I see it, I owe you nothing. So, anything you do you will clear through me. Is that understood? Another thing, any-time you're ready to discuss the circumstances of your birth and your . . . Mickey, you have only to ask. Right now I like you about as much as you like me, so you see, in all areas we're starting off even."

Philippe stood at attention and clicked his heels together the way he'd seen the Gestapo do in Paris. "Yes sir, Mr. Tarz, sir," he said, saluting smartly.

Left alone in his new office, Philippe sat down with a thump on the swivel chair. Well, he'd lost that round, but the war was still in progress.

Guilt rippled through Philippe. The feeling that he'd made an ass of himself in front of his father rankled. Maybe it wasn't guilt he was feeling, maybe it was something else—anger and fear that he was out of his depth here and his father was secretly laughing at him, this upstart who'd appeared out of the blue, threatening and making demands. He needed to take time to get his thoughts together, to make a constructive, productive plan that would give him some authority in running the studio.

Philippe looked around his office, noticing it for the first time. The nine-by-ten cubicle had one window with a view of the parking lot, a door that had at least sixteen different coats of paint on it, a bare wood floor that was dusty, a beige swivel chair, and a scarred wooden desk that was completely bare. Humble beginnings, to be sure. His eyebrows shot up suddenly, and his eyes widened. Was this the way his father had started when he'd first come to Fairmont? It seemed logical. If he asked, his father would probably say that surroundings didn't make a difference, it was what you did in your surroundings that counted. And, of course, he would be right.

A wave of homesickness surged through Philippe, and he felt tears burn in his eyes. He'd had such a good life growing up, the best of everything, and it wasn't just the material things he was missing. His mother, Yvette and Henri, his godparents, and all his friends had loved him. But he'd been a boy then. Now he was a man—a man following in his father's footsteps. Everything he did and tried to do would be considered in light of Reuben Tarz's accomplishments. Everyone would be watching him; he would be able to read in their eyes the comparisons they were making, and he knew he would come up short. Reuben Tarz *was* Fairmont Studios.

With no time clock to punch and no calendar to enforce time limits, he was his own boss and the equal of his father . . . on paper. But he knew that his father would never, ever consider him equal until he proved himself. But how? Philippe laced his hands behind his head and leaned back in the swivel chair, unaware that it wasn't the tilting kind. He went over backward, toppling onto the dusty floor. A yelp of surprise escaped him, and it was at that moment that his father knocked and opened the door.

Reuben reached out a hand to his son. His face flushed with embarrassment, Philippe grabbed hold and rose to his feet. "The chair doesn't tilt," he muttered.

"I see that." Reuben grinned. "This won't be the last time that you land on your ass. I was in that position more often than on my feet when I first started to work here. I came by to tell you maintenance will be up shortly to fix this office. We've been using it as a storage room. I'm sorry it's not bigger. I don't know if this will interest you or not, but this was my office once and that was my chair and desk. I'm not being sentimental, it was just left here."

Philippe felt something alien attack his throat. He nodded, not trusting himself to speak.

"If there's anything you need or want, you have only to ask," Reuben continued. "I've requested a secretary for you. She'll start on Monday. I believe her name is Lucy and she'll be coming from the production offices, so she's no greenhorn. Until they know and recognize you here, you'll have to wear this badge if you plan on walking about the lot. It's mandatory." Reuben handed over a white tin badge with Philippe's name typed neatly on it.

Philippe stared at the badge. Philippe Bouchet. His eyes questioned his father.

"You'll take a lot of crap around here from people wondering why you aren't in the service. We're all very patriotic. Your French accent will serve you well. It was my idea, and I'm not trying to denounce you. If you prefer Philip Tarz, that's okay, too." Reuben turned on his heel to leave the office.

"I would like to keep the office as is. I wouldn't mind someone cleaning up the cobwebs and dust, though, and for now I'll go with Bouchet. What you said makes sense," Philippe said grudgingly. This time it was Reuben's turn to nod. Once the door had closed behind him, he grinned from ear to ear. The boy was a puppy, but puppies learned quickly or they felt their master's hand.

With his father's commanding presence gone, Philippe picked up the phone and asked the operator to ring Daniel Bishop's offices in Washington. He announced himself, said he was well, and immediately asked if there was any news of his mother.

"Nothing, Philippe," Daniel replied. "I check with the Red Cross every day. My friends are working on it. I've sent several messages. We can only wait. I'm sorry my news isn't better."

"So am I. I'll be in touch, Mr. Bishop." Philippe hung up, then rang the operator a second time and gave the Bishops' number in Georgetown.

Nellie answered the phone breathlessly. "Bishop residence, Nellie speaking."

"Good morning, Nellie, this is Philippe. You sound out of breath. Did I take you away from something?" he asked.

"I was watering the garden, and no, you didn't take me away from anything. How are you, Philippe? I miss you."

"I . . . I have nothing to do here . . . yet. I'm in my new office with no pencils or papers, just dust. You're the second person I called. I called your father first to ask if there is news of my mother, but he said he's heard nothing. I decided to call you." He was babbling, saying words that meant nothing to her. "I . . . I miss you, too," he blurted out. He smiled at the sigh in her voice.

"I'll write you a letter tonight and send it to the studio. I'll be your first piece of mail. Will you save it? My letter, I mean?" Nellie demanded.

"Of course," Philippe said gallantly. "I will respond. I'm going to walk over to the production offices and meet Miss

Perkins. That's where you're going to be working. I'll get, how do you say, the lay of the land for you.''

"Everyone says Jane is a crackerjack, I'm sure you'll like her. She started in the studio when Uncle Reuben did. He gave her her first break. Daddy is very fond of her.''

"I bought a house and a car,'' Philippe said boyishly. "And a phonograph and a lot of jitterbug records.'' Nellie squealed with laughter. Philippe flushed and then laughed along with her. "If I'm going to be an American, I have to start acting like one. I don't want to be a . . . puffed shirt.''

"That's *stuffed* shirt, Philippe. Do you know how to jitterbug?''

"No. I thought you could teach me when you get here.''

"It's a deal. And you can kiss my hand the way Frenchmen do in the movies.''

"It's a deal.'' Philippe laughed. "Well, it's been nice talking to you.''

"Will you call me again?''

"Certainly . . . you bet!'' They were both laughing when they hung up.

Philippe sat for a long time contemplating the square black telephone. It was such a marvelous instrument. Then he began to drum his fingers on the dusty surface of his bare desk. He couldn't spend all his time thinking about a lovely young girl he'd just met. That's what boys did, not young businessmen. But the truth was he didn't know *what* to do. What direction should he take? He knew what his mother would advise: research, study, know his facts. Never be unprepared if something is important. And the sooner he started, the better.

Philippe decided he'd had enough of his dismal surroundings. Pinning on his badge, he headed for the studio lot. His first stop, the reference library. There he would research Fairmont Studios from day one until the present.

The door to his father's office was open, so Philippe poked his head in and asked for a pad and pencil. Reuben rang for his secretary, who fetched them immediately.

"What's that?'' Philippe asked curiously as he watched his father attempt to slide a large yellowed square of cardboard under the blotter on his desk.

Reuben looked up at his son, a strange expression on his face. Hesitantly he withdrew the cardboard square and held it up. His voice was unlike anything Philippe had ever heard before—tortured and yet vulnerable. "Years and years ago

Mickey gave me this. In a way it was a joke, I suppose—on her part, at least. I thought . . . I wanted it to be important, and it was . . . to me. I had such grand plans then, I was going to . . . As you know, Château Michelene produces, at least it did, quality wines. I wanted to expand it and export the finest. Mickey gave me this . . . winemaker's calendar. I . . . I know it by heart. When I left France for America it was the only thing I brought with me as a reminder of that time. The calendar and a sizable debt," Reuben said ruefully. "A debt that was repaid within the year. I don't suppose you're interested in all of this. I'm . . . I'm sorry I've been rattling on."

Philippe thought his father's eyes looked peculiar, until he reached down for his reading glasses. Of course, they were misty with memories. "This is the time when the third cultivation of the soil is required to protect the vines against the weeds," he said softly. "The Bordeaux mixture is best. You have to trim the long shoots so the vines spend their energy on making fruit. If there's a heat wave, the cellar doors have to be closed at night and a sulphur candle burned. The vine growth slows down that way and then you can bottle again when there's time. I . . . when my mother told me the story of the calendar, I was nine years old. I had it memorized in two days. You see, I was so sure you would appear any day and then you and I would have something to talk about. I wanted you to be proud of me. That calendar was my litany until I was about twelve, and then I realized you were never going to come. But I didn't forget a word of that calendar." Philippe stared at his father coolly and was pleased to see that he had turned pale. Turning on his heel, Philippe walked out of the office. Reuben's hands trembled as he carefully slid the brittle calendar under the blotter.

"Inspect and clean the vats to be used for vintage so vine growth and fermentation can start at mid-month. Low strength, less stable wine can turn in the warm weather so it must be carefully . . ."

"Mickey, this is so unbearable . . . Where, why . . . ?"

Chapter Eleven

THE NIGHT WAS PITCH-BLACK, THE FAT, SWOLLEN CLOUDS overhead just as dark. Thunder growled intermittently, promising a steady downpour, the kind of rain that lasted for hours. Other than the thunder, the night held a funereal silence. All sounds had ceased hours earlier with the stealthy footsteps of the Resistance members as they made their way into a deserted farmhouse on the outskirts of Cherbourg. When it did come, heavy rain would be welcome, for it would hide any sounds the partisans might make as they worked to free their beloved France from German hands. Rain also washed away the ever-present stink of death.

The loyal group of Resistance fighters numbered fifteen. They were quiet, smoking and drinking thin, sour wine, and glad to have it. They were waiting for the man who was the leader of the Mauier network. When he arrived, if he arrived, they would be given their orders, divide into groups, and leave. All was in readiness; their backpacks were full of explosives, their carbines lay at their feet, the transmitter was packed safely away.

Mickey and Yvette were new to the Mauier network but had been welcomed by the second-in-command, Jean Duclose. He'd asked only one question when the two women arrived:

Can you and will you be able to kill Germans if you have to? Mickey had nodded vigorously; Yvette's head bobbed fearfully.

"Most of us have some training in the art of killing. It isn't a simple matter. You can break a neck with a trained blow. You need to know how to break a stranglehold, how to knee your attacker in the thigh as well as in the crotch. Simple rules, easy to master."

Mickey had no trouble, but Yvette had been unable to apply the simple rules until Mickey had hissed in her ear, "Pretend this is the German who slaughtered Henri. Always think of Henri. That's why we're here." That had been at the last stages of twilight. Two hours of practice sessions later, every man in the small group had felt Yvette's wrath.

"You'll do," Jean said gruffly. Mickey beamed her pleasure. For days she'd been worried that Yvette would fall apart and not be able to do her share, and Mickey was unwilling to have her partner with anyone else because of that fear.

The inch-high candle in the tin plate was starting to sputter. The group's thoughts were one: Where was Raoul? The night would be wasted if he didn't appear soon, for without his direction and his orders from England they would be useless.

Fifteen minutes later, as the candle hissed to blackness, Raoul Berne arrived with the rain that sliced against the farmhouse windows. Silently he advanced to the circle of people, a small torch in his hand. He was tall but squat-looking somehow in his bulky peasant clothes. The battered British cap he wore in no way disguised his French face. His mouth was thin and tight, his nose aquiline. In the yellow light from the torch, Mickey noticed that his eyes were a peculiar shade of gray, almost translucent. There was a sense of power and competence about him that relaxed her. Yvette inched closer to Mickey as he began to speak.

"We'll work in threes. Each of you will be given a paper with your instructions. I'll give you five minutes to memorize it, then you burn the paper. Be sure nothing is left behind, for we will not be returning. Ninety minutes before dawn you will make your way to the next house that will be safe. If you are wounded, you will be left behind, is that understood? I have . . . pills, each of you will be given one in case you are captured by the Germans."

Mickey's blood ran cold as she reached for the lethal white capsule. For a moment she thought Yvette would refuse it, but when her friend reached for it her hand was steady. For a full moment Raoul's translucent eyes locked with Mickey's. Although she wanted to look away, she couldn't tear her eyes from his burning gaze.

"We'll transmit at exactly two minutes after four o'clock. You," he said, jabbing a long finger at Yvette, "will do the transmitting. I like women with red hair and green eyes." His voice was a friendly growl, and Yvette yelped in fright. Mickey bit down on her lip to hide her smile.

"How many Germans do you think he's killed?" Yvette whispered in Mickey's ear.

"Ask me directly, mam'selle," Raoul interjected. "Twenty-eight, and I loved every minute of it. How many fearsome Germans have you killed for our country?"

"N-none," Yvette stammered.

"That will change tonight. You will be with me and the woman next to you. You will be my lookout, and you," he said, pointing to Mickey, "will help me with the explosives." Mickey nodded. "The Brits tell us if we are successful in blowing up the Cherbourg communications center; they can bomb the German sub base at dawn. Our timing is crucial, so let's run through it one more time. This rain is a godsend," he muttered to no one in particular.

Minutes later they separated, each group heading in a different direction. The rain beat down, soaking them to the skin in seconds. It took the best part of three hours to reach their objective, fighting the beating rain and slashing winds. Suddenly Raoul drew up short, then turned to Yvette and hissed through his teeth. "I smell your fear, and that's not good for any of us. You will concentrate on what has to be done, lock your mind on our people and what these filthy bastards are doing to them. In Nantes today they gunned down forty people—women and children. Think of that."

Raoul next addressed himself to Mickey. "We are less than a kilometer away from the center. There are patrols from here on in. Usually no more than three, one for each of us, eh? We crawl now, on our bellies, and make no sound."

As if they would, Mickey thought fearfully. Would she die here attempting to blow up a communications center she wondered. Who would tell Philippe and Reuben? There would be no one to identify her body, and she would be listed simply as missing. The thoughts were driven from her mind as she inched her way forward, directly behind Raoul.

Harsh, guttural German words swirled about Mickey, carried

on the wind. Suddenly Raoul stopped, and Mickey's chin thumped down on his boot. Less than ten feet from them stood two German soldiers. They began to walk away, and once they were past, Raoul whispered to Mickey, who in turn whispered to Yvette: "They'll return in less than seven minutes." Mickey knew without being told that she and Raoul would come up behind, pull back the man's head and drive the knife home, right through the jugular vein.

The German's torch was pointed low, lighting their way. This was their signal. Mickey and Raoul stepped out into the road, their arms outstretched. The sound of the snap as the first German's neck broke was so loud, it was like thunder in Mickey's ears. With Yvette's help she dragged the corpse into the brush at the side of the dirt road.

Raoul took a moment before dropping to the ground. "The first one is the hardest. After that it gets easier. Remember that."

Mickey believed him implicitly. She'd actually enjoyed snapping the man's neck. There was blood on her hands, but she didn't care. As long as it wasn't French blood, she could live with what she'd done.

"Slow and easy now," Raoul murmured, "we're less than half a kilometer from the center. The Germans are everywhere. Maybe not too many tonight because of the rain. The Boche likes comfort, so my estimate would be half the usual number." The women nodded.

Fifteen minutes later the communications center loomed ahead of them, blacker than the night and sky. A dim yellow light could be seen through the rain. Inside, the Germans were laughing and joking, undoubtedly congratulating themselves on their daily victories over the defenseless French. Maybe some were sleeping on a night like this, dreaming of their families or of Adolf Hitler, the maniacal leader of the German Reich.

Raoul glanced at his watch. Earlier he'd been fearful that the women would slow him down, but they were actually seventy seconds ahead of schedule. Time to take a deep breath. Time to bolster the redheaded woman. "We have exactly seventeen minutes and twelve seconds to string the explosives. In six minutes two or three Germans, depending on their manpower in this weather, will walk right by us. They must be taken care of. Their shift ends in twenty-five minutes, so no one will look for them until that time."

"How . . . how do you know this?" Yvette whispered.

"Because, madame, I have been sitting on that rise every night for the past fourteen days. I know what the Germans are going to do before they do it. They are predictable, and this group is lazy." Raoul waited, his eyes glued to his watch. "Now," he hissed.

Mickey slithered to the right, followed by Yvette's ample body. Even before she saw them, she could smell the cigarette smoke. Nodding to Yvette as she came upward in a knee crouch, she ticked off her fingers to the count of ten with the point of the knife. Then she moved forward, making a sloshing sound in the muddy road. The Germans turned, their torch shining upward, bathing Mickey's face in its yellow glow. She froze in her tracks, her thoughts rushing to Philippe and Reuben.

Yvette sprang to life, diving for the legs of the German closest to her. Her knife went in lightning fast, and then she shoved and pulled upward. Confident that she'd ripped the man's heart in two, she fell backward. The torch was on the ground, and she could hear Mickey panting close by. When she rolled away, straining to see, her body touched something soft yet solid. Mickey or the German? She reached for the torch and picked it up. It was the German, blood spouting from his mouth.

"Yours is still alive," she whispered, hoping Mickey could hear her. Holding the light closer to the man's face, she smiled down at him, enjoying the fear in his eyes. Then, still smiling, she lifted her foot in its heavy boot and smashed it down on the man's face. When she raised her foot there was nothing left of the man's face. "For Henri and all those poor souls in Nantes," she snarled.

Mickey had left to take her place with Raoul and the explosives. Yvette realized she would have to drag the two bodies herself. At that minute she felt an enormous surge of strength. Whatever had to be done, she could do. For the coward that she was, she'd done well this evening, and Raoul was right: the second one was easier.

Later, when they were a kilometer away from the communications center and waiting for the moment the plunger shot downward, Yvette whispered to Mickey, "I finished him off for you. He would have died anyway within minutes; I just hastened his death. He burns in hell now."

Mickey shook her head. "I was thinking about Philippe and Reuben. I froze, Yvette."

"Yes, but you recovered and did what was expected of you. He was right, Mickey; the second was easier. What do you think?"

"Yes, much easier."

Raoul held up his hand. "Ten seconds, nine, eight, seven, six, five, four, three, two, one . . ."

The sky was a giant roman candle as charge after charge of explosives rocketed upward. Raoul gave them no time to savor their victory. "Come, we still have work to do, ladies. Until we hear the British bombing the sub base, all we did was blow up a communications center that can be operational again in twenty-four hours." His voice was harsh but not unkind. "Keep up with me now, the rain is letting up."

Yvette cursed under her breath. "So much for being enamored of my red hair and green eyes."

Mickey smiled, her thoughts far away in America with the two men she loved most. But this was the last time she would give free rein to her thoughts. Tonight she'd almost been killed because she'd indulged her emotions. She had to stay alive to see Philippe again—and maybe, God willing, Reuben, too. From now on she would be positive and aggressive, concentrating on sabotaging the Germans any way she could. Philippe and Reuben belonged to another life.

Later, when their night's work was finally over and they were approaching the safe farmhouse, Mickey realized she was almost happy. She'd contributed to France's fight. Now she had time to enjoy the countryside, at least for a few minutes. How clean and fresh it smelled. How safe it looked.

"We'll wait here for the others," Raoul announced. "We have a perfect vantage point; we're hidden and can watch the farmhouse for a while. Because it was safe two days ago doesn't mean it's safe today." He raised his binoculars. When he was satisfied that the house was empty, he passed a cigarette to Mickey and Yvette. They smiled at one another as the RAF planes dropped their bombs on the sub base. Later Raoul and the two women welcomed the rest of their party as they straggled in in small groups.

"This is our biggest coup to date, and we have reason to be proud and thankful that we've all returned," Raoul congratulated them. "Now let's see if we can find some food at the farmhouse, for my belly is growling."

With the night's work behind them and a meager amount of food in her belly, Mickey took her turn resting. The fear she'd lived with all night long was dissipating slowly, to be replaced with a strange kind of exultation. Her eyes strayed to Yvette, who was crouched in the fetal position, thinking God knew what.

Mickey wished she were clairvoyant so she could reassure Yvette of the future. Not for the first time, she wondered what lay in store for them. The moment they had joined the Resistance, her old life had slipped away from her. Even her name had been changed; one could not be betrayed if one's name wasn't known. She was called Chapeau and Yvette was referred to as Maman. Only in whispers did the two friends refer to each other by their given names, and Mickey knew even that was a mistake. Somehow, though, it helped to make sense of their situation.

She'd heard bits and pieces concerning their next strike and the next safe house run by an aging farm couple who had spirited shot-down RAF pilots and fleeing Jews over the mountains—thirty-seven French-Jewish children, parentless and seeking refuge. Her heart had turned over when she'd heard about the children who would be her responsibility. So many little lives, and none of them past ten years of age! How would the little ones make the climb over the mountains? How many would they lose? She prayed for the strength and stamina to see her through the coming days. And when she'd finished those prayers, she prayed anew for those of her countrymen who had betrayed their own for food and the promise of life. She couldn't judge those people. What would she herself not have done to protect Philippe? No, there would be others to judge French traitors someday.

Chapter Twelve

AUGUST'S VICIOUS HEAT WAVE GROUND TO A FINAL HALT and gave way to normal temperatures during the last days of the month. It was a particularly trying time, with the war news going from bad to worse to devastating. Daniel Bishop was fretful and fearful and half angry. Fretful and fearful because there had been no news of Mickey. Reuben called every day, and he was now at the point where he dreaded the calls, although he did his best to make his voice as cheerful as possible. Philippe usually called right after his father, and as the days wore on, the boy grew frantic—which did nothing for Daniel's frame of mind.

Nellie would be ready to leave for the coast in a few days, and he was already feeling his loss. Rajean was sullen most of the time, curled on a chair with a book he knew she wasn't reading. They spoke very little these days, and when they did she snapped and snarled at him. Something was bothering his wife, and it wasn't the fact that Nellie was leaving. On the contrary, he'd perceived a definite sense of relief in his wife at their daughter's coming departure. Tonight he was going to have a talk, a serious one, with his wife. Nellie would be out, so they would have the house to themselves and could argue as loudly as they wanted.

Enough was enough. His spirits perked up momentarily at the thought he'd had earlier this morning of going to the coast with Nellie for a week or so. Rajean would probably be glad to be rid of him so she could get into whatever kind of trouble he was keeping her from at the moment. If Nellie didn't mind having him tag along, that's exactly what he'd do. It would be good to see Reuben and Jane, and even Max. And his desire to discuss Mickey and the war in Europe was so strong, he felt light-headed.

Daniel glanced down at his desk. Every pending piece of work could be assigned to a junior man at the office. Besides, he would be a telephone call away if a snag occurred. In the meantime he could concentrate on Mickey, Reuben, and Philippe.

Yes, Philippe . . . Daniel paused a moment, recalling the most recent telephone call from the boy, the one he'd asked Daniel to keep under his hat. Something about a gut feeling he had about a new phenomenon called tele . . . tele . . . Daniel frowned, trying to remember. Tele-something—a technological breakthrough, apparently, and one that Philippe was currently looking into. Tele*vision*—yes, that was it. Seeing a picture on a box in one's living room was the way the boy had described it. Philippe wanted to get the jump on the other studios and hoped that by working on the project secretly he could even override Reuben's opposition when the time came. Daniel admired the boy's determination; perhaps that was why he was using Nellie and her trip to California. Going along with her gave him an excuse to look into the matter. This television would be a challenge, the boy said, not of the decade, but of a lifetime.

Daniel slammed his desk drawer and stood up. It was time to go home. Christ, he hated the thought. If he had anyplace else to go, he'd never return to the house in Georgetown. Of course, when Nellie was there it was different. But with Rajean there alone, the place resembled a war zone—and he had to do something about it before he became mortally wounded. He wanted to breathe again, to laugh and smile, to joke and cry. Goddammit, he wanted his life back!

Ten days before he'd hired a firm of private detectives to observe his wife, but so far all they'd been able to report was that Rajean made daily phone calls from a phone booth in the Rexall drugstore. Hardly grounds for divorce.

So . . . if Nellie agreed to his accompanying her to California, he would bait his trap for Rajean. He'd had her on short shrift these last weeks, and she was staying grudgingly in line. Before he left he'd give her some money and let her dig her own hole. It was a sneaky maneuver, but it would get him back his life— and at the moment that mattered more than anything else.

To Daniel's relief, no steam billowed upward from the cobbled Georgetown streets. It was actually pleasant driving home, with a perfect light breeze that ruffled his thinning hair through the car window. Most important of all, the oppressive humidity was gone.

The umbrellalike elm rustled overhead, a friendly sound to Daniel's ears, when he pulled the car to the curb. For a moment he just sat in the car and savoried the early evening. Unfortunately his house loomed before him, a solid reminder of the task he had yet to perform. He'd never liked this Jack Sprat house from the first moment he'd first set foot in it. Back then he'd acquiesced to just about anything Rajean wanted just to see her smile at him. Now he knew that he'd never been truly in love with his wife. Love, that wonderful heart-singing feeling when all you wanted was the other person's happiness was what he'd hungered for. And he'd been so naive, thinking if he gave all of himself emotionally, physically, and financially, his happiness would come back twofold. All he'd gotten was misery. And Nellie, although Nellie and his happiness did not go hand in hand. But for that part of the light in his life, he would not short-change Rajean. With a weary sigh he prepared himself to leave the car and go inside.

The small foyer with its white tile floor, so sterile-looking, seemed dim. There were no flowers on the hall table, and no light shone from the narrow living room. In the kitchen he found a bowl of salad and a cheese sandwich on the table, wrapped in wax paper. Ignoring them, he poked his head out the back door. Someone had watered the flower beds recently. The little walled garden smelled earthy and damp. The four tomato plants held up by thin stakes had been his contribution, and now there were two ripe tomatoes on one of the vines. He loped down the steps to the garden and pulled one of the tomatoes off the vine, then rubbed it on his pant leg before biting into it. His very own tomato, nurtured by Nellie with water and fertilizer. He had to remember to thank her. Grinning wryly, he entered the deserted kitchen, banging the screen door behind him.

* * *

Rajean watched her husband from her position at the front window. When he didn't come upstairs immediately she followed his progress with her ears, listening to him walk through the house to the kitchen and then out to the small walled garden. When the screen door closed behind him she knew he was on his way up to their room. Quickly she settled herself on the chaise and flipped open a magazine. When she heard Daniel stop at her daughter's bedroom door, she smiled. His love for her daughter was so touching . . . and so fortunate. For it was through Nellie that she would be able to get from her husband what she wanted. Not for the first time she realized that she could bring Nellie and Daniel's plans to a grinding halt if she wanted to. After all, she was Nellie's mother. If she vetoed the trip to California, Nellie would have to go to college in Washington. So this evening she was going to tell Daniel that Nellie could go to California—for a price. Daniel would pay it, too. Daniel would do anything for Nellie's happiness. Her features took on a smug look when her husband walked past her on the way to the bathroom.

"I hope you don't mind the sandwich and salad for dinner," she called to Daniel's retreating back. "Nellie didn't want any dinner, and I didn't feel like bothering for just the two of us."

"I ate a tomato and I had a big lunch," Daniel replied as he closed the door behind him. He turned and locked the door, something he rarely did. But only here in this large tiled room could he think. It was his sanctuary of sorts after a long, grueling day at the office.

Twenty minutes later he emerged from the bathroom, one towel around his neck and one around his waist. As he walked behind the chaise and dressed, he spoke to his wife in the even tone he'd affected over the last few years. "I'll be going with Nellie to California. I'm not sure how long I'll be there, and I'm sure you'll have no objection."

"Oh, but I do, Daniel," Rajean replied, smiling. "I want to talk to you about this little matter. I know I can't stop *you* from going, but I've been thinking . . . California is such a wicked city, and your friends Reuben and Bebe—well, I don't think that's the place I want my daughter to be. No, I think she should stay here and go to college in the city."

Daniel stared at his wife a moment, eyes narrowed. Then he gave a grim little smile. "How much, Rajean?"

"Ten thousand . . . for now" was Rajean's immediate response.

"You realize, of course, that you're selling your daughter. I adopted her legally years ago, so I have as much say in her welfare as you do."

Rajean's lip curled. "I'm selling and you're buying. Don't they call it supply and demand or something like that?" she asked sweetly.

Daniel regarded her with contempt. "As soon as I get back I'll be filing for a divorce. I've had enough of this . . . existence."

"That will cost you, too," Rajean replied languidly. "And remember: the courts always award custody of a minor child to the mother. So be prepared, darling." The flutter of fear she always felt at the word *divorce* subsided a bit. After all, the "*ex*-Mrs. Bishop" didn't sound altogether bad—provided Mr. Bishop paid and paid and paid. How much could she zap Daniel for until Nellie came of age? Probably not all that much, she mused. Well, it would have to be *all that much* if Daniel was serious about the divorce—and she had no reason to think he wasn't.

"Did you have a figure in mind?" Daniel asked conversationally.

"A hundred thousand, this house, and my car," Rajean responded after a moment's thought. Her husband's peal of laughter sent chills up her arms. "Cash! And some kind of annuity for my . . . advancing years," she added, frowning as Daniel laughed again and walked out of the room.

He was still laughing when he entered his home office. Laughing because Rajean's demand matched exactly what he'd been prepared to give in return for his freedom and sole custody of Nellie. The detectives he'd hired would take care of the rest.

It was then he saw the copy of the *Star* on his desk, neatly folded along with two bottles of his favorite beer in an ice bucket. Nellie, of course. The ice had melted, but the water was cold to the touch, with little beads of frosty water trickling down the sides of the bottle. Just the way he liked it. Sweet Nellie. He shuddered to think what would have happened to her if he hadn't come along to marry her mother. The note he'd left in her room made him grin again, picturing her face as she read it. Nellie would appreciate his taking time off from the office to accompany her to California.

Daniel shook the paper free of its confines. This was the moment he dreaded every day, the moment his eyes scanned the front page for news of the war in Europe. He never knew quite what it was he dreaded or expected each day when he put the paper aside after reading it from beginning to end. The war offices and news correspondents didn't even know of Mickey Fonsard's existence. His heart felt sore when he realized that another day was almost over and still there'd been no word concerning her safety.

At the thought of the torment Reuben must be going through, his head began to pound. Inside of a week they'd be commiserating together. Ever since Reuben had told him he hadn't taken Philippe to see Bebe, he'd had the uncanny feeling that Bebe knew more about Mickey than any of them. But he doubted she'd share her information with Reuben. It was a damn shame; for a while he'd thought that things would work out between his old friend and Bebe, particularly after Reuben was honored at the Academy Awards years before. Reuben had thought so, too, and said he'd tried, but Bebe wanted more than he had to give. Bebe always wanted more, expected more, just like Rajean.

Daniel likened happiness to the commodities market. One minute you had it and the next it was gone unless you were an expert trader.

In the world of business both he and Reuben were kings. In the world of love and happiness they were both king-size duds.

With a sigh Daniel leaned back in his leather chair. Together he and Reuben would find a way to deal with their concern over Mickey.

Rajean drew in her breath and let it out slowly when the door closed behind Daniel. For several moments she sat quietly trying to take deep breaths, unsure of what she was feeling—exaltation or dismay. Ten thousand dollars now and a hundred thousand for a divorce. If she sold the house, perhaps another sixty or seventy thousand. Then she could move to New York, be near Teddie.

Her hand was on the phone to place a call when she drew it back into her lap. Long-distance calls showed up on telephone records. It was also time she stopped being so impulsive. Tomorrow would be soon enough to call Teddie. This was what she wanted, wasn't it? Freedom to come and go as she pleased, free to spend money, to give gifts, free of Nellie and the responsibility of motherhood. Nellie was an independent young girl, able to take care of herself now. Besides, long-distance family relationships were best. Maybe she wouldn't sell the house, maybe she would keep it to have a home base. In a strange kind of way she rather liked the narrow house with its crazy-shaped rooms. She also liked the atmosphere of Georgetown and the cobblestone streets.

A small prick of fear tickled Rajean. She wished she hadn't been so verbal about Daniel to Teddie. Why was it lovers always confided things they shouldn't? Deep in her gut she knew now that she shouldn't have said a thing about her husband. Teddie knew too much about her as it was, and lately . . .

Suddenly Rajean jumped up from the chaise and ran to the bathroom mirror. Yes, there they were—the tiny lines around her eyes, the slight droop at the corners of her mouth. Dammit, it wasn't fair! Men became distinguished as they got older, and women . . . women just aged. Cosmetics went only so far. She lifted her arm and tweaked the fleshy part with her two fingers. Sagging! God! Even her breasts were squishy now and her belly button was sinking into her stomach. Her thighs jiggled, too. Quick as a flash she hiked her skirt to her waist and whirled around, craning her neck to look at her rear end in the mirror. Drooping, too. Gravity. Who cared if a man's ass drooped? No one. Who cared if a man's thighs jiggled? Men had hair to cover their thighs, so it wasn't as noticeable anyway. No one cared. And men's belly buttons simply weren't worthy of thought.

Tomorrow she'd look into plastic surgery and find out how much of a chunk it would cost.

Rajean leaned over the sink to scrutinize her reflection. Honesty demanded she assess herself now, before she committed to the divorce. The Pan-Cake makeup hid a multitude of defects and announced others. Her skin wasn't that good, it never had been even with the assiduous care she'd give it. Acne had left scars, and no matter how careful she was with her makeup, it settled into the little pits, often making her look grotesque. She'd tried sunbathing to tan her face and arms, but somehow the little pits speckled instead of tanning. She'd stayed indoors for a long time after that fiasco. She looked hard and she looked worn, and no amount of cosmetics and no new hairstyle was ever going to change that. What would she look like if she let her eyebrows grow back, she wondered, scrutinizing her reflection in the mirror. She tried to imagine herself without the Pan-Cake makeup, without the artificial eyelashes and highly arched, penciled brows. Like a hag, she decided. God! She leaned as close to the mirror as possible to stare at the tiny wrinkles above her upper lip.

Rajean dropped the lid of the toilet seat and sat down with a thump. Was this the way Teddie saw her, or was she being overly critical? Tears welled in her eyes. Of course Teddie saw her like this; Teddie had a trained eye. It would explain so many things—the fights they had over long-distance calls, the times Teddie had refused her calls altogether. Teddie never calling her during the day when Daniel was at work. Teddie staring at Nellie's graduation picture and practically salivating over it. Teddie liked young girls with firm flesh and silky hair. She was kidding herself if she thought the affair with Teddie was going anywhere but down the drain.

Damn, tonight she was going to have another one of her horrendous nightmares. Two nights earlier she'd had a dilly and woke up drenched with perspiration, or at least that's what she told herself the next morning, but by afternoon she realized what she'd had was a hot flash. The realization had been so awesome she'd fled the house and walked for hours trying not to think about the hateful word—menopause.

Yesterday she'd flounced into her doctor's office demanding to know all there was to know about menopause. She'd lied to the doctor and said her periods were normal and not as erratic, as they really were. The doctor had tried to console her by saying she was lucky she was late in starting, and there was medication for the hot flashes. He'd even given her a little pamphlet that she'd thought too stupid to read and tossed into the trash only to pick it out later to read. She threw a tantrum then in her room, stamping her feet and beating her clenched fists into the pillows. The three-page pamphlet had been informative, too damn informative. What she remembered now were the words *dryness* and *estrogen*. Another remembered word flashed through her mind: *lubricants*! "Oh, God," she moaned.

Rajean got up and flushed the toilet, not knowing why. She noticed that her hands were shaking. Earrings would cover the wrinkles in her earlobes. Big earrings, the button kind that was all the rage these days. Dryness. "My ass, I'll take estrogen. If I have to, I'll take a bath in olive oil!"

Back on the chaise with her legs stretched in front of her, Rajean once again reached for the phone. Only Teddie had the power to drive these nasty thoughts from her mind. She could call collect so it wouldn't show up on the telephone bill. Her hand was on the phone, her thoughts with her lover. She could feel the accelerated beat of her heart, and her throat felt dry. Her foot twitched nervously as she waited for Teddie's voice to come over the wire. Only the voice she heard wasn't Teddie's—it was young and trilling with intimate laughter:

"Rajean? No, sorry, Teddie can't come to the phone right now."

In the background Rajean could hear Teddie's husky laughter. The phone dropped from her hand onto the hardwood floor. It was a long time before she obeyed the operator's querulous order to replace the receiver.

"Damn you, Teddie!" she cried. "Damn you to hell!"

Chapter Thirteen

HOW WARM THE SUN WAS, HOW COMFORTING, BEBE thought as she strolled through the fragrant garden. This was going to be her next project. It was time the tangled vines and shrubs were fed and trimmed before the yard turned into an emerald jungle. The only problem was there weren't enough hours in the day to do everything that had to be done. The pool alone took her an entire morning to clean. Eyes narrowed, she examined her appointment book. If she hurried home from her temple committee on Thursdays, she could work in the garden until dark.

Bebe's pencil flew down the week's list of things to do. Because of extended meetings with her attorney to discuss her divorce, she was off schedule by almost two days. And she'd worked so hard these past six weeks, come so far, she couldn't let a series of meetings throw her off course. Perhaps if she tried to get by on fewer hours sleep . . . Quickly she made some adjustments in her book, and when she was satisfied that her life, according to her notebook, was back on schedule, she leaned back for a half hour that was hers to relax.

In the whole of her life she'd never felt this good, this confident. She drank thirstily from a tall glass of ice water. Quite by accident, she'd discovered that drinking water was good for the skin. Now she consumed eight to ten glasses a day, and her skin was more supple, softer to the touch.

These days she didn't have a single complaint about her life. Everything, including her divorce, was under control. Even her thoughts about Reuben were under control. Once she'd had the locks on the door and her telephone number changed, she'd installed a security fence around her property. Now there was no way Reuben Tarz could invade her life or her property. Then she remembered the stack of letters on the central hall table, all from Reuben and not one of them opened. It was almost a game now, avoiding Reuben.

Bebe drained the glass of ice water and set it on the table next to a single sheet of white paper that had been taped to the front door. It was from Reuben, and the message was so blinding, she couldn't have missed it if she'd tried. He'd used a heavy black grease pencil on the stark white paper:

IMPERATIVE YOU CALL ME IMMEDIATELY IN
REGARD TO FIRSTBORN SON.
                    REUBEN

Bebe had no intention of responding to Reuben's summons. She wasn't ready yet to lock horns with her husband over John Paul. Just learning that the boy was here and would want to meet her at some point had jeopardized her recovery program. Every time she thought of him, her heart ached and she could barely keep from drowning her guilt in liquor. No, better to avoid the entire issue until she was stronger. . . .

That night the phone began to ring—twenty, thirty rings at a time. By eleven o'clock Bebe thought she'd go out of her mind. Defiantly, she took the receiver off the hook and stuck it under the cushion of a chair.

At twenty minutes past midnight the doorbell shrilled to life and continued to ding-a-ling for over an hour. "Go ahead, Reuben, ring it till it wears out," Bebe muttered. "I'm not opening this door to you now or ever again!"

At a quarter to three in the morning, fresh from her bath, Bebe marched down to the cellar, flashlight in hand. She yanked open the fuse box and twisted the quarter-size fuse. The doorbell stopped in midpeal.

"So there!" she snarled. Gathering the hem of her robe, she stomped her way back to the second floor. If he was still there in the morning, she'd call the police.

The clock on her nightstand read four o'clock, and she was still wide awake—so wide awake she almost jumped out of her skin when she heard the sound of a pebble hitting her bedroom window. Angrily, she stormed to the window and pushed at the screen. "Either get off my property, or I'm calling the police!" she bellowed. "Do you hear me, Reuben! I'll have you arrested for harassment and trespassing. I mean it!" When Reuben's harsh words filtered up to her, she grasped the window ledge, her knuckles whitening.

"Won't that look nice—you, me and our son plastered all over the front pages. Now open the goddamn door so we can talk in private. I swear, Bebe, I'll smash every window in this house! Your son is coming to see you tomorrow. Now, open the goddamn door!"

Trancelike, Bebe slid her feet into slippers and pulled on her dressing gown. At the front door she drew in a deep breath and held out her arms to prevent Reuben from entering. "This is the last time you're coming into this house, Reuben. I want that understood. So say what you have to say and then get out of here!"

Reuben shouldered his way past her, forcing her to follow him into the living room. She watched as he turned on every lamp in the room. When he was satisfied there was enough light, he turned to her and said, "Philippe is working at the studio now, Bebe. I think you should know he still hates my guts—and as far as I can tell he hasn't forgiven you yet, either. But I don't think this waiting game you've been playing with him will work anymore. I guess he wants to meet his natural mother even though he doesn't seem to harbor much love for her. He said he was coming here tomorrow to camp on your doorstep. Now, that's the only reason I'm here. Are you going to see him when he comes?" Reuben asked coldly.

What was there for her to say? She'd never actually thought that a confrontation would be forced on her. Slowly she sank onto a chair and buried her head in her hands. Bebe reached out as the world slid away from her and she toppled to the floor. Reuben was at her side instantly, gathering her into his arms. He was stunned at how tiny and thin she was underneath the robe she wore. Thin, but not skinny. Actually, she was hard as a rock, he thought, massaging her arms. He saw the blunt-cut nails and felt the calluses on the palms of her hands. He noticed her hair then, short and curling around her face, giving her a gamin look. He noticed the streaks of gray around the temples. He frowned as her skin looked soft underneath the cold cream. Brown as a nut. He knew she was healthy and happy. The thought disturbed him. He tried to remember the last time he'd seen her, actually paid attention to her. Months before, which didn't say much for him.

Bebe's lashes fluttered and Reuben found himself staring into the clearest, the greenest eyes he'd ever seen. Green eyes filled with pain and . . . oh so vulnerable. Surely, this wasn't the Bebe he knew and was married to for so many years. All the sharp words, all the recriminations, were forgotten. "I'm sorry, Bebe. I didn't want to blurt it out like that, but you didn't answer any of my letters. My God, I came here every day. I wanted to be the one to tell you. I'm sorry as hell you had to find out like this. Here, let me help you onto the sofa."

Bebe sat hunched over, her hands folded between her legs. When she spoke her voice was soft and gentle. "You say he hates us both."

"Surely you don't expect love and devotion." It was a statement.

"When you first told me about John—about Philippe, you said Mickey kept him and raised him. I never knew, Reuben. They told me they would give him out for adoption. Over the years I stopped to see Yvette every time I was in Paris, and she never gave the slightest indication that Mickey had the boy. A lot of things are clearer now. I never asked about him in . . . in any of my visits. I could never bring myself to verbalize anything in regard to him," Bebe said in an agonized voice. "I . . . knew if I ever . . . I wouldn't be able to leave."

"You should have told me," Reuben said gently. "I was his father. I should have been told."

Bebe raised her head to meet her husband's eyes. "And what would you have done, Reuben? Tell me, what exactly would you have done?"

"I don't know, but I know I should have been given the chance to make up my own mind. Jesus Christ, Bebe, do you know what kind of shock it was when Daniel brought him to me?"

"I would imagine," Bebe said shakily, "it's something like it was for me when you first told me. Look, why don't I just keep playing the game; just tell him I—I don't want to see him right now. I've worked very hard these past months to get myself back together, and I don't know if I can handle any emotional setbacks. I don't ever want to be dependent on anything or anyone again. I'm doing fine now.''

"How . . . who . . . You do look wonderful," Reuben said sincerely.

"The details? You always did want to know every little detail. Okay, I'll tell you: guts. That's all it took. I knew if I didn't do it this time, I might as well lie down and die. I climbed the walls, I puked my guts out, I crawled on my hands and knees, I scrubbed and scrubbed, hard physical work so I could pass out from sheer exhaustion. And I did it by myself. Every hour, every minute, of my day is filled. I have no time now for might-have-beens. I cannot change anything for that young man. If Mickey raised him, then he's had a wonderful life. I don't see that he has anything to complain about. He simply wants to satisfy his curiosity about me. *I have no wish to see him.* Pass that along, Reuben. Now, if you'll excuse me, I think you've taken up enough of my time this evening. . . . By the way, have you figured it out yet?"

"Figured what out?" Reuben asked, puzzled.

"The reason Mickey never wrote you or Daniel. It's obvious now, isn't it? All those years, she knew. She let you leave and never said a word. She knew, Reuben."

Reuben's voice was full of sorrow. "Yes, I figured it out. . . . Mickey and Yvette have joined the French Resistance, Bebe. No word has come through yet regarding their safety. I thought you might like to know. . . ."

Bebe shook her head. "You're wrong. I don't want to know. I live one day at a time. I have no interest in the past. Nothing can be undone. My future is unknown to me. I'm making a new life for myself with my own two hands, and none of you are included in this life. We'll be divorced soon enough, and that will put an end to any communication between us."

Without another word Bebe rose and walked Reuben to the door. She was so tiny, just a slip of a woman, yet she seemed ten feet tall, Reuben thought. And then he saw the tears glistening in her eyes. Before she could move he tilted her chin so he could look into her eyes. His touch was gentle when he put both hands on her shoulders.

She cried then, like a wounded animal in a trap. "Don't do this to me, Reuben. Take your son and go away. He's yours, my gift to you—late, I grant you, but . . . Get out!" she shrieked, jerking free of him and running up the steps.

"Bebe . . . I . . . Goddammit!" He cursed himself for barging into his wife's fragile new life like a bull in a china shop and ripping her world apart. Well, he argued with himself, she's not exactly blameless here. Maybe not, but you could have spared her feelings a little. She's right, the kid had a good life, better than either you or she could have provided. She's in a fragile place right now, and if Philippe comes to see her, she could go over the edge and she knows it. She's fighting to survive the only way she knows how. You are a fucking son of a bitch. You'd like to see her fall back into her old ways when she was dependent on you and . . . other things. You never saw this side of your wife. You didn't know she had guts. You didn't know she could make it on her own. That has to smart a little. And of course you are never going to forgive her for the boy, right? But then, what about Mickey? She kept your son all these years and never said a word to you. Let's divvy up the blame in the right proportions here. Shut up!

Reuben slammed out the front door and stormed to his car. Without turning on the headlamps, he jerked the Cadillac into gear and raced backward until he heard the crunch of metal on metal.

"Son of a *bitch*!" What the hell had he hit?

He hopped out of the sedan, aware for the first time of the other parked car in the circular driveway. It was just a pile of junk, but still, it belonged to somebody. Now he had to go back into the house and see Bebe again.

He waited a moment to see if the crash would bring her to the upstairs window. When he was certain she wasn't going to appear, he let himself back into the house and crept up the stairs to the second floor. He was almost at the landing when he heard Bebe's gut-wrenching sobs. They tore at his heart; this wasn't acting or pretending. There was no audience for her to play to.

At the door to his wife's room, Reuben hesitated. He was an intruder here, hated by his wife and all his children. His thoughts whirled crazily as he listened to Bebe pour her heart into the pillow she was clutching.

"Do you think it was easy giving you up?" she moaned. "It was the hardest thing I ever had to do, almost as hard as trying to hate your father. I said all those horrible, nasty things so I could leave. I wasn't any good for you, and neither was your father. I had to give you away; I had to do what was right for you. I gave you a name, though, and every time I thought of you I called you John Paul. I loved you. I never forgot your birthday, and I knew that someday you'd grow up to be a wonderful human being, so much better than your mother and father. I gave you that chance, and it was the hardest thing in the world for me to do. God, please don't make this any harder for me. Don't let him come here. Don't make me see him. Make him change his mind, let him write to me and tell me how much he hates me, but don't let him come here!''

Reuben was backing away from the doorway when Bebe sat up in bed, her eyes wild when she spotted him. "Sneaky *bastard*! You listened to me. Damn you, have you no shame? Get out of here. You're ugly, you're hateful. I hate you!'' she screamed. "You're a low-down, nasty man. You cheated my father, you stole his studio, and, goddamn you, you stole my virginity. All you do is take, take, take, and you never give anything back. You are a son of a bitch, Reuben Tarz, a pure, unadulterated son of a bitch, and I *hate* you!'' Eyes flashing with the force of her rage, she reached for an enamel vase on the nightstand and flung it at Reuben with all her might.

"You're right on every count,'' he cried, ducking as the vase flew past him and shattered against the door frame. "Look, I came back only to tell you I hit your gardener's car, and I want to pay for the damage.''

"I don't have a goddamn gardener, so don't tell me any more lies. You sneaked in here to . . . to . . . Just what the hell *did* you come here for?''

Reuben took a few steps into the room, careful to remain near the threshold. "I told you: I hit the car out front, smashed into the front of it. I want to make good.''

"Damn right you'll make good; that's *my* car. You give me the money right now, this goddamn minute!''

"That sardine can is yours!'' Reuben cried, astonished. "What the hell are you doing with a piece of junk like that?''

"I sold my car to pay for Mattie's pension. It runs,'' she said defiantly.

"Not any more it doesn't,'' Reuben said. "Why didn't you tell me? I'd have gotten you a car. Aren't you embarrassed to be seen in it?''

Bebe took a deep breath. "You know, Reuben, somehow I knew you were going to say that. Yes, it's an eyesore, and yes, I'm embarrassed to drive it, but I drive it anyway. I call it my lesson in humility. It's all I can afford. I don't want anything from you—not until we're legally divorced.''

Reuben shrugged. "I only thought—''

"I know what you thought," she interrupted. "You know what you are, Reuben? You're a damn robot. You walk, you talk, you eat, and you sleep, but you aren't real because you don't know how to feel. You're nothing but a cheap copy of a human being. And before you can say it, yes, I am what I am and I am real. I hurt, I cry, I make mistakes, and I make some of them over and over again, but I am learning from my mistakes. I know now what I *don't* want. It's taken me a long time, and it might even take me longer now that you've come here and upset my life. But I'm going to do it, if only to outsurvive you and to make you pay for what you've done to me over the years. Now give me the money for my car and get out of my house."

Out of the corner of his eye Reuben could see that she'd backed him to the top of the stairs. Three steps at the most and he'd topple over. It was not a comforting thought.

The moment the fear in her husband's eyes registered, Bebe turned and walked back to her room. Reuben watched her until she'd entered her room, for the first time truly proud of his wife. When he heard a muffled cry of pain, he followed her back to the room in time to see her wrap a towel around her foot. "What happened?" he asked, hurrying to her side.

"Oh, I must have stepped on some broken glass from the damn vase," she muttered.

"Let me take a look at that," he said quietly. Obediently Bebe held out her foot. "It looks pretty deep, and there's some glass in it. Do you want me to try to get it out, or would you prefer I take you to a doctor?"

"Is it going to hurt?"

"Probably. The antiseptic will hurt even more. Do you have a tweezer?"

"On the dresser. Don't dig, just pull it out."

"All right, hold still now. Grip my shoulders, but don't jerk your foot."

Thirty minutes later Bebe's foot was bandaged and she'd gulped down the aspirin that Reuben handed her. They were sitting on the floor in front of the open window watching the dawn creep over the tops of the trees. Reuben's arm was around Bebe's shoulders, and she leaned into him, weary after the evening's turmoil. Reuben found himself nuzzling his chin in her sweet-smelling hair.

"If you want to talk about Philippe," he murmured, "I'll listen and not say anything." Bebe shook her head. "Do you want to discuss the divorce?'' Bebe shook her head. ''Mickey?'' Again Bebe shook her head. ''Is there *anything* you want to say?''

Bebe moved slightly. ''Yes. I want to say good-bye to you. In bed. That's how we started. Now that we're going to end it, it seems fitting somehow.''

An unseen hand jerked at Reuben's heart, sending a flurry of fear into his throat. Somehow he'd thought she wouldn't go through with the divorce. But now that she was working so hard at changing her life, she didn't *need* him anymore, didn't want him. All she wanted was to say good-bye in her own way. Too much, too little, too late, he thought. Sound roared in his ears as desire coursed through him. ''No, no,'' he cried hoarsely as he brought his lips down on hers.

With a sound that resembled a groan and a plea, he brought her to him, crushing his mouth against hers, tasting her, feeling her lips yield to his. When he broke away he saw the flush in her cheeks, the way her lips parted, rising once again for his kiss.

Hating himself, Reuben brought her closer, aware of the lemony fragrance in her hair. Her skin smelled of flowers and a delicious womanly scent that was hers alone. Her arms wrapped tightly around his neck, pulling him closer.

She lay in his embrace, fragile as the first flower of spring. He buried his face in her hair, luxuriating in its softness, surrounding himself in her warmth.

As Reuben gazed at her form in the golden lamplight, all of his pent-up yearnings, feelings he hadn't realized existed until this day, rose to the surface, and he moved closer. The feel of her satiny skin, the voluptuous curves beneath the silk gown she wore, exhilarated him.

Once again his lips clung to hers, and Bebe's head spun as she felt her body come to life beneath his touch. He was gentle, more gentle than she remembered, his hands unhurried as he explored her body intimately. His mouth moved against hers, and her senses reeled as she strained against him, trying to be closer to him, trying to make them one.

With infinite tenderness, Reuben loved her, realizing that in spite of her past, she was inexperienced. He put a guarded check on the growing fever in his loins, waiting for her, arousing her patiently until her passions were as demanding and greedy as his own.

His hands burned her flesh as they traveled the length of her, stopping to caress a pouting breast, a yielding, welcoming thigh. The silken gown was now an irritant, and Bebe wished to be rid of it. Hasty hands found the pearl buttons, opening them, exposing her skin to his touch.

His lips left the sweet moistness of her mouth to find the tender place where her throat pulsed and curved into his shoulder. Down, down, his mouth traveled, turning her in his arms, finding and teasing the places that brought consummate pleasure and sent waves of desire through her veins. The ivory luster of her breasts beckoned him, their rosy crests standing erect and tempting. Her slim waist was a perfect fit for his hands, her firm velvet haunches accommodating the pleasure of his thigh. He placed a long, sensual kiss on the golden triangle her nudity offered, and Bebe gave herself in panting surrender.

As the last of the stars twinkled overhead, his lips touched her body, satisfying his thirst for her and yet creating in him a hunger deep and raw. The intricate details of her body intoxicated him with their perfection. The supple curve of her thigh, the flatness of her belly, the dimples in her haunches, the muscled length of her legs. But it was always to the warm shadows between her breasts that he returned, imagining that they beckoned him in a silent, provocative appeal.

Bebe's body cried out for him. She offered herself completely to his seeking hands and lips. And Reuben, sensing her passion, furthered his advances, hungry for her boundless beauty and placing his lips on those secret places that held such fascination. He indulged in her lusty passion, which met and equaled his own.

Beneath his touch her skin glistened with a sheen of desire. She slid her hands down the flat of his belly, eager to know him again and to satisfy her yearning need. She strove to learn every detail of his flesh so she could remember it later, touching his rippling muscular smoothness, feeling the strength beneath. She kissed the hollow near the base of his throat, tasting the scent of his after-shave. And when she cried his name, the sound tore from her throat, painful and husky, demanding he put an end to her torment and satisfy the cravings he'd instilled in her.

The galaxy of stars overhead became one world, fused together by the blazing heat they created. Together they spun out beyond the moon, reveling in the beauty each brought to the other, seeing in each other a small part of themselves. Two spirits, one pale as starlight, the other dark as midnight, came together in their passion, creating an aura of sunlight in the dark, endless night.

What seemed a long time later, Bebe wiped at the tears trickling down her cheeks. Her voice when she spoke was solemn and full of sorrow. "Do you know, Reuben, in all the years we've been married, you made love to me only once. The night when I was sick you slept with me so your body warmth would . . . Only once. And then tonight. It's not much of an epitaph to a marriage, is it?"

Reuben's eyes snapped open. He had to answer her, say something to take the finality out of her voice. But what? He didn't know this new Bebe. In the end all he could do was nod.

Bebe sat up and swung her legs over the side of the bed. As she reached for her robe she said, "You'd better leave now. I have a full day ahead of me, and I want to take a bath. I need to wash you out of me." When Reuben made no move to get up, she walked around to his side of the bed, leaned over, and lightly brushed her lips across his cheek. "Good-bye, Reuben."

Reuben's eyes narrowed. "Are you telling me that after . . . after what we just . . . you're really saying good-bye?" he asked, astonished.

"Yes. It's time. You never could say it in actual words, but in other ways you said it every day of our married life. I don't *need* you anymore. I know in the days and months to come, I will *want* you, but I can live with that. Needing and wanting are two very different things." She turned on her heel. "I expect you to be gone by the time I'm finished with my bath."

Reuben turned at the sound of the closing door. By God, she meant what she'd said! He felt his loss then, so keenly he wanted to cry. His eyes were frantic as they raced around the room, Bebe's room, which held nothing of his.

The words Bebe had spoken just moments before now pushed him out of her bed and into his clothes. As he walked down the corridor to the stairs, he realized that he hadn't felt this devastated since the day he and Daniel had been gassed and blinded during the war. He'd thought then that his life was over. He *knew* now that his life, as it had been until now, was never going to be the same.

The cool early dawn wrapped itself around him as he made his way to his car. Even in the dim early light, he was shocked at the sight of Bebe's rusty, decrepit car. For some reason a lump settled in his throat as he walked around to view it from all angles. Without stopping to think, he pulled his billfold from his inside pocket and peeled off ten hundred-dollar bills, wedging them in the crease between the backrest and the seat. Bebe would see them when she opened the car door. A smile spread across his face when he pictured her tootling down the road into town in the horror sitting in front of her house. In his gut he knew that she would return all but three hundred dollars of the money.

With a sigh, Reuben slipped his sleek Cadillac into gear. Right now he had to think of Philippe. If he hurried, he could make it home, shower, change, and get to the studio in time to explain and hopefully prevent the boy from going to Bebe's house.

Driving home, Reuben realized he couldn't fault his wife for the stand she was taking with Philippe. If anything, he admired her guts, but the decision must be ripping her apart. If mother and son did come face-to-face, he was positive that Bebe would stand tall, stare down her son, and tell him his mother was Mickey Fonsard. She would not give in to his curiosity. Would he himself have the guts to do what she was proposing? He doubted it. If Daniel hadn't initiated a meeting between himself and his son . . .

Grinding the car to a halt in front of his house, Reuben sat for a moment with the key still in the ignition. He liked the Bebe he'd been with—in fact, he more than liked her.

"Too much, too little, too late," he mumbled, and wearily made his way into the quiet house.

Chapter Fourteen

PHILIPPE CHOSE HIS CLOTHES WITH CARE, REJECTING JACKET after jacket. He wanted something that would say he was Philippe Bouchet and not a carbon copy of Reuben Tarz. Finally he selected a soft gray cashmere jacket that was lightweight and a pair of charcoal trousers. To complete the outfit he would wear an open-necked white dress shirt, but no tie. His visit today was not really formal.

In front of the mirror he made faces at himself as he rehearsed what he was going to say. "I'm your son, the one you tossed in the trash. Hello, I'm Philippe, your son. I wanted to see what kind of woman would throw away her son. I'm Philippe and I'm here to tell you if I never see you again, it will be all right with me. Hello, I'm Philippe. Please, Mother dear, tell me what it feels like to give away your flesh and blood. Hello, I'm Philippe, and I came here to tell you to go to hell. I don't need you. I don't want you, either." End. Finis.

In a nervous gesture, the boy smacked his fist into his open palm. Finally, after all this time, he was going to meet his real mother. Reuben had scheduled the meeting for midmorning. If he hurried, he could arrive at the studio before his father. So far, he thought glumly, it had never worked—no matter what time he got up. Secretly he thought his father slept at the studio.

Philippe was standing at the window of his office with a cup of coffee in his hand when his father entered the room. For some reason the knowledge that he'd beaten his father's arrival by at least ten minutes brought him no satisfaction.

"Philippe, I spoke to your—to Bebe last night," Reuben began, clearing his throat nervously. "And . . . well, there's no way for me to say this except straight out. She doesn't want to see you. She feels . . . actually, what she said was that there's no room in her life for you, and the reason she gave . . . you up was so that you would have a better life than she could give you. I tried . . . but she's adamant about not wanting to meet you. I'm sorry, I can't stop you from going to her home if you insist on it. But I would advise against it. I never realized until this . . . last night just how strong-willed your mother is. I know this must be a blow. . . ."

Philippe whirled around. "Blow? Hardly. I merely wanted to satisfy my . . . curiosity."

"That's strange," Reuben said, smiling. "Your mother said those exact same words. Look, I'm going to get some breakfast. Would you care to join me?" He wished he could see the boy's eyes.

"No. I've eaten," Philippe said, his back to the room. "But thank you."

When the door closed behind his father, Philippe's shoulders slumped and the coffee cup in his hand trembled. God, he wished he were back in France, wished he'd never heard the name Tarz, wished he still believed Mickey Fonsard was his real mother.

He'd been so arrogant in his thoughts, so mocking in regard to his real mother and father, and now he'd just been put in his place by two . . . masters of the art. Words—he'd been mowed down by words.

In a flash, Philippe was out of the office and bolting down the steps. Alone in the building, Reuben walked to the window, grinning wryly. If he were in Philippe's position, he'd have done exactly the same thing. Like father like son. . . . The thought pleased him.

The early morning sounds of the birds soothed Philippe. For a moment he almost felt as if he were back at the château in the country. He looked around at the lush vegetation, overgrown and untended. From his position inside his car he could see thin blades of grass poking up through the cracks in the concrete driveway. One blade in particular held a drop of dew that sparkled like a diamond. It was so quiet, he thought. How lonely it must be living here. In particular he missed the sounds of animals: a dog's bark, a cat's meow.

On arriving he'd parked his car across the driveway, completely blocking it. Then he'd walked up the long drive to see if there was any sign of activity. The stillness disappointed him; he'd been hoping for some sign of his mother. There was a rusty, dented car in front of the pillared mansion, which had to mean someone was in the house. Still, he had all the time in the world, so he could wait as long as need be.

It was important for him to meet his mother, not because he wanted to exorcise old dreams and desires, but simply because he was curious. She meant nothing to him; he had a mother, a mother who . . . lied to him. That he could forgive, had forgiven. If there was one thing in this world he knew, it was that Mickey Fonsard loved him with all her heart and soul.

Philippe slouched down in the driver's seat of the car, expecting a long wait. While he waited he did something he'd promised himself he wouldn't do: he honed his thoughts to Mickey and Yvette and the war. Deep in his gut he knew that his mother hadn't gone to Spain as she'd said she would. Loyal Frenchwomen would be in the underground with the Resistance doing what they could for their country. When his heart began to pound, he forced himself to think about his boyhood, when things were pleasant and wonderful. A bright red wagon painted by Henri, the wonderful pony cart, old Jake and Jake's pup, Dolly . . .

The redwood planters full of colorful flowers welcomed Bebe in the early morning dawn. It was so peaceful, so colorful, and so inviting, she found herself sighing with pleasure as she attacked her melon and toast. This delightful sanctuary was hers and hers alone and didn't invite worry or distress. Here, at this sparkling iron-and-glass table, under the striped canopy, she was at peace with herself.

Her farewell to Reuben had been painful, but she was still alive and eating her breakfast. Life went on; she had to go on, too. Reuben was her past, over and done with. Now all she had to do was deal with the news he'd showered on her last evening.

Earlier she'd heard the car's engine and looked out her bedroom window. Without investigating she'd known who was calling on her at this ungodly hour—her son. She'd known he would come simply because he was Reuben's son. The word *no* probably wasn't even in his vocabulary; he would think he could change things because of who he was, just as Reuben thought he could change things. This boy, this son of Reuben's, would think he could change her mind. Probably right this second he was sitting somewhere at the end of her driveway, waiting for her so he could present himself, thinking his presence would make her feel guilty. If he was like Reuben, he would hope to chip away at her defenses until he triumphed over her—and destroyed her in the process. "No!" she said emphatically.

Bebe finished her breakfast and carried her dishes into the kitchen. Today she had three meetings, one at the temple to organize a children's outing, one at the Red Cross, where she volunteered to answer the phone for three hours, and the last at St. Joshua's Hospital, where she was in training to counsel family members of accident patients. She was also having lunch with Muriel James, Fairmont's biggest star.

There was no time in her busy schedule today for Philippe Bouchet.

Drawing upon a store of strength she'd never tapped deep inside her, Bebe walked out into the bright morning sunshine. Her eyes widened in dismay at the damage Reuben had done to her car. However, a few more dents, a shattered headlamp, wouldn't prevent the engine from catching. When she saw the stack of hundred-dollar bills stuffed into the seat cushion, she frowned—then peeled off four of the bills and stuffed them in her purse. The other six were clutched in her hand as she started the old car. The engine kicked over immediately, and Bebe smiled. Old didn't mean useless at all. Actually she was beginning to like the rickety old jalopy; she'd even given it a name, Bebe Two, but she'd never admit it to anyone but herself.

As she started around the semicircular driveway, the sun glinted off the car's hood ornament and reflected through her windshield. She sounded the froggy horn and slowed down. When she was three feet from the car, she leaned her head out the window.

"This is private property and you're trespassing. Please move your car!" she called. When there was no movement she sounded the horn a second time. *I will not get out of this car and approach him. I will sit here all day if need be.* When there was still no activity in the car, she actually leaned on the horn. She hated the noise and after five minutes withdrew her hand. "If you don't move your car, I'll go back to the house and call the police!"

At last Philippe opened the car door and stepped out, walking around to the front of the car so his mother would have a full view of him. He waited, expecting her to step out of her car.

Reuben, you didn't tell me he looked just like you. Dear God, how is it possible that this young man could be so like his father? Looking into the sun as she was, Bebe was stunned to see that none of the boy's features were her own. *Reuben's son. Mickey's son.* She felt tears burn her eyes as time raced backward. *Oh, Reuben, how I loved you. Everything was for you, Reuben. I destroyed my life because of my love for you. Leave, leave, I don't want to see you,* her heart cried. *Don't come into my life now, it's too late. Leave, please leave.*

"I'm Philippe Bouchet," the young man said arrogantly.

"Yes, I know," Bebe replied coolly from inside the car. "I'd appreciate it if you'd move your car. I'm going to be late if you don't. I really don't want to take the time to return to the house and call the police." *Dear God, he even had the same arrogant-sounding voice as Reuben.* She felt a wave of dizziness attack her.

"I'd like to talk to you . . . Mother," the boy said, advancing a step.

"I don't have time to talk, and your mother is Mickey Fonsard. Don't show her disrespect by calling me Mother. I want you to leave!" *Mother. Oh, God, yes, she was his mother but in name only. Don't come any closer, please don't come any closer.* "I know your father told you not to come here, but you came anyway. You are your father's son, that much is obvious. Now I'm not going to ask you to move your car again," Bebe snapped. "If you don't, I will simply ram this car into it. I hope we understand each other."

There was a catch in the boy's voice when he asked, "Why did you . . . abandon me? Why didn't you tell my father about me?"

Why? Bebe thought her heart was going to rip out of her chest. She reached down deep, digging for the strength she needed. "I made sure you had a good life; you have no complaints. I owe you nothing, not even an explanation. Speak with your father." She slipped the car into gear and eased up on the gas pedal, watching through her tears as the boy scurried back to his car. As he backed and swerved, grinding the gears unmercifully, Bebe bit down on her lower lip. The salty taste of her own blood made her cry out. The moment the boy's shiny new car was on the shoulder of the driveway, she roared past him, looking neither to the right nor the left. Philippe Bouchet belonged to the past.

Once Bebe Two had made its way down the curving canyon road, Bebe turned the car at the first cutoff and parked. Her shoulders shook with the sobs she'd held in check. Why didn't he understand that this was best for him? Why had he insisted on coming to see her? Reuben must have told him not to come.

You must be your own person, just as your father was. There's no room in my life for you, but that doesn't mean I don't love you. I remember everything, every detail of your birth; I remember all the hateful, terrible things I said. I remember all the nightmares over the years; I remembered each birthday, each Christmas, the start of each school term. Only I know what I felt and only I know how you felt in my arms. To this day I can still remember the ache when I left you behind. I gave you a name, and in my heart you have always been John Paul. Now I have to say good-bye a second time. How much am I to endure? How much? I need to know so I can live in peace with myself . . . how much more?

Philippe drove erratically, his mind everywhere but on the road. Twice he almost careened into a car only to swerve to safety at the last moment. He didn't understand any of what had just transpired. He'd thought all women were like his mother in France. This . . . this person who was his real mother was a . . . cold, heartless bitch. Threatening to call the police, ordering him off her property because it was "private" . . . What she'd said about his having a good life was true, but it was her fault that his father had never come to see him, her fault for keeping his existence a secret. What a tidy little group they were, he thought miserably as he remembered Daniel Bishop's words: "We were all abandoned at some point in our lives, and I think that's what drew us together, by Mickey of course. I was an orphan and brought up in an orphanage, Reuben's parents died and he was sent to live in a home where there was no room for him. Bebe's mother died and left her as a child. And now you, abandoned by both your real mother and real father. In the end, as much as it will hurt you, you'll realize that what Bebe did was for the best."

Now he was driving slower, his thoughts under control. He needed to talk to someone who could look at his situation objectively. Thank God Nellie would be here in a few days. She would understand and explain the way women thought and acted on their thoughts. Nellie's life hadn't been all that wonderful, but she'd managed to survive, and she liked him, really liked him. And he liked her, too. Nellie understood. Nellie would help him get through this transition from France to America. Together they would help each other.

Philippe roared into the studio parking area and swerved into his assigned space with such force that he ran over the cement block separating his space from the one in front of him. The impact jolted him backward. He uttered his favorite American word that seemed to sum up most of his situations.

"Shit!"

Reuben winced as Philippe leapt out of the car, slamming the door behind him. He moved quickly then, timing his arrival in the hall to coincide with Philippe's. "How'd it go with your mother?" he asked casually.

"How did . . . She told me to get off her property or she would call the police," Philippe said bitterly. "She wouldn't get out of the car but sat there blowing the damn horn. She sat there in that goddamn beat-up car and told me she'd made sure I had a good life and had no complaints and to get out! Jesus Christ, what kind of woman is that!"

Reuben sighed. "I told you not to go out there. I told you she said she didn't want to see you. You should have listened."

"Do you know what else she did?" Philippe blustered. "She threw these out of the window as she drove past me. Six hundred-dollar bills! I picked them up. She yelled something like 'Give these to your father.' You Americans, you're all crazy!" Philippe yelled over his shoulder as he raced into his office.

Reuben grinned at the sound of glass shattering on the upper part of the door. He'd done the same thing years ago, but now he couldn't remember why. Time . . . When he glanced down at the money in his hand, he grinned again. He'd been off by a hundred dollars. "Bravo, Bebe," he murmured. "Keep it up."

Reuben checked his watch. If he didn't hurry, he'd be late for his appointment with the attorney Daniel had retained for him in regard to his divorce. . . .

Forty-five minutes later he found himself sitting in a comfortable burgundy chair across from Andrew Blake, Esq., a thin, bald-headed young man with penetrating hazel eyes and a penchant for custom tailoring and footwear. Each took the measure of the other, and as if by some unspoken agreement both concurred that they would do business together.

"What I see here," Blake said in a deep voice that surprised Reuben in one so young, "is either a messy case or a simple, cut-and-dried affair. I heard from Mrs. Tarz's attorneys several days ago." Paper crackled as it was shifted from one pile to another. Reuben leaned back and crossed one leg over the other. If nothing else, he was here to be amused by his wife's demands. "Actually, what we have here are two proposals," Blake continued. "First, Mrs. Tarz wants the forty-nine percent of the stock that was turned over to you some years ago. If you're willing to give her that, she'll agree to your continuing to run the studio at whatever salary you think is fair. She wants nothing else. The second proposal, of course, is predicated on the first. If you can't see your way clear to the forty-nine percent, she wants everything else. And when I say everything, I mean everything, which means you leave the studio and get a job somewhere else. I think you should know the attorneys she's hired are almost as good as I am." This was said without conceit. "It could become a bloodbath. All your dirty linen will be aired. Now, have you given any thought to what it is you want to counteroffer?

"Oh, one other thing," Blake continued. "Mrs. Tarz is going to take back her maiden name. She said she sees no problem concerning the children." He sat back steepling his fingers beneath his chin as he watched the man across from him. There had been only one show of emotion—when he'd said Mrs. Tarz wanted to take back her maiden name.

This is really happening, Reuben thought. She's going through with it. He uncrossed his legs and leaned forward. "What are my chances of keeping the studio?" he asked quietly.

Blake frowned. "Not good. She can prove that her father gave the stock to your sons and she gave it to you when you decided on a reconciliation. The studio was her father's. However, there's a way in and out of just about anything if you're willing to pay the price. You have to be the one to decide."

Reuben stood up and buttoned his jacket. "Give her the studio. Only I'm not interested in staying on under those circumstances. I'll hand in my resignation tomorrow. As of this moment, I've just retired."

"Mr. Tarz, do you know what you've just said?" Blake asked, sitting up in astonishment. "I think you'd better go home and think about this a little more. This . . . Daniel Bishop told me the studio was your life."

"Mr. Blake, Daniel told you the truth. Therein lies the problem. I won't change my mind, so get the paperwork started. I'll have my secretary bring over the stock shares."

After Reuben left, Andrew Blake sat for a few moments with his mouth hanging open. When he'd recovered sufficiently he picked up the phone. "Get Daniel Bishop on the phone," he ordered. Five minutes later he was told Daniel was on his way to California. "Thank God," he groaned. He wasn't starting any paperwork until Bishop arrived. Notifying opposing counsel was something else, however. He picked up the phone a second time, his fingers drumming on the shiny surface of his desk. He'd say it was tentative. Everything was tentative until it was signed . . . in blood, Reuben Tarz's blood.

Bebe was pruning a prickly rosebush when the kitchen phone rang at fifteen minutes past six. It was her attorney. She listened, her face registering shock. "He said that! He's willing! Not even an argument? Fine, I accept."

In a daze she walked back to the garden and immediately sliced her finger with the pruning shears. Back in the kitchen she held her bleeding finger under the cold-water tap. It had to be some kind of trick. Reuben would never . . . last night she'd thought Reuben would never . . . and he had . . . She wrapped her finger with the end of a dishcloth and placed a call to her brother Eli.

"I don't want any part of that studio, sis," he told her when she gave him the news. "It's all yours. I guess I should offer my congratulations. Maybe Pop will stop spinning in his grave now that Fairmont is back in the family. And I do mean family."

Bebe frowned. "What are you talking about, Eli?"

"You and Philippe now own the studio, that's what it means. Don't tell me you didn't think about that!"

Bebe sat down on a kitchen chair, her face drained of color. "No, I never thought of that. My God, I can't . . . I don't want . . . Eli, I never . . . What am I going to do?" she wailed.

Eli's voice grew thoughtful. "I don't know, Bebe. Do you really want the studio, or do you just want to get back at Reuben? You don't know the first thing about running the place, and I doubt the boy knows anything. If Reuben has resigned, where does that leave things? He's giving you what you want. You shouldn't have . . . Listen, Bebe, why don't you think about all of this for a few days. I don't see any real big hurry to make a decision right this minute.''

"Eli, there's more. I didn't tell you everything." In a shaky voice she told her brother about Reuben's visit and their lovemaking. Then she rushed on and told him about her early morning meeting with Philippe. "Eli, are you still there?" she asked when there was no response.

"I'm here, sis. You still love Reuben. And you love the boy, or you wouldn't have sent him away. It's all right to love. I know you're afraid of getting hurt again, but that's what life is all about. If you can't love, you can't feel. Do you want to go through the rest of your life anesthetized? Right now you're filling your hours with busy work and I'm not negating any of it. You could, if you wanted to, take an active part in the studio. You're far from stupid. You'll probably make some mistakes, lose some money, but you'll learn. Reuben was green when he started. You'll have the advantage now, no one but your son will be there watching over you. Do you want my advice?''

"Yes, I do.''

"Go for it. Call your attorneys and tell them you agree to the studio as your share of the divorce settlement and you regretfully accept Reuben's resignation. Make sure you use that word, Bebe, *regretfully*. Resign from all that busywork you've been doing and take over the studio. I don't think the boy will fight you, but if he does, simply put him in his place. Motherhood has a lot of rank, if you know what I mean. Use it to your advantage. Learn the business from the ground up; do your homework. You'll be surprised at how much you're going to remember. Don't forget how in the old days we used to hang out there whenever Pop would let us. Things aren't all that different, but whatever you do, don't fire anyone till you know what the hell is going on.''

"Eli, I'm a woman, who's going to pay attention to me?''

"Everyone, as long as you sign the paychecks. Remember that.''

"Do you really think I can do it?" Bebe asked fearfully.

"I *know* you can do it. Look, do you want me to come down for moral support?''

"Yes, I do . . . but, no, I don't want you to come. What I

mean is, if I'm going to . . . do this, I'll do it myself, and if I fall flat on my face, I won't have anyone to blame but myself. How far behind are you on your commissioned paintings?''

"Two years," Eli said ruefully.

"Right," Bebe laughed. "And you're going to come down here and wet-nurse me."

"Yes, I would."

"Thank you for that, Eli. I needed to know that someone I love is in my corner. Thanks for listening to me. I'll probably be calling you every day for a pep talk."

"That's what I'm here for. Take care, Bebe, and good luck."

"Bye, Eli."

Five days later *Variety* screamed to the movie industry: HOL-LYWOOD'S WONDER BOY RESIGNS! GIVES STUDIO TO WIFE!

Reuben Tarz grinned when he read the headline. Bebe Tarz fainted on the front steps of the Benedict Canyon house.

Chapter Fifteen

IT WAS AN OMINOUS SILENCE, ALMOST AS OMINOUS AS THE first pale gray slices of dawn, for none in the farmhouse knew what the new day would bring, nor did they know what would happen when the silence was shattered by the arrival of their leader, code-named Pier. Pier, the partisans were told, was a burly giant, more a bear than a man. His body, whispered one partisan, was as thick as a hundred-year-old tree; his arms like huge cut-off stumps; his hair like moss grown wild; but his eyes—*Mon Dieu!*—they could see all the way through to one's soul. His ears, the partisan confided, could pick up sounds miles away. He and he alone had killed more Germans than any other member of the underground.

Mickey leaned back against the quarry stone, relishing the feel of the coolness against her weary body. If only she could strip off these filthy clothes and have a bath. If she had a kingdom, she would relinquish it right now for a cake of soap and some toilet paper, things she'd taken for granted for years and never thought she would be without. The urge to scratch her body was so commanding she dropped forward to her knees and then stood up. Lice. Everyone had lice except herself and Yvette. From the beginning they'd tied their heads in scarfs, and in the early dawn they'd crept off by themselves and inspected each other's heads. The moment Yvette pronounced her head clean of the hateful creatures, she would heave a sigh so loud she thought it could be heard in the next province.

She was so proud of Yvette these days. Her friend had become so expert at thwarting the Germans and so incensed with killing them, she had become a force to be reckoned with. At some point, and Mickey wasn't sure how it happened or when it happened, Yvette had taken control and proved to be a worthy partisan. Mickey was the only one to hear her friend whimper in her sleep and see the tears roll down her cheeks.

Mickey sat down next to her friend, wrapping her arms around her bent knees. "I am so hungry I think I could eat one of my own fingers," she grumbled.

"Don't think about food, Mickey, it just makes you hungrier. As starved as I am, I know I could not eat another red beet. Ah, my stomach has turned over at the thought. I've been thinking—wishing, really—that I were back at the farm having an argument with Henri. There are times when I think I can actually smell the barnyard and see the dogs and cats and chickens. I was so happy, so blissful, back then. A warm bath at night, making lusty love with Henri, sleeping next to him . . . that was happiness, Mickey. Why is God doing this to us, why did He take that away from me? I will never understand. Never!

"And you, Mickey," she continued, "all you do is think about Philippe and Reuben. You, too, are like a machine. How much longer are we going to . . ."

Mickey wrapped her arms around her friend. "Until we are a free people again, that's how long, *chérie*."

"Did you have the leaders send your signal?" Yvette asked.

"No. I know I should have. Well, yes, I did, but it didn't happen the way we thought it would. They told me . . . actually, what they said was that my code name would go in and only one department and one English-speaking man would know that I am Chapeau. It is for our own safety. Did you ever in your wildest dreams think that our Paris gendarmes would join forces with the Germans? No one can be trusted. So Philippe and . . . and Daniel will pray for our safety and continue to call our friends in England and will be told the same thing: they know nothing of our whereabouts. It breaks my heart, but there is nothing I can do. I will make a confession to you, old friend. I am keeping my sanity by thinking of Reuben. I force my mind to go back over the years when I was younger and in

love with him. I relive each and every moment. In here"—
she tapped her head—"I have my own time clock and calendar.
I tick off each memory, and when I have a moment to myself,
I think of the next one. You, on the other hand, are dealing
with your loss the only way you can. We are a sorry team, are
we not?"

Yvette nodded solemnly. "Twenty years is a long time to
love a man, a man you haven't seen in all that time. I've always
envied that love because it was so constant. It never wavered,
not even when you found out about Philippe."

"It keeps me going, Yvette. The poets say hope springs
eternal. If I don't see him in this life, then perhaps in the—"

"Stop it," Yvette hissed. "We talk only of Germans and
death, not ourselves. Remember that!"

"Yvette, we are mere mortals. How we've managed to survive so far is a mystery to me," Mickey said sadly. She wished
Pier would arrive with their assignments so she could get some
sleep. These whispered conversations with Yvette were beginning to take their toll on her. More than anything she wanted
time to relive her memories, to remember how it was when
she was happy and in love and living in a world that didn't
include Germans and survival and killing. Just for a little while,
so she could wake and . . . and kill again and again and again.

Yvette straightened up and glanced at Mickey. Her eyes held
concern and worry that her friend of so many years was slowly
losing touch with reality, preferring to slip in and out of her
past at will. Her disturbing thought was shattered as the rough
wooden door burst open.

The others were right, Yvette decided, the man did look like
a bear. From her position she noticed two things immediately—
his hands, which were as big as ham hocks, and round eyes
the color of muddy coffee that saw everything at a glance.

There were no greetings; there never were. The man simply
dropped to his haunches and spread out a map. Yvette nudged
Mickey to wakefulness. The man's voice was hoarse and
croaky, his eyes never leaving the map spread out at his feet.
A stub of a pencil drew lines and made deep gouging X's with
the speed of a cat in flight. Mickey shuddered.

"Chapeau and Maman, identify yourselves," he rasped.
Mickey raised a finger, as did Yvette. He nodded. "Pay careful
attention. You will take the children this way. We—" There
was a long pause, so long that Mickey found herself holding
her breath. "We expected perhaps thirty or so children. There

were . . . there were that many when they started out. You will
be in charge of ten of them. Hopefully, all ten will arrive tonight
after dark. The youngest is five and the oldest is eleven.''

"*Mon Dieu!*" Mickey and Yvette whispered in unison.

"He's not helping this time around," the bear said gruffly.
"That's why there are only ten left. Their survival depends on
both of you. You, Maman, will have charge of the wireless.
You," he said, addressing Mickey, "remove your boot and
stocking. I'm glad you have big feet, madame," he said as he
busily traced a map on Mickey's foot with waterproof dye.
"You," he said, addressing Yvette, "will be the one to refer
to this map, as Chapeau will be unable to decipher it under
her toes. Clever, eh?''

Yvette thought it stupid but kept quiet. Did this man have
any idea how much time it took to unlace a boot, pull off socks,
and stare at feet? And then it took twice as long to shove the
same swollen foot back into the sock and boot.

"Look at it now, Maman, so it is fresh in your mind. The
first leg of your journey only and the first two safe houses.''

"Are they boys or girls?" Mickey asked.

"Does it make a difference?" rasped the man.

"To me it does," Mickey replied coolly.

"Six boys and four girls. The oldest is a girl and the youngest
is a boy.''

"When do we . . . when do we leave?" Yvette queried.

"As soon as they arrive tonight. It promises to be a dark
night, possibly some rain before morning.''

"They will be tired, and there's no food here," Mickey
pointed out.

"You are wrong, madame, they will be exhausted, not simply tired, but they understand what is at stake. They also understand empty bellies. You will act as their guide, not their
mother, is that understood?''

"Perfectly," Mickey replied, her eyes cold. Yvette nodded.

The bear looked uncertainly from Mickey to Yvette. Was
he making a mistake? If so, he would have to live with it. The
others, experienced men with knowledge of ammunition and
explosives, were needed here.

As the bear's voice droned on to the men in the circle, Mickey
rose to stretch her legs, and Yvette did the same. Both of them
itched to poke about in the canvas carrybag Pier had dumped
on the table, certain it contained food and possibly a jug of

wine and some cigarettes. It wasn't much considering that there were twelve of them all told, thirteen with the bear.

"The transmitter?"

Yvette stiffened at the bear's words. "Here," she said, dragging a heavy case across the room.

"You've been using this?" When Yvette nodded, the respect in the man's eyes brought a smile to her lips.

"This is the one you'll be taking with the children." From inside a valise he withdrew a small, compact transmitter. A finger as thick as a sausage tapped the green coils of the antenna, the key she would use to transmit her messages. The stubby finger poked at several small compartments. "Your extra quartzes are stored here." They were the size of a small matchbox, and by changing to a new quartz the operator was able to alter the broadcasting frequency. "Keep changing and the Germans will have difficulty locating you. Never transmit for more than ten minutes without changing your quartz," the bear said harshly. "Eight minutes is even better. In an emergency, never, ever transmit for more than thirty minutes. If you have the least inkling that you're in some serious trouble, get rid of this case. As with your other transmitter, the keys to the codes are wrapped in a silk scarf underneath. We even have a strap for this little baby; it will go right on your back like a book bag."

Yvette nodded. "Did you bring any food?" she asked brazenly.

"Some potatoes and some carrots. A few cigarettes, no wine." His voice was almost apologetic. "When I arrived I saw a well in the back, the kind the farmers store food in. I expect it was dark when you arrived and you didn't see it. Check it out, you might find enough food for some soup."

"I'll do it," Mickey volunteered. Twenty minutes later she was back, her arms full of wilted turnips and withered onions. Each pocket of her shirt bulged with small cabbages. "There might be enough for the children if we don't eat too much," she said quietly. "Is it safe to make a fire in the stove?"

"Don't stoke the fire," Pier replied. "We've posted a lookout. Let the food simmer."

It was the middle of the afternoon when the bear gathered his maps and gear together. There were no good-byes, no handshakes. He and the man he traveled with would leave as silently as they had arrived. At the door he turned to Yvette. "You have the most dangerous job of all. If you are caught, there is nothing any of us can do for you." His eyes swept over to Mickey. "Take care of the *enfants,* mademoiselle."

The moment the door closed behind him, Mickey doused the fire. Carefully she measured out the thin soup into dusty bowls. "Can we save some for the children?" she asked apologetically. Ten gaunt-eyed men nodded. Mickey's hand trembled as she slammed the lid tightly onto the soup pot. Under cover of darkness she would retrieve the small sack of dry, withered apples that were at the bottom of the small well. Children needed nourishment.

Rubbing sleep from his eyes, a man whose code name was Fish motioned to Mickey. It was her turn to sleep. Over the past few months she had learned how to sleep at odd times of the day, but lately her sleep wasn't restful. Instead, it was tortured with memories, memories she deliberately dwelled upon, the way she would do now when she settled herself in the corner of the farm kitchen.

The rag rug was her mattress, her knapsack her pillow. If she didn't think about Reuben, she would fall asleep instantly. She knew she should close her eyes and blot everything else from her mind, but if she did that, Reuben would start to fade from her mind and her heart. Now that she had a sense of her mortality, it was crucial to remember every little detail of their love.

Her head in the crook of her arm, Mickey forced her thoughts back to the past. Her tired brain sifted and shifted the happenings in chronological order. The last time she'd slept, she'd gotten as far as Reuben and Daniel's arrival at the château and the game she'd played with Reuben, teasing him in her own way, tantalizing him until she could hardly bear the ache within her.

She'd gone to her room early that evening to hide from her desires and emotions. . . .

First, she'd turned off the lamps, remembering how good the darkness felt. One could hide in the darkness of a room or in the darkness of one's mind. One could hide from the world in any number of ways, and that world would pass by.

She was feeling sorry for herself. In the whole of her life she'd never felt this way. That large world out there was full of emotional cripples, it didn't need one more. Go after him, take what you want. Give what you want but never give all of yourself, for when it's time to walk away there will be no reserve to carry you through. She smiled wickedly. All right, Reuben Tarz, you shall have ninety percent of me. Right now!

Her room was bathed in moonlight, the bed turned down, her silky white nightgown folded neatly on her pillow.

She ripped at her clothes, fingers feverish in their haste. The silky nightgown rustled softly as it fell about her. She looked in the mirror to see how much this night had ravished her. With lightning-quick motions she removed what little makeup remained, washed her face, and applied a light dusting of powder. She washed her mouth as well as her hands to rid herself of the smell of nicotine and wine. A light spritz of her favorite perfume, and she was finished.

All the lamps were off with only the thin remnants of moonlight streaming through the windows, creating silver shadows everywhere. The room looked exquisite, she decided, perfect for making love.

Impatiently she waited until the sounds she heard outside her door were right. Then, feeling as giddy as a schoolgirl, she stepped down the hall to Reuben's room. Softly she opened the door. His room was also bathed in moonlight, which lay across his bed in a giant beam. It seemed to Mickey that the young American glowed in the near darkness. She wondered fleetingly if it meant anything, if it was a sign of some sort. In the end, she simply didn't care.

Kneeling by his bed, she whispered in his ear, her fingers trailing gently the length of his cheek and down his neck. The coverlet had slipped from his neck. How broad his chest was, how muscular his arms. How very, very young.

"Come, *chéri*," she whispered.

Reuben woke, instantly aware of her presence. He lay quietly, giving himself up to her touch and her scent. When he shuddered, she smiled, her teeth flashing in the moonlight.

"Come with me now, to my room."

Reuben swung his legs over the side of the bed, his hands clutching the edge of the plump mattress. Mickey dropped her head into his lap, whispering as her tongue did strange things to him—things he wanted never to end. He drew in his breath, expelling it in a loud hiss. With all the force he could muster, he grasped her shoulders and pushed her backward. He stood in his nakedness, staring down at her. At last he reached for her and drew her up close. With one fluid motion he enfolded her into his arms and in seconds they were both in bed.

Eager to be close to him, Mickey abandoned herself to sensation. Her fingers tore at her gown as she hurried him with hushed whispers and moist kisses, eager to lie with him and teach him her special secrets.

His mouth sought hers, his arms locked her in a hard embrace. Wave after wave of desire coursed through her as she answered his kisses and inspired his caresses. Her tongue darted into the warm recesses of his mouth, her arms wound around him, making him her prisoner. Soft hands caressed and stroked her back, smoothing along the curve of her waist to the fullness of her hips and bottom, pressing her close to her desire. Her breasts were taut and full beneath his hands. Soft moans of ecstasy escaped her parted lips as he aroused her to the heights of passion. He devoured her with his eyes, covered her with his lips, igniting her sensuality with teasing touches of his tongue against her fiery skin. His fingertips grazed the sleekness of her inner thighs, and, helpless, she felt her body arch against his hand with a will of its own, to aid in his explorations.

His mouth became part of her own, and she heard her heart beat in wild and rapid rhythms. They strained toward each other, imprisoned by the designs of yearning, caught in an embrace that ascended the obstacles of the flesh and strove to join breath and blood, body and spirit.

Gently, in the darkened room, he laid her back against the pillows, leaning over her, nuzzling her neck, inhaling the heady fragrance that was hers alone. Blazing a trail from her throat, his lips covered her unguarded breast, and she shivered with exquisite anticipation. She became unaware of her surroundings, oblivious to time and place; she knew only that her body was reacting to this man, pleasure radiating outward from some hidden depth within her. She allowed herself to be transported by it, incapable of stopping the forward thrust of his desires, spinning out of time and space into the soft consuming mists of her sensuality.

Her emotions careened and clashed, grew confused and wild, her perceptions thrumming and beating wherever he touched her. And when he moved away from her she felt alone. When he returned, she was whole again, wanting and needing, wanting to be needed in return. The feverish heat of his skin seemed to singe her fingers as she traced inquisitive patterns over his arms and back and down over his sleek, muscular thighs.

He had never touched a woman this way, but somehow he knew he could touch a thousand women and none would feel the same to him as this one. None could have the unexpectedly smooth skin that tantalized his fingers and tempted him to seek more secret places.

Suddenly the room grew dark, jealously keeping the sight of him from her eyes. She wanted to see him, to know him, behold the places her fingers yearned to find and her lips hungered to kiss. "The lamp," she whispered, hardly daring to make a sound, afraid to break the spell. She barely recognized her voice; it sounded husky, throaty, sensuous, even to her own ears. "I want to see you. I want to know you, like this . . . naked. All of you." It was a plea, a demand, exciting him with its fervor, arousing his desires for her to a fever pitch.

Soft golden light flooded the room, and he stood before her, just out of reach. Her gaze covered him, sizzling and searing, lingering at the swell of his manhood and grazing over his flat, hard stomach. Dark patterns of lustrous and black curling hair molded his form into planes and valleys, covering his chest and narrowing to a thin, elongated arrow that seemed to point below. Thighs thick with muscle supported him, the scars of his wound breaking her heart. His torso tapered and broadened again for the width of his chest. Her arms stretched out for him, beckoning him to her.

He was filled with an exhilarating power that came from the knowledge that she wanted him, unabashed and unashamed . . . the power that a woman can give a man only when she reveals her desire for him, welcoming him into her embrace, giving as well as taking, trusting him to lead her to the realms of the highest star, where passion is food for the gods and satisfaction its own reward.

In the lamplight he gazed down at her, possessing her, held in the spell of the moment, reveling in watching her eyes travel the length of his body. Her lips parted, full and ripe, revealing the pink tip of her tongue as she moistened them. She was leaning back against the pillows, one knee bent, hiding her most secret place from his sight. Breasts proud, their coral tips erect, she invited his hands and his lips. As he reached out to touch her, an answering voluptuous stretch revealed her womanhood where a fine feathering of downy hair caught the light, gilding her body with a soft, shimmering glow. She was beautiful, this lioness with the hungry eyes, beautiful and desirable, setting his pulses pounding anew, unleashing a driving need in him to satiate himself in her charms, to quell this hunger she created in him and to salve an appetite for her that was ravenous, voracious.

He stepped into her embrace, felt her arms surround his hips, aware that she rested her cheek sweetly against the flat of his stomach, rubbing against his soft, curling hairs. His hands found the pins in her hair, impatiently pulling them, removing them, eager to see its dark wealth tumble to her shoulders and curl around her breasts. Silky chestnut strands, scented and shining, rippled through his fingers, tumbling and cascading from his hands, down the smooth length of her back and onto the pillows. She lifted her head, looking at him with eyes heavy with passion. He had been right in likening her to a lioness, a wild cat of the jungle. Dark lashes created shadows on her high cheekbones; upward-winging brows delineated her features. The full, ripe body, tinged with gilt, tempted his hands, invited his lips.

Her teasing touches fleetingly grazed his buttocks and the backs of his thighs, slipping between them and rising higher and higher. She took in with her eyes all she touched with her fingers, the masculine hardness of him, feeling it pulsate with anticipation of her touch, and when her hand closed over him, a deep rumbling sounded in his chest, escaping his lips in a barely audible moan.

He lay down beside her, reaching for her, covering her breasts with his hands, seeking them with his lips. But her appetite for him had not been satisfied, and she lifted herself onto her elbow, leaning over him, her hair falling, draping over her shoulder, creating a curtain between them.

She touched him again, running the tips of her fingers down his chest, hearing his small gasp of pleasure. The flat of her palm grazed his belly, and her lips blazed a trail following her hand's downward slope.

The swell of her hips and the rounded fullness of her bottom filled him with a throbbing urgency. Nothing short of having her, of losing himself in her, would satisfy. He was afraid the touch of her lips would drive him over the edge, past the point of no return. Impatiently he drew her upward, pushing her back against the pillows, trapping her with his weight. He wanted to plunder her, drive himself into her, slake his thirst, knowing his needs could be met only in her.

Her mouth was swollen, bruised, and tasting of himself. Her arms wound around him, holding him close as she pressed her nakedness against him. His hand made an intimate search over her breast, skimming its tip, and his lips followed hungrily, tasting and teasing until a golden warmth spread through her veins, heating her erratic pulses. Her hair became entangled around his neck, and he brushed it aside before resuming the moist exploration with his lips, lingering now in the place where her arm joined her body before tracing a path again to her full, heaving breasts. She clung to the hard, sinewy muscles of his arms, holding on to him for support, afraid she would fall into a yawning abyss where flames were fed by passion.

His hands spanned her waist, tightening their grip and lifting her above him. His mouth tortured her with teasing flicks of his tongue, making her shudder with unreleased passions. She curled her fingers into his night-dark hair, pushing him backward, away, pleading that he end the torment, only to follow his greedy mouth with her body, pressing her flesh against his.

A throbbing ache spread through her, demanding to be satisfied, settling uncontrollably in her loins, causing her to seek relief by the involuntary roll of her hips against the length of his thigh. He held her there, her bottom forward, driving her pelvis against him.

Suddenly he shifted, throwing her backward and settling on top of her, looming over her. For a thousand times, it seemed, his lips and hands traveled her body, starting at the pulse point near her throat and ending at her toes.

He whispered French words of love, words she'd taught him, praising her beauty, celebrating her sensuality. Her body seemed to have a life of its own, and she succumbed to it, turning, opening, like the petals of a flower. His searching fingers adored her, his hungry mouth worshiped her. Lower and lower his kisses trailed, covering the tautness of her belly and slipping down to the softness between her thighs.

She felt him move upon her, demanding her response, tantalizing her with his mouth, bringing her ever closer to that which had always eluded her and kept itself nameless for her. Her body flamed beneath his kiss, offering itself to him, arching and writhing, reveling in the sensation that was within her grasp, reveling in her own femininity. She felt as though she were separated from herself, that the world was comprised only of her aching need and his lips. Exotically sweet, thunderously compelling, her need urged him on, the same need that lifted her upward, upward, soaring and victorious, defeating her barriers, conquering her reserves, bringing her beyond the threshold of a delicious rapture that she had never dreamed of or suspected, even in her fantasies.

And when his mouth closed over hers once again, he had

proved her a woman and had not cursed her for it. He had allowed her to rise victorious in her passions, leaving her breathless and with the knowledge that there was more, much more. She was satisfied yet discontented, fed and yet famished. She wanted to share the ecstasy he had given her, participate in the sharing, and only with him.

Grasping her hips, he lifted her as though she were weightless. He brought her parted thighs around him, and when he drove downward, she felt as if she were being consumed by a totally different fire—a fire that burned cooler, leaving the sensibilities intact. Yet there was that same driving need deep within her, deeper and more elusive than she had experienced the first time. She struggled to bring herself closer, needing to be part of him now, needing him to be part of herself. These fires burned deeper, brighter, fed by the fuel of his need for her, of his hunger to be satisfied.

Tears glistened on her cheeks. She was triumphant, powerful—a woman. In this man's arms she knew she had been born for this moment, that all her life had been leading up to what she was experiencing with this magnificent American. Together they had found the secrets of the universe.

The purple dawn was wrapping its arms around the château when she crept from Reuben's bed and made her way down the hall to her own room.

How cold and forlorn her bed felt. She wanted to be back in Reuben's bed with her head on his shoulder. Tears streamed down her cheeks. She'd known it would be like this. And now there was nothing she could do. She'd tasted her fill of the American, and like an alcoholic she wanted more. Would always want more. Better to say she was "addicted" than in love with a man half her age. More than half. She'd lied when she said she was forty; she was actually forty-three. Old enough to be his mother. Old enough to be a grandmother. *Mon dieu!*

How long would she be able to keep him? Six months, a year? Would he be the one to ask to leave, or would she be the one to send him on his way? Where in the world would she get that kind of strength? She'd known. Why hadn't she listened to herself, to that little voice that warned her?

Yvette crept close to Mickey. With a gentle finger she brushed at the tears on her friend's cheek. How much she'd given and how little she'd gotten in return. And now this trek with the children to lead them to safety. Her heart told her it would be Mickey's undoing. Guiltily she made the sign of the cross. "Please," she whispered, "don't let anything happen to her. Help me to help her." Was it a foolish prayer? Was it ordained somewhere that this would be a fateful trip?

Yvette swore then that she saw Death enter, grimly stalking the perimeters of the room. She squeezed her eyes shut, not wanting to see the dark shadow move forward and then stop.

She slept, her sleep full of demons from the past, the present, and the future.

Chapter Sixteen

THE SWEET SMELL OF ORANGE BLOSSOMS AND THE TANG OF salt sea air flirted with Nellie's nostrils. She savored it for a moment as she drank in the sight of her father and her uncle Reuben together. Misty eyes, good-ol'-boy slapping, and then the bear hug made her own eyes narrow, but only for a second. Blinking in the bright sun, she looked around, hoping that Philippe had come to welcome her to California. For the whole of the trip she'd kept her fingers crossed, something she'd always done as a child when she wanted something desperately. Over the Grand Canyon she'd made a wish that Philippe would be the first person she saw and that he would sweep her off her feet and plant a warm, welcoming kiss on her mouth. Wishes were for little children, she thought sourly.

"I think my daughter has a burr in her undies," Daniel murmured into Reuben's ear. "I think she was expecting Philippe to be here."

Reuben slapped his forehead. "Jesus, I didn't think, or I would have asked him along. To tell you the truth, we don't do a whole lot together these days, and I'm not . . . I haven't been at the studio for several days now. But we can talk about that later. She's a knockout, Daniel. When did she grow up? It wasn't all that long ago that I saw her in Washington. Jesus, she's a young lady!'' Reuben's voice held stunned surprise.

Daniel kept his voice low so it wouldn't carry to the young girl walking ahead of them. ''I came home from work one day and there she was, with a new hairstyle, high heels, and this dress that looked as if it were made of gossamer. She had a date with a young man who drooled when he saw her. I don't mind telling you I had a few bad moments, and the lecture I handed that young man is probably still ringing in his ears.''

Reuben grinned. ''This is only my inexpert opinion, but I'd say the boy doesn't stand a chance. If there's one thing that can turn a surly, hostile young man into a human being, it's a girl.'' He hesitated a moment, then added soberly, ''He hates me, Daniel. He went to see Bebe, and she ordered him off her property. Told him Mickey was his mother. He's been like a butterfly in a wasp's nest ever since. Jesus, we have so much to talk about. You are staying with me, aren't you?''

''I'm not paying for a hotel, that's for sure. I have to start saving my pennies because Rajean is going to wipe me out. We're getting a divorce. We'll talk about that later, too.''

Reuben nodded. ''Have you given any thought to moving out here? This is where we got our start, you know. Hell, if you're going to make a new life for yourself, this is the place to do it. And if you're interested in some big bucks . . . well, the studio could use a brain like yours.'' His heart thudded as he realized he couldn't offer Daniel a job at the studio; he'd resigned. Bebe, then—Bebe would be more than glad to take Daniel on.

Daniel breathed deeply, and he offered Reuben an appreciative smile. ''I swear to God there were times when I could smell these orange blossoms. But to answer your question, yes, I have given it some thought. Nellie said there wasn't enough sunshine in my life. And she's right; the kid is always on the money when it comes to me.''

''Nellie, hold on,'' Reuben called. ''This is the car. Hop in; our next stop is the studio, where I know a young man is waiting for you with his tongue hanging out.''

Nellie gave her uncle and father what Daniel referred to as her Christmas-tree smile. ''I was hoping he'd be here, Uncle Reuben.''

''It's my fault. I didn't think to ask him, and his European manners wouldn't allow him to invite himself. I was so caught up in my own selfish happiness at seeing your father that I—''

''It's okay, Uncle Reuben, don't apologize.'' She flashed

her smile again, and Reuben's heart melted. *Philippe, if you let this girl get away, you are a fool.*

"What about our bags?" Daniel asked.

"All taken care of. They'll be delivered to the house. I hate standing around waiting for something even if it's your luggage, pal. By the time we get to the house later on, they'll be there. Now, hop in and let's get this young lady to Fairmont. Daniel, Jane has been fussing and fretting ever since she found out Nellie is going to be working for her. She's . . . she's what I call good people, but then, you know that. She asks about you constantly. Wait till you see her, she's turned into a beautiful woman. And what a producer! She has this incredible sixth sense, this finely tuned . . . thing that enables her to pick a winner out of nowhere. She's never married," he added, watching Daniel out of the corner of his eye. He bit down on his tongue to stifle a laugh when he saw Daniel straighten his shoulders and finger his tie.

"And now for your tour. The building on your right is . . ."

The studio's commissary was filled to capacity, which puzzled Philippe somehow. As he took his place in line he noticed that all conversation ceased. Even the rattling dishes and clanking silverware seemed muted. Something was in the air. He looked around, trying to lock his gaze with just one person so that he could get a feel for what was wrong. He didn't think it was his imagination when he saw heads and necks lower over plates of food.

Eating alone had never bothered him before, and now, today, he wished he'd made at least one friend so he would have someone to sit with. Then he felt himself grow angry at his insecurity. His father would never tolerate a situation like this. None of these technicians and actors would ever dare cut a conversation short or refuse to look at him if he walked into a room. They simply wouldn't dare. Philippe felt his shoulders square imperceptibly and his jaw tighten as he paid for his meal. His eyes were bold as he stared around the full dining room. Not an empty table anywhere. He was saved from stalking out of the room when he heard a voice call his name.

"Philippe, over here." It was Jane Perkins. Philippe felt as though he'd been thrown a lifeline as he weaved his way to the producer's table.

Jane moved her tray to accommodate Philippe's. "I'm taking

an early lunch hour so I can be on hand to meet with Daniel's daughter when she arrives," she said cheerily.

Jane Perkins, Fairmont's leading producer, was a pretty woman, a quiet woman with warm soft brown eyes and a gentle smile. She was dressed in a tailored tweed suit with a crisp white blouse that rather enhanced her femininity. In many ways she reminded Philippe of his mother—like now, when she knew he was hurting and was doing her best to make him feel comfortable.

"What *is* that on your tray?" she asked inquisitively, a smile in her voice.

Philippe looked down at his tray, noticing the assortment of food for the first time. He smiled ruefully. "I kept pointing and they kept piling it on. I'm not even hungry. I came in here just to kill some time until Nellie gets here. You're going to like her, Miss Perkins."

"I know I will. One can't get a higher recommendation than Reuben Tarz. Did anyone ever tell you how we all met, your father and Daniel and myself?" There was no surprise in Philippe's face when she acknowledged Reuben as his father.

"No. My father and myself . . . we . . . aren't that comfortable with each other—yet," he added hastily.

Jane leaned across the table, her eyes sparkling. "It was like this. I was coming out of the studio and I'd landed a part in a crowd scene. I was so delirious, I was doing a jig. These two young men were leaning on a wall, smoking a cigarette, and we had this little conversation. I said something about always leaning on the wall for a cigarette if I got a part, but that day I was flat broke and didn't have a cigarette. I guess that's why I was doing a jig. Anyway, they offered me a cigarette, and then when I left your father gave me the whole pack." Her eyes grew misty with the memory.

"A while later, out of the blue, I got this message to come to the studio," she continued, "and lo and behold, there were your father and Daniel. Reuben was Mr. Rosen's assistant, at least I think that's what his title was. He gave me something to eat, a doughnut, I believe, and said I was going to have a screen test. I fainted, can you believe that? From hunger, of course. Lord, I was so stupid in those days. The long and short of it was they liked my test and cast me in the Dolly Darling series. The success of the series was so phenomenal, there are days I still can't believe it all happened. I even did a skit or two in the Red Ruby films. They were good, too. Then, as all good things do, it came to an end with the success of talkies. Your father hired a voice teacher for me, but I couldn't cut it, so he literally dumped me in the production office and said, 'Get to work.' I loved it from the first moment, and I've been here ever since. It's so wonderful to see a creation on paper come to life under the lights. I owe your father my very livelihood. He's a wonderful man, Philippe. If you give him half a chance, I know you two can meet on some common ground. He's been a wonderful friend to me all these years.''

"I appreciate your sharing that with me," Philippe said glumly. He poked at his food, moving it from one place to the other on his plate.

"But you aren't going to make the effort to change things, is that it?" Jane asked quietly.

"I didn't say that."

"You don't have to. I can see it in your face. I'd like to say one more thing on the subject, then we can lay it to rest. I have no intention of being a buffer between you and your father. One of you will have to make an effort to right things. If you don't, it will be *your* loss."

"Miss Perkins, can you tell me what's going on around here?" Philippe asked, glancing around the commissary. "When I came in everyone stopped talking. No one will look at me. Did I do something I'm not aware of, or has it come out that I'm Mr. Tarz's son?"

Mr. Tarz's son. Oh, Philippe, she wanted to say, bend a little, meet him halfway. "I guess the whole studio is buzzing with your father's resignation. It came as such a shock, out of the blue, really. I don't think any of us were prepared for it. I mean, Reuben *is* Fairmont Studios. With Bebe taking it over, it's anybody's guess what will happen. I don't think she knows that much about making movies. I guess she can learn if she's determined. We all learned. . . . Philippe, what's the matter?" she asked. The boy was staring at her with a horrified expression on his face. "Don't tell me you didn't know? Oh, Lord, I'm so sorry, I thought, I expected you would have been the first . . . I never would have blurted out. . . . Keep calm, people are staring at us. . . . Smile, Philippe, or tomorrow you will have a terrific problem. That's it, now let's both get up and go over to my office, where we can talk in peace. Leave the damn tray," she said tightly. *Reuben, I could strangle you for this. No wonder this kid feels the way he does.*

Outside in the flower-scented air, Philippe found himself

taking deep breaths to ward off the dizziness that assailed him. Jane watched Reuben's son helplessly, searching for the words that needed to be said at this moment. "All my life, Philippe, I've been careful never to say anything that would hurt another human being, and I've just knocked you off your feet. Reuben's resignation was so . . . public, in a manner of speaking. Everyone knew, and I don't honestly know how it came about. It was such an important decision, I just assumed you knew. Please, forgive me."

"It's all right, Miss Perkins," Philippe said, grinning wanly. "There's nothing to forgive. If my father wanted me to know, he would have told me. There really isn't much else to say, so I think I'll go back to my office . . . and play with my pencils and papers. I guess I'll see you later. Thanks for sharing lunch with me."

Jane fought with herself not to run after him. If she gave in to her desire, she would be breaking a cardinal rule she'd set for herself years ago, which was not to get involved in Reuben's private life unless he requested she do so.

Until today she had honored that commitment. "Damn," she muttered as she made her way back to her suite of offices.

Reuben swung the powerful car down the narrow alley behind the production offices. He had no desire to drive past the parking lot that until last week had held his assigned car space with his name on a stark white sign. Things moved fast at Fairmont. By now his name would be gone and the sign would read Bebe Rosen. No, he didn't want to see *that* today.

Intuitive as he was, Reuben knew immediately that something was wrong when Jane greeted them at the door to her office. Oh, she smiled, took Nellie in her arms, and welcomed her like a long-lost daughter. She kissed Daniel and hugged him until he bellowed for mercy. But her eyes, Reuben noticed, were half-angry, half-full of worry.

"Nellie, we have the rest of the week to get you settled in," she said, smiling. "I had lunch with a young man who is chewing his nails to the nub waiting for you. Why don't you go over to his office while we three old people talk about yesterday. Go outside, make two lefts, one right, and walk straight up the stairs. Philippe's office has his name on the door. We'll stop by and pick you up in, say, two hours."

Nellie flashed her brilliant smile and was off before anyone could comment. Daniel raised his eyebrows. "Aiding and abetting?" he teased.

"Young love." Jane smiled tightly. "He's eager to see her, she's eager to see him. Simple."

"Mind if we sit down?" Reuben asked.

She gestured at the couch and chairs adorning her office. "Please do. . . . Reuben, I have a bone to pick with you. Do you know what I just did? I blurted out . . . He was so shocked . . . he was like a pariah in the commissary. He didn't know you'd resigned! Why in God's name didn't you tell him?" she demanded angrily. "Do you have any idea how I felt?"

"Would somebody mind telling me what's going on?" Daniel asked, looking from one to the other.

"Reuben resigned from the studio," Jane told him. "Everyone knows about it except Philippe. I blurted it out over lunch. The boy was stunned. I felt as though I'd knocked the world right from under him. Apparently Bebe is taking Reuben's place."

"You resigned!" Daniel said, shocked. He looked across at Jane. "If that's the case, then there are two of us who didn't know. What the hell's going on?"

Reuben sighed and shook his head. "Bebe wanted the studio as part of the divorce settlement, and I gave it to her. It was never really mine, Daniel. I wanted it to be, but it wasn't. It doesn't matter if I busted my ass making it what it is today. There were days when I thought I'd earned it, but I knew in my gut it would always belong to Bebe. You should see her. She's done a complete turnabout. I think she can handle it. Philippe will keep her in line, or she'll keep him in line. It'll be interesting to watch what happens."

"And that's what you're going to do—watch?" Daniel said incredulously.

"No, as a matter of fact I won't be around to watch. I was sort of hoping you'd make the decision to move back here and keep an eye on things."

"Just like that," Daniel said, his eyes narrowing.

Reuben chuckled. "More or less."

"Let's say I do agree, what will you be doing?"

"What I should have done years ago. I'm going to France."

"There's a fucking war going on!" Daniel shouted. "Excuse my language, Jane."

Jane shrugged. "Not to worry."

"Just how in the goddamn hell do you think you're going

to get to France, and if you do, how in the name of God do you think you can find Mickey?"

"I don't know, Daniel. I may never find her, but I won't know that unless I try, now, will I? In any case, my mind is made up. I'll be leaving on the next Red Cross plane as a news correspondent." Reuben grinned. "Good cover, don't you think? And before you can ask how I arranged it all, I have a friend who works for the *Times* in New York. He sent me all my credentials. As a matter of fact, they arrived yesterday. I have four days to wine and dine you before I leave."

"You damn fool, you'll get yourself killed," Daniel blustered. "I'm going, too!"

"No, Daniel, this is something I have to do alone," Reuben said firmly. "You already made the trip to bring Philippe here. I have to do this, don't you understand? I should have done it years ago, and I didn't. It's settled. If you want to talk it to death, I suppose we can do that, but it won't change anything."

Daniel threw his hands in the air. Jane closed her mouth with a snap. Reuben smiled happily.

"Bebe . . . did you tell her?" Daniel asked.

"No. You and Jane are the only ones who know. Listen to me, Daniel. Bebe is almost there. I mean she's giving it everything she has. Right now the only thing she has yet to resolve is Philippe. Now I'm giving both of them that chance by removing myself. I have to find out about Mickey for the boy's sake. I don't want him going through the rest of his life worrying and wondering the way I did. He'll have Nellie, but Nellie won't be enough. You've been the brains of this outfit for a long time, so don't tell me you can't see the sense to what I'm doing."

"After all these years you still love her," Daniel said in awe.

Reuben turned from the window. His voice was low and husky. "No, Daniel, I love what we shared. A man can't love a memory, I learned that a long time ago. Over the years you've heard me say some strange things and you've seen me do some things that were stranger still. Listen to me now. I love Bebe. Bebe loves me."

"But you're getting a goddamn divorce!" Daniel shouted in exasperation.

Reuben smiled. "You have to end something before you can make a new beginning."

Jane ran to Reuben and threw her arms about him. "Oh,

Reuben, I'm so glad you've finally come to your senses. I don't want you to go, but I understand. We'll keep things humming here. If he'll let me, I'll watch out for Philippe. The same goes for Bebe.'' She turned to face Daniel, her eyes moist and pleading.

Daniel joined his friends at the window and wrapped them both in his arms. "Two wise men and one wise woman. Not bad. What can I do, Reuben?"

"Continue to be my friend," Reuben said quietly. "Otherwise there's nothing you can do; things are under control."

Daniel looked doubtful, but he smiled for Reuben's benefit. Jane's soft hand on his shoulder made him turn, and in doing so he read the concern in her eyes. And in that moment of time he fell deeply and passionately in love with his friend of many years. Neither he nor Jane noticed Reuben's contented smile.

Jane looked away, confused. Was it possible that what she herself was feeling was mirrored in Daniel's eyes? After all this time? She looked up at Reuben, her anger at him forgotten. His grin was contagious . . . and sly. Why, he's manipulated this whole thing, she thought in amazement. "Touché," she said so quietly only Reuben heard her.

"If anyone wants my opinion," she continued, suddenly feeling a bit giddy, "I think we should leave the young people to themselves. I also think we three should take off for the Lily Garden and . . . and tie one on."

"Hear, hear!" Daniel cried.

Grinning, Reuben clapped Daniel on the back and put his other arm around Jane. "I'll tell you what, you two go ahead and I'll meet you there. I'll tell the young people their time is their own. Actually, what I want to do is walk around the studio and say good-bye in my own way. After today I won't be back. You don't mind, do you?"

He was manipulating again, Jane thought. If he stayed, she and Daniel would have to drive to the Lily Garden alone. Suddenly she laughed, a delightful sound that warmed the senses. "Wonderful idea!" she said enthusiastically.

Alone in Jane's office with only the sound of the soft whirring fan for company, Reuben settled himself. He was in no hurry to visit his son's office. Abruptly he felt a flutter of panic. Perhaps he was cutting things a little too close. There were so many good-byes to be said, so many things for him to do in only four days. What he should have done was call a meeting to announce his resignation instead of leaking the news. Once he made the decision he knew he had to act on it immediately, before he could change his mind. And he himself had given the order, by phone, to have Bebe's name replace his on his parking space. Al Sugar, the head of the prop department, had expressed his disapproval, but Reuben knew he would do it immediately.

Maybe the good-byes weren't such a good idea after all. After all, he'd already said good-bye to his secretary and given her a smashing bonus. Wonderful, loyal Margaret. But he wouldn't miss her, and he wouldn't miss anyone else, either. Why had he stayed all these years, working like a slave, getting by on only a few hours sleep each night? To prove what to whom? So much of his life was gone now, and while he couldn't recapture the past, he could try to start a new life. In order to do that, he knew he had to start that life where his old life had ended—back in France. Whether it made sense or not, he had to go ahead with his plan.

First he had to clear out his desk, not that there was anything he really wanted . . . except for one thing. He might as well go there now and get it. One of the secretaries could pass on Jane's message to Philippe; no need for him to deliver it in person.

Reuben whistled as he made his way to his office. He took the stairs two at a time and was barely winded when he reached the top. Margaret's office was empty now, her desk cleared, waiting for the next secretary to take her place. He hoped she was happy in her retirement.

Shouldn't he be feeling something, he wondered as he walked around his office. Anger or remorse? Or perhaps gratitude that he'd had the chance to make Fairmont one of the "big three" studios? No, relief, he decided. Now he had time to fill his life with sunshine. He certainly had enough money to last him three lifetimes. Everyone was provided for—Simon, Dillon, and, of course, Bebe, if she saw fit to avail herself of his generosity.

Once inside his office, he realized he didn't want to go through his desk; didn't want to touch any old memories, each with its own story worthy of a movie script. Let someone else do it. Hastily he penned a note and clipped it to his blotter. Throw everything in the trash. Done.

One last thing, the reason he'd come here. His hands trembled as he lifted the blotter from the desk and stared down at the winemaker's calendar. He was holding it in his hands, trying to decide how to carry it home so that the brittle paper didn't fall apart.

"Try this," a voice said. Reuben whirled to face his son, who was holding a large cellophane envelope. A lump lodged itself in his throat. He didn't attempt to speak, merely nodded. "Allow me," Philippe said as he held open the envelope. "There are places that can preserve this for you," he said with a catch in his voice.

"I know, but it wouldn't be the same," Reuben said. "By the way, Jane said to tell you both that the rest of the day is yours. She and Daniel went to the Lily Garden. I'll be joining them. If you care to come along, you're welcome. If not, bring Nellie home. Before midnight."

"Oh, Uncle Reuben, I don't have a curfew!" Nellie said, flushing.

"I'll have her home on time. We'll decide later about the Lily Garden. Will you be coming back here?" Philippe asked.

"Not on your life. It's all yours . . . son. Yours and your mother's."

Panic rivered through Philippe. "There's no reason . . . you don't have to—"

"Yes. Yes, I have to do this. I'll be leaving for France in four days. When I have news of your mother, I'll send it on. If I can."

Philippe felt sick to his stomach. "But the war . . ."

"I've been to war before. I know your country as well as I know my own."

Philippe licked at his dry lips. When Nellie nudged him forward, he dug his heels even deeper into the pile of carpet. "Will you . . . can you . . . tell her . . . I'm . . . tell her I love her and I think of her every day. I don't see how you can possibly find her with what's going on. It's impossible!"

Reuben looked his son straight in the eye, speaking slowly and distinctly. "I never make a promise I can't keep. I never give my word if there is the slightest chance it will be broken, either by me or by circumstances beyond my control. If it's humanly possible, I'll find your mother. Now, you young people run along and enjoy yourselves."

Philippe led Nellie down the stairs. "Did you see him, did you hear him? Who the hell does he think he is? He . . . I found out . . . never mind, we went through all this before. This is a hell of a way for us to start your first day here. Come on, I'm giving you a tour of the studio."

"Philippe, I think he was waiting for you to . . . to . . . I don't know, act like a son, I guess," Nellie said. "How can you hold him responsible for something he knew nothing about? It's not fair, not to him or yourself. I won't say any more, but I want you to think about it."

Philippe smiled sadly. "I'll think about it."

While her husband was happily toasting old memories with Reuben and Jane, Rajean Bishop was hailing a cab to the Waldorf-Astoria, where she'd called ahead to book a suite of rooms. Her eyes were glittering, her pulses pounding with exhilaration. She had eighty-five hundred dollars in cash in her purse, a new designer nightie, a daytime outfit the color of rich coral from the same designer, and a smashing evening frock in case Teddie wanted to take in Broadway. Already she'd made a serious dent in the money Daniel had given her.

As soon as she checked in and unpacked she would head for Tiffany's to buy a present for Teddie, something absolutely outrageous and so meaningful Teddie would see once and for all that she was the one, the one who loved and wanted to commit until eternity.

Suddenly her exhilaration evaporated. Teddie didn't know she was in New York. What if Teddie had other plans? Maybe she should have checked before she made the trip. But she so wanted to surprise Teddie! This way she'd stop by Teddie's shop in the middle of the afternoon, after she left Tiffany's. In the coral suit she'd be dressed to advantage, and Teddie would immediately know the Tiffany's shopping bag was a gift. She'd pretend she was in town to shop, to take in a play. Then she'd casually suggest dinner at the Waldorf—her treat, of course. Dinner would lead to the rest of the evening and, possibly, the entire night. If Teddie wasn't in the shop and she couldn't make contact this afternoon, she would take a cab to the brownstone on East 74th Street that Teddie called home. She'd ring the bell, trill, "Surprise! Surprise!" and hold out the gift. Teddie did so love gifts. They'd have wine and cheese and talk and talk. Eventually she'd mention that she was considering a move to New York because Daniel was going to be generous with his divorce settlement. Of course she wouldn't say *how* generous and she wouldn't mention the fact that she was going to keep the house in Georgetown. The designer nightie would be tucked in her oversize purse, wrapped in soft tissue, along with her small makeup case. Plan C . . . Plan C would go into effect if Plans A and B didn't work out, and she didn't want to think about that now.

"That'll be two-fifty," the taxi driver called over his shoulder, interrupting her reverie.

Rajean climbed out of the cab and handed the driver the fare and a dollar tip. He smiled his thanks as he looked into his rearview mirror, then frowned as he watched Rajean dance her way into the hotel. He'd seen enough broads in his time to know what she was here for. He'd also seen men like the one climbing out of the taxi behind him. A gumshoe; the city was full of them. For a moment he debated. Should he go in and warn his passenger? After all, she had given him a nice tip. Nah, he decided, live and let live, it wasn't any of his business.

Rajean looked around the suite of rooms, impressed with the spacious luxury. What she should do, would do, was send herself some flowers on her way to Tiffany's. Huge baskets of flowers, enough to keep the bellhops busy for a while, and she'd sign the cards with initials, as an indication that she had a secret lover. The flowers would add to Plans A, B, and C.

Champagne, of course, for either plan, in a silver ice bucket. She'd brought the Baccarat glasses from home, the kind Teddie adored, saying it was elegant and decadent at the same time when you drank from crystal with a name.

She lifted the silky nightgown from its nest of tissue and smoothed it out on the bed. Thin straps made of lace and ribbon, the bodice shirred in black organza, so sheer the nipples of her breasts would show through. The Empire waist was cinched under the bodice with clusters of tiny satin rosettes set with pin-tip pearls. The skirt was a double layer of organza, the scalloped hem heavy with two rows of rosettes. It was positively wicked-looking. Rajean glowed when she remembered the way she'd looked in it. Of course she'd paid far too much for it, but she wouldn't worry about money now. Now she had to calm herself, freshen her makeup, and decide how much she was willing to spend for Teddie's gift.

Two hours later she walked out of Tiffany's with an exquisite statue of Aphrodite fashioned from Belgian crystal. It had cost her $1,700, far more than she'd wanted to spend, but there hadn't been a thing in Tiffany's aside from the statue that Teddie would like. When another customer—a rather shabbily dressed man—also expressed interest in it, Rajean decided she had to have it.

Now, should she walk or take a taxi? She glanced down at

her fashionable high heels and decided to walk. That way her entrance to Teddie's decorator shop would be breathless, more natural. Of course, she'd have to do some other shopping on the way. Perhaps a new purse and scarf, something to give her a few other parcels to carry.

Rajean made a second stop at a specialty store on Madison and bought a box of assorted candles of different colors and shapes, a beaded evening bag for twenty-five dollars, and a scarf for three. Her purchases were gift-wrapped, and she was given a small colorful satchel to carry them in. On her way up Madison, she found a florist and ordered two hundred dollars' worth of flowers, demanding the tired clerk agree to deliver them by six o'clock.

"Sign them L. E.," she said briskly. L. E. for love everlasting. She knew it was a silly thing to do, but she didn't care.

By this time her feet were aching and she felt hungry, so hungry she knew she'd shortly be cranky and irritable. Maybe that was good: this way she wouldn't take any nonsense from Teddie. She'd show some spirit, some guts, and not allow herself to be walked over. Thus resolved, she hailed a taxi and asked to be let out at the corner of 50th and Second Avenue.

She'd never been to Teddie's shop before; it was off limits. Teddie didn't mix business with pleasure. But this was an exception, she told herself. Ten minutes later she thrust open the door emblazoned with gilt lettering that read INTERIOR DESIGNS BY TEDDIE—and gasped. This shabby, dusty, moldy shop was so unlike what Teddie had described, she could scarcely believe it was the right place. A wizened old man with gravy stains on his tie crept out from behind two rolls of purple carpeting. Rajean stood statue-still, not wanting to touch anything. "Is Teddie here?"

"No," the man said curtly. "This ain't Teddie's day to come in. Try tomorrow afternoon." He turned to retreat behind the purple carpeting."

"Wait a moment. Where can I find—"

"I ain't no one's keeper. Teddie pays me to keep the name on the door and that's all I know. I got a good Oriental I can let you have for three hundred dollars. You interested?"

"No," Rajean said, and retraced her steps out the door to the rusty sound of the bell clanging overhead. Back on the street, she felt disoriented. Should she go left or right? Not that it mattered now. Teddie had lied to her; Interior Designs by Teddie was anything but famous and certainly not international. She was so engrossed in her unhappy thoughts that she collided with another pedestrian.

It was the shabbily dressed man she'd seen in Tiffany's.

"Well, this is a real coincidence!" he boomed happily. "I was just going to go into that shop to see if I could pick up a good Oriental carpet. The purple kind. I just bet you beat me out like you did at Tiffany's."

"No, I didn't buy anything. Look, if you really want this statue, I'll sell it to you," Rajean said desperately.

"Well, little lady, you're too late. I bought another one. Don't tell me yours has a flaw in it."

How bright his eyes were, how inquisitive. God, maybe he was a lecher or a thief who followed women around waiting to snatch their purses. Fingers clutching her bag, she stepped away from him and out to the curb where she flagged a taxi. "East Seventy-fourth between Second and Third," she told the driver.

When she rang the bell, Rajean knew Teddie wouldn't be home, but she'd had to come, she didn't know why. To beg, to plead, to pretend she hadn't been to the shop, hadn't seen the dirty old man with the stained tie, pretend that things were all right. She would slide a note through the brass mail slot. "Darling," she wrote.

> I came to the city to do some emergency shopping and stopped by, but of course you weren't home, hence this note. I'm staying at the Waldorf, Suite 1112. I'd love to see you before I leave for the West Coast on Saturday. Give me a call or stop by.
>
>   Rajean

She'd given herself an extra day, which was stupid. What was she going to do, sit around a hotel and suck her thumb, hoping Teddie would give her some precious time?

Rajean opened the door to her hotel suite forty-five minutes later and gasped. She'd had no idea two hundred dollars would buy so many flowers! They were everywhere—on the bureau, on the night tables, on the tables next to the sofa and chairs, on the floor, in the corners. Even the bathroom held two baskets of yellow-and-white pompons. The smell was so sickeningly sweet that she felt dizzy. And somehow the sight was depressing, not exhilarating, as she'd hoped; it made her want to cry.

For no matter how the cards were signed, the reality was inescapable—she had sent the flowers herself. There was no secret lover, and even Teddie was beginning to tire of her.

Well, she hadn't burned *all* her bridges. There was still Daniel. She could get Daniel back with a crook of her finger if she wanted to. Nellie would help her. She would call them in California, ask them about their trip, and tell them she missed them. That's exactly what she would do. If things *really* didn't work out with Teddie, she would join her husband and daughter in California whether they liked it or not.

Rajean picked up the phone and had the long-distance operator try the Tarz home in Benedict Canyon. There was no answer. When she called the studio, she was cut off in midsentence. Finally she called person-to-person and asked for either Reuben Tarz or Philippe Bouchet. When the boy came on the line, she identified herself and asked for Daniel. A moment later she was stunned when Nellie took the phone from Philippe, sounding faint and far away.

Rajean forced herself to sound motherly and concerned. "I'm trying to locate Daniel, Nellie, do you know where he is?"

"I sure do, Mother. He's having lunch with one of the prettiest, smartest women here at the studio," Nellie teased. "They went to the Lily Garden. If it's important, I can have him call you."

"No, it isn't earth-shaking that I talk to him this minute, but I would like you to have him call back if he has time. No, no, better not have him do that!" Rajean said, remembering where she was. "I'll catch up with him tomorrow or the next day. Enjoy yourself, honey. . . ."

Rajean stared at the phone as though it were a coiled snake ready to spring—at her throat. The prettiest, smartest lady at the studio. That could mean only Jane Perkins. They were the same age, and she was as career-oriented as Daniel. They would have much in common. . . . And where did that leave her? Holding a Tiffany shopping bag worth $1,700. She wondered if the prestigious store had a return policy.

Angrily, Rajean connected with the operator and asked for room service. She ordered a cheese sandwich and a bottle of gin that she didn't really want, then removed her makeup and ran a hot tub. The hell with all of them. First thing in the morning she'd return to Washington. Somehow she'd find a way to regain Daniel's interest.

An hour later Rajean realized her skin was starting to pucker. Quick as a flash she hopped out of the tub and kicked at the bathroom door with her bare foot; she had to get away from the nauseating smell of the flowers. Naked, she made her way to the bedroom of the suite.

The long evening stretched before her. She remembered her intention of taking a sleeping pill. Instead of one she took two, swallowing them without the aid of water. The cheese sandwich stared up at her, the bread dry and curling around the edges, the cheese darker on the sides. She ate the sandwich because there was nothing else to do. It would take a while for the pills to work, at least an hour. The gin might help speed up the sleep process. She poured a tumbler full and added a single ice cube. While she gulped the fiery liquid she placed a call to Teddie. When Teddie's voice came over the wire, she sat the glass down with a thump, the gin splashing over the sides.

"Hello," she said throatily.

"Rajean, is that you? I just got in and found your note. It was sweet of you to stop by. I was out on a business call. How are you, sweetie?"

Sure you were. Sweet of me to stop by. Sweetie. God, she was a mess, no makeup and about to pass out from the pills. "I'm just fine and looking forward to California. I can't remember, have you been there?"

"Several times. Did you get much shopping done?" Teddie purred.

"Quite a bit, as a matter of fact. I picked up a little something for you, that's why I stopped by." *Fool, fool, fool!* her mind screamed.

"Rajean, you are just the kindest person. Always thinking of me. What are your plans for this evening?"

Already the pills and the gin were starting to fog her brain. She sighed. "I was going to turn in early. Shopping simply wore me out." Damn, she sounded as though she were in a tunnel. By God, she would not ask Teddie to stop by, she simply would not. "I know you must be busy if you just got in, so I won't hold you up. It was nice talking to you, Teddie." Rajean said from her tunnel.

"Darling, is that rejection I hear in your voice? After all these years. I know, you found someone else, is that it? And now you don't have time for me. I thought more of you, Rajean. If I'm not mistaken, we had an agreement, you and I, that we'd tell each other if we found someone new."

"I don't remember that agreement," Rajean said thickly.

"Listen, sweetie, I have to run now, I'm meeting a client for a drink. I'll stop by, oh, let's say nineish, and you can give me that little gift you picked up for me. I have one for you, too. I've been saving it for just the right time. I'll call before I come over, is that okay? In case you have . . . other company," Teddie said slyly.

Rajean didn't bother to respond; she couldn't, her tongue was too thick and glued to the roof of her mouth. She lurched her way to the hotel dresser, where she'd placed her watch. Narrowing her eyes, she tried to decipher the time. Seven-thirty. That meant she had an hour and a half to shower, fix her face, and dress in the scandalous black nightie.

She couldn't do it, Rajean decided when she climbed from the stinging shower, gripping the shower curtain so she wouldn't fall. Her hair felt sticky and stringy, and her face was stiff from the effort it cost to keep her eyes open. She slapped haphazardly at the steam-coated mirror with her sodden wash-cloth which came back to slap her in the face. A hag stared at her from the streaky mirror. She had to do something; Teddie would be here soon.

Frustrated, she kicked at one of the baskets of flowers she'd moved out of the bathtub. Purple shasta daisies spewed onto the tile floor, little pieces of greenery scattering about. "God-damn flowers!" she muttered as she opened her purse for the vial of Benzedrine Teddie had given her a long time before. She reached for the gin bottle, knocking over a second flower arrangement. The pill bottle dropped from her hands, and the sodden towel slipped as she bent to search for the tiny pills among the flowers. "Goddamn stupid flowers," she muttered as she dropped the pills back into the bottle. She had to get herself together before Teddie arrived! She cried as she struggled to reach for the pills and the gin bottle.

The moment she swallowed the three pills she knew she'd made a mistake: she'd taken the sleeping pills instead of the Benzedrine. God, she'd sleep for a week if she didn't . . .

She staggered to the bathroom and stuck her finger down her throat. Nothing happened. "Damn, damn, damn!" She sat back on her haunches at the edge of the bathtub and picked up one of the wilting daisies. "Teddie loves me, loves me not, loves me, loves me not." When the last purple petal fell she blubbered, "Teddie doesn't love me."

Her hands on the edge of the bathtub, Rajean used it for

leverage to get to her feet. She laughed then, a sickly sound, as her toes squished the flowers on the floor. "Stupid, stupid, stupid," she muttered. She had to get dressed, Teddie would be here soon. . . . Teddie, Teddie, Teddie. Why weren't the damn pills working? Then she remembered that she'd taken the wrong ones. To sleep. To sleep in bed.

The black nightgown was a gossamer web threatening to choke her. Squealing, Rajean yanked it away from her face. The damn thing just didn't feel right on her skin. She staggered to the closet door and stared at herself in the full-length mirror. No damn wonder, she had it on backward! Her left breast was spilling from the tight band on the back reinforced to keep the straps intact.

God, she was so tired; she had so many things to do yet before Teddie arrived, but her brain wouldn't function. Clumsily she yanked at the black gown, hiking the fullness of the back up over her breasts. Teddie would like the rosettes. The hell with it, she'd lie on her stomach for Teddie to admire them. The hell with everything. "Daniel, where are you?" she moaned.

Rajean whirled around, stumbling against the bed, her eyes on the colorful flowers all about the room. As soon as she took the Benzedrine she would get rid of them. Teddie would never believe she had another lover who would send her a ton of flowers. She'd made a fool of herself.

On hands and knees, Rajean crawled around to the side of the bed, doing her best to fight the blanket of sleep that threatened to engulf her. By sheer will alone she searched until she was sure she had the right pill bottle in her hand, then tossed a handful of Benzedrine pills into her mouth. Grasping the pitcher of water on the night table, she raised her head and slurped.

She was on the floor now, at the foot of the bed, flower baskets all around her, the designer nightgown hiked up around her thighs. Strange mewing sounds escaped her lips.

"Daniel, take me home, I'm sorry. I didn't . . . I'm sooooo sorry, Daniel. I need you, Daniel," she cried.

Twenty minutes later Rajean's eyes popped open and her head snapped backward. She was on her feet now, walking jerkily about the room, touching this and that, trying to straighten things and making even more of a mess. Catching sight of her reflection in the floor-length mirror, she started to cry again, the same sick, mewing sounds as before. Everywhere she looked there were flowers, more on the floor than in the baskets now. How had that happened, she wondered. The hotel manager was going to have a fit. Well, let him have a fit, she didn't care. Love Everlasting, she snorted. Love never lasted. There was no such thing as love. Love was a game. One person gave and gave and gave and the other one took and took and took. "All my pride, all my self-esteem, all my money, all my emotions, and all of my conscience. Teddie St. Claire, I hate your guts! Daniel, I need you, Daniel," she moaned.

What time was it? Teddie should have been here by now. Rajean jerked her way to the dresser, her arms puppetlike as she reached for her watch. Quarter past midnight. Teddie wasn't coming. Daniel wasn't coming. No one was coming.

"The hell with all of you!" Rajean screeched as she reached for the sleeping pills. If no one was coming, she might as well go to sleep. She downed three of the tablets and crawled into bed. "You can all go to hell," she muttered as she drifted into a drug-induced sleep.

At twenty minutes of two, Tedra St. Claire sashayed through the door Rajean had left open for her, her jaw dropping in shock. Her eyes began to water immediately with the thick, choking smell of the flowers and burning candles. She plucked a card from a luscious arrangement of pink roses. "Who the fuck is L. E.?" she muttered.

She looked around the room, her narrowed eyes taking in the half-empty gin bottle, the pill bottles, the strewn flowers, the messy bed. Then she saw Rajean sprawled across the bed, her nightgown on backward. "Must have been a hell of an orgy," she said, slipping out of her coat as she approached the bed. "I'm sorry I missed it."

She sat down next to Rajean and placed a gentle hand on her shoulder. "Rajean, darling, wake up, Teddie's here, darling. I'm sooo sorry I'm late. I see that it doesn't matter; obviously you had . . . other things to do and didn't miss me at all. I am so disappointed, darling. Rajean, wake up. Come on, Rajean," she called harshly, forgetting to sound loving and concerned. "Where the hell is my fucking present?"

Teddie was strong, muscular actually, and regularly worked out with weights, but Rajean's inert figure was almost more than she could handle. She was angry with herself even for coming to the hotel, and she wasn't leaving until she had her present. If there was one thing Teddie hated, it was a woman who couldn't handle her liquor or her drugs.

"Dammit, Rajean, wake up, I want to talk to you!" Teddie snarled. How had she ever allowed herself to get involved with this stupid woman? Abruptly she poured the contents of the ice bucket all over Rajean's head. The moment Rajean started to sputter and struggle to wakefulness, Teddie yanked her upright with one hand. "I thought you were going to wait for me. Shame on you, Rajean, after all we've meant to each other."

"What time is it?" Rajean asked thickly.

"After midnight. What a beautiful gown," Teddie said, fingering the soft material. It must have cost a fortune. I hope he or she was worth it. "Darling, who is L. E.?"

"Love Everlasting," Rajean said, flopping back against the pillows.

"How . . . cute," Teddie drawled. "Male or female?"

"Does it matter?" Rajean responded groggily.

"I thought we were as . . . one. The present you mentioned is my good-bye gift, is that it?"

"It's on the dresser. Lock the door on your way out."

"No, no, darling, I don't accept any tacky gifts. Where's the *real* present?" Teddie cooed, searching in Rajean's shopping bags.

"Don't you dare go through my things!" Rajean cried as she tried to make her arms and legs work.

"Oooooh, how absolutely stunning!" Teddie exclaimed, having unwrapped the Tiffany's gift box. "You have such exquisite taste. Thank you so much. I can't believe you'd give me such a generous good-bye gift. I'll treasure it, darling, forever and ever and ever." She leaned over and brushed her lips against Rajean's cheek. "Poor darling, you look so . . . tired. Here, sweetie, take these pills and you'll sleep like a baby. Sorry, I used all the water, so you'll have to take them with gin. You're going to sleep like a log if you don't die first from all these flowers. Sleep now, darling, and I'll stay right here with you until you're fast asleep. It's the least I can do for this wonderful gift. Teddie loves you," she crooned over and over.

"Do you really, Teddie, do you really love me?" Rajean asked pitifully.

"Darling, you know I do, and I don't want you to forget me when you go to California. Promise me you'll send a Christmas card." When Rajean didn't respond, Teddie pulled the spread up to her chin and smoothed out the wrinkles. How peaceful she looks, Teddie thought. She reached out to pluck a rose from the closest flower arrangement and placed it on the coverlet.

Teddie danced her way to the door, careful to lock it with the key, which she slid back under the door. Then she flipped over the Do Not Disturb card. Rajean would need her rest in the morning. Her hands caressed the crystal statue. Joyce was going to love this little trinket. "Bye, bye, Rajean," she chirped happily.

Seven days later Rajean Bishop was buried in Mary Mount Cemetery on the outskirts of Washington, D.C. It was a private service attended only by Daniel, Nellie, and the detective Daniel had hired to follow his wife.

The coroner's report read: Possible cause of death, suicide. Above-normal readings of alcohol and drugs contributed to this death.

Daniel put the Georgetown house up for sale the day after Rajean's funeral. On the second day he set the wheels in motion to close his Washington law office. The third day was spent settling all his accounts, paying bills, and transferring his personal affairs to Los Angeles. On the fourth day he left for California with Nellie.

Neither of them looked back.

Chapter Seventeen

REUBEN TARZ CONTEMPLATED THE CERULEAN SKY FROM HIS position in the hammock, wondering if a cloud would appear anytime soon. The dazzling jewellike sky was beginning to give him a headache, or was it his thoughts that were causing the dull ache in the back of his head? The last time he'd seen such a vast expanse of blue was in a meadow in France that was covered with bluebells. Mickey's meadow. Mickey's bluebells.

Was the brilliance overhead an omen? Possibly, since he was leaving the next day for Andrews Air Force Base, where he would be flown to England as part of *The New York Times*'s foreign news team covering the war.

Today was his to do whatever he wanted. All his good-byes had been said but one. The servants were dismissed with generous paychecks, and his sons, Philippe included, had been notified. It was the last good-bye that was bothering him; until this moment he'd more or less decided to ignore Bebe. By now she probably knew he was leaving, so what was the point in making the trip to Benedict Canyon?

Now he was annoyed, and when he was annoyed like this he argued with himself, and he always ended up doing what he didn't want to do. He owed his almost ex-wife a good-bye, not that she would care one way or the other, he told himself. But he wasn't going to argue; he was going to do it, later, after the sun went down and it got dark. This day was his to plan a new life—a life without Fairmont Studios and the power he had wielded there, it was true, but nevertheless one that carried with it an element of danger and, yes, excitement. He was almost to the halfway mark in his life, a successful man by most standards, but unhappy for all that. Now he was going back to France, to find Mickey and set things straight, twenty years after the fact.

Reuben laced his hands behind his head. The years hadn't dulled his memories of Mickey; if anything, they were sharper than ever. How beautiful she'd been, how loving—and so very lusty. Older, yes, but that hadn't made one bit of difference to him then. How would she look now, he wondered. Daniel had said she was the same, still as beautiful. His heart began to pound as he tried to envision their first meeting. That is, he thought dismally, providing I can find her. Now that the time to leave was drawing near, he was starting to realize the enormity of the task he'd set for himself. It had been pointed out to him by his friends at the *Times* that he could lose his life. But he was adamant—right or wrong, he was going, and that's all there was to it.

Reuben's eyes fell on the notepad on the glass-topped table, the journal he was planning to keep for his . . . memoirs. The story of his life, from the beginning, of course, from his first meeting with Daniel and up through the present with this war in progress. It would be a tale of friendship, of love, of success and failure. Perhaps it might even make a fairly decent script for a film. Of course any story, any film, had to have a beginning, a middle, and an end. Yes, yes, yes, and there would be an end; that's what this trip was all about. But could he get it all down on paper? The acid test. He had to do it, not just for himself, but for everyone involved.

Reuben gazed out over the wide expanse of apple-green lawn. A sparrow sailed gracefully from its perch to light in one of the flower beds. Immediately it began to search for worms. There was a nest high overhead; Reuben had seen it from his bedroom window. The feeders and birdbaths he'd set out were used constantly by the winged inhabitants of his yard. He made a mental note to load the feeder. How would the birds manage while he was gone, he wondered. They would survive; after all, they were creatures of the outdoors. Feeders and birdbaths just made things a little easier.

This . . . thing he was considering, his memoirs, if done right could ace Selznick's *Gone With The Wind* and reap huge box-office rewards. It would have everything *Wind* had, even more, except the fire. For Christ's sake, he had two wars going for him, and a love affair that spanned twenty years. Women were addicted to love stories and handsome actors. And according to box-office receipts, women were also the principal movie-goers.

So, he asked himself for the hundredth time, is this why you're going to France, to find the ending to your story? You could make one up, he argued with himself. It wouldn't be the same. I want it to be factual. So factual you could die over there and it won't get finished. I have to try, I owe . . . I owe so much. I have to put back, pay back somehow. . . .

And exposing Mickey, not to mention everyone else, to the public will be acceptable to everyone? You can't please every-one. It's what's best for the majority, in the final analysis. The box office is the ultimate test. But you don't work at the studio anymore. That's true. There are other studios, other actors beside the ones at Fairmont. Jane might like it enough to want to produce it. But what about Philippe and Bebe? They control the studio, they call the shots, Jane works for them. "I'll find a way," Reuben muttered.

Reuben jammed his hands into his pockets and started down the flagstone steps. He walked quietly so as not to startle the bathing birds. He grinned. "It's okay, ladies," he said, turning his head. For Christ's sake, Daniel's trip to France while the war was going on would be so stupendous, the public would gobble it up and beg for more. He was a filmmaker, and he knew what the public wanted and didn't want, and he knew they were just waiting to sink their teeth into this one. As soon as he had an ending.

"You are a son of a bitch, a real bastard. You'd go to these lengths just to come out on top," his other self picked up on the previous argument. "Yeah, if that's what it takes, then that's what I'm doing. I don't want any more argument from you. I've thought this through, I've planned it, and I'm going ahead with it. Enough!" he roared to his conscience. Startled birds took wing, their feathers rustling with indignation as they lighted in the branches of the trees.

His thoughts beginning to race along the corridors of his

past, Reuben stared down at the blank pad. Already he itched to put words on paper, but it wouldn't be real if he started now. No, he had to begin on the plane and then whenever he had a few moments to scribble. If this was going to work, it had to be authentic, from word one.

Reuben stared at the notepad so long, he grew drowsy, his thoughts far away, not in France this time, but in Benedict Canyon. He was tempted to go into the house and call the studio to see if Bebe had taken over yet. Some instinct told him she hadn't, that she was waiting for him to leave first. This pleased him, it meant she wasn't the vulture she used to be, waiting to pick at his bones.

What was he going to say to her this one last time? Make apologies, explanations? Ask her to be more generous than he deserved in forgiving him? "You had it all, the whole ball of wax, and you didn't know what to do with it," he muttered. To kill his thoughts Reuben allowed himself to drift into sleep, where only nightmarish demons prevailed. Those kinds of demons he could deal with in the bright light of day.

The sun inched its way across the blue sky, fluffy white clouds in its wake. Orange blossoms fluttered downward, some of them settling on Reuben's sleeping shoulders; birds flitted close at hand, eyeing the still form in the chaise longue. Reuben slept deeply and peacefully, so deeply he remained unaware of the steady progression of people coming to visit him for one more good-bye.

Philippe was the first, his dark eyes full of sadness and fear. He wanted to shake his father awake, wanted to confide every emotion he'd ever felt and confess that he didn't hate him, had never hated him. More than anything he wanted to tell his father that he'd work night and day at the studio, alongside his mother, to keep it going and preserve the reputation it had maintained all these years. There were so many things unsaid, so many apologies unspoken. The need to touch his father was so strong, Philippe clenched his trembling hands into fists. How was it possible the sleeping man didn't feel his presence?

He walked a little closer, his quiet steps disturbing the birds clustered around the feeder, and bent down to whisper in his father's ear. "I forgive you, Papa. *Au revoir.*" He cried then, all the tears he'd harbored since the age of twelve, tears of bitterness, tears of love and forgiveness. His sins of pride were gone now, the door to his heart open and ready to accept whatever this new life had to offer. Then, quietly, he left.

Daniel and Jane were the next visitors to the house in Laurel Canyon. Daniel rang the bell three times and then kept his finger pressed to the bell for several moments. At last he turned to Jane, his eyes full of worry. "He said he was going to stay home today and do nothing. I can't let him go like this without saying . . . something."

Jane's voice was soft and soothing. "We shouldn't have come here, Daniel. We said our good-byes yesterday. Reuben wants it this way. We should respect his wishes. I know it's hard for you, but if this is what Reuben wants . . ."

Daniel's voice was agonized. "This is so . . . he should have done this years ago. Why now? The war is . . . this isn't the time to go to Europe. He's always listened to my advice before. This time . . . this time I couldn't reach him. I know he heard me, heard the words, but . . . Jane . . ."

"I know what Reuben means to you, and that special feeling you have for him, that love, is the reason you have to let him go," Jane said quietly. "All these years you've been his friend, his confidant, his conscience. It's time to let Reuben be Reuben. He has to do this, he has to go in order to live. You should understand that. Your reasoning is selfish, Daniel. It can't be happy ever after for Reuben until he puts his life in order. I for one am glad he's finally going to do this, and yes, the timing is . . . incredibly bad. Perhaps this is precisely why he chose this particular time. It's taken the war and Philippe's arrival to . . . to make this decision. Daniel . . ."

Daniel turned to the pretty woman at his side. The worry left him as he stared into her warm, concerned eyes. What he was seeing was for him, not for Reuben. "When and how did you get so smart?" he asked, marveling.

Jane flushed, her thoughts scattering at what she saw in Daniel's face. Her heart skipped a beat and then fluttered wildly in her chest. It had been a long time since anyone looked at her this way. Her voice was unsteady, girlish. "I'm sorry, what was the question again?"

"I said how and when did you get so smart?"

Jane laughed self-consciously. "I like to think the people I care about deserve more than a passing thought. I think the reason Reuben and I have remained good friends all these years is that neither one of us trespassed on the other's private life unless asked."

Daniel smiled at her in obvious approval. His touch was possessive when he took her arm to lead her around to the gate at the rear of Reuben's property. "I need to do this, Jane, I need to see him again."

Jane placed a gentle hand on Daniel's and nodded. "It's beautiful here, isn't it?" she asked quietly.

"Yes, and I'll bet you five dollars I can count on one hand the number of times Reuben has noticed how beautiful it really is. Beautiful and . . . lonely."

"Look, he's sleeping in the hammock. Please, Daniel, don't wake him," Jane pleaded. "I feel like I'm trespassing. Even though we both love him, there's something . . . something about seeing him like this . . . not in control, vulnerable. He wouldn't like us being here."

"I know, but I had to see him one more time." He closed the gate and slipped the latch back into place. "Listen, I have an idea. Let's you and me play hooky today, what d'ya say? Let's do everything you always wanted to do but never had the time for. Production won't fall apart without you for one day, and I'm still getting my feet wet. No one will even miss us. You said yourself when we came out here that things were under control. Well?"

Jane was quick to note the unhappiness in Daniel's eyes. He'd been through a lot lately. "That's a wonderful idea, Daniel," she replied warmly. "If you hadn't suggested it, I was going to. And at the end of the day when you drop me off at my door, will you kiss me good night?" She held her breath for his answer.

"Do I have to wait till I drop you off?" he asked. "Why not here, now, right in front of Reuben's house? I hate to put off till later something that can be done right now. Pucker up, Jane Perkins."

It was a silly, friendly kiss that spoke of many suppressed feelings, feelings that would surface and be dealt with possibly later in the evening or in the very near future.

"I wonder, Daniel, if you are the person I've been waiting for all my life, that one person I might want to share my soul with," Jane said, and smiled at him. "I've never said that to a man before, possibly because I knew in my heart it wasn't time. Do you think I'm being forward?"

"No. I was thinking along those same lines, but I didn't quite know how to phrase it. Do you know what I've hungered for all my life? Well, let me tell you . . ."

* * *

It was almost dusk when Reuben woke. Instantly he realized he'd slept the better part of the day. He knew he had to do two things, fill the bird feeders and the birdbath and say good-bye to Bebe.

He enjoyed pouring seed into the feeders and sprinkling a few extra handfuls around the ground. The birds were sleeping now, secure in the thought that morning would arrive with food and clean water. Suddenly the birds' welfare was the most important thing in the world to him. Daniel . . . Daniel would come out and take care of the birds. Hell, why hadn't he thought of that before? Daniel should come here and live in the house while he was gone. He slapped at his head in annoyance. "Sometimes, Tarz, you are downright stupid," he muttered. He'd write a note, put the key in it, and drop it off at the studio on his way home from seeing Bebe. He felt better immediately as he gazed around the peaceful garden. "I hope you guys are satisfied that I'm securing your future," he murmured. Over-head the trees rustled softly, and he thought he heard a soft chirp in response. He smiled all the way to the shower.

Bebe sat on the front steps of her house, her hands laced around her knees. Would he come? All day she'd crossed and uncrossed her fingers while she waited. She'd done so much, just to keep busy so she wouldn't think. Now, she was tired and she still had to walk her dog, the golden-haired spaniel she'd picked up at the pound. In the ten days she'd had him he'd proved to be a wonderful companion. The man at the pound said he'd belonged to an elderly man who had passed away. She'd loved him on sight, and Wilbur, as she had named him, loved her, at least she thought he did. He followed her everywhere, waiting outside the door while she bathed, sleep-ing at the foot of her bed, walking down the steps with her, bringing her his leash when he wanted to go for a walk.

Now she whistled softly, and the dog trotted over to her. She fondled his silky ears, which dragged down to his first leg joint. Dark, chocolaty eyes stared up at her adoringly. "I don't know if he's coming or not, Willie." The dog laid his head in her lap, licking her hand. "Tomorrow, we're going to work. I'll bring your bed. I expect you to snap and snarl if things get sticky."

Willie cocked his head to listen to the sound of her voice, then licked her hand again, his signal that she should continue to scratch his ears. Bebe laughed. "My best friend. You are, you know. It's just you and me, Willie."

Twice Bebe got up to stretch her legs, Wilbur panting anxiously at her feet. When were they going for their nightly walk? When her watch read 9:30, Bebe reached for the leash on the wicker table. "He isn't coming, Willie, so let's go for our walk. No tugging, no pulling, you are to be a perfect gentleman. Walk at my side," she admonished the frisky dog.

Wilbur usually took an hour before he found just the right spot to relieve himself. They walked, they jogged, they circled each tree and shrub that lined the long driveway leading in from the canyon. Bebe was wondering how long Willie would continue his search for the ideal tree when a pair of headlights blinded her and the purr of a car's powerful engine roared in her ears.

He had come.

Bebe hated to do it, but she tugged on Wilbur's leash. "We'll do this again later. This is important."

Reuben stopped the car alongside Bebe as she led Willie back to the house. His voice held amusement and something else . . . Sadness, Bebe wondered.

"Out for an evening stroll?" he asked.

"It's that time of night. Reuben, this is Wilbur, Willie for short. I guess you could say he's my best friend these days. He's loyal, loves me unconditionally, and doesn't fight back. A pity I didn't look for those attributes in my friends years ago."

"Do you want a ride to the house?" Reuben asked. Bebe shook her head. "I'll wait for you, then," he said, and continued on. In his rearview mirror he could see her and the dog loping after the car.

Bebe unhooked the dog's leash and sat down on the steps. "It's a beautiful night, isn't it? Sit down, Reuben. I know why you're here, so I don't expect it will take long."

Reuben sat down and stretched his long legs out in front of him. She was right, it was a beautiful night—warm but not too sultry. The crickets were chirping, a pleasant sound in his ears. The half moon smiled down on them benignly. His heart began to thud in his chest. "I wasn't going to come, but then I thought that would be unfair to you. I realize we're getting a divorce and I take full responsibility for that. There are a lot of things I wish I could change, but I can't. For whatever it's worth, Bebe, I'm sorry for what I've put you through."

They were words, words with meaning. Words she needed to hear. "I can't allow you to take full responsibility, Reuben. I've learned so many things lately, and I think the most important thing is that each of us must take responsibility for his or her actions. And because of what I've learned, I must tell you something. I wish it were a different time and place and not the night before you leave, but . . . ."

Bebe cleared her throat nervously. Wilbur inched closer; his eyes on Reuben were unwavering. "All these years you wondered why Mickey never wrote to you or Daniel. I'm the reason, Reuben. It wasn't because of Philippe. She was away and her mail at the château was sent on to Paris. I was staying there for a little while. I opened the mail, read your letters, yours and Daniel's, and I burned them, all of them. She . . . I guess she thought you were too busy and didn't want to be bothered, which was what I wanted her to think. I did send her a note telling her we were married and deliriously happy. I wrote it on our wedding night while you were downstairs getting drunk. I . . . I also stole the letter you wrote to her that was in your jacket pocket at the studio. It was the one where you . . . where you said . . . I guess it was an ultimatum of sorts. I tore that to shreds after I read it. I . . . I couldn't let . . . I can't let you go back there without knowing what I did. I'm sorry. I don't expect you to believe me, but I am."

She paused, staring at her hands in her lap. "You see, I was so in love with you, so jealous of what you and Mickey had. All I wanted was your love, and you couldn't give that to me because it was all parceled out to Mickey. I literally stole your life away from you. Twenty years that I can never give you back. I wish I'd listened and believed Mickey when she told me you can't make someone love you. God, how I tried. All the trouble, the drugs, the liquor, I did that, indulged, so you would pay attention to me. I lived for your smile, a kind word from you. If you patted me on the head, I would have died for you. I realize now that I was sick, so sick I was out of my mind half the time. Saying I'm sorry almost sounds silly, even to me, but if there is anything I can do for you, for Mickey, I'll do it. I wrote a letter to her explaining my part in this. It's on the table on the porch. I was hoping you would stop by so I could give it to you. Reuben, I don't want you to say anything, and I don't want you to even look at me. For too many years I saw disgust and hatred in your eyes when you looked at me. I can't bear to see it again."

She stood up and turned away, tears glistening in her eyes. "You should go now, Reuben. I appreciate your coming by and letting me get this off my shoulders. I hope for your sake that Mickey is well and that both of you . . . well, I hope your meeting after all this time is what you want. She loves you with all her heart. I know what I'm talking about because I feel the same way. And because of those feelings, I can let you go. That's what love is, wanting the other person's happiness more than you want your own."

In a flash Bebe had the leash on Willie's neck and was sprinting around the side of the house. She raced through the gate, slamming the bolt home. "Good-byegood-byegood-byegood-byegood-bye," she cried. "If one of us is to be happy, I'm glad it's you. Good-bye, Reuben."

The dark night hovered around Reuben, sheltering him from his shame. The dog's yips from the back garden sounded so happy. He wasn't sure, but he thought he heard a soft dirge playing on the wind through the rustling leaves.

For the first time in his life, Reuben Tarz truly mourned his loss.

Chapter Eighteen

BEBE ROSEN, AS SHE THOUGHT OF HERSELF THESE DAYS, started the first day of what she referred to as her career. The anticipation she felt quickly turned to annoyance as she pulled up to the security gate at Fairmont Studios in her rusty car. The guard, his tie loosened at his neck, shirt-sleeves rolled up, and his cap set back on his head, approached and asked to see her pass. She explained who she was, noting scattered gum and candy wrappers littering the entrance. If Reuben were here, the man would be at attention, properly attired and there would be no sign of debris.

Bebe climbed from the car and looked for the man's name tag, which was supposed to be pinned to his creased shirt pocket. "Your name, please," she said coolly.

"Eddie Savery, ma'am."

"Well, Eddie, it's like this. I'm taking over for my husband, who has left the country. I'm going to give you exactly ten minutes to straighten your tie, adjust your cap, roll down your sleeves, and find your identification pin. Then I'm going to give you another five minutes to clean up this debris. If you are one minute past my deadline, you are unemployed. Oh, one more thing, don't ever criticize my car, either mentally or verbally. The clock is ticking, Mr. Savery." Bebe kept her eyes glued to her watch. You head them off at the pass and never give an inch, she thought, and their respect will be automatic. As Reuben was often fond of saying, everyone wanted discipline and an overseer.

With one minute to spare, the guard was back at his post, the offending debris clutched in both hands. He swallowed hard and did his best to smile at Bebe.

"Thank you, Mr. Savery," Bebe said, shaking down the sleeve of her suit jacket. "Now, if you'll open the gate, I'll be on my way. Have a pleasant day."

The guard touched his hat respectfully. "You, too, ma'am." Obviously he wasn't going to be able to do much reading the way he'd planned. He let his breath out in a loud *swoosh*. He'd come *that* close to being fired. The moment he saw a director's car approach, he snapped to attention.

Bebe pulled her car alongside a snappy Cadillac roadster, probably her son's. She grinned when she stepped back to look at her own vehicle next to the impressive line of sedans, coupes, and sports convertibles. Her car, she decided, would give the entire studio something to talk about for days.

Upstairs in the executive office building, Bebe stared at Reuben's closed office door for a long time. Twice she reached out to twist the doorknob and both times she pulled back. It seemed sacrilegious, somehow, to cross the threshold of Reuben's private space, the place where he'd spent twenty-odd years of his life. She looked around, delaying the moment when she could stall no longer. This place where she was standing was the outer limits of the secretary's office, an austere kind of room, functional, but not elaborate or eye-appealing. Margaret, Reuben's loyal secretary, obviously hadn't been much of a decorator. But that could be changed with very little effort. Al Sugar, the head of the prop department, would help her. Some plants, a few comfortable chairs, some decent pictures on the walls, a new carpet, some up-to-date magazines, and it would all take shape.

Bebe noticed her hand was trembling as she reached out once again to grasp the polished brass door handle. A hand snaked ahead of hers and the door flew open. "You just open it, it's simple," a voice said coolly.

Bebe looked up and stared into Reuben's mocking eyes, another ghost from the past. "Thank you," she said, managing to sound quite normal. "I have this feeling that I'm trespassing somehow."

"Yes, I felt that way, too, in the beginning. In fact, I still feel that way." Philippe waited, wondering if his mother would prolong the conversation.

Her back to her son, Bebe drew in a deep breath. She was going to have to turn, face him, and she was going to have to do it now. What would Reuben do in this situation, she wondered. Whirl around, be blasé, and put him on the defensive, something he excelled at. When she turned, her features were composed, her voice even. "I noticed something when I walked into the building; in fact, I noticed it outside, too. It's quiet, too quiet, almost gloomy."

Philippe found himself searching his mind for something his father would say in a situation like this. "Rather like a funeral after the funeral, a wake, I believe is the way Americans refer to it. I suppose it is. Mr. Tarz . . . my father is gone. Most of the people here, at least I find it so, think of him as *the* studio. I've noticed the past few days that people are being quiet because they're unsure of what's going to happen, and of course their jobs are uppermost in their minds." He'd said too much, dragged out his response, but his mother was paying attention, actually seemed interested in what he'd just said.

"Yes, I can understand that. Well, I'll have a memo sent around as soon as I get a secretary. Business as usual until I . . . I understand the workings of this studio. It's been a long time since I've been here, and even then I was here in a visiting capacity only. As a child, Mr. Sugar let me play in the prop-room. It was a wonderful place of make-believe." Damn, she was talking too much. The boy was looking at her as though she had two heads.

Philippe shuffled his feet. "If there's anything . . ."

"I'll call you," Bebe said, locking eyes with her son.

When the door closed behind him, Bebe's shoulders sagged. How was she going to work here, day after day, with Reuben's image so near? Her heart was beating so rapidly, she had to sit down. She bolted up a second later when she realized this was Reuben's chair, his indentations in the soft material. "Damn!"

For God's sake, this wasn't a shrine, she scolded herself. It was an office, used by a man who had run Fairmont Studios. Calmer now, she took the time to look around, to savor the place that had held her husband captive all these years. It was comfortable but fairly Spartan, much like the outer office. A workplace with no frills and no doodads. Well, she would change this and the outer office. It was what she wanted now, a conducive atmosphere for her to work in. Earth tones would be nice, with splashes of bright color. Perhaps a smaller desk that wouldn't dwarf the room and the occupants that came to . . . check on her out of curiosity. This had been fine for Reuben because he was larger than life and twice as intimidating. No leather, but soft nubby material on the chairs. Cushions with bright colors. Several green plants. Some brass or bronze on the walls. Maybe a collage of Fairmont's biggest box office hits.

Bebe perched on the edge of Reuben's chair and drummed her fingers on the desk. Obviously refurnishing the office was to be her first priority, a secretary second. And there was no time like the present to get things under way. With something like relief, she rose and left the office.

Outside, Bebe knew people were looking at her covertly as she walked along the newly paved walkways. When she reached her destination—the proproom—she found Al Sugar and outlined her request; ever-accommodating, he promised her that Reuben's old offices would be transformed by four o'clock. Her second stop was the personnel office, which agreed to send several "possibles" for her to interview at four-thirty.

"How many people does it take to make this studio what it is?" Bebe muttered to herself as she walked around, staring at the crowds of people hurrying along from one destination to another. Actors and extras in makeup and costume, propmen and stagehands hauling scenery, directors, producers, writers . . . Fairmont was, literally, a dream factory.

This place, this studio, created temporary happiness and entertainment. And because of Reuben it was a better place than when her father had operated it. She had to give her husband that much credit. Reuben had diversified, buying this and that and adding to the studio's enormous wealth. Tonight she would take a set of books that she would requisition from legal and study them at home. Will I ever be able to take hold, absorb the whole of it, she asked herself.

Where was Reuben now, what was he doing? Was he in the East or on his way to Europe? Last night had been hard on her, so emotionally hard that she'd sat up in the kitchen all night drinking coffee. Where had she gotten the guts to confess to her past misdeeds? And how and when would Reuben retaliate for her sins? She shivered in the warm air.

An hour later Bebe had completed her walk around the perimeters of the studio lot. In her mind she now held a mental picture of each building that rested on each lot. She decided she'd earned her lunch.

She was just brushing the crumbs from a meat pie off her green silk dress when she spied Daniel and Jane Perkins walking arm in arm toward her. If she didn't speak, they wouldn't notice her; their eyes were intent on each other. They're in love, Bebe thought in surprise. She'd always thought of Jane as rather plain, but smiling as she was now, she was pretty. And Daniel . . . well, Daniel wore the silliest smile she'd ever seen.

A few moments later Philippe and Nellie approached on their way to the lunch wagon. She was beautiful, this proper-looking young lady who was laughing at something her son had said. He wore a wicked grin as he playfully poked Nellie's arm. So, Bebe thought wistfully, they all had someone, Daniel and Jane, Nellie and Philippe, Reuben on his way to Mickey. And what did she have? Wilbur. A damn dog.

To while away the rest of the afternoon, Bebe walked over to the studio's massive library. There she was observed looking through the chronological stack of books relating to the studio. Studio personnel watched as she flipped through the dusty tomes, scribbling notes on some kind of chart.

At four-thirty she folded the long yellow sheet of paper and stuck it in her purse. It was time to see what the head of the prop department had accomplished with her office.

She would have gasped in surprise if the four women from personnel hadn't been sitting in the outer office. Instead, she gave them a curt nod and marched through to her own office. Inside, with the door closed, she clapped her hands and whirled around delightedly. It was beautiful. Warm and inviting. She could definitely work here. It wasn't exactly sparkling—in fact, it was rather dusty—but that could be changed when she hired one of the four women in the outer office. Secretaries cleaned offices, watered plants, and made coffee.

By six o'clock Bebe made her final choice. Tillie, a petite middle-aged woman with no aspirations to be anything other than a secretary, had an infectious grin that Bebe adored, and impossibly curly hair that stood up in tight ringlets. When Bebe had asked what her skills were, she'd debated a moment and then replied, "I could lie and say I'm a whiz at office work, but I'm not, and you'd find out sooner or later. I taught myself to type and my dictation skills are so-so if you go slow. But I know how to file,'' she'd added brightly. "Other than that, I'm addicted to soda pop, long, clanking earrings, and I think most men stink." This was said out of the corner of her mouth, sotto voce.

"You're hired!" Bebe grinned. "What's your feeling on dogs?"

Tillie grinned. "They like me and I like them."

"Good, because I have one and he'll be staying here in the office with me. You can start tomorrow if you like."

Tillie nodded agreeably, and they went on to discuss salary. Bebe knew she was paying twenty-five dollars more than she should, but since Tillie had agreed to walk Willie and clean up, it would be worth it.

Bebe Rosen was on a roll.

Chapter Nineteen

THE MOMENT NELLIE BISHOP SET FOOT IN REUBEN TARZ'S mansion, where she was to live with her father, she knew with dead certainty that she wanted to be rich and famous, and she didn't want to have to struggle to reach that end. Tucking Philippe Bouchet under her wing wasn't going to do it for her, but marrying him might. If she wanted to make inroads quickly, she would have to shed her carefully cultivated sweet-young-girl image. However, she would have to do it by degrees. If she charted her course and stuck to it, she could be married to Philippe Bouchet within a year. It wouldn't take *that* much doing to break down his old-world courtliness. After all, he was a man, and a man had certain biological needs, needs she could fulfill if she wanted to, or she could hold out for the ring and the marriage certificate. Perhaps this very mansion would be hers someday. She swooned in ecstasy when she envisioned herself sweeping down the elegant mahogany staircase in a designer gown while hordes of actors and actresses waited below to curry her favor.

Nellie walked through the downstairs rooms touching costly figurines, rubbing her hand over the brocade on the sofa, staring at her image in the polished cherrywood. Everything looked so new . . . so unused, waiting for her to breathe life into it.

Parties at poolside, Japanese lanterns, tons of food, music, servants waiting on her hand and foot. Yes, this was what she wanted.

For now, though, she and her father were caretakers of this splendid mansion, seeing to the birds, making sure pipes didn't break, and doing all the things that went with living in a house.

Nellie's eyes glowed with pleasure as she climbed the wide, curving staircase that led to her room. She drew in her breath at the top when she leaned over the balcony to stare down at the marble foyer. "Mine, all mine," she murmured as she made her way to the bedroom that was to be hers.

The bedroom was larger than the whole of the second floor of the Georgetown house, and it was hers. Done in mauve and dove-gray silk, the room was exquisite. If she removed her shoes, she would sink into the luxurious carpeting up to her ankles. The wall-length-mirrored closet would surely hold hundreds of outfits, each prettier than the next. Racks and racks for shoes, other shelves for handbags and gloves, perhaps one for hats, although she didn't like to cover her head except for funerals.

The bathroom made her gasp with its sunken tub and black marble walls. The first thing she would buy would be crystal decanters for perfume, bath salts, and powders. The towels were thick and luxurious beyond anything she'd ever seen. "All mine," she crooned as she wrapped one of the misty-rose towels around her torso and danced her way into the bedroom, where she dropped the towel in front of the mirrored closet.

"Soon," she breathed as she set about unpacking her bags. The collegiate-looking clothes and simple playsuits looked so out of place on their scented hangers. Nellie's eyes narrowed speculatively; from now on her paychecks would go toward filling this closet. Perhaps if she sweet-talked her father, she could convince him her simple clothing was not suitable for California. Maybe tonight she'd talk to him if he wasn't seeing Jane.

Jane . . . Jane Perkins with the sweet smile and observant eyes. Jane saw right through her, of course, and it had amused her at first. Amused her because Jane knew Philippe was interested in her, and that interest could be swayed, placing Jane's job in jeopardy. Still, she would have to be careful since her father was obviously enamored with the production head, she thought craftily.

Bebe Rosen Tarz would have to be cultivated, too. Perhaps she could bring Philippe and Bebe together in an emotional way so that Philippe could take over the business end entirely. If things were left the way they were now, Bebe would only be in the way, a thorn in her side. And she knew enough about Bebe to play the game, the same game she'd played over the years. Match and checkpoint, she gurgled. Oh, yes, it would behoove her to align herself with Bebe. Tomorrow she would "drop in" on Bebe and begin the game, a game with one set of rules—hers.

Chapter Twenty

THE SHEER CURTAINS ON THE FRENCH DOORS DANCED WITH a gentle midnight breeze, bathing Daniel's naked body with coolness. Overhead, stars sprinkled the heavens, surrounding the silvery moon like a halo.

Jane stirred in the crook of Daniel's arm, causing him to tighten his hold imperceptibly. He was never, ever, going to let this woman get away from him, he thought with a contented sigh. Making love with Jane was the most wonderful thing that had ever happened to him. His other life had been a mere passage of time to get to this place, this moment, with this warm, gentle, caring woman whose passions, like his own, had exploded into millions of stars.

"I didn't know . . . I never felt . . . How is it I've lived all these years and never—"

"Shhh," Jane said, placing a finger over his lips, not wanting to spoil this perfect moment.

It had happened so naturally, so innocently. Daniel had kissed her good night at the door, and she'd clung to him, savoring the feel of his arms about her. Then she'd asked him in and held his gaze steadily until he'd weakened and said, "Well, I could use a cup of coffee." Coffee in the kitchen turned to wine in the bedroom. Jane wasn't sure who had initiated the second kiss, not that it mattered now. A second glass of wine led to a third and the courage to remove her clothes, her eyes clinging to Daniel's to see if he noticed the slight sag to her once-firm breasts and the extra flesh on her hips. What she saw in his eyes was mirrored in her heart and gave her the confidence to lead him to her bed. She smiled. Within minutes she knew she had a sleeping tiger by the tail. They'd been like wild animals at first, ferocious and vociferous as they'd explored, touched, tasted, and savored. They'd teased, petted, kissed, and kissed again and again, tasting each other. They'd laughed, giggled, pinched, and nibbled until neither one could bear it another moment. Then they'd made slow, wonderful love as though they'd been doing it for years. When their passions exploded simultaneously, they'd laughed together in exultation. And then she'd cried, never having experienced anything so total, so completely hers, and she knew Daniel felt the same way.

"I've waited all my life for this," Daniel whispered.

"So have I," she whispered in return.

"Do you feel like we were meant for each other?"

Jane smiled in the darkness. "I knew it the day I met you and Reuben outside the studio, but you never noticed me. The few times we met over the years, you were . . . I don't know, it seemed to me as though you had a mission in life, and there was no room for me even if you had noticed me. And, of course, you were married."

"Jane," Daniel said, hiking himself up on his elbow to stare down at her, "my marriage to Rajean, as I told you, was . . . a desperate move on my part. I wanted to belong to someone, to be connected, if you know what I mean. I think it was Nellie I loved, not Rajean. We were a family of sorts. I knew it was a mistake almost immediately. In side of a week, really. We were pals more than anything. One day I said, 'Do you want to get married?' and she said, 'It sounds like a good idea,' and we got married. At first she tolerated sex, and after a while she made excuses. She made it very clear that she didn't have much use for men, and while I was a man and her husband, it didn't seem to make much difference. Later on I found myself staying later and later at the office, even sleeping there. It was no marriage, not ever. Some men channel their sexual drives into work, and that's what I did. If there was any energy left at the end of the day, I showered it on Nellie. After the first year I legally adopted her. I know this sounds terrible, but

Rajean's death was a blessing... for me, and for Nellie as well. I'd made up my mind to divorce Rajean before I came out here and told her so. Nellie... Nellie accepted it, at least I think she has. She's a remarkable young lady. She didn't cry at all. I know she's grieving inside, that's the way she is. Working with you will be good for her. Isn't she a wonderful kid?"

Jane chose her words with great care. "She's asked a million questions, and she took stacks and stacks of folders home with her. She said she wants to learn the business from the ground up. That shows initiative, don't you agree?"

"It certainly does. Do you think Philippe and Nellie are... I think they go together very well. You know what I'm trying to say." Daniel laughed.

"I think it's safe to say Philippe is very interested in Nellie. I've seen the way Nellie looks at him." *But not the way you think, Daniel. She's calculating and manipulative. Daniel, you are so wrong about your daughter; you don't know her at all.*

"They'll be good for one another. Now they each have someone," Daniel said happily.

Just like Bebe and Reuben, who fed off each other. Can't you see Nellie is just like Bebe? Can't you see it, Daniel?

Daniel kissed her, a long, lingering kiss. "I don't want to leave, but I have to. Nellie always waits up for me, and I'm going to have a devil of a time explaining where I've been. It's, my God, it's two o'clock!" He jumped out of bed.

"Are we... does this mean... are we a secret, Daniel? If so, I must tell you I can't accept that. I have never sneaked around with a man, and I don't plan to start now. Nellie's old enough to understand her father having a relationship with a woman," Jane said tightly.

Daniel took her face in his hands and gazed tenderly into her eyes. "No, Jane, I would never ask you to sneak around. I would never expect that. I'll talk to Nellie, of course I will, and knowing her, she'll be thrilled for the both of us. But not tonight. Tomorrow," he said, leaning over to kiss her again. "You do like Nellie, don't you?" he added anxiously.

Once again Jane chose her words with care. "She's a charming, beautiful young lady, and she has an equally charming and handsome father."

Daniel left Jane Perkins's house feeling confident that his was a wonderful world. He had Nellie and now he had Jane.

"Jesus, what a lucky man I am," he murmured. He smiled all the way home.

The smile was still on his face when he pulled his car alongside Philippe's in the circular driveway. The fact that his daughter and his best friend's son were parked together in front of the house at two-thirty A.M. didn't surprise or bother him at all.

"And where have *you* been?" Nellie chirped through the open window of Philippe's car.

"Gathering orange blossoms," Daniel quipped. Then he remembered his promise to Jane and walked around to the passenger side of Philippe's car. "Actually, I was with Jane and time . . . got away from me."

"Reminiscing will do that." Nellie laughed. "I'm going to remember that line the next time I'm late."

Daniel smiled fondly at the two young people. He wagged his finger under his daughter's nose. "Not too much longer, Nellie, tomorrow is a workday. Good night," he said affably.

"Your father's right, Nellie, it's time for you to go in," Philippe said quietly. "Tomorrow is here already, and I have to be at the studio by seven."

"Why?"

Philippe frowned. "Why? Because . . . because those are my hours."

"But you're the boss, with your mother, of course, so you shouldn't have to adhere to a time schedule. I do because I am a lowly apprentice, but you, you can sleep late, you don't even have to go in if you don't want to." She opened her purse and withdrew a small compact in order to examine her face. "Philippe," she said casually, "what do you think of Jane?"

"The dossier the studio has on her is quite complete. I'd say she is a remarkable, efficient, knowledgeable woman," Philippe replied. "She's also a very nice person, from the little I've seen of her. She's rather gentle, warm, and kind. In many ways she reminds me of my mother . . . in France. Why do you ask?"

"Working with her as I do, I see only the business side of her. I don't think she likes me. No, I *know* she doesn't like me." Nellie looked up to catch the surprise on Philippe's face. "Oh, it isn't anything she said or did," she added hastily, "it's something I picked up on these past few days. I catch her staring at me, and she has this strange look on her face. She doesn't like me, but she loves my father!"

"That's strange. I had the impression Jane liked everyone. She's well thought of at the studio. In fact, production would fall apart without her. I guess that's why my father gave her a ninety-nine-year contract." Philippe smiled. "It was sort of a joke, I'm told, but he insisted. If she ever decides to leave for any reason, the studio would be forced to pay out an astronomical sum of money to her every year if she chose to exercise the contract to the letter. Like my father, Jane *is* Fairmont. Your father is, too, but in a different way. His job in legal has been waiting for him all these years. Sifting through all the records and files, I came to the conclusion that the workings of the studio, the personnel, are all part of my father's master plan, for want of a better word. There won't be any changes made in the near future, I can tell you that much."

Nellie suppressed a yawn. "It all sounds very interesting, Philippe, but it is late and I do have to get up early. . . . By the way, I just realized that *I* don't have a contract. Does that mean I'm just temporary?" she asked coyly.

"I'll check it out tomorrow." He squeezed her hand. "Will I see you Saturday evening for dinner?"

"Oh, I'm so sorry, Philippe, I can't have dinner with you. Jane made . . . well, what she did was, she arranged a meeting—actually, it's a date because she told me to get dressed up—with one of the young actors at the studio. Carlo Santini, do you know him?" She waited for what she knew would be Philippe's response, and she wasn't disappointed.

"That gigolo!" he cried indignantly. "That doesn't please me at all. I insist that you break this . . . this date!"

"Philippe, I can't do that," Nellie protested, forcing herself to sound distressed. "Jane's my boss; how would it look if I said no? She said she's going to arrange for me to meet every eligible young actor on the lot. Imagine that!" On that note she breezed out of the car and blew Philippe a kiss as she started up the steps to the front door. "Good night, Philippe," she called. "I'll see you tomorrow."

Philippe seethed and fretted on the drive home. He stormed into his empty house, his footsteps loud on the marble floor. Until tonight he had liked Jane Perkins. Tomorrow he would take a second look at her iron-clad ninety-nine-year contract.

His head was pounding unmercifully as he climbed the stairs to the second story and slammed his way into his overly decorated bedroom. His mother would laugh if she could see it. The decorator had gone wild with her black-and-white zebra wallpaper and speckled black carpeting. The tailored black-and-white-checked drapes made his eyes water, as did the black lampshades. He hated it, and yet he was stuck with it.

The urge to smash something, to shatter that something into oblivion, was so strong he grew light-headed with the thought alone. His hands to his temples, he lay back on the black and white flowered pillows. If Jane Perkins were standing in front of him, he would have pushed his fist through her warm, gentle face. Nellie Bishop belonged to him.

As Philippe reached out for troubled sleep, he wondered whose side his mother would be on. Then he tried to imagine Nellie in his arms, here in his bed. He reached for the pillow and buried his face in it, willing the ferocious headache to dissipate.

While Philippe struggled with his headache and sleep, Nellie danced around her bedroom wondering what it would be like to be married to the head of a major studio. A true Hollywood mogul. Would that make her a mogulette? She smiled at herself in the smoky mirror in the bathroom. Anything was possible; her father had said so time and time again. And her father was always right.

Chapter Twenty-one

BEBE'S OFFICE CRACKLED WITH ELECTRICITY—HERS, AS SHE
paced up and down to Tillie's amusement. Today she would
preside over her first company meeting. On the ride in to the
studio she'd made up her mind that after she called the meeting
to order, she would sit back and listen.

Thoughtfully she fingered the small spiral notebook she'd
found in Reuben's desk. It looked to be his business bible, the
pages old and tattered, the wire half gone from the side, replaced with adhesive tape. It was impossible to know if he'd
left it behind deliberately or had simply forgotten it. Whatever
the case, it was going to prove invaluable—Reuben's
dictionary for success, and who could quibble with what he'd
done over the years?

Know your adversaries. If superior, retreat; if evenly
matched, fight; if they're weak, close in for the kill. And always
find the skeleton in the closet. Give generously so you can take
back and your adversary thinks he's willingly giving up that
which you want and need. Obviously, it had all worked for
Reuben, Bebe thought with a grimace. The only thing was she
wasn't Reuben, and she didn't know if the members of the
board would be her adversaries. There was every possibility
they would work with her once she herself knew the inner
workings of the studio.

She was dressed tastefully and professionally in a glen plaid suit with a frilly white blouse. She had on pearl earrings, the one gift from Reuben that she still treasured, a businesslike watch with a black leather strap, and her wedding ring. That, of course, would be removed when the divorce was final. Her hairdo was almost severe, pulled back from her face with a black onyx comb on the side. She felt it gave definition to her profile.

If only she could stop her hands from shaking. A drink would do that, but those days were behind her. Either she was going to make it on her own or not at all. "Damn you, Reuben, you gave in too easily," she whispered.

At least she knew what the seating arrangement was because she'd had Tillie place name cards around the table. Jane Perkins would be on her right, Philippe on her left, directors on the right, production heads on the left. Daniel Bishop would sit a quarter of the way down on her right so she'd be able to see his eyes during the meeting; Tillie, of course, was directly behind her.

Willie whined from his position under her desk, desirous of his mistress's attention. Bebe dropped to her haunches to caress the spaniel's silky head. "You have to wait here, pal, until this meeting is over. I'm going to need your support then. Look what I brought along for you to chew on while I'm out of the office."

The dog's satiny ears picked up and then flopped over to rest on his paws as he waited for his treat. When Bebe offered him a soup bone that had been wrapped in waxed paper, the dog yipped his delight. His soft brown eyes gazed at her adoringly.

"It's time," Tillie said, poking her head in the doorway. Bebe straightened up and followed her secretary down the corridor to the conference room. Tillie, she decided, was one of the flashiest dressers she'd ever known. Today she was attired in a red and white polka-dot dress and bright red shoes. Startling red earrings the size of lemons hung from her ears, and on her wrist jangled several gold bracelets. Yet Tillie herself was comforting, just as Willie was—a port of calm for the impending meeting. Thank God, thought Bebe, I had the good sense to hire her.

At the door to the conference room Tillie halted and smiled confidently at Bebe, reminding her of a precocious squirrel ready to invade a backyard full of acorns. Then she thrust open the door and stood aside for her boss to enter.

Every seat at the long, polished table was taken with department heads. They stood as one when Bebe entered the room, Jane, too, a warm smile on her face. Bebe nodded and motioned for everyone to be seated. She took her seat and leaned forward, hands clasped in front of her, the picture of calm confidence. All night she'd practiced this pose and the words that would come next.

"Jane, gentlemen," she said briskly, "this is going to be a very short meeting. I'm sure all of you are wondering about my plans and objectives. It's simple. I want this studio to remain the thriving enterprise it's been in the past. If we can do better, we'll work together to that end. For the time being, I anticipate no changes. It'll be business as usual. My office doors will be open to you at all times." Bebe smiled warmly around the table before she fired off her closing statement. "I hope none of you will—" she paused a full five seconds before she continued "—be reticent about opening the door to my offices because of my . . . gender." She was pleased to see the self-conscious smiles and nods. Out of the corner of her eye she noticed Daniel's thumbs-up salute.

"And now I think we can get on with the business of the day. Among other things, I believe Mr. Bouchet has a research report on television."

The meeting droned on for over an hour, coming to a close when Philippe handed around his thick reports to all those present. Bebe thanked him and adjourned the meeting. Tonight she would study her son's contribution—carefully, to make sure she didn't miss a thing.

Outside in the hall, Tillie was ushering Bebe ahead of the mob behind them. "You were swell," she hissed in her ear. "If you were scared, I sure couldn't tell. They couldn't tell either." Bebe sighed with relief.

"Bebe! Hold on," Daniel called. "Are you becoming so professional you don't have time for old friends?"

Bebe's eyes glowed warmly. "Daniel, I . . . I thought it might be better if I didn't let the present situation get in the way of our very old and very wonderful memories. I wasn't sure how you felt after all this time, and then there was Rajean's passing and Reuben leaving . . ."

"I've been waiting for you to come by my office. When

you didn't call or stop by, I thought you . . . well, I thought you didn't want anything to do with me anymore."

"Obviously, we have a classic case of misunderstanding here," Bebe said, and took his arm. "Come along to my office and Tillie will make us some fresh coffee. I have something I want to show you."

Daniel felt light-headed with the change in Bebe. This couldn't be his old friend from France. Bebe the spoiled young brat, Bebe the jazz baby, Bebe the alcoholic and drug addict. Not this woman dressed so impeccably and walking so confidently at his side, not this warm, gentle-sounding woman. This striking woman who had so heartily endorsed his position at the studio was his friend. And, he realized suddenly, his boss. The thought brought a chuckle to his lips.

"What's so funny?" Bebe asked.

"You're my boss." Daniel laughed. "You have to admit that's funny."

"Why?"

Bebe's voice was so serious, the smile died on Daniel's face. He couldn't lie to Bebe and he didn't want to lie. "For so long I thought of you as a party girl, interested in a good time with no thoughts for anything but your own immediate feelings. I never thought of you in this capacity, but I always knew you were smart enough to do and be whatever you wanted. I even told you so one time—years ago, in France. And you said, and this is a direct quote, 'Oh, poo, that sounds like hard work.' "

Bebe sighed. "That was then and this is now. I hit bottom, Daniel. It was either stay there or climb out, and the only place to go was up. It wasn't easy, and I know I'm not out of the woods yet. I take it one day at a time, and at the end of each day I thank God and ask that tomorrow be just as good. I'm going to do my best."

"That's all any of us do. Congratulations." He hugged her, pretending not to see the tears glistening in her eyes.

Bebe whistled softly, and a golden whirlwind circled her legs, pink tongue wagging as fast as his tail. "Daniel, meet Willie."

Daniel was a young boy again as he dropped to his knees, his hands stroking the dog's silky body. "Jesus, Bebe, his ears are longer than his tail. I bet they get in the way, don't they, fella?" Bebe looked on, smiling indulgently.

"Willie is my roommate, my friend, and my confidant. He

loves me unconditionally, he's loyal, and he doesn't argue. We get along fine."

"I can see that. I don't suppose you'd loan him out once in a while," Daniel asked hopefully.

"Not on your life. You have all that room at the canyon house. Get your own dog. Reuben won't mind. It just might give the old place a little sparkle and life. This is *my* dog!" she declared firmly, and laughed as Willie romped around her, barking and wagging his tail furiously.

"By the way," she asked, changing the subject, "has anyone heard from Mickey?"

"No, and I'm worried. Philippe has to be in torment, but he's carrying it off well. I'm hoping that you two . . ."

"Don't, Daniel. If it's meant to be, it will be. Among other things, I've become a fatalist these days." Bebe smiled at her old childhood friend; he grinned back.

"Old times, eh."

"No, Daniel. Those old times, as you call them, are memories now. Memories best forgotten, at least by me. Tell me," she said, changing the subject again, "how is Nellie?"

"Doing just wonderfully. She loves production, and she can learn so much from Jane. Speaking of Jane, we've been seeing each other. She's a wonderful person," Daniel said, his eyes glowing.

"I'm happy for you," Bebe said sincerely. "And for Jane. I think you two will make a wonderful couple. How is Nellie taking it?"

"Very well. I think she's fond of Jane. Of course, she's seeing Philippe almost every evening. They are, as the saying goes, enamored of each other. I for one couldn't be happier."

Bebe nodded and then rose and came around the other side of the desk. "Well, it was nice chatting with you, Daniel, but I have an office to run. Not that I have a lot of work on my desk. I'm still doing my research on the studio. I want to fully understand the entire system before I make any decisions. I also want to study Philippe's television report. He seems to think it's the wave of the future. If he's right, this industry could fall apart. But let's get together again, real soon."

Daniel blinked in surprise. Bebe had just dismissed him. Nicely, of course, but it was still a dismissal. This pretty, intelligent woman standing in front of him was definitely not the old Bebe. Now he understood all Reuben's conversations.

How easy it must have been for him to fall in love with this new Bebe. And so terribly sad.

"Anytime you want a sitter for your friend, I'll be glad to oblige," Daniel said cheerfully.

"I'll remember that. I'm glad you're here, Daniel, and I'm serious about getting together."

"I'll call you," Daniel said, and he meant it.

When he was almost to the door Bebe called him back. "Daniel, is it true that you hold two percent of Fairmont voting stock? Reuben gleefully informed me of that fact before he left."

"Yes, it's true. Mickey gave it to me when I was in France. I won't take sides, Bebe, I want you to know that. If I have to vote, it will be what's best for the studio, in my opinion. Right now I'm in the same position you're in. I'm learning what makes this place work. From a legal standpoint I don't suppose that makes a lot of sense, but it's the way I do things."

"As long as you're fair," Bebe said briskly.

"Do you doubt me?"

Bebe hesitated. "I'm not sure."

There was no response to that statement, Daniel decided, so he merely nodded and left the office with a last scratch to Willie's ears.

After he left Bebe stared out the window for a long time, reliving memories of her friendship with Daniel. Sweet, honest Daniel. Loyal, too, not to mention caring and compassionate. Reuben's best friend in the whole world. Daniel would report to Reuben, of that she had no doubt. But she had one ace up her sleeve from the past if she chose to use it: the silly agreement she'd tricked him into signing years ago, whereby he agreed to . . . what? They'd made a bet and he'd lost. She'd boasted she could get Reuben to make love to her. Daniel, his eyes full of loyalty and love for his best friend, had disagreed, saying Reuben was too much in love with Mickey to give her a tumble. Instead of making love to her, Reuben had raped her in the barn. How delighted she'd been to inform Daniel that his idol had clay feet. And, devastated, he'd scrawled his name on the bottom of the contract he himself had drawn up. Would he remember it now, she wondered. Would she use it if she had to? It was part of her other life, the part she'd left behind. Maybe, maybe not, she decided.

"I think this is everything," Tillie said, slapping a pile of folders on Bebe's desk. "This batch is pending, this is definite, this represents last week's rejections. I've been through them all, and . . .''

"And what?"

"I don't agree with half of the decisions. It seems to me—and I'm no authority, bear that in mind—but it seems to me that anything by a new writer is automatically rejected in favor of contract writers who have 'names.' Some of those names are lousy, if you don't mind my saying so. I don't understand why the studio would pay out more money for something so inferior."

Bebe looked at her secretary sharply. "I'll go through them. Did you find anything else?"

"I'm waiting for the balance of the contracts to come over from legal. If you want my opinion, I think everyone around here is overpaid, from the janitor to the guards at the gate. I don't have a college degree, so maybe that's why I don't understand why everyone, myself included, has to have a contract. But I've been told that's the way Mr. Tarz wanted it. It's great for job security from the employee's point of view, but I'm not sure it's in the studio's best interest."

Bebe nodded. She had no desire to tear down anything that had proved successful for Reuben. The studio was in the black, which was all she was interested in at the moment. Until she understood the studio's policy one hundred percent, she wasn't going to tamper with anything, and that included employment contracts.

Bebe dove into the mound of folders on her desk while Willie snoozed contentedly under her desk. By four o'clock she had a fairly good idea how scripts were acquired and why some were chosen over others that were rejected outright.

Two things happened when she tossed the last folder onto her "finished" pile: Tillie ushered Nellie Bishop into her office and at the same time announced that the United States Army was on the phone. Bebe blinked in surprise and motioned Nellie to sit down across from her desk. On the telephone she announced herself briskly and then listened while the person at the other end of the line boomed out his request.

"General Barrows, let me see if I have this straight. You want my studio to make three featured shorts with scantily clad girls selling war bonds. You did say scantily clad, did you not?" She listened carefully. "I see; you want female Uncle Sam outfits on the girls, short skirts full of sparkles and pretty smiles. You want the shorts filmed at actual bond rallies and

not here at the studio.'' She looked up to see Tillie holding a
card with huge dollar signs on it and had to bite down on her
lower lip to keep from laughing. ''Gratis, General! Tell me
something, how many of the other studios turned you down?''
This time she did laugh when the general sputtered into the
phone. ''Everyone here at the studio is extremely patriotic, but
our stars have contracts and clauses in them that forbid outside
employment. . . . Of course I understand that we control our
stars. I'll take the matter up with our board tomorrow and get
back to you by the end of the day.'' She copied down a phone
number where the general could be reached. When she hung
up the phone she signaled to Tillie.

''Find out who handles any charity work we do and which
department could take this on. I think we should do it, what
do you think, Nellie?'' she asked suddenly.

''I think it's wonderful!'' Nellie cried. ''It's very good exposure for the studio and patriotic as well. The public will
double its efforts. I'll be glad to help. When I'm finished in
production, of course. On my own time,'' she added.

Bebe smiled at her. ''That's very nice of you, Nellie. My
goodness, you're all grown-up. It's been years since I've seen
you. Your doting father was telling me this morning how pretty
you've become, and he didn't exaggerate a bit.'' Nellie flushed
becomingly. ''I was sorry to hear about your mother.''

Nellie lowered her eyes. ''Thank you. It . . . it was so sudden. She was so . . . so very unhappy for a long time.'' She
sniffed delicately. ''If you don't mind, I'd rather not talk about
it.''

''I'm sorry. Tell me, are you grasping how things are done
in production?'' Bebe asked.

Nellie nodded. ''More or less, but I have a lot to learn. I'm
going to be an apprentice for a long time. It's fascinating
work.''

Bebe riffled through the folders on her desk. When she found
what she was looking for, she handed the folder to Nellie. ''Do
you by any chance know why Jane rejected this?''

Nellie pretended to read the proposal inside the manila folder,
although she knew exactly what it was. Jane had asked her
opinion on it, and she'd criticized the outline as being rather
silly, nothing more than an inane idea for a Saturday afternoon
serial. Of course she'd known that Jane had been considering
the proposal seriously until she'd voiced her opinion. Now she
realized that Bebe must like it, too, since it was the only file

she had pulled from the thick stack on her desk. After a moment's hesitation, Nellie gambled.

"I think *Danny's Raiders* is a wonderful idea. As a matter of fact, I even interjected some ideas of my own for plots. I'm not so old I don't remember what it was like to be fourteen and fifteen. I also made one other suggestion, that Danny should have two girls in his group to offset the whole thing. Girls go to matinees, too, and they like to have adventures just the way boys do. I told Jane that young people with brothers in the military needed some respite from their concerns. Maybe I'm not expressing this in the right way." She was careful to allow just the right amount of anxiousness to creep into her voice. She relaxed when she saw Bebe smile.

"Did Philippe see this?" Bebe asked.

Nellie's mind raced again, and she gambled a second time. "I don't know if he actually saw it, but we talked about it. He liked the idea, we both did, but because Jane is such a good friend of his father's, he was reluctant to . . . step on her toes. Uncle Reuben has told me more than once that Jane never makes mistakes. It wasn't my place to . . . you know." Nellie hesitated, then added delicately, "You won't say anything to Jane about what I just said, will you? She isn't . . . what I mean is she . . . she isn't that easy to . . . work with."

Bebe had never really known Jane Perkins on a personal level, but she'd heard Reuben talk about her often enough. He'd ranked her so high in the industry, she'd been jealous of the plain woman with the plain-sounding name. Jealous of her ability and her position at the studio.

Now, as head of the studio, she had final script approval, as did Reuben. Should she go ahead and option *Danny's Raiders* and undermine Jane, or should she let it go? She had a gut feeling about the script, an instinct that said it would work if properly developed, and Nellie's suggestion was a good idea. After all, young people and women were the biggest moviegoers.

Nellie was sitting on the edge of her chair waiting for Bebe's decision, and something in the young girl's eyes—some hint of speculative anticipation, perhaps—led Bebe to rise, signaling the end of their meeting.

"I understand, Nellie. Of course I won't say anything. And I'll let you know when I've made my decision on *Danny's Raiders*. We'll talk again . . . soon."

Nellie's direct gaze shifted to the open door as she stood in response to Bebe's dismissal. She's annoyed, Bebe thought. The tight set of the girl's slim shoulders reminded Bebe of herself when she was her age. When things didn't go the way she planned, she used to draw into herself, tightening her shoulders as she started to scheme to make things work the way she wanted.

Bebe laughed at herself when the door closed. Nellie was Daniel's daughter. No, Rajean's daughter, she corrected herself. In the future she would have to pay attention to that.

Sensing his mistress's distress, Willie whined and slinked out from his position under the desk. He belly-whopped over to Bebe, his tail thumping on the carpet. "I don't know why, Willie, but that girl unsettles me," Bebe murmured. Willie growled low in his throat, his way of showing support.

Nellie was bristling with suppressed anger when she returned to her cubicle outside Jane's office. She hadn't meant to come back to the office, but she'd stupidly forgotten her purse. Jane was talking on the other side of the partition, and she listened shamelessly, knowing her boss was unaware of her presence. Some sixth sense alerted her that Jane's phone call had something to do with her. Her eyes narrowed as she continued to listen.

"It isn't any one thing, and I can't quite put my finger on what it is exactly that's bothering me. She's amenable, she takes direction well, she asks the right questions, perhaps she asks too many, I don't know . . . more than anything, I'm just not comfortable with her. Sometimes I have this feeling that she's waiting . . . waiting for me to make a mistake. And then she'll pounce. Tell me I'm being silly."

Nellie's hands clenched into tight fists. She *was* talking about her. But to whom? Bebe? Certainly not to her father or Philippe. A friend, obviously a close one, someone she confided in. Nellie continued to listen as Jane's voice changed subtly.

"Daniel is a gift, something I never thought I'd have in this life. Every time I see him it's like getting a present; now, isn't that silly?" She laughed softly. "Oh, Aaron was nice and comfortable, but there was no sparkle, no deep, heavy breathing, if you know what I mean." She laughed again, an intimate sound, one shared only between friends who understood each other. "Daniel makes my blood sing, and at my age that's a remarkable feat, don't you think?"

Nellie wished she could hear the person on the other end of the line. Jane's voice changed again, the worry and anxiety was back. "Daniel thinks the world of his daughter. He thinks she's more wonderful than peanut butter, and, yes, you're right, it's going to be a problem. He talks about her all the time, and he should, she's his daughter and he feels this tremendous responsibility toward her." Jane's voice grew stronger, more confident. "I'm sure I'm imagining things. Look, I have to go now; I'm meeting Daniel and I want to freshen up. . . . Good heavens, Gloria, I'm sorry if I gave you that impression. I don't think the girl is gunning for me or anything like that. . . . Yes, I understand, and I will be careful. Look, I'm sorry if I burdened you with . . . it was . . . I needed to talk to someone. Let's just forget the whole thing. Lunch on Friday sounds great. Off the lot, okay. I'll meet you at the gate and we'll drive down to the wharf for a nice fish lunch. Remember, fish isn't fattening."

Nellie moved quickly away from her cubicle. If Jane was going to freshen up, she would pass her desk on her way to the restroom. Quickly she left the office and ran across the lot to her father's office, zigzagging so she wouldn't bump into the work crews on their way home. When she reached the top of the steps she was gasping for breath. She burst through the private door to Daniel's office and planted a loud kiss on her father's cheek.

"I ran all the way," she said. "I wanted to get here before you left. I'm taking you to dinner, and I don't want to hear you say no. I never see you anymore. You're always with Jane. I might as well have stayed in Washington," she babbled, knowing guilt would get her what she wanted.

She was right, Daniel thought guiltily. Over the past few weeks he'd virtually abandoned his daughter. And now she wanted to spend a little time with him, take him to dinner for the pleasure of his company. How miserable she looked, how unhappy. My God, how could he have neglected her like this?

"Listen, honey, dinner sounds wonderful," he said warmly. "I'll even let you pay if you insist, but would you mind if Jane comes with us? I did make plans with her, and this is pretty much last minute."

"I don't mind," Nellie said listlessly, all the sparkle leaving her face. "It's, oh, I don't know, I see her all day at the office and I sort of wanted to be alone with you. But I don't mind. Look, Daddy, this was last minute, too, so why don't you go ahead with Jane. I'll take Philippe to dinner."

Daniel's heart turned over. How woebegone she looked. Jane

would understand if he explained it to her, and maybe if he and Nellie made an early night of it, he could see Jane later. She was so understanding; that was one of the things he loved about her.

"Not on your life," he said, squeezing her hand fondly. "I'll call Jane now and tell her you're taking me out. She'll understand. Honey, I'm so sorry I've neglected you the way I have. From now on we're going to do more things together. I promise. Forgive me?"

"Oh, Daddy, you are so wonderful! It's just that I get blue sometimes. I've been thinking about Mother all day today, and I guess it sort of got to me late this afternoon when I saw Bebe. You're all I have in the whole world and . . ." Nellie dabbed at her eyes and swallowed the way she had when she was little. "I . . . I'll go powder my nose while you call Jane."

Jane hugged her arms to her chest when she hung up the phone. How cold she felt . . . how very angry. She didn't like the feeling. She didn't like Nellie Bishop, it was that simple. Nellie Bishop was starting to frighten the hell out of her.

All day she'd looked forward to seeing Daniel, had worked conversations through her mind, things they would say to each other, imagined looks, soft touches. Dammit, she needed Daniel. Tonight was supposed to be special, at least she'd thought so. And now this. Something about it bothered her . . . it seemed a little too coincidental, Nellie's overwhelming desire to spend time with her father on this of all nights.

Impulsively, she picked up the phone and called Philippe's office. Without meaning to she blurted out, "Will you be seeing Nellie this evening?"

Philippe's voice was cold and sounded hostile to Jane's ears. For God's sake, what was *his* problem?

"Our plans were canceled." You should know, he wanted to say, you're the reason they were canceled, you and your determination to introduce Nellie to every available man in California. "Is there anything else?" he asked curtly.

"No, I'm sorry I bothered you, Philippe. It wasn't all that important, it can wait till morning."

The shiny black telephone glared at Jane. Suddenly she hated it. But how could she blame a telephone for what was happening? It was merely an instrument people used to convey their thoughts and opinions.

Jane felt shame and rejection as she prepared to leave the office for a lonely evening at home. And she wasn't overreacting; she wasn't being a silly, jealous woman. What she was, she decided later in the evening, was a frightened woman, afraid of losing the man she loved. She tried to quiet her jangling thoughts by remembering Daniel's last words. He'd said he would call or stop by if it wasn't too late. Yes, that's what would see her through the evening.

It was a quarter past ten when Daniel picked up the phone to call Jane. Nellie snatched the phone out of his hand. "Oh, Daddy, you are so inconsiderate. It's ten-fifteen, Jane is probably asleep. She was complaining today about how tired she was. She's probably sleeping right this minute. You'll wake her, and then you'll feel just terrible. I swear, Daddy, I'm going to have to teach you how to treat a lady," she said in mock seriousness.

"I suppose you're right, but I did say I'd call," Daniel said lamely.

"Daddy, ladies, especially ladies like Jane, do not sit around waiting for men to call late at night. Aaron was always a perfect gentleman."

"Aaron who?" Daniel asked.

"I guess he was her last gentleman friend. I heard her telling someone today what a gentleman he is and how fond she was of him. Maybe he's a business associate, and I . . . She's very fond of you, Daddy," she said hastily when she saw her father's face darken.

Without another word, Daniel kissed his daughter good night and went upstairs to bed. He would take his daughter's advice. She might be young, but she was a woman, and women understood other women. Men, as Reuben had pointed out, never did and never would understand the female species.

When the phone rang at eleven-thirty Nellie snatched it up on the first ring. As she'd expected, it was Jane. Nellie made her voice sound sleepy and groggy. "Wha . . . time is it? . . . My goodness, Jane, Daddy fell asleep the minute we got home, around eight-thirty or so. Do you want me to wake him? I will if you want me to, but Daddy is a bear when you wake him out of a sound sleep."

"No, don't wake him, Nellie. Just leave a message that I called."

"I'll do that." Nellie deliberately scribbled something on the pad by the phone that even she couldn't decipher. And why should she be expected to remember phone calls late at night, especially those that woke her out of a sound sleep?

Nellie waited a full five minutes before she picked up the phone a second time. She dialed Philippe's number from memory and waited until he answered on the fifth ring. His voice was gruff, and he sounded annoyed. Well, she would change all that in a second, Nellie thought. "Hi, Philippe, I just called to say good night. I hope you aren't angry with me for canceling our plans this evening. I had no other choice, you know." She rushed on, not giving Philippe a chance to respond. "I kept wishing I were with you and wondering what you were doing. I just got home this minute and decided to call you. What did you do all evening?"

Philippe's voice thawed and grew warm. "I read most of the evening. I wrote a letter to my mother I know will probably never reach her. A quiet evening. Did you enjoy yours?" He hadn't meant to ask the question, but he wanted to know.

"It was all right. He smiled all night long. I guess movie stars have to do that. He had so many teeth, Philippe, he reminded me of a shark. He talked a lot about himself and how much money he made and how really, really famous he was going to be someday. He said I was prettier than a movie star. Dinner was terribly expensive. I hardly ate a bite. You know, Philippe, now that I'm home I can't even remember what he looks like." She giggled, and Philippe laughed, which was exactly the response she wanted.

They talked for another ten minutes or so and then hung up. Philippe would dream about her all night long, and she would dream, too—about attending the Academy Award ceremonies as the wife of the most powerful man in Hollywood. In her dream she'd wear a virginal white gown, but when the time actually came, she'd wear a stunning red sheath, off the shoulder, and full of sequins or maybe rhinestones. Diamonds in her ears, of course, and on her wrists. She'd have her shoes dyed to match the dress and full of the same glitter, but maybe just on the heels so they shimmered and sparkled when she walked. Smiling, she reached out to sleep, welcoming it.

In the morning she was disappointed that her sleep had been dreamless.

Chapter Twenty-two

THE WINTER SUN BATHED THE FRENCH COUNTRYSIDE IN A dazzling, blinding light, but only for a moment. Clouds, thick and gray, were moving in, and new snow would fall, hopefully enough to obliterate the footprints of the Resistance members as they made their way in a single file to what they had been told was a deserted village—deserted by the French, but not by the Germans, who manned a command post outside the village church.

These members were new, so new that Mickey and Yvette had yet to be told their code names. The other members they'd come to know over the last months had either left for other networks, been reassigned, or joined God. Mickey dreaded the day she and Yvette would reach a rendezvous with no one to greet them, give them orders, share the latest news, and tell them yes, France would rise again. Her thoughts had never carried her beyond that particular moment.

She was cold now, numb actually, and hungrier than she'd ever been in her life. As always, she tried not to think about food and her stomach and a warm bath. Such luxuries were not for her at this time. Months earlier she'd given up the game she'd played with herself when they rested, the game of Reuben and Philippe, reliving memories of happier times. It had taken

Yvette and her stern, waspish tongue warning her she would get them all killed because her mind was not on the business at hand, and she'd been right. She wanted no loyal Frenchman's death on her conscience. There was no time for reveries of any kind if one wanted to stay alive.

Mickey felt her group had done well considering they were not trained soldiers. By military standards their efforts might seem puny, but she knew, as the others did, that people continued to live because of their efforts. The Basil network of which they were now members was more refined, with members who knew how to create believable identity papers, and tailors who could craft a German uniform by hand. Somewhere there was a storehouse of confiscated German weapons, uniforms, transmitters, and anything else the Boche had unwillingly given up to the patriots. So far, though, she and her colleagues had been unable to avail themselves of these necessities because the storehouse was outside the perimeters of the Basil network. Others used it and lived to tell about it, which was all to the good, she thought.

It was snowing now, large, feathery flakes that would get smaller as the wind shifted. Once she'd thought snow beautiful, so clean and pure, but she'd since seen it stained with her countrymen's blood, seen others frozen to death. It was hateful now, but unlike the rain, the snow was a smothering blanket to sound that they used to their advantage. It would help them now when they sent out a member to reconnoiter the village. If they were lucky enough to eliminate the command post, they could build a fire and warm themselves. There would be food, and it wouldn't matter if it was German food or not. Silently, she prayed that there would be enough for the second group of children due to arrive tomorrow.

This would mark the second trip over the mountains to safety. The first trek across the Pyrenees had been in September, and weather conditions had been tolerable; only one grave had been dug.

Mickey shuddered. "Yvette," she whispered, "this weather . . . the higher we go the worse it will be. The children . . . even we won't be able . . . There must be a better way."

"There is no other way," Yvette grumbled. "I think God will watch over the lot of us. They say He watches over drunks and little children. And foolish women," she added.

"It's not myself I'm worried about, it's the children." Mickey's eyes misted. "I can still see myself digging that grave with my hands and those children, their sad eyes. They trusted us, and we . . . we lost the little one.''

"We didn't just lose him, Mickey, we lost him to God—and that's what makes the difference. I heard you tell Philippe on more than one occasion when he was little that when a child died, it was because God needed another angel. Did you lie to your son?''

"Stop it," Mickey panted as she came to a halt behind the man in front of her. "I was responsible for that child, and he died. It is on my conscience. I saw the way the others looked at me. I'll see their eyes until the day I die.''

Yvette was saved from the sharp retort that was on her lips when the man in front of them turned. "There is no room for martyrs in this movement, nor for foolish sentimentality. Take my advice and don't look at their eyes and don't ask them their names, either. You are not their God, their mother, or their relative. You are their guide and nothing more.''

Mickey shrugged. The man was right, and she knew Yvette meant well, but that wouldn't change the way she felt and thought. Children were children. Someday these same children would be France's future. Never again did she want to see condemnation in a child's eyes when he looked at her. Never!

By this time the fat, lacy snowflakes had given way to hard dots of icy rain. It would change back to fine snow shortly, Mickey decided, looking around her anxiously. They were waiting for a man named Gage to return from the village. He wasn't really a man at all, but a seventeen-year-old university student who claimed to know the village as well as he knew his prayers. There was a tunnel, he said, that had been dug during the Great War that led from the rectory to the church and then to the hilltop a mile from the village. He'd argued vehemently with André, the group's leader, that the command post would be in the belfry of the church, for it was the highest vantage point, offering visibility to both ends of the road as well as to the entire village.

In the end André had acquiesced, but only because Yvette had given him not one but two resounding kicks to his shins. "If the boy knows the area, he's the one to go. I don't plan to stand here and freeze, so send him on his way," she'd said in the voice she'd used to order her husband about. André had waved his hand, a signal that the youth was to go ahead and report back as soon as possible.

"It's been too long," one of the men whispered much later.

"Too long," whispered another. "The snow is coming down harder. Maybe he can't find his way back."

"You talk too much," Yvette snapped. "He's young, his eyes are sharp, and he's resilient, not like this group of old men and women. He said he'll come back, and he will." He had to come back; she'd given the order for him to go. Unlike Mickey, who relied on prayers, she was depending on luck. Now she crossed her fingers in their thick gloves.

When the boy returned an eternity later, he was as frisky as a newborn pup, his eyes shining with his news. He addressed himself to Yvette, probably because she reminded him of his mother, Mickey thought sourly.

"Their machine guns are in the belfry, as I thought they would be. I was standing right under them in the tunnel. I heard everything they said. There are six of them, I think. The floor was warm, so they have a fire. No smoke can be seen the way the snow is blowing."

"What did they say, these bastard Germans?" André demanded.

The boy gave a Gallic shrug. "I don't understand German," he said. "Do you?"

"How do we get in there?"

"Through the tunnel, of course. It opens in the small room off the sanctuary. I think they're clustered at the back of the church, near the confessionals. There's more room there. They're using lamplight. I cracked the trapdoor and it was black as hell. I know of no other way. Besides, the snow is worsening," he said pointedly.

He was their Pied Piper; they were his mesmerized followers, slipping and clawing their way to the hill opening that would lead them into the tunnel. Muttered curses and sharp expletives were strangled in the swirling snow, all made by the men in the marching column. Yvette kept her lips clamped together, as did Mickey. I hope I live long enough to talk about this, she thought crazily. To her dismay she'd found out over the past months that men were not the superior force she'd believed them to be all these years. After all, she and Yvette were alive and had done everything that these men had done, possibly more. But unlike the men they hadn't whined or cried or complained except to one another.

The church was large by most village standards, Mickey reflected a while later when she peeked through the partially open door into the sanctuary. It had eight pews divided into fours, made from Austrian walnut, and in the back of the church a cavernous fireplace and stove that could be cooked on, as these filthy Germans were doing now. The aroma of frying sausage and potatoes made her dizzy. In the faint yellow light she could see guns and boxes of ammunition stacked against the wall near the one confessional. God alone knew what the Germans had stashed behind the confessional curtain. Quickly she blessed herself, asking forgiveness for carrying her own gun into the house of the Lord. It was sacrilegious. She wouldn't think about the killing that would happen shortly.

André motioned for the patriots to gather together in a circle. His whispers sounded harsh in the quiet sanctuary. "We must wait till we see how often they go to the belfry and how often they transmit. It's possible we'll be here for a very long time, so get comfortable. Gage will monitor the door."

"We are going to take one prisoner, aren't we?" Gage asked excitedly, his boyish face lighting in anticipation. "Since none of us speaks German well enough to use the wireless, we need a prisoner, and we need someone close enough to hear what they're saying. It would help if we could watch their transmittal."

The boy was right, Mickey thought morosely. "I speak German—quite well, as a matter of fact," she said. "I can listen, and Yvette, if she can get close enough, will . . . she can try to get a feel for his touch. But it's tricky."

André scowled at his little band of freedom fighters. Through no fault of his own, he seemed to be losing control. The eager young boy had shown him up several times, and the red-haired woman had a tongue like a viper. Christ, he hated working with women; they were too emotional and temperamental in his opinion. Only four months with the Resistance and already his head was clotted with too many deaths, half of them women. These two, though, he admitted, were different, older and more dedicated, if that was possible. Although he worried about them, he'd never let them know it, for they'd think him soft and weak. He worried about the boy, too, who hadn't even tasted life, probably had never had a woman in bed. For a moment he felt unsure of himself as the others looked up at him expectantly. His scowl deepened. There was no room here for ego or personalities, it was what was best for the lot of them and their country.

He moved closer to Gage. "Is there any way to reach the back of the church without going down the center aisle?"

Gage shook his head. "If the wind picks up a little more and they keep on drinking, one of us could crawl on his belly under the pew and get close enough to hear what they're saying." He shrugged; it was the best he could offer in the way of a solution.

One of us, Mickey thought. What he meant was, she should be the one to crawl on her belly since she was the only one who understood German. Yvette would transmit. There was no other choice. Without being told, she knew that their weapons would be left in the sanctuary. A knife up her sleeve would be her only protection. Without a word, she nodded at André.

"We'll give you an hour," he told her. "At the end of that time one of you crawls back here to tell us what those bastards are saying. Take off your boots and remove your jackets. Buttons make noise and boots might hit the footrests. Maman to the left, Chapeau to the right. One hour. Go!"

Mickey's heart pounded as she dropped to the floor to crawl through the half-open door. She bellied her way across the front of the altar, blessing herself and then slithering down the step to the communion rail, fumbling with her numb hands to find the latch on the center gate. The latch clicked beneath her fingers when she held her breath, then gently, she inched it backward, allowing just enough room to crawl through.

For a moment she hesitated; had her movements alerted those at the back of the church? A light touch on the heel of her foot by Yvette urged her on. By now she was in front of the communion rail, straining her eyes to see exactly where the footrests were. One to each side of the pew . . . If the last parishioner had raised it on leaving, there would be no problem. When she reached the first pew, her gloved hands straight in front of her, she crawled forward. The footrest was up, as were the second and third. Five more to go. The fourth was down, without enough room to crawl over it. She sucked in her breath as she gripped the hard wood in both her hands. Then she heard a sound, a whispery, scratching sound as the footrest moved upward. Mother of God, it wasn't the footrest at all, but a rat crawling over her arm! She wanted to scream, to drop the footrest and run. Her eyes were wild, her arms stiff as the rat scurried up her arm to her shoulder and down her back. It would be right in Yvette's face. She felt rather than heard Yvette move, then something sailed up and past the pew she was under. The rat made a screeching sound that was followed by an arc of light and a gunshot so loud it deafened Mickey's ears.

"A rat, nothing more," she heard one of the soldiers say in German.

After a few moments, she began to move again, slower this time, her eyes straining for other vermin. When she reached the seventh pew the footrest was down, which was fine this time, as it afforded her more protection in the faint light and shadows at the back of the church. When she moved to the side so Yvette could crawl next to her, she could feel her friend's trembling body. She reached out to offer a comforting pat on her arm.

The Germans were playing cards, eating, and drinking. Their talk was desultory—the storm, one soldier's wife who was due to have a baby by the new year, a superior they all seemed to detest, a woman named Renée who, according to one of the soldiers, was the commandant's French mistress and fucked like a rabbit.

Boots scraped the hard wooden floor and chairs were pushed back suddenly, the sound like thunder in the quiet church.

"Ach, no fool will be out in this weather. Who will know if I climb that damn belfry? You can't see your hand in front of your face," one of the soldiers grumbled.

"Orders," another said harshly. "These French are fools. We do what we are told. I want to see my wife again. Quickly, so I can transmit."

It was impossible to tell how long they remained under the pews—perhaps close to an hour, Mickey thought. They'd been in the sanctuary for well over an hour, which meant the Germans must be transmitting every three hours.

Mickey's entire body was so numb, she thought she'd never be able to move again. The floor was ice cold with drafts blowing from every direction. She could feel herself start to shiver.

The German returned from the bell tower, his boots stomping across the floor. "I told you there is nothing out there but snow. These French, they are probably lighting Christmas trees," he snarled.

Mickey's eyes widened in the darkness. Christmas! Surely it wasn't Christmas. If it really was Christmas, that meant they would . . . be killing . . . she didn't know for sure that it was Christmas. Killing is necessary no matter what day it is, she cautioned herself.

"Send your message, Kort, so we can divide our shift. I need some sleep," ordered the officer from the belfry, tired now and half-angry. "And while you're at it, find out how much longer we're going to stay in this damned church. There are no R.A.F. pilots around here, or we'd have seen them. There are no tracks in the snow, and we searched every damned house in this miserable village. They went over the mountains. They're probably all dead by now." His voice was angrier now and sullen.

"Yes, my general," the transmitter mocked as he prepared to send his message to God only knew where.

Mickey could feel Yvette tense at her side. She knew her ears were straining to hear the taps of the keys.

Fifteen minutes later they were back in the sanctuary, where it was colder still. Mickey slipped into her heavy jacket, grateful for the warmth it offered. "At least two of them will sleep, possibly three," she whispered.

André nodded. "You two will be the last in line. The transmitter stays alive. Which one is he?" he asked Yvette.

"We saw only boots, nothing above the knees. He has very large feet, and he sits like this," she said, demonstrating a wide-legged stool position.

"I think it's Christmas," Mickey said in a hushed voice. The others were silent as they digested her words, each of them remembering other Christmases with family and friends.

"It makes no difference," André said with a catch in his voice. Mickey wondered then how old he was and if he had a family. Suddenly she didn't want to know; it was enough to know he was human and had feelings he kept hidden like the rest of them.

André turned to stare at his group. In a low, harsh voice he whispered, "For thousands of years a church has been designated as a place of sanctuary. This is our church, it belongs to every French Catholic in France, and we are protecting it from those German killers. I don't know if God will forgive us or not for what we're about to do. I hope He will," he said, blessing himself.

Mickey felt calm suddenly, almost peaceful as she dropped to her belly. God would forgive them because they were His children. He alone knew there was no other way.

The Germans were sluggish with the warmth of the fire and the wine and food they'd consumed. It was to the partisans' advantage as they attacked—brutally. Mickey thought she would never get used to the sight of blood spilling from a man's throat, or the sound of the death gurgle, but this time she barely noticed, wondering if it really was Christmas.

Two men with braided rawhide strips around their necks were alive. Tethered as they were, they could signal only with their eyes.

"Call this one a horse's ass in German," Yvette said to Mickey as she spat in the soldier's face. "Look, see the fear in his eyes. He's afraid of us foolish French. Damn you, Mickey, say it!" she shouted. The soldier cringed, knowing his life was almost at an end. At that moment he would have confessed anything—unlike these men and women. Small in number, these partisans fought loyally and to the death. In his mind he admired them. He was a horse's ass; well, he'd been called worse in his life, mostly by his wife, who loved him dearly. Now he wished he'd told her more often how he felt about her.

"Who is the transmitter?" André asked coldly. Neither man acknowledged his question. "Let me put it to you another way: the one who does the transmitting is the one who stays alive." The man Yvette called a horse's ass jerked forward. When André nodded, the remaining German was pulled backward into the darkness of the church. There was a moment of light scuffling and then silence.

André himself tied the German to his chair, the knots in the stout rope cutting deeply into the man's wrists. He made no sound. He was alive and they needed him. For what, he didn't know, but whatever it was he would help them, for he wanted to stay alive to tell Ilsa how much he loved her.

"We get warm, we eat, and then we dispose of these miserable excuses for human beings. How nobly they died for the Third Reich. Pigs! Swine! You should all die with that paperhanging bastard. If I ever hear the words *Heil Hitler* again, I will shoot to kill on the spot!" André cried passionately.

Mickey had heard it all before, so many times that she found herself drifting into sleep with the warmth of the fireplace at her back. These hard-fighting Frenchmen gave voice to their thoughts because they felt so helpless against the German machine. Now she would sleep, her belly full of the thick greasy sausage and heavy black bread. When she woke she would cook for the children and make up parcels of food to take with them.

For three days they ate, slept, and ate again and again as

they waited for the children, whose arrival was delayed because of the heavy snow. The German named Kort did as he was told, sending out his dispatches and receiving others. The deciphered messages made no difference to their situation, Yvette pointed out.

Mickey was busy cutting turnips and cabbage into the soup pot when she heard Kort ask André a question in his broken French. "If I tell you a safe way to get over the mountains, will you let me go free?"

Mickey finished her task and walked over to the German. "Why do you think we would believe anything you say? There are Germans all along the border. We'll find out our own way. The German hasn't been born that I would trust," she said viciously. "Unless of course you want to come with us," she added.

"No . . . yes . . . If that is what is necessary for me to remain alive, I will go with you. Your guide."

"No!" Yvette shouted.

"Why not, Yvette?" Mickey said. "Think about it. He could carry the food and, from time to time, the children when they tire. He is strong, burly, well fed, and he's lived well on our land and our food. I think we should take him. I think he should pay for our country's generosity. Look how strong he is, my friend. He'll be better than a pack mule. We will load him down so heavily he cannot escape. And"—she wagged a finger under Yvette's nose—"he will walk in front of you." To the German she said in a voice she could have used to discuss the weather conditions, "My friend hates Germans; they slaughtered her husband in Paris because he walked in front of the commandant. She held him in her arms and watched him die. She watched that same commandant kick her husband in the ribs when he didn't die fast enough."

Kort stared up at Yvette and in the whole of his life had never seen such hatred. Fear crawled around his belly, but he knew he would do what these two women asked of him, do it gladly if they allowed him to live. "I will give you no trouble," he said.

"André?"

"As you say, he will be better than a pack mule. I say take him, but watch him." Later he would tell Mickey to kill the German bastard the moment they set foot on Spanish soil.

Nine children arrived the following day, cold and hungry, but warmly dressed for the bitter weather outside. Mickey and

Yvette bustled about ladling out food and spreading blankets and pillows by the fire. Young Gage had proved to be an apt scavenger, looting the village houses in anticipation of the children's arrival.

If we could only stay here for the winter, Mickey mused as she stared at the sleeping children. There was certainly enough food in the root cellars and plenty of firewood. And more than enough Germans to go around. Her thoughts were bitter and angry as she stared at the defenseless children.

"I'd say the oldest is eight, possibly nine," Yvette whispered. "I wonder which ones we'll lose."

"Yvette, for God's sake, we haven't even left yet and already you're worrying about . . . about . . ."

"You're thinking the same thing, don't deny it, Michelene," Yvette said calmly.

A sound, foreign to their ears in the small church, startled them. The men at the table stopped talking, and André ran to the door, his rifle in readiness, Gage on the other side. When they heard the sound again, it came from the direction of the children.

"It's all right; one of the little ones is making sounds in his sleep," Mickey said quietly as she made her way to the little group of children. One boy with golden curls was sleeping on his side, his hand under his cheek. An angel, Mickey thought, a sweet little angel no more than five or six that God was going to put to the test. Bitter tears scalded her eyes.

"So," she muttered, "this is what we all heard." Leaning over, she opened the buttons of the child's bulging coat. A dog with warm, wet eyes stared out from his nest against the little boy's chest. Careful not to awaken the sleeping child, Mickey gently withdrew the small dog and held him up against her cheek. How warm and soft he was. His little pink tongue crept out of his mouth to lick at her, hesitantly at first and then lavishly.

"*Mon Dieu!* What are we to do with this little rascal?" Mickey demanded.

The men all looked at one another. There was none among them who had not had a dog as a child. They looked on helplessly, not wanting to be the first to say the dog had to be gotten rid of.

"Food, Yvette. This warm bundle needs food and some water," Mickey ordered in a strangled voice. She wiped at the tears on her cheeks, remembering Jake and Dolly.

At the table the men were making quiet wagers as to whether or not they would take the dog with them over the mountains. The German Kort offered to carry the dog along with his other load, but Mickey ignored him. Of course he would be eager for the dog to go along, so he could bark and give away their positions. But if the dog's sense of smell was developed, it could work to their advantage. Puppy or not, the animal would be devoted to the little boy who had carried him through the snow. He would smell danger if it threatened his master.

Sitting on their haunches, Mickey and Yvette watched the little dog gobble down more food than they themselves had eaten all day. When he was finished he lapped water from a cracked cup, then looked at them solemnly and piddled at their knees. Hearing no sharp reprimand, he wobbled over to the boy with the golden curls and within seconds was snug inside the boy's coat.

"This could be a problem," Yvette said, watching.

"If we leave him behind, he could die. He's too little to forage for himself," Mickey said glumly.

"Yes, but if he barks when silence is called for, we could *all* die," Yvette reminded her.

"Yes, that is a possibility. We must decide, you and I. The dog is probably the only thing left to this little angel. I cannot be the one to . . . to . . . say . . . I cannot be the one who says he must be left behind."

"Well, don't expect me to be the monster."

Mickey smiled. "So where does that leave us?"

"I guess he goes with us," Yvette said with a sigh. "We can take turns carrying him. He's a beauty, isn't he?"

"It's been settled," Mickey crooned to the little dog who was peeking out of the boy's coat. He seemed to understand her words. His eyes closed and he was asleep in seconds, safe and secure against his young master's beating heart.

It was three days before the snow let up. Three long days for the children to eat and sleep and get warm. Three days to become attached to the frisky pup who was now everyone's friend, even the German's. Three long days with enough hours to become attached to the solemn-eyed children who would be Mickey's charges. They were so little, so young, she thought. She'd laid aside any last doubts about the German even though Yvette hadn't changed her mind about him.

Kort didn't need prodding when it came time to make his

transmission. Mickey carefully translated the French words into German, and Yvette stood over him, her pistol pressed against his temple as she watched him make the three-hour transmittal. And always it was the same message: Heavy snow conditions, the village was deserted, and there was no sign of any R.A.F. flyers or French partisans.

One more transmittal was scheduled for the noon hour, during which Kort was to ask questions and read off a statement Mickey had translated for him. He was to say two of his men spotted tracks in the snow and followed them south, and he had not heard from them since. Mickey and the children would start out immediately, heading north, while the other partisans headed west. They would all have a three-hour start.

"The question is," Yvette said, "will they believe him?"

Mickey translated the question.

Kort nodded. "I see no reason for them not to believe me. My superiors have a great respect for your Resistance movement. Your people have killed many of my countrymen and given safe passage to many English flyers. They will believe me," he said defiantly, his eyes on Yvette and the pistol in her hand. For some reason he wasn't nearly as afraid of the men in this group as he was of this redheaded witch.

The children and the dog were fed one last time. Trips to the privy were urged, coats buttoned, caps fastened tightly under little chins, and gloves pulled up under coat sleeves. The fires would remain, for no German would care about a church burning down, and the equipment was packed and ready. They would all exit at the same time.

Mickey fastened her eyes on the children. She knew them now, much to her sorrow. Anna with the sad eyes was going on nine and the oldest. Marie, almost the same age, cried a lot, upsetting the other children; she was the only one who wouldn't go near the dog. Bernard was seven, as was Marc. Sophie and Stephan were six-and-a-half-year-old twins who clung to each other and stayed apart from the other children. Sophie's eyes were constantly filled with tears that never spilled onto her cheeks. To her dismay, Mickey had discovered that Sophie was the leader of the two. Max, a solemn-eyed six-year-old, stayed close to his cousin Mariette, who was the same age. Bruno somehow remained outside the group of children, preferring, Mickey supposed, to get his comfort from the warm, furry little body inside his jacket.

Mickey's eyes filled with tears. How unfair that these little ones had to learn at such a tender age that they couldn't become friends with their companions. If a friend died, there would be tears and sadness, an unwillingness to continue, to live another day. God alone knew what had been drummed into their little heads when they started on their journey.

Anna was the toughest. There was determination and defiance in her eyes. A methodical girl, she ate slowly and carefully, and her manners were impeccable. At least once a day she insisted on combing her hair and washing her face. As a result she was neater than the others, and her clothes were also thicker and warmer. Twice, Mickey had heard her chastise Marie when the younger girl broke into tears, telling her to grow up and act like a proper young lady. Marie had only wept harder at the girl's criticism, and no amount of comforting could bring a smile to her face. She was not a robust child, and Mickey worried about her.

Marc and Bernard, on the other hand, were friends from the same province. Like cohorts they whispered among themselves, not caring what orders they'd been given. They ate with relish, sharing their food with each other, although Marc was the more generous of the two. These two, Mickey knew, would be no problem; they would look out for each other.

Sophie and her tears puzzled Mickey, as did Stephan. They were exceptionally close, out of fear, she decided. She had yet to see the color of Stephan's eyes. Both appeared to be physically healthy, and she prayed that their mental condition wouldn't deteriorate with the long trip ahead of them. Sophie was much too young to shoulder the responsibility of her twin. Max and Mariette were little more than babies who sucked their thumbs constantly and should have been playing in a sandbox in the south of France with their mothers looking on indulgently. Although both appeared to be healthy, their eyes were trustful one moment, and filled with a deep sadness the next.

If she had a favorite, it would be Bruno, who was a chatty, sturdy little boy who said whatever popped into his head. If any tricks were to be played, Bruno would be the one to play them, with his mischievous eyes and wicked little smile. The others shunned him, possibly because of the warm, furry little dog he clutched to his chest.

It was time now for what Yvette called the children's marching orders. Standing tall, she saluted smartly to the group of children. "I am your general, and as such you must take my orders. Listen sharply, for our lives are at stake, and not one of us can make a mistake. We are going on a very long, very hard journey. You are soldiers now and must be brave and strong. There will be no talking whatsoever. Mademoiselle Mickey and I will speak only in English. If you speak English, you may talk; if not, you must be silent. Bruno, do you understand what I just said?'' The little boy nodded meekly. ''And the dog, he must not bark. If he barks, other soldiers, the Germans, will find us.''

''Do not worry, mademoiselle, my dog barks only in French, not English,'' Bruno said, grinning. ''I am ready, and I wish to be your lieutenant.''

''Then that is what you shall be,'' Mickey said with a catch in her voice. ''You will walk with me. Remember now, we speak only English from this moment on.''

''Fall in,'' Yvette ordered. When the children didn't move she shooed them out the door like pesky chickens.

The German waited for his instructions. ''In front of me, all the way,'' Yvette said, trying to hide her smile at the way he was loaded down. She felt a moment's grudging respect when the man moved off, his steps sure and firm.

Days later, when Mickey and her group stopped at the foot of the Pyrenees, she thought her heart would thump out of her chest in fright. In September the mountains hadn't looked this monstrous, and the children had been older. She gazed at a wall of solid rock, slippery with snow. It seemed to go up, up, up to the snow-capped peaks. The last time she'd been stupid, confident in her ability to conquer the unknown, but now that she knew what lay ahead, she felt stark terror.

''It is impossible, Yvette,'' she whispered. ''I don't even know if I can make it. They are so little, and it is so bitterly cold.'' Yvette nodded miserably.

''We must go now,'' Kort said briskly. ''There is a border patrol less than two klics from here. Do not think about how treacherous and frightening it is. Take one step and then another. Do not look up and do not look down. Instruct the children now!''

Yvette bit down on her lower lip. Kort was right. She nodded at Mickey, who shepherded the children into a small knot. She spoke quickly, but her voice was soothing.

Marie hung back, tears streaming down her cheeks. Anna stared at her in disgust. ''Leave her behind,'' she said in excellent English.

Startled by the girl's words, Mickey turned to face her. "You speak English?"

"And German and Italian, and I understand Spanish," the girl said soberly. "She is a baby, that one, she cries more than Sophie, and Sophie is only six. She is a coward, she whines and cries and she wets her pants." This last was said in French. Marie cried harder.

"We have no time for this," Kort said, his eyes on the sky. "We have to make camp soon, and it's going to snow again. Take some of my load, and I'll sling her over my shoulder."

Terrified, Mickey led the parade up the beginning of the rocky trail. Twice she slipped, but Anna's stiff arm against her back helped to keep her balance. Bruno trotted along at her side, his little feet nimble and sure on the rocky, slippery trail.

"I am not heartless, mademoiselle, I merely wanted her to realize how important this journey is," Anna said quietly in English. "I thought if I called her a coward, she would show some spirit."

"I know that, Anna," Mickey said, her breathing shallow and labored. "Please, no more talking."

Yvette's eyes were cold and merciless as she trailed behind Kort and the girl on his shoulder. "How is it you know this path and where the patrols are?" she snarled in broken German to the man's heaving back.

"Because I have a map," he replied. "I would have offered it to you, but you would have said it was some kind of trick. When we make camp I will give it to you if you wish."

"I damn well wish," Yvette snapped. He nodded, and her grudging respect for the German escalated.

When Mickey called a halt a long time later, it was because she herself could walk no farther. Everyone sank down gratefully and huddled together for warmth. "I'm sorry, but we can't make a fire today. Perhaps later on, and then maybe not. Do not look forward to it. What you are feeling now will just get worse," she said softly as she parceled out food for the hungry children. An extra portion was given to Bruno for his friend, who lapped it up in the blink of an eye. Grudgingly, Yvette handed Kort his share. Nodding his thanks, he ate quickly. When he was finished he handed Mickey his map. Her eyes widened as she showed it to Yvette in the thin beam of a flashlight.

"We cannot relax until we are above the tree line, and even then I am not sure we'll be safe," Kort said quietly. "I cannot carry the girl any longer. The terrain will become steep, and it will be impossible not to make sound. She must walk when we start out. You see, one-quarter of a klic from here is a patrol. Sound carries, as do sobs, in the quiet of the night.''

"Are we to believe then that you will make no sound?" Yvette asked, eyeing him contemptuously.

"I am a soldier, madame, I do not kill children. Soon I will be a father myself. Believe what you like," he replied with an air of righteous indignation.

Mickey volunteered to take the first watch, saying that only her legs were tired; her eyes and ears were keen and alert.

An amused expression on her face, she watched as Yvette strategically assigned everyone his or her own space in the tight circle. She poked Kort to indicate he was to take a position between herself and Mickey.

Satisfied that they were all more or less sleeping, Mickey settled back, her eyes on the trail that crisscrossed the one they had just left to make camp. A quarter of a kilometer wasn't much. She prayed quickly then, afraid to get too involved in supplication for fear she would miss some sound or indication that the patrol was coming closer. She wanted to think of Philippe and Reuben, but she didn't. Instead, she thought about chocolate cake, meadows filled with daisies, and a bright red wagon that Henri had once fashioned for Philippe when he was Bruno's age.

Kort had been right: it was snowing lightly now. Mickey crossed her fingers and offered up another prayer for the snow to ease off. But she knew it was an impossible plea, just as this journey was impossible.

They all heard the sounds at the same time. Mickey felt Kort grow rigid and knew Yvette had her knife at his throat. All at once she saw Anna spring to the left and clamp a hand over Marie's mouth. She could almost feel the girl's struggles as Anna used one of her legs to pin her in place. Bruno's hand snaked inside his coat to grasp the little dog's mouth. Bernard, who was next to him, also reached in and whispered, ''Let me hold his mouth, you rub his belly.''

As the German patrol grew closer, Mickey picked up three voices. She held up her fingers in front of Kort, and he nodded. They were cursing the weather, the mountain patrol, the lack of lusty women, and poor food. The anger in their voices was unmistakable. Mickey cringed, her heart pounding. It hadn't snowed enough to cover their tracks as they'd made their camp.

If the patrol used their flashlights or strayed off the trail, they would immediately see her ragtag little group.

Sophie buried her terrified face into her brother's coat sleeve. If Stephan hadn't moved his arm just then, the little girl might have been able to stifle her sneeze, but it exploded from her mouth like a gunshot.

Kort's arms shot out, knocking Yvette's knife from her hand as she reeled backward. Before either woman could stop him he was shouting to the patrol as he whisked Yvette's gun into his hand.

Yvette's eyes were murderous as Mickey prayed, "Please God, have mercy on the little ones' souls."

Chapter Twenty-three

REUBEN SIMPLY STARED, UNABLE TO COMPREHEND WHAT he was seeing. This couldn't be London. Half the city was gone, at least the half he was in. All around him were bombed-out buildings, sky-high piles of smoking rubble, and plaster dust. From somewhere to his far left he thought he heard a woman cry. He stopped, his boots crunching on the shattered pavement, trying to ascertain exactly where the cry had come from. It was quiet now; the cry, if that was what he'd really heard, had been snuffed out. He looked down and stumbled into a pile of rubble. All about him were crimson bloodstains, and he thought he saw a finger among the rubble, but he was too angry, too appalled at what he was seeing, to check it out.

"You best move smartly, Yank, this is no time to sightsee," his guide muttered. "The Frenchie you're supposed to meet isn't going to hang around waiting for you. They operate on strict time schedules, otherwise their whole network gets blown to hell. Why the hell you want to go to France is beyond me. You had a soft berth in America, and you're too old to fight." This last was said slyly, as though hoping to bait the tall American in his official army clothes into saying something. But he was disappointed. No one talked these days. "Go on now, mate, straight down the alley and around the corner is the Press Club.''

Reuben spoke then, his voice harsh and gruff. "What's the man's name? How will I recognize him?''

"He'll find you, not to worry. Get yerself a pint and he'll find you,'' the man said, turning to pick his way through the rubble to collect the pound of coffee and round of cheese he'd been promised to escort the American to the Press Club.

There was no electricity inside the club, which probably meant there was no running water either, Reuben thought as he made his way to a table at the back of the room. He'd been told he could get food and wine if he wanted it. He did.

Music played softly from the depths of the room, an American tune he'd heard before but couldn't place now. There was liquor behind the bar—not much, but enough. The stew, when it came, was thin but substantial, particularly when sopped up with several slices of homemade bread. He hardly tasted the sour wine, and he kept his eyes on the doorway as he chewed. Every so often he gazed around the room, surprised that it was still intact. There were chunks missing from the walls, loose plaster on the ceilings, and blackout curtains on all the windows, but an effort had been made to keep things as normal as possible under the circumstances. No matter what, life went on, he thought grimly.

He smoked and waited, waited and smoked. Twice the music stopped, only to start again, a melancholy refrain that worked a kind of magic if you were deliriously happy, which he wasn't. Grimacing, he did his best to tune out the sad words by drinking more wine as he kept his eyes peeled on the door.

The room was filling up now. Conversation wafted about him, some laughter, but mostly he observed quiet men, some in uniform, their faces intent, their voices just as intense. He was the only man sitting alone, he noticed, and no one was paying any attention to him except the waitress, who kept filling his wineglass. When she approached to fill his glass for the sixth time, he waved her away and lit a cigar.

Half an hour later, Reuben pulled out his pocket watch. His contact was four hours late. The word *contact* had amused him when he first heard it. It reminded him of a spy novel, with the contact arriving in the rain, a hat pulled low on his forehead, a sloppy coat belted at his waist. In fact, the studio had made a movie with a character like that. Now, however, he was no longer amused, and this wasn't a movie; this was reality, and he was scared almost shitless.

There wasn't anyone in the club who was even near his age. The uniforms were all young men whose bodies were lean and hard, soldiers trained to fight. The others looked just as fit and trim, with great reserves of stamina from which to draw. His good life in California just might prove to be his undoing.

By now Reuben was out of sorts, anxiety having given way to suppressed anger. It was the army's creed—hurry up and wait. He was helpless now, dependent on a faceless, nameless Frenchman who would take him into that beleaguered country.

The backpack he'd slipped out of when he entered was at his feet. He rummaged for his notebook and pencil and started to write. Quite a few pages were filled with his cramped writing, enough to send off to Jane to hold for him. The note that was to go in the envelope had been written while he was still on the plane. It was midnight when he licked the flap of the envelope and handed it to the waitress with instructions to give it to the *Times* correspondent when he came in. Eventually it would get to the States, along with packets of photographs the photojournalists sent out when mail moved.

His contact was now seven hours late. Reuben ordered more food and wine, then settled in to wait all through the night, getting up every so often to go to the bathroom or stretch his legs. Once he walked outside, but the acrid smell drove him back indoors. Twenty minutes later a man walked into the club, his eyes searching the candlelit room. Immediately he approached Reuben's table and sat down, speaking rapidly in French, neither explaining nor apologizing for his late arrival. He waved to the waitress for food and wine.

He was young, no more than twenty-five, if that. His eyes were ageless, though, as he stared across at Reuben. It was hard to believe this young man was accepting the responsibility for getting him into France.

His food finished, the man handed Reuben a packet of papers. "They are, how do you say, exquisitely doné. Another few days and your beard will be exactly like the one on this," he said, tapping the false identity card. "From now on we talk only in French. I talk and you listen. It is agreed?" Reuben nodded. "Take this," he said, indicating a parcel wrapped with string. "Be quick. You will keep your boots . . . for now, since we have none to give you. This must go, too." He pointed to Reuben's backpack. "Use this instead," he said, fishing a moth-eaten wool sack from his own pack. "I will see to trans-ferring the contents while you change clothes."

The young man, code-named Jean Dupré, dumped Reuben's bag onto the table, sorting through the contents to determine what was safe to carry. The razor and two bars of soap were tossed aside, while socks and underwear stayed on the table. The aspirin were emptied into the bag, the bottle left on the table. Jean was patently surprised to see the brush and comb were French. They went into the bag along with the pencil and pad, but only after he'd scratched off the gilt lettering on the pencil and torn off the top of the pad.

It was the first of September when Jean Dupré led Reuben out of the Press Club. On December 10, three months and ten days later, Reuben was within twenty-five kilometers of Mick-ey's château in Marseilles.

There was snow on the ground, more than he'd ever seen in his life. It was so blinding, Reuben's eyes watered constantly; his eyelashes froze and caked with beads of ice. His head pounded constantly, but he hadn't complained. With only seven aspirin left, he had vowed to endure the pain unless it felt like his head would blow off his neck.

No man with his wits about him would go through what he'd been through the past months, he mused. Sleeping in barns with only rats for company, hiding in garbage dumpsters that made Jean smell like a flower in comparison. Twice he'd been tempted to kill a rat for food, but he knew that would be madness indeed. He hated everything about France now, and the madman who controlled the country he'd once loved so passionately. Along the way he'd listened to the stories Jean and his compatriots had to tell—horrible stories he wanted to forget. Stories about women and children starving, stories about beaten old men and women, stories about people being carted off in trucks and never seen again. Lines and lines for every-thing, people, little children freezing in those lines waiting for thin soup or a piece of bread. All he wanted to do now was kill. When he slept, which wasn't very often, he dreamed of killing whole columns of German soldiers; and when he wasn't gunning them down, he was slicing out their tongues, ripping off their testicles, and burning their feet to their ankles. And still it wasn't enough. And when he woke from his nightmares he wrote, quickly, one word running into the next in his frenzy.

After the first month he'd given up the idea of writing his memoirs for the studio. What he was writing now was about truth and feelings and anger. He was obsessed with his writing, his thoughts never still.

He was French now; this was his country, the country that had given him back his sanity after the first war. He spoke in French, his thoughts were in French. He was one of them.

At some point during the second month he became an active member of the Resistance. Willingly he made dynamite charges, helped blow up bridges, knocked out power lines, destroyed water systems, set off homemade bombs that killed Germans. But it was never enough. For every German they killed, three more took his place, but still they continued with their puny efforts, certain the day would come when they would drive the Germans out of France. Reuben became an expert with the garrote, knew the anatomy better than any first-year medical student. He could kill with a blow, with a blade, with his stiffened fingers, and when he walked or crawled away he was glad he'd killed. His network had a saying when they killed a German: This bastard will not father any more bastards. His network's biggest coup to date had taken place a week earlier when they'd wiped out an entire convoy with the help of two other networks. It had been so organized, so meticulously done, Reuben could only marvel afterward that they'd lost just seven members. The honor of the kill went to his network, and there was much backslapping and camaraderie. They now were mobile with trucks and several tanks, along with several cars. Weapons filled one entire truck. Another held ammunition that would go to their storehouse. He'd rejoiced with the others and refused to think of the reprisals.

Jean was shuffling his feet in the snow, looking everywhere but at Reuben. His voice was low and husky, and he spoke now in English. It was his way of complimenting Reuben for the work he'd done with his network. "We part here, monsieur. You are certain you can find your way to the village alone?" Reuben nodded. "You will recognize old landmarks, eh?" Again Reuben nodded. "When you . . . you will remember where you are to join up with the Monet network. They are searching for the woman you are trying to locate. Perhaps they will have news for you. Here," he said harshly, "this is a Christmas present early." He handed over a small parcel.

Reuben removed the wrapping and withdrew a pair of dark glasses. Jean blushed furiously when he saw the American's eyes grow moist. "They come from a dead German major.

They will not harm your eyes; wear them over your own. They are for the . . . the . . .''

"Glare," Reuben said, nodding.

"Yes, the glare. Good . . . good luck, my friend."

"And to you." Reuben clapped both his hands on Jean's shoulders. He knew he'd never see Jean again, but his life was richer for having known him even a short while. He wanted to say the right thing, something important and meaningful, to this stalwart Frenchman, but he couldn't find the words. "*Bonne chance,* my friend."

Then he pressed on, for to stand still too long would add frostbite to his other problems. Now that he had the dark glasses he could travel faster, be more alert.

Five days later Reuben walked into the village nearest the château. Half the shops were nothing but rubble now; the steeple had been blown from the church, and its door hung drunkenly from a single hinge. Staring inside, he could see snow on the pews. He'd gone to midnight mass here once with Mickey, Daniel, and Bebe, sitting in the second pew from the back. When he left he tried to close the door, but it was too heavy, the hinge solidly rusted.

There was blackness all around him as he made his way down the lonely road that would take him to the château. It was going to snow again, he thought sadly, remembering the happy times with Mickey in the snow-filled meadows behind the château. His footsteps slowed as memories rushed to the surface. The chestnut trees were bare now, but he remembered when they were in bloom, remembered kissing Mickey under the leafy green umbrella. If she were at the château now, he'd be able to see smoke from the chimney, but she wasn't there. The entire village and surrounding countryside had been strafed by the Germans.

Reuben dropped to his knees in the snow, his hands folded in prayer. As with Jean, the words he was seeking wouldn't come. He looked down at the whiteness, wondering what it was he wanted to pray for. "Let it be there," he said over and over as he trudged down the road and around the bend.

The château stood, majestic and ghostly in the darkness, the ageless trees protecting it. Reuben drank in its beauty like a thirsty man in the desert. An overwhelming sense of peace flooded through him. How well he remembered the last time he'd walked away from this magical place. His heart had been breaking, and his eyes were full of tears when he'd looked back, looked back because he had fallen in love here. He should have run back, he never should have left. So long ago, so many years, so much heartache, and all because of Bebe. No, he wouldn't allow Bebe to intrude now. Not here.

The moon sailed gracefully from under its cloud cover, and he saw the trees clearly. They'd taken the brunt of the strafing, but still they lived. He tried to wrap his arms around the closest one, but he couldn't, it was too large. It lived, as did the others, and that was all that mattered.

Slowly Reuben walked through the snow, not sure if he was on the flagstone walkway or not. The front door beckoned him. It wouldn't be locked; Mickey never locked her doors. Once he'd asked for a key, and she'd told him she didn't even know where it was, if there was one. Now the door yielded to the pressure of his shoulder. "Are you ready for this?" he asked himself before he set foot over the threshold, back into his memories.

It was cold and dark, with little piles of snow scattered on the floor near the blown-out windows. He could find his way in the dark to the place where the candles were kept. He knew where everything was in this house. When he found the candles he lighted them with care, his hand cupped around the dancing flame.

Then he began a tour of the house, walking through the rooms one by one, touching an object, staring at another, remembering, always remembering. In the library his eyes widened in horror when he saw that the painting of the Three Musketeers was no longer over the mantle. He held the candle higher, hoping it had been moved to another wall, but bookshelves lined every other wall in the room. Then he saw it, leaning crookedly against the chair Daniel used to sit in. The heavy gilt frame was broken and cracked in several places, but the painting was intact. Angrily, Reuben ripped at the old wood and yanked the painting free. Its border of slatted wood remained intact, so he propped it up on the mantle and then stepped back to absorb its beauty. His heart pounded as he stared at Mickey's likeness.

"My God, you're more beautiful than I remember," he murmured. "I loved you so much. More than life. More than . . . than Daniel. And you loved me so much, you let me walk away. All those years, the days, the hours. Gone. I was so young, so greedy, so power hungry, and all it did for me was bring me here now. And now you're gone," he said brokenly.

"You took my son when no one else wanted him, you raised him, and then you sent him to me, your greatest treasure. You thought I would come back, I know you did, but I was young and afraid of what I would see in your eyes, what I see in my son's eyes now. I failed you, darling Mickey. You had such hope for me, such confidence that I would become rich and famous as well as powerful, and I am those things and they mean nothing. All these years I thought I was doing it for you, but I was doing it for myself, to prove to myself that your faith in me was justified. I lied to myself, I did it all for me. I'm glad you can't hear me say these things. I am so ashamed. I should have come back; I should have listened to my heart." Reuben dropped his head into his hands and wept then for his memories and for the man he had become.

Upstairs on the second floor he fared no better as memories attacked him like fierce warriors assaulting his every sense. In Mickey's room his eyes flew to the mantel and the jar of flower petals. He'd known it would be there. She'd saved it. Dizzy with relief, he removed the lid. After all these years the scent was still discernible. He wept again as he sank down on the bed, the petals sprinkled on his open hand. "I'm so sorry, so very sorry," he said over and over.

At last he slept out of sheer exhaustion, in Mickey's bed with the crushed flower petals in his hand, his apology on his lips.

Chapter Twenty-four

THE WINTER SUN SHONE THROUGH THE DIRTY MULLIONED windows of the château, warming Reuben beneath the dusty bedding. His eyes were open now, scanning the once-familiar room. Although he had no memory of it, he must have awakened during the night and crawled beneath the covers. He stretched in his bulky clothes, his dark head pressing into the pillow, which smelled ever so faintly of Mickey's perfume.

Here in this familiar place where he'd been so happy, Reuben gave in to his grief. At last he'd come home, but too late. Where in the name of God was she? He closed his eyes, wishing he never had to leave the cocoon of safety he'd created for himself. In frustration he threw the covers to the side and immediately felt the cold, crisp air wash over him. In the old days there was always a fire going in the grate during the winter months. It had always been warm and toasty here in this splendid room, which received the sun on three sides.

He knew he had to fight his memories before he set out on what he thought of as the last leg of his journey. And after the memories he had to write in his journal, so it would be ready to give to one of the members of the new network he would be joining.

Thus resolved, he started on the ground level and worked

his way back upstairs, storming and thundering his way from room to room, cries of anguish escaping him as he made his way through twenty long years of memories. In Mickey's room again, he made the bed and caressed everything that belonged to her. He cleaned the grate and laid firewood for when she returned. From time to time he wiped his eyes. "No man should have to go through this," he muttered to himself. Once Mickey had told him that happiness and sadness belonged together like a shoe and a sock. One could not know happiness if one had no knowledge of pain. How wise she'd been, how warm and caring. His sense of loss was so unbearable, he wanted to lie down and die.

Suddenly his other self rose to the fore, demanding to be heard. *I thought you said you were in love with Bebe. Which is it? What kind of man are you that you can't make up your mind?* "I love them both," Reuben said defensively. *That's impossible,* argued his inner self. "They're both in my heart and I can't carve them away. That's been my problem all these years, I love both of them in different ways. That's it!" he roared as he slammed the door behind him.

He pounded his way down the hall to his son's room, the one Bebe had used when she'd visited. This door had been closed while the others had been open. Had Philippe closed it against him deliberately, knowing he would come someday?

Inside, Reuben's eyes devoured the sight of his son's young life. This was nothing like Bebe's frilly, feminine room. Was Mickey aware of the irony of having Philippe use this particular room?

As he walked around the room, he imagined Philippe's evolution from infancy to boyhood to manhood. It was a wonderful room for a child. Stiff-legged wooden soldiers resplendent in their coats of red paint stood at attention on a shelf above the bed. A rocking horse full of nicks and gouges attested to many hours of play, as did the basket of brightly colored blocks. A red wagon with one rickety wheel stood next to the rocking horse; it, too, had seen years of hardy use. A vision of Mickey pulling his son in the wagon made his heart constrict. A tricycle with fat rubber wheels and rusty handlebars and one missing pedal had been pushed into the farthest corner.

The small-boy corner gave way to a section of the room designated for boyhood. The remains of an ant farm stood on a shelf along with dozens of books. Colorful miniature cars and a variety of balls took up a second shelf. Puzzles of every description were stacked neatly alongside roller skates. A scooter and a larger bicycle with chipped blue paint leaned against the wall under the eaves next to a magnificent castle fashioned from stone and wood. Reuben dropped to his knees to peer into the tiny windows that held little people and scaled-down furniture. A king sat on a gilt throne, his crown tarnished, his robes faded to a dusty pink. Reuben leaned closer, his eyes straining to see into the dim interior of the castle. A tiny piece of paper was pasted to the king's crown. He knew if he reached in to touch the crown, the paper would disintegrate at his touch. He could barely make out the word: Papa.

His eyes misty with unshed tears, Reuben made his way to the area that represented Philippe's adolescence. It held a desk, a comfortable chair, more bookshelves, and a bulletin board. Tacked to the board was the winemaker's calendar, almost as yellow and brittle as his own; Reuben stared at it, finding it difficult to swallow past the lump in his throat. The desk held the usual assortment of pens, pencils, tablets, books, and rulers. A number of language books were piled next to notebooks full of written assignments, all bearing a large red A in the top corner. Clippings from newspapers, yellowed and dry, were all quotes from Teddy Roosevelt. A packet of photographs, most of Mickey, Yvette, and Henri, stared up at him.

The cupboard that held Philippe's clothes was slightly ajar. Reuben smelled a mixture of orange and spice, something Mickey placed in all the closets to ward off moths. Everything was neat and clean, and the clothes had all been hung close together. The shelves held more books, folded sweaters, and heavy jackets. Shoes were lined up like soldiers next to several pairs of galoshes. There was a sled in the corner with a pair of boxing gloves hanging from the steering rudder. Four pairs of ice skates of different sizes rested in a wooden box, their blades dull and rusty. Tucked away in one corner, as though meant to be concealed from all other eyes, was a wooden toy chest. On his knees, Reuben tugged and pulled until he had it in front of him. Then he rocked back on his haunches, knowing somehow that what was inside was going to upset him, change him somehow. Twice he reached out to lift the heavy brass hasp. The lid groaned, the hinges sending out splatters of rust. Inside were stacks and stacks of letters, twenty or so to a packet, each parcel tied with stout string. Some were written in crayon, some in colored chalk, others in pencil, and a few in ink. Hundreds of letters addressed simply to "Papa."

Reuben sat down on the cold floor with a thump, his eyes glued to the contents of the trunk. He fought the tears in his eyes, struggled against the desire to read the letters. True, they were written to him, but they had never been mailed. Philippe had kept them in his closet for years and years, which could only mean they were for the boy's eyes only. Reluctantly, Reuben closed the lid of the small chest and replaced it in the dark corner of the closet, exactly where he'd found it.

His thoughts and motions frenzied, he made his way back to the room he'd slept in. Grabbing his journal from his knapsack, he raced back to Philippe's room and sat down at the desk. His pencil moved freely as thoughts and emotions tumbled from his mind. He ached with feeling, his heart bruised and battered; in those moments he truly believed a person had a soul and truly believed his intangible soul left him the moment he laid aside his pencil and journal.

By the time he'd finished writing in the journal, it was close to noon; he'd used up the valuable early morning hours, and traveling would be dangerous. His sentimental memories were cast aside in an instant. He had to find Mickey, had to ask her about the letters in the chest. Did she know of them, had she read them, or were they Philippe's secret?

Reuben's steps were sure and confident when he struck out from the château without a backward glance. First he'd head north to Avignon and then west to Nîmes, where he would rendezvous with partisans willing to take him to Montpellier and Beziers; from there he'd board one of the ancient buses that trundled by once every two or three days on its way to Carcassonne. He hadn't allowed himself to think beyond Carcassonne because he wasn't sure that Mickey would be in Spain. His heart told him she would head for safety via the Pyrenees, regardless of what she'd told Daniel, but logic told him she belonged to one of the networks he was hoping to encounter. Wishing and hoping she was safe simply wasn't good enough. What he'd seen and heard since coming to Europe had convinced him that as a loyal Frenchwoman, Mickey would do whatever she could for her country.

Five days later he made contact with a man named Didier who told him there was every possibility the woman he was searching for was one of two female partisans who had joined up with a network to the west. Reuben's blood ran cold when Didier told him that Chapeau and Maman, the code names these women used, were waiting for clear weather to guide a group of orphaned children over the Pyrenees to safety. "Hopefully," Didier had added gruffly. "The two women did it once before in the autumn, when it wasn't cold and treacherous as it is now."

"Draw me a map and tell me what you can about the network they belong to," Reuben said harshly, his heart thumping in his chest.

"In the snow I will draw you a map," Didier said. "Nothing is put on paper, even one's mother's name. You must trust your memory." Reuben nodded.

At that moment he was twelve days behind Mickey. If he and Didier could reach Carcassonne by rail instead of by bus, he could save an extra four days. If he slept only a few hours a day and traveled by daylight, which Didier refused to do, he could make up another four days. If he reached Carcassonne alive, he would go it alone and not involve the man, who was needed elsewhere. He made up his mind to say nothing to the young Frenchman until the right moment.

He felt close to Mickey now, so close that his heart started to hammer in his chest. Possibly only four days from seeing her again.

"Monsieur, Merry Christmas," Didier said quietly.

Startled, Reuben could only gape at the man standing next to him. "Today is Christmas?"

"Tomorrow is Christmas, this is Christmas Eve. We must pray that our luck holds and the Germans will let us travel on this religious day. I truly think they will not be too critical of their passengers. They control every train and bus in France. Did you know that?" Again Reuben nodded.

Four days. Four days . . . Christmas Eve. Was Bebe celebrating the holiday, or he wondered was she attending a party somewhere? Jane always had an open house for the entire studio on Christmas Eve. Lord, the number of Christmases he'd shared with Jane simply because he'd had nowhere else to go. His feet picked up a cadence he'd marched to once before when he'd been a soldier. Four days. Four days . . .

"Merry Christmas," Reuben whispered.

Chapter Twenty-five

THE SCENE BELOW PHILIPPE'S WINDOW WAS ONE OF INTENSE activity. The studio was filming what he called a shoot-'em-up-bang Wild West movie. The lot was filled with covered wagons, cowboys, and rangy-looking cattle. A saloon, complete with swinging doors and ladies of the evening, beckoned to weary cowboys in search of a twenty-five-cent bath and shave. Fake gunshots echoed in his ears. Sometime during the next fifteen minutes there would be a shoot-out on the main street, and one of the black-clad figures would die. The remaining cowboy would holster his smoking gun and either ride off into the make-believe sunset or carry off the good girl, victim of a vicious land baron trying to steal her family homestead. Philippe shook his head wearily as he returned to his desk.

He didn't like it here, didn't like making movies or watching movies being made. The past months he'd tried to convince himself he could do what his father had done, but he realized now that he didn't want to walk in his father's shoes. No, he wanted out, wanted to make his own way in the world without interference, particularly of the parental kind.

A scream rent the air—the familiar ''damsel in distress'' cry for help—and Philippe shuddered. He had to get out of there, get some fresh air, anything, just so he was away from that place.

In his car with the engine running, he knew he didn't want just "anything"—he wanted a certain something. Once again he pulled the wrinkled piece of paper he'd been carrying around with him for weeks and looked at it, not that he needed to. The address of Al Sugar, the recently retired prop department head, was burned in his brain. He was taking a chance driving out to the Valley without calling ahead, but he didn't care. If he had to, he'd wait all night. Besides, it was a nice day for a drive.

Twice Philippe managed to get lost, but the city map on the seat helped him out, and at best he wasted only twenty-five minutes.

Al Sugar was spraying his fruit trees, a bucket of whitewash at his feet, when Philippe pulled his car to the curb. The elderly man had the neatest house on the street and the prettiest trees and flowers. His retirement, Philippe thought. This was how he occupied *his* time. Was he happy puttering with his fruit trees and flowers?

A young boy whizzed past him on a bicycle, laughing as his friend tried to catch up. School must be out for the day, Philippe mused. Sounds of laughter and play echoed from up and down the street. Memories of his old blue bicycle and other boyhood treasures assailed him, and he hungered for the sight of them. He kept his eyes on the pedaling boys until they rounded the corner.

Carefully Philippe stepped over a hedge, pausing to admire a tidy little border of yellow flowers with bees buzzing at the blooms. "Mr. Sugar?" he called. The old man turned, his glasses speckled with whitewash. "Mr. Sugar, I'm—"

"Lord love a duck! I know who you are, boy. You're the spittin' image of your father. Fine man, real fine man. All this," he said, waving his hand about, "is because of him. He made sure I retired with dignity. He gave me a generous bonus that paid off this house. Fine man, real fine man. He still calls once in a while to see how I'm doing."

Philippe stared at the friendly old man with curious blue eyes. He could see why his father liked him. He liked him, too. "Philip Tarz," he said, holding out his hand. The bone-crushing grip startled him. He grinned, realizing it was the first time he'd referred to himself as Philip Tarz, either in his mind or aloud. "I need your help, Mr. Sugar. On my way over here from France Mr. Bishop told me how you . . . created credentials for him to go to Harvard Law School. I need the same kind of credentials now to get into the military.''

"Lordy, lordy, lordy, I think this calls for a glass of lemonade. Come along, youngster, we'll wet our whistles and talk about this,'' Al said excitedly.

Inside, Philippe looked around the bright, cheerful kitchen with its yellow and green wallpaper and braided rugs by the stove and sink. The room sparkled. Al set out a pitcher of frosty lemonade with two glasses and a plate of cookies. "Store-bought,'' he said, winking. "I never did master the oven on this stove. Hell, the truth is I can't bake worth a darn.''

Philippe bit into the soft, gingery cookie and nodded his approval. The lemonade was tangy, not too sweet and not too sour. The old man beamed his pleasure when Philippe asked for a second glass.

"It's like this, Mr. Sugar. . . . Jesus, I don't know where to begin,'' Philippe said miserably.

"Try at the beginning, son, that's always a good place. I have all day and night, too, if it takes that long.''

Philippe cleared his throat. "You see, Mr. Sugar,'' he said carefully, "I'm not exactly planning on defrauding the navy. I do have an education equivalent to four years of college. Actually, I was three-quarters of the way through graduate school when we had to leave Paris. Our schooling in France is far more advanced than it is here. All I need is a set of papers saying I finished college, and a new name. All my other papers are in order. I spoke to several recruiters to find out exactly what I need to go to Officer's Training School. I want to fly planes, Mr. Sugar,'' Philippe said forcefully. "I want to go back and bomb the hell out of Germany. I know I can do it. I can be the best damn pilot the navy has ever seen.''

"You know, young man, your father came here to say goodbye before he left. He talked a little about you, not a whole lot, mind you. I know all about your mother in France, and I've known Miss Bebe for years. So . . . I'll do it!'' he blurted out happily. "Now, hold on a minute,'' he said as Philippe reached out to grasp his hand. "That last handshake almost did me in.'' He grinned. "Now, just how soon do you need this done?''

"A couple of days.''

Al Sugar laughed and smacked his knee. "That's exactly what your father said the first time. Son, I will never forget the day Mr. Bishop drove off the studio lot with a car from the prop department, a suitcase full of Rudolph Valentino's clothes, and my . . . creative endeavors. He was driving cross-country with only four or five driving lessons under his belt. I was never sorry I did that. When I saw that boy's law degree I was as proud as your father was. I want your promise that you'll be the best goddamn pilot the navy turns out.''

"You have it, Mr. Sugar," Philippe replied solemnly.

"That's good enough for me. You bomb hell out of those Krauts, you hear.''

Philippe nodded. "I hear. I only hope my word is as good as my father's.''

"It is. You know, son, when you first came up to me in the yard, I couldn't believe how much you look like your father. Just seeing you makes me feel young again.'' Al got up from the kitchen table and carried the empty pitcher to the sink. "Well, I think we chewed the fat long enough. I'll call over to the prop department and have my son—he's working there now—bring everything we need out here to the Valley. We'll start on it tonight. You're welcome to stay for supper—pork chops, apple sauce, and bulldog gravy. Apple pie . . . store-bought, but I make my own ice cream. Am I tempting you, son?''

Philippe laughed. "If the apple pie is as good as these cookies, you have a deal. Mr. Sugar, can we talk about my father? I'd like to know what he was like when he first came back after the war. . . .''

Four days later, Al Sugar handed Philippe his diploma from the University of Southern California. His college transcripts were impeccable, as were those from graduate school. In addition to his academic credentials, there was a letter on crackly white paper with the navy seal at the top, signed by William F. Halsey himself, recommending Philip Reuben as an exceptional candidate for Officer's Training School. It was signed "Bull.'' Halsey's nickname. Philippe's eyes popped.

"Son, that paper is the real thing, and so is the seal,'' Al said proudly. "Hollywood typed it. It'll pass muster. The rest is up to you. Make me proud and your father, too.''

"I will, Mr. Sugar, you can count on it,'' Philippe said in a choked voice. This time their handshake was a little less bone-crushing.

Al Sugar watched until Philippe's car was out of sight. "You come back, boy, you hear me?" he whispered.

Sighing, the old man picked up his fresh bucket of whitewash and proceeded to spray the rest of his fruit trees. He looked up once and muttered, "You watch out for him, You hear?" The sun dimmed for a second, and Al smiled. "Yeah, I thought You'd see it my way. He's a good kid, he just has to find himself, and with You looking out for him he'll be okay. Amen."

Chapter Twenty-six

JANE PERKINS OPENED THE FRENCH DOORS LEADING TO HER terrace. Christmas in California. Another year almost gone, she thought sadly as she stepped onto the terrace.

The early twilight was her favorite time of day. Out in the cool evening air it didn't seem like Christmas at all. Come to think of it, it didn't seem like Christmas indoors, either. Even trimming the fragrant balsam hadn't lifted her spirits. Now the empty boxes had been carried back to the attic, the floor had been vacuumed, the presents placed beneath the tree.

The long, swirling red gown she had donned for her annual party was supposed to make her feel gay and relaxed. Instead, she felt tense and irritable, emotions unknown to her until four months earlier, when Nellie had arrived.

If only she didn't love Daniel. If only . . . if only . . .

Suddenly she wished for snow and freezing temperatures—anything that would keep people away from her party. All she wanted was to be able to retreat into her bedroom and nurse the sorrow building in her breast. If Reuben were here, she could tell him what was going on and how she felt. But, she thought ironically, if Reuben were here, she wouldn't have the problems because he would have cut Nellie off at the pass, even if she was Daniel's daughter—stepdaughter.

There were so many things she didn't understand. Or was she merely pretending not to understand because she didn't want a head-on confrontation with Daniel's daughter and Reuben's son?

These days the studio resembled ten acres of quicksand, deadly and treacherous. Things simply weren't going on as before. There were subtle little changes, changes that affected revenue, buys, and rejections. They hadn't turned out a quality movie in the last four months, and the projected schedule was so horrendous that her head ached every time she thought about it.

She was still smarting over the loss of *Ambrosia*, a script she'd wanted very much to buy. It was a perfect vehicle for Joan Crawford, who wanted to do the movie desperately. It would have been next year's feature film, capable of winning several Academy Awards. Now it was in the hands of M-G-M, who had paid twice what she could have gotten it for. Negotiations were under way to loan Crawford to M-G-M. Nellie had called the script schlock, and Philippe had said it was a sticky mess of sentimentality. Daniel had patted her on the head like an errant child and said, "Jane, honey, business is business, you can't win them all. Don't fret, something better will come along." It was then she'd realized what was happening—she was fighting not just a battle, but a war, one she couldn't hope to win because she had no allies. Not one.

Maybe she should have gone to Bebe, but that wasn't her style. She didn't know how to backbite, wasn't up on infighting. Unfortunately, integrity and honor seemed to count for nothing on the open market.

Two days earlier she'd made up her mind to resign the day after the New Year. In fact, she'd typed her resignation and sealed it in an envelope, intending to hand-deliver it to the legal department at nine A.M., January 2. It was short and to the point, asking that the studio waive the thirty-day-notice clause in her contract.

Jane's heart fluttered wildly when she thought about the four heavy brown envelopes that had arrived in the mail over the past months, sent to her personally here at home. They were from Reuben, of course, all from Europe and bearing the *Times*'s name in the upper left-hand corner.

The first packet had arrived on a dreary, rainy day, when she'd been home with a severe cold. Hands trembling, she'd opened it and sat at the dining room table reading the cramped writing that covered twenty sheets of paper, front as well as back. The short note scribbled on the top margin read: "Jane, I think you'll know what to do with this when the time comes." He'd scrawled his initials underneath. Sniffling and sneezing, she'd read the whole thing three times. She smiled, she cried, and she agonized at what she was reading. Reuben had entrusted the story of his life to *her* hands, not to Daniel and not Bebe, the closest people in his life. Obviously it was to be kept secret, otherwise he wouldn't have sent the packets to her home. All four of the heavy packages were locked in her wall safe.

The past few days she'd toyed with the idea of setting up her own production company once she'd definitely made up her mind to tender her resignation, but such an endeavor would wipe her out financially. She'd have to mortgage the house, sell her car, liquidate whatever investments she had. Max would help if she needed extra capital, that much she knew. Everybody thought of Max as Reuben's gangster friend from the old days. But gangster or not, Max was as loyal a friend as she was to Reuben. For years now he'd anguished over the fact that he'd never been able to repay Reuben for getting him back into legitimate mainstream society. This payback would be a pleasure for Max as well as for her, if she decided to film Reuben's life. It must be what he had in mind. If he'd wanted to write a book, he would have said so. Any number of publishers would jump at the chance to buy what she had in her safe. No, it was a film Reuben wanted.

All her life she'd trusted her gut feelings, and now her stomach was rippling at the thought of filming Reuben's life. If she handpicked her crew and used unknown actors and actresses and filmed on location . . . The challenge frightened and delighted her.

The defeated look had left Jane's eyes when she stepped back into the house. How she loved Christmas. She vowed to make this holiday as enjoyable as the ones in the past. Daniel would be arriving soon. Weeks before they'd agreed to have a private hour before the party got under way, enough time to toast the season and exchange their presents. Her heart was beating now in anticipation of the moment Daniel walked through her door and saw the huge tree and the festive decorations. His eyes would light with approval at both the house and herself. He loved her as much as she loved him, and it was a wonderful giving and sharing love—a love that was gentle and quiet one moment and wild and exhilarating the next. There was only one flaw in their relationship, and that was Daniel's obsessive love for Nellie.

Jane glanced at her watch. Daniel was always punctual; he should be arriving . . . right now. When the doorbell rang, she tensed. Daniel usually let himself in with his key. This formality could mean only one thing. Anger sparked in her eyes as she walked to the door, and she made no attempt to smile when she opened the door to admit Daniel and Nellie.

"Merry Christmas, Jane," Daniel said exuberantly.

"Merry Christmas," Nellie gushed over her shoulder as she made her way to the Christmas tree.

"I didn't think you'd mind if I brought Nellie along. There didn't seem to be much sense in having Philippe drive all the way out to our side of the canyon, and there's so much traffic." His smile faded when he saw the anger in Jane's eyes.

"But I do mind, Daniel, I mind very much. However, it seems I can't do much about it at the moment," she said coolly, then turned on her heel and marched into the living room. "What will you have to drink? Nellie? Daniel?" Thank God her hands weren't as shaky as her stomach.

"Wine, just a little," Nellie said happily. "This is the most gorgeous tree. I've never seen one more beautiful, have you, Daddy? I'm so glad you allowed me to share this intimate time with you and Daddy. Once everyone gets here it will be just a party. I brought you a present, Jane. I put it under the tree."

"Thank you," Jane said flatly, handing Nellie her wine.

"I brought you one, too," Daniel said boyishly as he dug a small box out of his pocket. Jane had been expecting—had hoped and prayed for—an engagement ring, but Daniel's gift-wrapped box was long and narrow. Disappointed, she watched as he carefully placed the gaily wrapped package on the table. An engagement ring was what she wanted, had dreamed of all these months. A ring meant marriage, togetherness for always, and nothing would have made her happier. But that was then, this was now, she thought sadly. She held out Daniel's drink but made no move to touch the package.

Daniel accepted his glass of Scotch with sober eyes. It had been thoughtless of him to bring Nellie along without even calling Jane first to let her know. He saw that now. But the change in plan had been made so suddenly, it seemed. One moment Nellie was on the phone with Philippe, and the next she'd had no way to get to Jane's party. And after all, it *was* an inconvenient, out-of-the-way drive for the boy, while he, Daniel, was already heading that way himself. . . . He simply hadn't thought Jane would mind. But she did. She minded very much. The spark was still in her eyes, ready to burst into flame any second if he didn't do or say something. Later, of course, she would apologize and so would he. But there were hours to get through until then.

"You know, Jane, when I first heard about your famous Christmas parties, I thought it was only for the stars at the studio," Nellie said exuberantly. "You know, all that glitter and sparkle. Then I heard, and I don't know who told me, that your party is for all the people who work behind the scenes. I just can't tell you how wonderful that is. And your Christmas party for the children at the studio was . . . well, I just want you to know I think it's absolutely swell of you. You are just so . . . wonderful, isn't she, Daddy?"

Daniel grinned. "She is the marvel in marvelous. Everyone says so. Reuben made a wise choice when he hired you to head production."

"Thank you," Jane said curtly. At the bar, she poured herself a drink and took it neat, slapping the empty glass on the countertop. Daniel's eyes popped. This was one angry lady. Compliments alone weren't going to make things right. Not this time.

If Nellie was aware of the tension between her father and Jane, she gave no outward sign but rattled on about the array of gifts under the tree. "I guess I'm just Daddy's little girl, especially at Christmastime. Jane, you'll never guess what my Christmas present is . . . was . . . from Daddy," she said breathlessly. "I don't have to go to college next September if I don't want to. Needless to say, I don't want to. UCLA won't miss me at all. I'm learning so much from you. She's such a patient teacher, Daddy. I know exactly how things are done now, but it will take me at least a skillion years to be as good as she is."

Daniel grappled for something to say, suddenly aware that whatever was wrong with Jane had something to do with Nellie and wasn't stemming just from this one incident. He watched as Jane belted down another drink, her eyes on Nellie. If she kept this up, her party would be minus a hostess. Now he was annoyed—with himself, with his daughter, who had placed him in this position, and with Jane, who couldn't accept a little inconvenience without an unnecessary display of temper.

"Excuse me, I think the caterers are here," Jane muttered, and headed for the kitchen in a rustle of red chiffon before Daniel could voice his thoughts.

"Is Jane upset about something?" Nellie asked innocently as she poked at a package under the tree.

Daniel chose his words carefully. "I imagine preparing this party, decorating the tree and house, was an awesome job. Jane is such a perfectionist. You ladies are such fussbudgets when it comes to parties. Maybe you should go out to the kitchen and see if there's anything you can do to help."

Nellie shook her head. "Oh, Daddy, you don't know much about women. Jane has this party organized to the last detail. She won't want me interfering. She sees enough of me at the office. But"—she wagged a playful finger in her father's direction—"you're wrong about her being a perfectionist. She's made some colossal mistakes, and her mind definitely isn't on studio business. Some of her approvals have been so bad, I didn't want to say anything. It's a good thing Philippe and Bebe caught them and vetoed her bad decisions. This is just between us, Daddy," Nellie whispered conspiratorially. "I think you're her problem. She's in love, and her mind is on you."

Daniel felt a sudden urge to slap his daughter, and he didn't know why. Yes, he knew Jane was in love with him and he with her. But he also knew that her love wouldn't interfere with studio decisions. He gave his daughter a brief smile that never reached his eyes, and, apparently satisfied, she shifted her playful gaze and poked at another present under the tree.

A long time later, just seconds before the first guest arrived, Jane returned to the living room, a drink in her hand. She smiled, but like Daniel, the smile didn't touch her eyes. With her guests, however, she was her normal, affectionate self, offering drinks, often linking arms with them, and then moving on to another cluster of people, where she'd hold vibrant, intense conversations. There was always a drink in her hand, and she refused to meet Daniel's questioning gaze.

Philippe arrived an hour into the party with a lavishly wrapped gift that he presented with a flourish. Jane accepted the gift graciously and nodded in Nellie's direction. Watching the young man walk toward his daughter, Daniel stared in dumb surprise at what he saw in Philippe's eyes. Hostility! For whom? Definitely not Nellie. Jane? Well, he'd certainly look into *that*.

Bebe arrived a short while later, full of apologies. "You won't believe this, Jane, but my car broke down. Do you have any idea how hard it is to get a mechanic on Christmas Eve?"

Jane laughed, her eyes full of merriment. "I heard your car all the way in the kitchen. Have you given any thought to retiring that piece of junk to the scrapyard? How about a glass of ginger ale or a Virgin Mary?"

"Ginger ale will be fine, and no, I'm not about to junk that car," Bebe announced. "I've grown very fond of it. I plan to ride it into the ground."

"It is into the ground." Jane giggled. "Oh, Bebe, I'm so glad you came. I wasn't sure . . . it's been so long . . . and I was never sure if you . . . I guess this isn't the time to talk about such things. Listen," she said impulsively, "do you have any grand plans for after this party or for tomorrow?"

"Not a one. I'm going to watch Willie open his Christmas bone and then I'll open the present I bought myself and that's it."

"Spend it with me, then. Stay after the party. I need . . . I'd like to talk to you . . . about . . . Will you stay? If you have to get back to Willie, I can come with you," Jane said desperately.

Bebe shrugged. "I can stay until breakfast, but aren't you going to be spending the evening with Daniel and . . . Nellie? I more or less thought that the four of you, including Philippe, would be together since everyone is predicting you'll all be a family soon."

"No, I've no plans to spend Christmas with . . . I mean, I'd rather be with you—thanks, Bebe. I . . . appreciate it. Look, I have to circulate. Daniel is on the sofa over there, just make yourself at home. I'll see you later. Bless your heart, Bebe, for . . . We'll talk afterward." The red dress swished out of sight and Bebe was left alone with a goblet of ginger ale in her hand.

She walked around the room, speaking to electricians and cameramen, shaking hands with their wives and smiling. This was a social gathering and it was almost Christmas. Here she was simply a guest, not the head of the studio. She enjoyed the feeling.

This was the first time she'd been in Jane's house. Compared with Reuben's canyon mansion and her estate, this was small. It wasn't elegant, but it was pretty and comfortable and reflected

Jane's taste and personality. Everything was old, but not shabby. Again the word *comfort* sprang to mind. There was nothing ostentatious about Jane's house, just as there was nothing phony about Jane.

Bebe meandered over to the huge Christmas tree, delaying the moment when she would have to join Daniel and his daughter and her son on the sofa. Why were they sitting there like outcasts, she wondered. And why wasn't Jane . . . Releasing her puzzling thoughts, she inhaled the fragrance from Jane's tree and felt tears sting her eyes as she remembered another Christmas many years before. A Christmas with Reuben, Mickey, and Daniel. They'd decorated the tree together. Reuben was poised on the top step of the ladder getting ready to place the Christmas angel, and he'd asked her to hand it to him. When she'd climbed up the ladder, their hands had touched and their eyes had met. She would never forget that heady moment because she was already in love with him, and it was one of the rare occasions when he'd really noticed her and reacted to her as a woman. No, she would never forget that moment. *Where are you, Reuben, on this Christmas Eve,* her heart cried.

A moment later she approached the sofa. "Merry Christmas, Daniel. I was wondering as I stood by the tree if you remembered that last Christmas in France."

Daniel stood and wrapped Bebe in his arms. "Merry Christmas to you, too. And yes, I thought of that earlier. I was hoping this Christmas would somehow be like that one, but I've managed to spoil it for Jane. If I wasn't a man, I think I'd cry." This last was said so quietly, Bebe had to strain to hear the words.

"Then you must fix whatever is wrong before it's too late. Things left unsaid can do irreparable harm, Daniel. I don't know Jane all that well, but I believe she is a fine person. Do what you have to do, and if that isn't enough, do more. That's my free Christmas advice."

She turned to Daniel's daughter. "Merry Christmas, Nellie. You look lovely, rather like the spirit of Christmas in that sparkling gown."

From Nellie she moved on to Philippe. Thank God she'd already observed him from across the room. The shock she'd felt at seeing him in formal attire, looking so much like Reuben, had been considerable. How handsome he was, how arrogantly sure of himself. "Merry Christmas, Philippe," she said formally. "Tell me, why are all of you sitting here alone? Christmas parties are for fun and camaraderie."

Nellie shrugged. "I don't know any of these people. They're mostly just technicians. Philippe and Daddy don't know them, either. I thought . . . we all thought . . . the party was for the studio stars."

Bebe's eyes narrowed, and her voice was cool when she responded. "You really should circulate and get to know these people. The studio isn't made up just of stars, you know. The people in this room make Fairmont what it is. I for one am glad Jane gives this party every year. If just a quarter of them walked away from the studio, it couldn't function. I'm sorry if I sound . . . bossy, but, Daniel, you should know better. Reuben would throw a fit if he knew what your attitude was—and yours, too, Philippe. What right do any of you have to sit here and pretend you're better than they are?"

Daniel was on his feet in a moment. "Hold on, Bebe, it's not like that at all. You have us all wrong. Apparently, you're—"

"No, Daniel, *you* have it all wrong," Bebe interrupted. "I can comment only on what I see. And what I see are three Fairmont Studios employees deliberately isolating themselves from the other guests at a lovely party, remaining exclusive . . . as if they thought they were too good to mingle with ordinary people. And that upsets me. Have a nice holiday," she said, and walked away.

"I think we've just been put in our places," Daniel said quietly. "And she's absolutely right." He sat down, his eyes searching the crowded room for a sign of the brilliant red dress. Jane was angry with him and he didn't blame her. He hadn't stopped to think how his sitting apart would appear to the guests. Now, three-quarters of the way into the party, it didn't seem a good idea to get up and mingle. Damn it to hell! He wasn't doing anything right. This was his and Jane's first Christmas together, and he'd wanted it to be perfect. His hand reached into the pocket of his jacket to touch the small velvet box that rested inside. It was the ring he'd picked up earlier in the day—a flawless solitaire that would look beautiful on Jane's finger. Engaged . . . He wanted it more than anything in the world. The present he'd laid on the table, a diamond bracelet, hadn't even aroused Jane's curiosity. All evening long he'd waited patiently, hoping she would make her way across the room to say something, to acknowledge the gift. But she hadn't.

"Well, if you want *my* opinion, I think Aunt Bebe is wrong," Nellie said petulantly. "I don't know any of these people, and they don't know me. What can I possibly have in common with them? I think this is a stuffy, boring party, and I want to leave. Are you coming, Philippe?"

Philippe did not respond; he was struggling to suppress the anger he felt—at himself and at the situation in general. Twice he'd made a move to get up and talk to some of the men he knew slightly, but each time Nellie had pulled him back as though she'd sensed his intention. His mother was right. Now he felt about two inches tall and wanted nothing more than to run to her and apologize. The disgust he'd seen in her eyes, and what he was hearing and seeing from Nellie bothered him.

"I think we should just sneak out. No one will even miss us," Nellie said impishly to Philippe. "Come on, let's go. Are you staying, Daddy?"

Reluctantly, Daniel shook his head. There didn't seem to be much point in staying now.

"Well, Philippe?" Nellie prodded.

"If you're sure you want to leave, it's okay with me," Philippe said, rising. "But shouldn't we say good night to our hostess?"

"To Jane!" Nellie trilled. "Hardly. Let's go before she takes it into her head to introduce me to some other eligible bachelor." That was all Philippe had to hear. Taking her hand, he hurried her to the front door, grabbed her coat from the hall closet, and ushered her outside.

In the cool night air Nellie pressed closer to Philippe and kissed him. "I've been wanting to do that all night," she murmured. "That's why I wanted to leave. I want to be with *you* on Christmas Eve, Philippe, not a room full of strangers. Sitting with my father all night isn't my idea of a good time, either." She kissed him again, more ardently this time, her leg insinuating itself between his. "Let's go to your house," she whispered.

Philippe practically tripped over his own feet as he walked with her to the car. "Are you sure, Nellie? Your father . . ."

"Philippe, are you trying to talk your way out of making love to me?" Nellie demanded.

"No, of course not. It's just that . . . your father . . . I've asked you before, and you . . ."

"That was then. This is now. I was frightened. . . . This will be my first time, and I . . . I wanted it to be just right. Christmas sort of makes it right. I feel it's right." She squeezed his hand. "Don't you?"

"Hell, yes." Aching with anticipation, he climbed behind the wheel. At last he was going to make love to sweet, wonderful Nellie, the girl he wanted to marry. His first Christmas present. Jesus, how lucky could a guy get.

"Don't worry about Daddy, Philippe," Nellie said, snuggling close to him. "No matter what he said, I know he'll stay until the wee hours and get home in time for breakfast like he usually does. Then he'll probably spend all day with Jane. Or maybe he won't go home at all this time. Let's not think about Daddy, let's think about what you and I are going to do . . . to each other." Philippe almost swerved off the road when Nellie's hand loosened his belt buckle.

Neither Nellie nor Philippe noticed Daniel standing in the doorway as they drove off. Nellie was wrong; Daniel was going home to the empty house in the canyon, the engagement ring still in his pocket.

It was close to midnight when the last guest left Jane's house.

"Now, that was a hell of a party," Bebe said, laughing. "No drugs, not too much alcohol, good music, nice people, and excellent food. I want you to know that this is my first party since . . . turning over a new leaf, as they say. I'm so glad you asked me. Look, if we work together to clean up this place now, you won't wake up to a mess. It won't take long."

"That's not necessary, Bebe," Jane said, slipping off her heels with a sigh of relief. "Aside from having breakfast with you, I don't have . . . what I mean is, I don't have any plans at all for tomorrow."

"Is that another way of saying you and Daniel had a tiff?" Bebe said, stacking a load of dishes onto a tray.

"I think it's more than a tiff. Listen, why don't you leave that for now and sit down. I need to talk. We can do it later if you still want to help."

Bebe nodded and sank onto the sofa while Jane took a seat next to her and began to talk. The words tumbled out between tears and sobs, all the things she'd been feeling, suspecting, for months now. "I know Daniel planned on giving me an engagement ring this evening," she said at one point. "When I saw Nellie at the door with him, something in me snapped. I showed my anger and I acted on that anger. You saw him leave. I wanted to ask him to stay, I really did, but I couldn't.'' She hesitated, then rushed on. ''I'm resigning, Bebe, the day after New Year's. I just can't stay on with the situation the way it is. I'm sorry.''

''Jane, you can't resign,'' Bebe said, clearly shocked and disturbed by Jane's announcement. ''Reuben will never forgive you, and he'll never forgive me for allowing it. You can't let this girl force you out. I wish you'd said something sooner. The way I see it, we have two choices. We can transfer her out of production and into publicity or wardrobe, anywhere we want, or we can simply fire her. Look, I'll tell Daniel. I'm not bashful when it comes to something like this.''

Jane shook her head. ''I appreciate it, Bebe, but it won't work. You're forgetting Philippe. Philippe and Nellie aligned together will be deadly to the studio. I don't want to do anything that will cause Daniel heartache. I love him too much. Can't you see, I have to leave.''

''But that isn't going to work, either. Nellie will always stand between you and Daniel. You have to tell him how you feel. He . . . you can't build a relationship without truth and honesty. Take a good long look at me, Jane, for I am the living proof of what I say. I wouldn't wish that kind of thing on my worst enemy. Why don't we just think about this during the coming week. No hard-rock decisions need to be made this evening. Tomorrow I want you to call Daniel and spend Christmas with him. You don't have to accept his ring if you don't want to. Do it for you, Jane, it's what you want. Now, show me those mysterious packages you mentioned.''

''Yes, in a minute.'' Jane stood, licking at her dry lips uncertainly. ''I think . . . no, I *know* I'm doing the right thing by showing you what's in my safe. If you weren't the strong woman I know you are, I would keep these papers to myself. I've done little else but think of this for weeks now. I think you can handle this. If I'm wrong . . . ''

Bebe could feel her pulses start to pound. Jane sounded so ominous. Whatever the packages contained must have something to do with Reuben. Summoning a smile to her lips, she said, ''Why don't you just get these . . . packages, and we'll take it from there.'' Her face remained expressionless when Jane returned a few moments later and handed her four battered brown envelopes.

While Jane cleared the room and washed the dishes and glassware, Bebe read. She was still engrossed as Jane moved the furniture back to its original position, vacuumed the rug, and straightened the remaining presents under the tree. Every now and then Jane glanced at her as she read Reuben's heart-wrenching words. Had she come to the part where Reuben said he loved her, she wondered. It was almost dawn when Bebe laid aside the last piece of paper, her eyes sad and moist.

"I think, Jane, that this is one of those miraculous gifts Gentiles talk about at Christmastime," she said quietly. "Thank you for sharing this with me. You were right to wonder if I was ready for something like this. Months ago I wouldn't have been able to handle it, but I can now." She gazed at the Christmas tree and smiled. "I wonder where he is and what he's doing at this moment. Christmas . . . I was standing by your tree earlier, and he came into my thoughts. He's always in my thoughts. I know I will love Reuben all my life and into eternity. I don't know why. He's never given me a reason to love him, but I do."

"Why don't I make breakfast and then you can go home to Willie," Jane offered. "I have a lot of leftover meat if you'd like to take some with you."

Bebe grinned. "On behalf of Willie, I thank you. He's getting a little tired of dog food. You won't believe this, but I cook for that animal. Reuben would die laughing if he knew."

Jane patted her hand. "Eggs and bacon coming up." It wasn't until they'd drained their third cup of coffee that Bebe spoke again.

"I want you to think about this after I leave. Let's start to film Reuben's . . . life. Right now. We'll requisition whatever we need in the way of sound stages, production crew, and all the rest of it—make it a top-secret, top-priority project. We'll scour the world for unknowns and turn this into another *Gone With the Wind*. You'll be in charge—which should get Nellie off your back for now. This will be our baby, from conception to birth to . . . Christ, we don't have the end!" Bebe cried suddenly.

"Not yet we don't, but we will," Jane told her confidently. "Another packet is due to arrive shortly. But you're right— everyone has to be sworn to secrecy. You know how this town gets when something is going on that isn't public knowledge."

Bebe smiled. "When they hear we're commandeering Fairmont's finest to make a top-secret film . . . God, Jane, can you picture the emotion of this town! I vote we do it."

Jane glowed. "I truly appreciate the confidence you have in

me. But what about..." She shifted uncomfortably, then turned to look Bebe straight in the eye. "What I mean is, you don't exactly come across as a sympathetic figure in this town. How are you going to feel when the whole damn industry starts raking over your past and questioning your ability to assume command of Fairmont this way?"

"I'll just stare them down. In my car!" Both women laughed.

"I have to be going," Bebe said, rising. "Willie gets... precocious if he isn't let out early. Merry Christmas, Jane, and thank you for the most wonderful gift I've ever received."

Ten miles away Philippe and Nellie sat in his car staring at the Little Chapel in the Hills. They'd been waiting since midnight, when Nellie had confessed that she couldn't make love without being married. Philippe had gaped at her in alarm, his erection dying instantly, as she'd sobbed and cried and apologized. "It's not that I don't want to, it's just that... I'm not that kind of girl. You said you wanted to marry me someday," she'd reminded him tearfully. "Why don't we make Christmas Day our someday. I don't care about a big wedding or anything like that. I just care about you. I'll marry you in a minute and make love to you twenty-four hours a day. If you... if you don't want to marry me or if you've changed your mind, I'll understand. Jane said Frenchmen aren't the marrying type the way American men are."

"I do want to marry you, but your father—my God, what will he think of me?" Philippe asked, disturbed.

"He's going to think you love me very much to marry me instead of taking me to bed without a wedding ring. He'll respect both of us," Nellie said in a determined voice. "A Christmas Day wedding. Isn't that romantic, Philippe? Neither of us will ever be able to forget our anniversary. Oh, Philippe, we can be so happy. I can help you run the studio. We'll be together night and day. But it has to be your idea; you must propose to me properly." She waited, eyes wide and imploring while Philippe stared at her in a daze. At last he dropped to one knee and took her hand in his.

"Will you marry me, Nellie?"

"Oh, Philippe, of course I'll marry you. Oh, darling, we're going to be so happy," she gushed. "With the two of us running the studio Bebe and Jane can retire. Daddy and Jane will get married, and Bebe will... she'll probably do whatever makes her happy. Oh, how romantic this is going to be!''

Philippe ignored the warning bell that was sounding far back in his mind. Instead, he stood up and pulled Nellie against him, nuzzling his chin against her soft, silky hair. ''I love you,'' he murmured.

''And I love you, darling Philippe, as much as I love life,'' she whispered.

Nellie and Philippe were married at two minutes past seven on Christmas Day. The ceremony was performed by the justice of peace and lasted three minutes. Nellie handed the bridal bouquet of plastic flowers back to the justice before she kissed her husband.

Mr. and Mrs. Philippe Bouchet drove to Philippe's house singing ''Jingle Bells'' at the top of their lungs.

Daniel spent the entire night staring at the artificial Christmas tree in the living room. It was so cold, so impersonal, with its dismal blue lights and blue ribbons on the tips of the branches. When dawn broke he called Philippe's house to find out when Nellie would be home, but there was no answer. Now he had two worries on his mind—Nellie and Jane. This was not the way he'd planned on spending Christmas, he thought morosely. He'd been so happy until Jane's party, and now he didn't know how to go about making things right. What was his first priority, Nellie or his relationship with Jane? Nellie was a proper young lady and she'd never stayed out all night before. It wasn't like her not to call.

It wasn't like Jane not to call, either. All night he'd waited for one or the other, and here he was still waiting—waiting for Jane to call, waiting for Nellie to come home. Anger raged through him. He'd give them one more hour, and if he hadn't heard from them by then, he'd say the hell with both of them.

His shower over, Daniel prepared a scrumptious breakfast of scrambled eggs and luscious pink ham, sliced thin just the way he liked it. It was one of the most dismal breakfasts he'd ever eaten.

Fed, showered, and shaved and nowhere to go on Christmas Day. It was a hell of a thing. His anger carried him back to the huge living room and the white Christmas tree. Rajean would have liked this tree, called it chic. Suddenly he upended it and gave it a vicious kick, and then another, venting all his anger on the toppled tree. Then, still seething, he left the house.

He was damn well going to Philippe Bouchet's house to find out where his daughter was, and then he was going to go to Jane's to apologize. He had enough of this damn bullshit. Today was Christmas, and he was going to celebrate it if it killed him and everyone he knew.

An hour later Daniel slowed his car as he saw Philippe swing his roadster into the driveway coming from the opposite direction. Damn kids were singing "Jingle Bells" at the top of their lungs. He found himself smiling. Nellie wore her sparkly gown, and Philippe was still dressed in evening clothes. They must have gone out to breakfast.

"Merry Christmas, Daddy," Nellie called gaily when he followed them up the driveway. "Do we have something to tell you! Do you want to guess, or shall we tell you? Philippe, you tell him!"

Philippe walked slowly down the driveway. It was obvious to Daniel that Nellie's exuberance hadn't rubbed off on him; he looked sad and bewildered. "Sir, there's no easy way to say this except to say it outright," he said reluctantly. He looked, Daniel thought, as if his head were going to be chopped off any second. "Nellie and I got married this morning. We sat outside the Little Chapel in the Hills until it opened." Daniel's shocked face drove him on. "It was my idea, sir. I love Nellie and she loves me. We . . . we wanted it to be right, and Nellie said she didn't care about a formal wedding. Later we can marry in church. . . . Sir?" Philippe said miserably when Daniel still didn't speak.

God Almighty, Reuben was going to hand him his head for allowing this to happen, Daniel thought, dazed. And Mickey, what in hell would she say when she found out? Why were the young so impulsive? When he saw that Philippe was waiting for him to say something, he forced himself to respond. "Congratulations. . . . But isn't this a little . . . sudden? I mean—"

"Now, look, Daddy, you aren't going to act like a silly father and say this marriage has to be annulled, are you?" Nellie broke in. "I love Philippe and he loves me. We're going to run the studio together, isn't that just too, too much?" She hugged him and planted a long, smacking kiss on his cheek. Then, seeing the concern in her father's eyes, she whispered, "Be happy for me, Daddy. It's what we both want."

"I am, I am, it's just that it's such a shock. When you didn't come home last evening . . ."

Nellie's gay laughter chilled Daniel to the very marrow of his bones. It carried the same undercurrent of disdain he'd heard when Rajean laughed at one of his silly jokes. "And of course you thought the worst of me, didn't you?" Nellie said lightly. "Admit it, Daddy. It's okay, in your place I would have thought the same thing. I thought you knew me better than that. I would never do anything to hurt you. Now," she said, clapping her hands together, "I am going to make a champagne breakfast for the two favorite men in my life. Come along." She laughed, making shooing motions with her hands. "I never saw such sad sacks. Liven up, be happy! Today is Christmas, and Philippe and I are going to be married for the rest of our lives. I'm so happy! So very, very happy!"

Daniel watched Philippe out of the corner of his eye. It might be Christmas and he might be married, but Philippe Bouchet was not a happy young man. Hadn't Nellie seen Philippe's misery? Or was she ignoring it? He wondered then whose idea it was to get married. Philippe had said it was his, but for some reason Daniel didn't believe him. He glanced at his daughter. How happy she was, and she deserved happiness. Rajean had never really provided a happy home life. Now Nellie was going to have a home of her own, one that wasn't too shabby by most standards. In fact, his daughter was going to be a very wealthy woman. In his heart he wished her well.

It was noon when Nellie and Philippe saw him out and stood in the driveway waving good-bye.

"Now, Philippe, you and I are going to have a little talk," Nellie said coolly after her father had left. "I am very weary at this moment, because you acted and are still acting as if we did something wrong. You didn't smile once the whole time Daddy was here. If you're having second thoughts, we can have this marriage annulled. You think I tricked you or something like that, don't you? Well, Philippe Bouchet, you can just drive me home now and . . . and I'll be out of your hair. . . . Well, why are you just standing there? Say something."

Philippe swayed dizzily as his head started to pound. Everything she said was true; he did think those things. Right this second he didn't give a damn if he never saw Nellie Bishop again. Nellie Bouchet. Suddenly the eggs he'd just eaten surged upward. With a strangled sound, he rushed to the first-floor powder room and emptied his stomach. Then he rinsed his mouth and swallowed four aspirins.

Nellie was waiting for him on the stairs, her elbows propped up on her knees and the long dress draped between her legs. Tears streamed down her cheeks. Philippe was reminded of a lovable homeless urchin. Contrite, he sat down next to her and put his arm around her shoulder. "Someday we're going to laugh about all this," he said huskily.

"Do you think so?" Nellie whimpered, and wiped at her tears with the hem of her dress. "I want to love you, Philippe. I want to know you belong to me and I belong to you. It's so important to me, to belong. I thought . . . I mean, in your situation with Uncle Reuben and Bebe and your other mother . . . it just seemed to me that we . . . My mother is gone, and Daddy—Daniel Bishop isn't my real father . . . I don't know what I'm trying to say . . ."

"It's me, Nellie, it isn't you," Philippe said quietly. "I do love you and I wanted to marry you, perhaps not as quickly, but now that we are, it will be fine. I guess I'm just in shock. I was thinking about my mother and worrying about why no word has arrived. My father . . . he should have managed to send some kind of message. I thought for sure that Christmas . . . I was so certain there would be word. Christmas is a day of miracles. Last evening at Jane's, my . . . Bebe . . . was so distant, so reserved. I will never get used to the idea that she—"

Nellie nodded. "Abandoned you, I know . . . but you must think of it as her loss, not yours. You have another mother who loves you. You know what they say about paybacks. . . . If the time ever comes when you want to get back at her, you have the power. Think about it—you could toss her out on her ear if you wanted to. Could you do that, Philippe?" She asked, leading her husband up the stairs.

"No. An eye for an eye isn't right. That would make me the same as she is. My father gave her half of the studio; he wanted her to have it. She'll do fine. Actually, I have to respect her in a way. She must have a lot of guts. In that respect she reminds me of my other mother. Besides, Nellie Bouchet, your father has the controlling two votes."

"Exactly!" Nellie said triumphantly. "And how do you think he would vote them? Our side, darling. If Bebe were *my* mother, I'd squash her like a bug for what she did. You are so kind and wonderful; I guess that's why I love you."

The warning bell he'd heard earlier sounded a second time. This time Philippe paid attention, watching as his new bride retreated to the bathroom to shower. Out of courtesy he used the shower in the guest bathroom, standing under the stinging spray for a long time, wondering how he knew he'd just made the most serious mistake of his young life.

Ten minutes later he was under the coverlet, naked as the day he was born. Nellie would expect him to be naked. His heart thumped crazily in his chest. He felt no desire, only dread. When he heard the bathroom door open, he almost shot out of bed. How pretty she looked with the towel draped around her, her damp hair hanging in ringlets around her face. She was smiling. Sweet Nellie. His wife, Nellie. The moment she dropped the towel, Philippe squeezed his eyes shut. After a slight hesitation Nellie lay down on her side of the bed. With Philippe lying rigidly on his side, there was enough space to fit several people between them.

"I'm the first to admit my ignorance in matters . . . what I mean is, I think one of us is supposed to move closer." Nellie giggled suddenly and bounced next to Philippe, who still had his eyes closed. "We are allowed to do this, Philippe. We're married now. We can do whatever we want in this bed. Or don't you want to do anything?" she asked, shifting slightly.

"Yes . . . no . . . I . . . can't," Philippe said miserably.

"What did you say?"

"I . . . I can't," Philippe repeated in the same tone of voice.

Nellie's mind raced. It was perfectly all right with her if he couldn't do anything. In fact, she was so relieved she felt like singing. She searched her mind for words and a tone that would convey just the right mood. "There are too many people in this bedroom, Philippe, and you brought them here. Your mother, your other mother, and your father and my father. They're your guests, not mine. I'm not trying to be cruel, darling, it's just that this has been . . . a traumatic day, and like you said, you've been worried about your mother and father. I understand, and I don't want you worrying about your"— she hesitated a moment—"inability to . . . you know. I think I'll sleep in the guest room, and later when you feel . . . we'll work into our marriage in degrees. It happened too quickly. I'll stay here with you till you're asleep, and then I'll go down the hall. All right, darling?"

Philippe almost cried with relief. Within seconds he pretended to have fallen asleep, snoring lightly. When Nellie slipped from the bed and left the room, he scrambled up and stared at the closed door. Should he get up and lock it? He *wanted* to get up and lock it. He *needed* to get up and lock it. But he didn't. He was a married man, and his wife had a right to return to his bed if she wanted to.

Frustrated and thoroughly wretched, Philippe Bouchet pounded his fists into his pillow. His last conscious thought before falling asleep was that he didn't love Nellie Bishop.

The Christmas tree lights winked at Jane. She'd forgotten to turn them off, even though she'd slept nearby on the sofa to be sure she heard the phone in case Daniel called. But he wasn't going to call now. It was ten-thirty A.M. on Christmas Day. If he was going to call, he would have done it before now. Depressed, she heaved herself up from the sofa, her eyes falling on the small gift-wrapped box Daniel had left on the table. A bracelet or necklace, possibly a lapel pin. How stupid she was, how incredibly stupid to think Daniel was going to give her an engagement ring. Well, she wasn't going to think about that now. First she'd take a shower, then have some breakfast and open her presents. Thank God she'd cleaned up last night. At least she wouldn't have to face the aftermath of the party this morning.

She was on the fourth step when the phone shrilled behind her. Jane's heart fluttered wildly in her chest as she made her way to the telephone table. Her hand snaked out to pick up the receiver and then drew back. She reached out a second time, her voice breathless with anticipation as she responded. Her eyes closed when she heard Bebe's voice.

"Merry Christmas, Jane! I just wanted to thank you for a truly lovely evening."

"It was my pleasure," Jane said dully.

There was a slight pause. "Oh, Jane, I'm so sorry! You thought . . . you hoped I was Daniel, didn't you? Look, I won't tie up your phone—"

"No, no, don't hang up. I've been sitting here all by myself staring at this damned tree and wishing Christmas would go away."

"Listen, I'm making a Christmas dinner. It's one of those things I have to do. I'd like it if you'd join me." Bebe giggled. "I have to warn you, though, my cooking leaves a lot to be desired. If you want to . . . if you'd rather wait to see if Daniel calls, I understand."

"Bebe, I think you just saved my life," Jane said with a catch in her voice. "I was just about to take a shower. I'll be there in an hour—and Bebe? Thanks."

"Forget it. I've been where you are many times. I know how it feels. I'll set an extra place. Listen, how do you feel about walking?"

"I love to walk, especially at night when it's cool and the crickets are out. Why do you ask?"

"Bring your walking shoes and a nightie. I think it's time the girls had a hen party. You game?"

Jane laughed. "I'm packing already."

The last thing Jane did before leaving her house was to open the present from Nellie. It turned out to be a framed photograph of herself, probably her high school graduation picture. She looked young and wholesome in her dark sweater and Peter Pan collar. Jane's first impulse was to pack it up and send it back; Instead, she shoved the picture back into the box and pushed it as far under the tree as she could.

Jane arrived at Bebe's at noon, her overnight case in her hand and an expensive bottle of perfume she'd been saving to share with just the right person.

Daniel Bishop rang Jane's doorbell, then let himself in with his key when she didn't answer. The first thing he noticed was his unopened present. Uneasy, he walked through the neat, tidy house, calling Jane's name over and over. Eventually he settled on her sofa and proceeded to drink himself into oblivion. At six o'clock he sank into a drunken stupor and didn't wake until four in the morning, at which time he walked through Jane's dark house calling her name again and again. Where in the goddamn hell was she at four in the morning?

Christmas was over, he thought bitterly as he drove home. The worst Christmas of his life.

Bebe raised her glass of club soda and made the first Christmas toast. "To Reuben, may he be successful in his mission."

"You really mean that, don't you?" Jane said in awe.

"Yes. I love Reuben and I want him to be happy." She held her glass aloft a second time. "Merry Christmas to you, Jane."

Jane smiled and held out her own glass. "Merry Christmas,

Bebe. Here's to our partnership and the success of our new film. Long live Hollywood!''

Willie barked under the table, and Bebe smiled. Life was almost perfect, she thought.

Almost.

Chapter Twenty-seven

THE WINTER'S SNOWS WERE HIGH NOW, AND NOT A DAY went by without more, always more. The incessant stinging sharp spray blew against Reuben now, making each step he took seem like two. Often he fell backward, and then anger at himself would drive him forward with a vengeance.

He was with a new guide, a youth named Marcel. The boy had the stamina of a mountain goat, his steps sure and deft even in the knee-high snow. Numberless times the boy had turned to reach out a hand and pull Reuben from his deep tracks. He'd promised snowshoes on their next stop, which wasn't scheduled for hours yet.

Twice he'd almost been caught, and his last guide, Didier, had saved his skin—once on the train to Carcassonne and again when they'd leapt off the same train minutes before it was due to arrive in Carcassonne. The Germans on the train had been lax, but there had been one sharp-eyed soldier who kept staring at Reuben's American boots. Didier had played the part of a drunk, melancholy because his lover had rejected him on the holiday. Staggering in his tracks, he'd spewed words about women wanting presents, laces, and fine stockings and cigarettes. And, he'd demanded of the Germans, where was a poor peasant like himself to get such fine things? The soldiers had laughed, poking him on the shoulder to show they understood his feelings. All except the soldier with the sharp eyes. He hadn't laughed. Reuben's heart pounded in his chest. There were four Germans in their car and probably four more at the other end. There would be more in Carcassonne.

"This is my uncle," Didier had said, pointing to Reuben. "I took his advice and now I am without a woman. He has had three wives and still I listened to him. I am a fool!" With an admirable show of despair, he'd thumped his chest in disbelief at what had happened. Reuben's heart continued to pound as he tried for a lopsided grin that didn't quite come off.

The sharp-eyed soldier moved to the back of the car, the other three moving forward to the middle car. Didier's hand snaked out to grip Reuben's thigh. A signal, but what did it mean? He nearly jumped out of his skin when Didier turned to the soldier behind him. *"D'urgence, sans delai, uriner."* For Christ's sake, thought Reuben, why did he want to take a piss now? The soldier shook his head, but Didier was already standing, motioning the soldier to follow him. Reuben rose, too, his hands on the fly front of his trousers. Now he understood.

At the back of the car Didier pushed at the heavy door and actually urinated. Then he stepped back for Reuben to take his place. It was now or never, thought Reuben. His bladder was completely empty. As he sidled up to the open doorway, he felt a violent push and hurtled through swirling snow, striking the ground with a hard thud. Although he hadn't actually seen Didier's next move, he knew the Frenchman had swiveled and caught the German soldier behind the knees, sending him flying after Reuben. Minutes later Reuben heard a sharp crack as Didier snapped the soldier's neck.

"We have ten minutes, possibly fifteen, before the others realize he's gone. We must be quick," Didier muttered, slinging the rifle over his shoulder. "All of them won't leave the train. Maybe three will come after us, but when the train pulls into the station the whole fucking army will be after us. This snow isn't heavy enough to cover our tracks. Move, monsieur!"

Reuben scrambled up the embankment on his hands and knees, Didier behind him. They ran then, as quickly as they could in the deep snow, trying to put as much distance between themselves and the Germans. Traveling as they were over flat land, and exposed to the elements, they were prey to any

German vehicle that came along—and there would be vehicles as soon as the Germans on the train alerted the checkpoint at Carcassonne.

Now they were no more than eight klics from Carcassonne, still on flat land that Marcel said would change within the hour. Reuben prayed that the youth knew what he was talking about.

"Monsieur, I have seen an old man move faster," the boy snarled impatiently. "I have a sweetheart I wish to see again. Slide your feet through the snow instead of lifting them up. Monsieur, you must hurry. If you look behind you, you will see a German truck. Once they see our path they will have no trouble following us as we are packing down the snow. Now do you understand me?"

"Yes," Reuben replied through clenched teeth. His lungs felt seared with the cold, and his entire body was numb with pain, so numb he couldn't feel his feet or his hands. But he kept on, moving as fast as he could, after Marcel.

"There is a ravine we must reach that will afford us some protection. The snow is worsening, and it will be dark in another hour. Faster, monsieur."

Yes, faster. Marcel had young legs, so it was easy for him to issue orders. Reuben's chest was on fire, his eyes burned by the cold. He could barely see where he was going, yet he had to keep moving. Desperately he tried to conjure up hatred, a hatred intense enough to drive him onward. But it wasn't working; his knees buckled, and he collapsed into the snow face first. Marcel's hand lashed out, grasping his shoulder. For a young boy, his grip was frightening. In another moment Reuben was on his feet and moving at the boy's sharp words.

"A puppy dog goes faster," he growled.

"You son of a bitch! A dog has four legs," Reuben snarled.

"It is easy to see you are no Frenchman," Marcel snapped over his shoulder.

"I never said I was a Frenchman." Reuben snapped back. "I'm an American, I'm three times your age, and I'm not apologizing."

"I didn't ask for an apology. I asked you to move faster. All of us who have helped you have placed our lives in danger. The least you could do, monsieur, is move your goddamn feet faster. Do you want me to tell you what those filthy swine do to partisans? Of course you do," Marcel said nastily. "If they catch someone like myself, they . . . they hack off his penis.

The older ones like yourself, they carve off your testicles. For sure you will not walk, monsieur.''

Reuben knew the boy was baiting him, doing his best to make him move as fast as he could. He heard the boy next to him chuckle.

"I think I would kill myself if that happened to me," Marcel said. "What would you do, monsieur?"

"In America we call testicles balls, and the man hasn't yet been born who will carve mine from my body. Just shut the hell up and leave me alone."

The boy grinned in the fast-approaching twilight. This American was crazy, but he was all right for a man his age. *Mon Dieu*, he was so tired himself that he wanted to drop in his tracks and sleep, but he'd promised Denise he would return to her.

He was a handsome youth with his dark hair and eyes to match, Reuben thought. Thin but sinewy, and tall, almost his own height. And his hands were strong, that much was certain. All in all a young boy on the verge of manhood, the way Daniel was when Reuben had first met him. This one was dedicated and motivated to kill for his country. Reuben doubted there was a more loyal Frenchman anywhere.

The wind was sharp as a butcher's knife as they slogged ahead. Reuben was on all fours more than he was on his feet, and in the end he stayed that way, crawling after Marcel, making better time. Snow crusted the top of his wool gloves and stuck to the fine hairs on his wrists, but it didn't matter, he couldn't feel the ice. Nothing mattered anymore, he thought groggily.

A violent gust of snow and wind slammed into him, driving him backward. He cursed in English and then in French. Marcel laughed, a boyish sound of delight, then stretched out his hand to Reuben, who grasped it gratefully. "We're at the ravine, monsieur. Now you will be able to rest, but you must not sleep. Slide down on your . . . ass." Reuben did as instructed. Almost immediately he felt warmer.

"For a while we'll be safe here," Marcel continued. "A while, monsieur, can mean an hour or it can mean days. You must prepare yourself. You will sleep only when I tell you, is that agreed?" Reuben nodded. "Good. It's snowing harder now, and the darkness will protect us. These Germans, sometimes they have dogs that can smell a man a mile away, but I heard no barking. I have very good ears." He grinned. "Here," he said a moment later, "eat this cheese and you'll feel your strength returning." Reuben bit off a chunk of the rock-hard cheese and chewed obediently.

"We can talk here, Monsieur American. I am sorry if I was, how do you say in America, too tough on you. It was for your own good. I hope you understand." If not, the boy implied with a shrug of his shoulders, it mattered little. "Tell me about the person you came all this way to find," he said. "The networks are all buzzing about this crazy American who seeks a woman from his past."

Reuben grunted and gave an indifferent shrug of his shoulders. But he talked then because he had to or he would have fallen asleep. He told the youth about his first meeting with Mickey and all about Bebe. When he got to the part about Philippe, his voice broke.

Marcel held up a hand. "It is enough, monsieur, you need tell me no more."

"No, I want to," Reuben insisted, and told him all about Simon and Dillon and his reaction to Philippe and the boy's reaction to himself. A long while later, after he was finished, he asked, "Well, Marcel, what is your opinion?"

"You are either very wise or very foolish, monsieur. You have come all this way, risked your life, to apologize for something that happened twenty years ago. I do not think I would have the courage to do what you are doing. Part of me thinks you are foolish and part of me applauds you. Tell me," he said, "what will you do when you find your old lover? Have you given any thought to how you will feel? What will you do if this wonderful woman wants to pick up where you left off years ago?"

"I don't know," Reuben replied honestly.

"I have heard of this woman and the other one she travels with. When this is all over they will be remembered. We will tell our children of her. I hope you find her, monsieur." He was silent for a few moments before he spoke again. "I am disappointed in your son. I think you are, too, eh, monsieur? A twenty-year-old Frenchman is a man. He should be with us, defending his country. He is not the man his father is. I mean no disrespect, for I believe you think the same thing. How will he ever be able to feel like a man when he knows he ran to safety? Yes, yes,I know his mother wanted it and that he is Jewish. All the more reason to stay and defend France. What must he be thinking, monsieur? His father comes here in the middle of the war, and he stays in your place and makes films. It is very sad.''

''You would not do what my son did, is that what you're saying? Even if your mother asked . . . insisted you be kept safe?''

''No, monsieur. My mother would never ask that of me, nor my father. This is my home, my country, my people. Your old lover has turned your son into a coward. I am sorry if my words offend you; it is how I feel.''

''Perhaps someday we'll know how he feels. A mother's love is very strong, very intense,'' Reuben said quietly.

''Understandable, but still wrong. . . . I think, monsieur, you can sleep for a little while. I will stay on watch. It is much warmer here, eh? The scrub brush and trees break the wind and carry the snow. Sleep and you will grow warm, the snow will be like a blanket.''

It was already light out, an hour or so past dawn, Reuben judged, when he grappled his way out of sleep. He was warm and hungry and had to go to the bathroom. And he was alone, he realized, his eyes going immediately to where Marcel had lain. The boy was gone, perhaps to check the area outside the ravine or possibly to relieve himself. Reuben looked upward through the snow and saw a ring of faces staring down at him.

All of them German.

Chapter Twenty-eight

THREE DAYS AFTER HIS MARRIAGE AND TWO DAYS BEFORE
the beginning of the New Year, Philippe Bouchet, also known
as Philip Tarz, climbed from his bed, dressed quietly so as not
to disturb his sleeping wife, jammed his newly forged American
credentials bearing the name Philip Reuben into the inside
pocket of his jacket, and left the house. His movements stealthy, he placed a whispered call to the local taxi company. Then
he closed the door quietly behind him and left the house without
a backward glance.

His hands in his pockets, he marched to the end of the street,
where he waited for his taxi. Ten minutes later he gave the
driver the address of his first stop: 5633 Laurel Canyon Road.

Bebe heard the sounds of a car engine the same moment
Willie barked furiously, his paws slipping and sliding on the
polished floors as he raced downstairs to growl and bark at the
front door. Curious, Bebe peered through the curtains at her
bedroom window. Whoever was calling was keeping a taxi
waiting.

Tying the belt of her robe with a jerk, she headed for the
stairs. Holding on to Willie by his collar, she thrust open the
huge heavy door and stared into the miserable eyes of her son.
Startled, she backed up one step, then another. Willie strained
at her tight grasp.

"I'm sorry to bother you," he faltered, "but I find myself in need of a . . . friend. Do you . . . would you take the time to speak with me for a few moments?"

Bebe stared as though mesmerized into his pleading eyes, then nodded and closed the door. "I must let Willie out and, if you like, I can make some coffee."

"I'd like that very much if it isn't too much trouble."

Some minutes later Bebe set a steaming cup of coffee in front of her son. "Use both hands," she said gently. "I used to do that when I was hung over from a party. And take your time, Philippe."

He nodded and obediently cupped his hands around the mug. "What should I call you?" he asked. "I don't want to offend you . . . that was never my intention . . . I don't know what the rules are in . . . situations like ours."

"Bebe will be fine. You said you needed a friend," she prodded gently, wondering why he hadn't gone to Nellie or Daniel.

Philippe swallowed the scalding coffee, barely aware that he'd just burned his tongue. "I came here for several reasons. I . . . I made a terrible mistake on Christmas. I . . . what I did was . . . I got married. To Nellie. I swear to God I . . . I don't know what possessed me to do that. For a little while I thought I loved her, certainly I . . . I wanted her, but she said . . . she said she wasn't that kind of girl. It was her idea, but I went along with it. She loves me very much and I don't want to hurt her. We never . . . I was so . . . the marriage was never . . . consummated," he blurted out. "My . . . my other mother would be so ashamed of me if she knew. It's all I've thought of these past days. We got married on Christmas Day and the day after I enlisted in the army," he lied. "I'd been thinking about joining up for weeks. I'm leaving today. I . . . you're the only one who knows. . . ."

Philippe leaned across the table to stare at his mother. "I don't belong here, my home is in France with my other mother. I don't even know if she's alive. She wouldn't allow me to stay and join the French Army or the Resistance. She was afraid for me. At the time I was afraid, too. I feel as though I betrayed my country and myself. I don't want to make films, I'm tired of spending money for meaningless things. None of that matters to me. If I thought I could make a valuable contribution to our film company, I might consider staying, but there's absolutely nothing for me to do. I play with paper clips,

I sharpen pencils, I look at contracts, I voice an opinion that is solely my own, and it isn't even an intelligent opinion. This studio belongs to my father. I don't want it, I never wanted it. I realize that now.''

Bebe thought her heart would shatter at her son's words. Married! To Nellie! She chose her words carefully. "I think I understand how you feel. I thought for a long time that I wanted the studio myself. Now that Reuben has given me his half, I . . . it's not that I don't want it . . . it's this fear that I can never measure up. For months now I've tried to learn the operation, and I think I know it, but to put it to the practical test . . . I'm just not sure. I do understand your feelings. You're much too young to tie yourself down to something you don't like or want. And that goes for marriage as well. You could have the marriage annulled if you . . . as you say, you didn't consummate the marriage. Of course the decision has to be yours. I don't think . . . no, I *know* that your mother would never, under any circumstances, be ashamed of you. Mickey loves you, she'd understand. It simply isn't in her to condemn or judge others, Philippe, even her own son. Your mother's only sin is that she loves too much.

"As for Nellie," she continued, "do you think it wise, or should I say gentlemanly, to leave her in the lurch like this? I don't know your situation, but don't you think she has a right to know? I found out a lifetime ago that you can't run away from your problems, you must face them head on and resolve them to the best of your ability.''

Philippe shook his head. "I wrote her a letter last night and left it in the dining room. She'll find it when she wakes up. Perhaps it is the coward's way out. But it is the best way for me as things are now.'' He hesitated a moment, then went on. "Before I leave, I would like to know why you abandoned me. I came here prepared to hate both you and my father. I tried to live off that hatred, but it was such an effort. I wanted both of you to look at me, to get to know me, and of course, to regret what you'd done. It can't matter now, so there is no reason to hide things from me. This might be your last chance to make things right between us. I couldn't fight for the country I thought was mine, so I will fight for yours.''

They talked then, mother and son. Bebe didn't spare herself at all, nor did she spare Reuben. What she said in closing startled her son: "I think, Philippe—and this is only my opinion—that you married a Bebe Rosen. I don't for a minute think

Nellie is the person she pretends to be.'' She told him then of her long talk with Jane Perkins on Christmas Eve and the time they spent together on Christmas Day.

"I've been so stupid!" Philippe cried.

Bebe smiled. "Everyone is stupid at some time in his life, Philippe. One learns from one's mistakes. It takes some of us longer, that's all. You said you came here because you needed a friend. Does that mean you want my advice?" Philippe nodded. "Then file for an annulment. I can speak to Daniel if you want. Do you want to give me your power of attorney?"

"I left it on the dresser for Nellie. I gave it to her."

Bebe's heart sank. "A later one will take precedence, I'm sure of it. I'll call my attorney, and we can write it out in longhand. I'll have Jane come over and witness your signature. Things like this are done all the time." I think, she added to herself.

It was a few minutes past noon when Philippe Bouchet signed his name to the document Bebe copied verbatim over the phone. Jane signed her name beneath Philippe's, then added the date and the time.

On the front steps of the house, Bebe watched her son leave, perhaps for the last time. Suddenly she panicked; she couldn't lose him again, she just couldn't! "John Paul!" she screamed. The boy turned and made his way back to her, his eyes as full as her own. "I've always loved you, every day of my life. But your other mother loves you more, and that's why . . ."

"You can let me go. I understand about partings. I'll be back. I'd like us to get to know each other. I want you to know that I . . . I like it that you gave me a name and thought of me all those years as John Paul. I hope I can live up to two such distinguished names." He wrapped her in his arms and hugged her warmly. "Good-bye, Mother," he whispered.

"Good-bye, John Paul. Now hurry, son, or you'll miss the plane. And I don't think my car would make it to Fort Dix."

Philippe laughed, sounding so much like Reuben that Bebe nearly burst into tears. In another two days it would be Philippe's 21st birthday. Happy Birthday John Paul, she whispered. Moments later the taxi rattled down the driveway . . . and he was gone.

The war at home was just starting; the first battle was scheduled for the second day of the New Year, when the studio reopened for business.

* * *

Nellie devoured an enormous breakfast of pancakes, eggs, and ham, along with juice, melon, and three cups of coffee. She was sitting in the sun on the small terrace wondering where Philippe had gone at this time of the morning. Earlier she'd cracked open one eye and watched him dress in casual clothes and then stuff a packet of papers inside his jacket.

The last several days had been hell for him, that much she knew. Not once had he met her steady gaze, and he'd barely spoken to her. Each night he'd retired early, and she'd joined him much later, careful to remain on her side of the bed. As far as she was concerned, the only thing that mattered was that the servants believe they shared the same bed.

The housekeeper appeared in the doorway, an envelope in her hand. "I found this on the dining room table, ma'am," she said quietly.

"Well, don't just stand there, fetch it here and clear the table," Nellie ordered.

The envelope yielded two pieces of paper, one of them a legal document—Philippe's power of attorney. In the note, Philippe announced that he had left her to join the army. To make up for her loss, he'd given her his half of the studio for the time being, his car, his house, and his bank account. How sweet of him, how gallant, Nellie thought sardonically, laughing to herself. The French were so noble.

First she would shower and dress, she decided, and then pay a special visit to the local bank that held a portion of Philippe's assets. She had a plan, and if all went well . . .

The battle lines were drawn now, by her missing husband: her father and herself on one end, Bebe and Jane on the other. For regardless of Jane's feelings for her father, she would align herself with Bebe.

"You lose," she crooned as she stepped into the shower. "My father will protect me and my rights with his last breath."

It was a conviction Nellie Bishop Tarz-Bouchet believed implicitly.

Ninety minutes later Nellie parked Philippe's Cadillac roadster, hers now, in the bank's parking lot. The power of attorney safe in her handbag, she climbed daintily from the gleaming car.

She had chosen to dress conservatively, much like Jane Perkins, in a tailored suit and crisp white blouse. Because of the tan she affected, cosmetics were largely unnecessary except for a little mascara to enhance her eyes. Her blond hair was done up in an elegant daytime chignon. All in all she looked like she was thirty years old instead of eighteen.

The bank's president received her cordially. He was a fussy, prissy man of sixty or so with a balding head that he kept touching and a mustache that was clipped and pruned like the border of a rose garden. His voice, when he spoke, was nasal, as though he had a cold, which he did. From time to time he apologized and blew his nose in a soft white handkerchief. Nellie handed him the power of attorney, which he accepted with an air of bemused attentiveness. The moment he finished reading it, Nellie had it back in her hands.

"My husband's attorney can furnish you with a copy," she said briskly. "I'm not here to withdraw monies. Actually, Mr. Evans, I'd like to have all our assets transferred to your bank. The Morgan Guaranty is"—Nellie wrinkled her nose—"too . . . stuffy and stodgy. I prefer to deal with younger institutions and bankers who have foresight. When all the transactions are complete, I'd like a full accounting. Can you do that?"

Ambrose Evans fingered his clipped mustache. He had a vague idea of Philippe Bouchet's accumulated wealth, and it had made him dizzy the day he'd opened the young man's account. The idea that someday his bank might handle the entire balance boggled his mind. Now he was going to be dealing with Bouchet's wife. He nodded, not trusting himself to speak.

"I wonder if your accounting department can give me some idea of our present bank balance. I'd also like an estimate of our accounts at Morgan. Now," Nellie said coolly, her heart thumping in her chest. Anticipation was so wonderful.

Evans cleared his throat. "Certainly I can do that, but don't you have your bank statements? What you're asking will take a little time. The statements would afford you a balance to the very penny." Something was wrong here, he could feel it. Yet the power of attorney was in order. He knew the law firm that had drawn it up and the lawyer in particular; he played bridge with the man every Saturday night.

"I'll wait," Nellie said sweetly. "I have all the time in the world now that my husband has gone off to fight for his country." With consummate delicacy, she allowed her eyes to moisten and dabbed at them with a lace-edged handkerchief.

"Yes, well, hrumph, I'll see what I can do," Evans said, and shifted uncomfortably on his chair. "In the meantime I'll

have my secretary fetch you a soft drink and a magazine while
I . . . get in touch with Mr. Bouchet's bankers in New York.''

"That's so very kind of you, Mr. Evans. Philippe, in his
haste to report in, forgot to give me the safe deposit key
where he keeps all his papers and records. I'm sure he'll get
in touch with me as soon as he can. He was so eager to be
off to defend our wonderful country that I guess it simply
slipped his mind. The very last thing he begged me to do
was come here today and straighten things out. It was his
wish that our accounts be transferred here to make things
easier for me.''

Evans tidied up his desk and nodded limply. Good, she was
throwing him for a loop, Nellie decided. His bald head was
beaded with perspiration. She sighed wearily and dabbed at
her eyes again.

By the time Evans resumed his seat behind his tidy desk,
she was halfway through the tattered copy of the *Saturday
Evening Post*. Without a word he handed Nellie a slip of paper.
The smoke spiraling upward from her cigarette covered the
shock in her eyes. If Philippe didn't come back, it would be
all hers. "That's more or less what I thought it was,'' she said
blandly.

"There is one problem, Mrs. Bouchet,'' Evans said just as
blandly.

"Oh, and what is that, Mr. Evans?'' Nellie said, gathering
up her purse and gloves.

"The accounts can't be transferred until Mr. Bouchet is
twenty-one years old. You can, of course, draw from them,
and if the trustees approve your withdrawals, the money will
be sent on to you. They requested a copy of your power of
attorney as well as your marriage license. I took the liberty of
telling them your attorney would forward the documents. Is all
this satisfactory?''

Nellie sighed. "Now, Mr. Evans, this is what I want you
to do. Tomorrow I want you to go to New York personally,
and by the close of business on Friday I expect this account to
register all of our assets. If you handle this satisfactorily,'' she
added pointedly, "I'll personally see about turning over some
of the studio business to your bank. And now I must be off.
Thank you so much for seeing me without an appointment,
Mr. Evans. I know my husband will appreciate it, and I'll be

sure to mention your cooperation when I write him this evening. Good afternoon.''

Nellie sailed from the office with the knowledge that she was a wealthy woman—an immensely wealthy woman if Philippe didn't return. His insurance policy alone would provide for her the rest of her life.

In a state of euphoria, Nellie drove home, undressed, removed her mascara, and put on a mint-green playsuit with matching skirt and white sandals. She was ready now, she told her reflection. Her destination, Reuben's house in Laurel Canyon, where her father was probably this moment changing the bird feeders and making sure the birdbaths were full of fresh water.

Nellie Bishop Tarz-Bouchet had learned to cry on cue at the age of six. Now she squeezed her eyes shut and willed the tears to flow. Sniffling, she rubbed her eyes. By the time she reached her father, it would look as if she'd spent the entire day weeping over Philippe's departure.

When she reached the mansion she ran straight to the back of the house and looked about wildly for her father. He was sitting on an iron bench under a rose trellis, a bag of birdseed at his feet and an open book on his lap. Screaming his name, she ran to him, arms outstretched. Gulping and swallowing, sobbing and coughing, she blurted out her unhappiness.

''Honey, it's not the end of the world,'' Daniel said, stroking her sympathetically. ''If you hadn't agreed, I'm sure Philippe wouldn't have enlisted. I'm so sorry, honey, but if, as you say, it's what Philippe wanted, then of course you had no other choice. He'll come back, Nellie, I know he will. He's Reuben's son, and I believe he's a survivor. Do you regret marrying so hastily, sweetheart?'' Daniel crooned against her golden head.

Nellie shook her head. ''Never, Daddy. We had a few glorious days together. We discussed this for hours and hours. He was so miserable, Daddy. First he didn't want to leave me, and then he kept talking about being a coward and not staying to fight for France. That was so terrible for him. Do you know, he actually cried in my arms. He's been so unhappy at the studio; he hates it there. He said he wanted to make his father proud of him. And you, too, Daddy. He knows I'm proud of him no matter what he does. I . . . I encouraged him, even though . . . Oh, Daddy, I am so miserable and unhappy,'' she wept. ''He kept talking and telling me what to do at the studio . . . Oh, he gave me this.'' She held out the power of attorney. ''I didn't want to take it, didn't want him to give me this, but he absolutely insisted. He said I should tell you . . . tell you—'' Nellie's voice broke, and she threw herself into her father's arms, sobbing uncontrollably.

"What, Nellie? What did Philippe ask you to tell me?'' Daniel said gently, his hands stroking her shoulder.

"He said," Nellie gulped, "to make sure I told you to send a copy of this to the bank in New York . . . I can't remember the name of it . . . and to transfer all his holdings out here to the bank he uses. He said it can't be done until he's twenty-one, but that you should start the paperwork. His birthday is just two days away. Oh, Daddy, I don't want his money, I want Philippe!" Nellie howled. "He made me promise, so . . . I'm telling you like I promised. I made so many promises, foolish ones. I had to for Philippe's sake. It's what he wanted. Oh, Daddy, do you think I can run his share of the studio? I'm so . . . scared. What if . . . what if . . . if Philippe doesn't come back? I can't eat, I can't think, all I do is think about Philippe.''

"Shhh, don't cry, honey, everything is going to be fine,'' Daniel reassured her. "We'll take it one day at a time. In the meantime, I want you to move back here with me so you won't be alone.''

"I can't do that, Daddy. I promised Philippe that I would be brave and strong and stand on my own two feet and manage things. If I hadn't promised, he wouldn't have gone." She squared her shoulders with heroic resolution. "I have to prove myself, to him and to me. He said I should sell the house and buy something grand, like this house, and that I should hire servants to look after me.''

"All right, now everything is going to be fine, honey. Why don't you go up to your old room and take a nap," Daniel cajoled. "You look exhausted. We'll have dinner on the terrace, would you like that?''

Nellie sniffed and hiccoughed. "Yes, I would. You are so wonderful and understanding. I love you as much as I love Philippe. Here!" she said, thrusting the power of attorney into Daniel's hands. "I don't want this . . . this paper. You take care of it.''

"I will. Now, run along. I'll look in on you after a bit. And you better be sound asleep," he teased.

After Nellie left, Daniel sat down with a thump on the iron bench. "I'll be damned," he muttered. So Philippe was a chip off the old block. He should have seen it coming, been prepared. He felt himself puff out in pride and couldn't decide whom he was more proud of—Nellie or Philippe.

What a remarkable young couple they were.

Hours later, his garden chores completed, Daniel set about readying the fire for his barbecue. As he was stoking the coals, he smelled a familiar scent. Jane! He whirled, his heart taking on an extra beat. Coming down the same flagstone steps were both Bebe and Jane. Grinning, he tossed his cooking utensils on the bench beside the open pit and approached them. "Just in time for dinner!" he shouted happily, his arms outstretched in welcome.

Jane neatly sidestepped Daniel's welcome, but Bebe allowed a peck on her cheek. "I'm sorry we didn't call ahead, Daniel, but we've been talking, and I decided we should just come over. This isn't a social visit, I'm afraid. It's business."

A nerve at the side of Daniel's eye twitched. His first thought was that Jane and Bebe were obviously allies, but against whom? Himself? Surely Jane wasn't going to allow their private lives to interfere with studio business. Recovering, he stepped aside and invited them to sit down.

"Let's go down into the garden," Bebe said quietly.

His eyes puzzled and apprehensive, Daniel followed them. "I didn't think there was any studio business this week," he said lightly.

"This business concerns . . . my son. I'm here because of Philippe," Bebe explained. "He came to see me early this morning before he left for Fort Dix, to say good-bye . . . and to tell me he made a mistake in marrying Nellie. He told me he didn't love her, and that she . . . he said she'd tricked him into marrying her. Apparently the marriage was never consummated. I told him he could get an annulment if he wanted. . . . Oh, Daniel, he was so distraught, so unhappy! He talked for a long time, and we managed to clear up a lot of the misunderstandings between us."

Bebe paused and glanced over at Jane, who inclined her head encouragingly. Bebe nodded and turned back to Daniel. "One thing that particularly disturbed him was the fact that he'd left his power of attorney with Nellie. At his insistence I called my attorney, who dictated another one over the phone. I copied it verbatim, and Philippe signed and dated it. The time is on it also to show that it superseded the one he left for Nellie. I called Jane to be the witness." She shrugged. "That's about it, Daniel."

"For Christ's sake, Bebe, surely you don't expect me to believe this . . . this bullshit you're handing me," Daniel exploded. "My God, woman! I can't believe you'd stoop this low. I thought you'd turned over a new leaf. No, I won't stand for this. Never!"

"No, Daniel, what Bebe is telling you is the truth," Jane broke in pleadingly. "I was there. I spoke with Philippe. This is what he wants. For months I couldn't understand why he took such a sudden dislike to me. I asked him this morning, and he said Nellie told him I was arranging dates for her with some of the stars and insisting she see older men, men affiliated with the studio. That simply isn't true. I would never do such a thing, and I think you know it.

"I don't like your daughter, Daniel," she continued after a slight pause. "She has undermined me every chance she could. What's more, she's lied—not once, but several times. Believe me, I feel terrible saying these things to you. I was so fed up, so disgusted that I drew up my resignation; it's locked in my desk." She gave a choked laugh. "I was going to let her push me out, Daniel, because I loved you with all my heart and I didn't want any problems. But now . . . I'm so sorry, Daniel. I wish . . ."

"You wish what? Nellie was right, you are a scheming know-it-all," Daniel said hoarsely. "She said you dumped all your frustrations on her. She told me what it was like working for you, but I didn't want to believe her."

Jane's eyes blazed. "Did she tell you about *Ambrosia*? It was a wonderful property, one I was determined to buy. Only we missed out because I let the option lapse—I thought we had two more days than we did. And the reason I thought that was because someone had changed the lapse date on the agreement; you can see the erasure marks. Then, after the deadline had come and gone, the agreement was tampered with again to reflect the original date." Jane paused and looked Daniel straight in the eye. "I think Nellie did it, Daniel—your daughter. And I also believe she tricked Philippe into marrying her. I saw that young man, and he wasn't lying, I can tell you that."

Daniel's eyes were wild behind his glasses. "I cannot believe you're saying any of this. You of all people, Jane. How could

I have been so wrong about you? Bebe, yes, her colors will never change, but you! Jesus, I loved you, wanted to marry you . . . And now this. Well, I'll tell you one thing—until I hear this from Philippe himself, I am discounting everything you say. And now I'd appreciate it if you'd both get off my property.''

"Whose property, Daniel?'' Bebe asked coolly. "My divorce from Reuben isn't final yet. I still own half this house. I can stay here as long as I wish. I can also fire you if I wish.'' She paused a moment, then sighed and shook her head. "Only I *don't* wish. . . . You were never pigheaded before, Daniel. You always listened to reason, one of the few people capable of seeing both sides of an issue. I admire your attitude toward your daughter; family is important. But truth is truth. If you turn this into a legal matter, we'll fight you every step of the way, which means Philippe's shares will be under contest until the matter is resolved. The entire studio could be jeopardized.''

Daniel's legal mind raced. It was true. Nellie would be out in the cold if he didn't do something. Christ, he wanted to laugh and cry at the same time. He was angry now, angrier than he'd ever been in his life.

"Are you going to fight me, Daniel?'' Bebe asked crisply.

"You're damn right I am—with my last breath if necessary. I'm not going to let you ruin these two young people.''

Bebe stared at her old friend for a long time before she spoke. And when she did, it was to Jane. "Show him.''

Jane drew a thick brown envelope from her purse. "I think if you read twenty or so pages, you'll know what you have in your hands. We've decided to go into production with this as soon as possible—even if your interference forces us to close down the studio! Because I warn you, Daniel: if you make a move against us, I *will* resign, effective immediately, and what's more I'll demand full compensation—in one lump sum. That means my termination settlement, retirement pension, every monetary remuneration Reuben set up for me according to the terms of my contract. It's a considerable amount, Daniel—and added to the financial burden of a legal dispute, it could even wipe out the studio. But I'm sure you know that.''

Daniel's eyes glittered coldly as he started to read from the thick folder. He continued to read until it was too dark to see Reuben's cramped handwriting. His hands trembled when he handed the thick envelope back to Jane, who was now a dim shadow in the early twilight.

It was to Bebe he spoke. "I have an ironclad contract. I should know, I drew it up myself." His voice was so full of pain, Bebe winced.

"I know that, but I can challenge it," she replied. "I don't want to do that, Daniel. All I want is what's best for the studio. That should be all you want, too. Reuben will never forgive you if you allow things to get out of hand. And because he isn't here, I must protect and respect our son's wishes."

"Not at the expense of my daughter," Daniel said in a choked voice.

"She's a bad seed, Daniel. She's not your blood daughter," Bebe reminded him. "You think about that and remember Rajean. Think back and remember."

Daniel reached out to Jane, who instinctively backed up a step. "Jane, I loved you. I don't understand . . ." he cried brokenly.

"I love you *now*, Daniel, I'll always love you, but I can't . . . I won't let Nellie destroy all that Reuben built up, and me along with it," Jane said quietly. "If I hadn't talked to Philippe myself today, I would have let that happen in the name of my love for you. But not now. Good-bye, Daniel."

Daniel sat with his head in his hands, hard, dry sobs racking his body. In the whole of his life he'd never lost his temper, never said a deliberate, mean, hurtful word to anyone. Yet just minutes before he'd verbally attacked Bebe, negated her as a person. Shame rivered through him. And Jane . . . God in heaven, he'd just about called her a liar to her face. How could he do that? He loved her.

They didn't understand about Nellie, didn't know what she'd gone through. They were overreacting, judging his daughter unfairly. There may have been granules of truth in what they'd said, but it was all blown out of proportion. Sweet, wonderful Nellie . . . how could they think such awful things about her? Jesus, she'd been through hell. Her mother had just died, not a normal death, but a suicide. That alone could scar anyone.

Nellie was merely shy, not aloof or cold. Cold . . . Jesus, the girl was so full of love! She fetched his slippers, rubbed his aching neck, made sure he ate balanced meals and got to bed on time, worried about him constantly. With Rajean for a mother she'd simply had to grow up too fast, take on too much responsibility when she should have been dating and having fun.

Daniel's frantic thoughts raced back in time. Even as a child Nellie had been a loner, afraid of close friendships, of getting hurt. While the other kids were skating and bicycling and going to parties, she preferred to study, write in her journals, spend time in the library, and listen to the radio. She had been an exemplary student, first at St. Margaret's and then at Bishop Ireton. Rajean had gone to the PTA meetings, had conferred with the austere nuns when they called. Yet . . . Daniel frowned, suddenly recalling that even though Nellie had been a straight-A student, the nuns still called the house and sent summoning letters. At the time, Rajean had shrugged off his questions—and he had always been left with the impression that the calls were of a complimentary nature. What else could they have been?

Jesus, what was he doing here, he asked himself uneasily. Looking for ways to condemn his daughter, to believe all the things Bebe and Jane said? Of course he was; justice demanded it of him. There were two sides to everything.

Philippe . . . Philippe needed to belong to someone, and Nellie felt the same way, so it was natural for the two young people to gravitate toward each other.

What the hell did Bebe know about love? Sick, obsessive love, yes. She was an authority on that. And Jane . . . she'd confessed that she'd never been in love until he'd come along. What did either woman know of that wild, wonderful, heart-wrenching emotion that overpowers a young person's life? That exquisite feeling of sharing, heart-pounding exhilaration? For that matter, what did he know about it?

Philippe loved Nellie. He'd seen it in the boy's eyes. And Nellie had looked at Philippe with . . . with . . . the empty look Rajean had used when she'd stared at him. No, that was wrong! Nellie smiled and giggled and blushed furiously when Philippe showed open affection. She was just shy and unused to handling open displays of affection. Surely once they'd been made man and wife . . . That business of the marriage not being consummated was pure rot on Bebe's part. Philippe was a virile young man at his sexual peak. Nellie was a beautiful, innocent young girl with a body young men craved.

Daniel's heart started to pound. Just married and he enlists. Nellie said it was what he'd wanted. New bridegrooms . . . he'd have thought Philippe would have wanted to spend more time with his new wife before going off to enlist.

The power of attorney was giving him the most trouble.

Everything Philippe owned was now Nellie's which meant she was a very wealthy young woman. Why would Philippe change his mind unless Bebe coerced him? Or . . . unless what Bebe and Jane said was true?

Where did his loyalties lie? With Nellie? Bebe? The studio? How in the hell was he ever going to explain all this to Reuben? Reuben trusted Jane, and Jane would never do anything to hurt him. Yet she was prepared to resign and claim all money due her—enough to bankrupt a studio already beleaguered by the exorbitant demands of a legal tug-of-war. In his heart Daniel knew she would never do something so drastic unless she believed totally in what she was doing. The pages Reuben had sent, they represented his life, and he'd entrusted them to Jane. The knowledge hurt him—the same way he'd hurt Reuben when he'd called on Rocky and Jerry to help him get to France.

If he forced the issue, Bebe was prepared to litigate as was Jane. The studio could be tied up for years. Somehow he had to learn the truth. Jesus Christ, Fort Dix wasn't on the other side of the world; it was in New Jersey—he could make the trip in two days and talk to Philippe personally. Bebe would know that, would assume that's exactly what he would do, and still she'd come here to make her intentions known. Therefore she must be telling the truth. Which meant Nellie had lied to him.

My God, what am I to do? he agonized. Whom should I believe? How could he allow the studio to go into litigation? Yet how could he simply turn his back on his daughter? And Reuben . . . if he lost Reuben's friendship over this, he might as well lie down and die.

Daniel glanced at his watch in the moonlight. It was twenty minutes past twelve. Too late to have a picnic supper. Nellie hadn't wakened, obviously; her bedroom window was dark. He should get up and go inside to bed, but suddenly, irrationally, he didn't want to be in the same house with his daughter. The realization was profoundly disturbing.

Tomorrow . . . tomorrow he would call Fort Dix. He would go to Jane and Bebe and talk to them. He would visit the studio and examine the option agreement for *Ambrosia*. If he had to, he would pry open Jane's desk to see if she'd actually drawn up a letter of resignation in which she'd waived her severance pay.

Nellie listened to her father's footsteps on the stairs and held her breath, waiting to see if he stopped at her door. She smiled

to herself in the darkness. Under her pillow was Jane's resignation letter and the old option agreement for *Ambrosia*. Just
hours ago she'd typed a new one, one that had no erasures and
no mistakes. It had been so easy to slip unseen into the studio,
so easy to remove the key to the executive offices from her
father's key ring. So easy to pry open Jane's desk with a hairpin.
And she'd done it all in less than two hours while her father
sat in the garden.

Philippe would be incommunicado for several weeks; everyone knew that new recruits were cut off from their families
until their training was over, unless, of course, there was a
death in the immediate family. Bebe Rosen would hold on to
her power of attorney and do nothing for a day or so, hoping
her father would switch his allegiance. By Friday Evans would
have transferred all of Philippe's funds to her name, and by
Monday morning she would be in total control of her husband's
inheritance.

Nellie Bishop Tarz-Bouchet slept like a baby.

Chapter Twenty-nine

HER HEART POUNDING, MICKEY STRUGGLED TO SEE THROUGH the falling snow. She could feel Yvette's hatred of the German Kort and knew she was probably thinking that he should have been killed along with the others in the village church. For the first time the children were huddled together like snow pillars, their fear as deadly as her own. Dear God, what would these terrible Germans do to the little ones? Would they be dragged off and made to march like puppets in the freezing snow, and if they faltered, would they be left behind to die? Or would they be gunned down in the name of the Third Reich?

Mickey inched closer to the children and put her arm around Bruno. She was about to open the boy's jacket to cover the dog's mouth, but Marc's hand was already there. Her eyes searched out Marie to see if the child was crying; she wasn't, but her eyes were filled with terror. Anna's hand was poised, ready to clamp down on the girl's mouth if she uttered so much as a sound, which was rather silly at this point since the Germans already knew they were below the embankment, thanks to Kort.

Her fear had been so overwhelming, she hadn't even realized Kort was speaking to the soldiers. "A grandmother and an aunt with their relatives' children," she heard him say. "I came across them this morning. I was searching for the nearest command post to turn them over to you, but twice I managed to get lost.'' He went on to tell the soldiers about the church and his surveillance for the R.A.F. pilots. ''My orders were to head for the nearest command post.'' There was a crackling sound as Kort pulled his map from his pocket. Mickey saw the blink of a flashlight and heard muttered curses when the biting wind whipped the paper from Kort's hands, carrying it away in a swirl of snow. She drew a deep breath when she heard the soldier's boots crunch down through the snow.

Yvette's hands went immediately to the knife in her pocket when she heard Kort tell the Germans that the women weren't armed. Laughing, he repeated his initial words—a grandmother and a pockmarked aunt as ugly as the English prime minister. ''They have no knowledge of weapons, see for yourself.''

Three sets of boots, plus Kort's . . . They waited, their eyes filled with fear and loathing. The flashlight circled around the group, coming to rest on each of them in turn. One of the Germans trained his beam on the ground to search for tracks. Seeing only their footprints in the snow, he seemed satisfied and clapped Kort on the back. ''Tell them to get on their feet,'' he ordered Kort.

''They don't understand German, but I speak a little French and some limited English,'' Kort said, adding proudly, ''That is why I was picked for the R.A.F. reconnaissance. They understand both languages.''

''Be quick about it, it's freezing out here. Tell them to go to the top of the embankment. We'll shoot them there.''

Kort spoke rapidly in English. Yvette's eyes widened at his words. ''There are three of them; there are three of us. Get up, you, Mickey, go for the legs; Yvette, you dive into the stomach, and I will cripple this one next to me. Be quick, for there will be no second chance.'' Then he stepped back, his gun held loosely in his hand. It wasn't hard for Mickey to pretend that her bones were stiff and aching as she struggled to her knees, her arms braced in the snow for leverage. Yvette did the same, and on the silent count of three they lunged. The moment the Germans fell backward, the children swarmed over them as one.

The attack was silent and deadly, the children huffing and panting, the little dog growling deep in his throat as his teeth ripped at flesh. The soldier Mickey charged was overpowered in no time: with her knee on his neck, she pinned his forearm and brought her knife down into his gullet in one swift motion. Blood spewed upward and then downward, staining the snow a bright crimson.

"Kill little children, will you! Never again! You'll never kill *anyone* again!" Yvette spat out as her knife found its mark again and again. She turned to Mickey. "They were going to shoot all of us, in the back." Her voice was so full of outrage, she had difficulty breathing. "They're vermin, lice, slime, a scourge on France. They don't deserve to live among decent people. Look at that one!" She pointed to the German Kort held by the throat with his suspenders.

Mickey was on her feet now, her eyes searching Kort's frenzied gaze. She understood he couldn't kill his own countrymen, but he wouldn't stop them from doing it for him.

"What are you waiting for, kill him!" Yvette ordered Kort.

"I can't," he cried. "I helped you, you and the children are alive. Don't ask this of me. If you want to kill him, you'll have to do it yourself!"

Yvette's eyes blazed. "I'll do it gladly, and if you so much as move, I'll kill you, too." The soldier was struggling, kicking out with his hard leather boots, his arms flailing.

The children huddled together, their eyes round with fear. All of them knew how close to death they'd come. The little dog, tight in Bruno's grasp, growled deep in his throat. The scene registered with Mickey in one blinding instant, and at the same time she knew there was something different about the children—and it wasn't their fear. But she had no time to dwell on them, she had to keep her eyes on the struggling German.

Later, neither she, Yvette, nor Kort knew how it happened. One moment Kort had eased his hold on the German while Yvette reached for him, and Mickey had braced herself for the lunge she knew the frantic soldier would make. All three were thrown off balance with the force of the thrust and toppled backward into the bloodred snow. The soldier had his hands around Yvette's neck as Mickey struggled to her knees. Suddenly Marie leapt from the tight little group, coming up behind the German, a knife in her hand. Stunned and taken off guard, they watched as the little girl attacked him from behind, stabbing him not once, not twice, but three times. In his pain he flopped over, blood spurting in every direction. The knife moved downward again, plunging deep into the hollow of the man's throat. Marie made no move to withdraw the knife but bent over him, her breathing harsh and ragged, sobs tearing at her own throat as she jabbed her fingers into his eye sockets. She was screeching about unbearable atrocities as she smashed at his nose and pummeled him with her hard little fists.

The other children were encouraging her now, shouting directions, their eyes wild as the little girl prepared to avenge them all. The knife slashed and tore, ripped and cracked, at the soldier's rib cage. A loud *swoosh* of air and heat emanated from the man's open chest. Satisfied at last, nine-year-old Marie tossed the blood-filled knife into the snow. Bernard picked it up, but only after he'd cleaned it with the snow.

"Now, do it now!" Anna gasped . . . as the others shouted deadly encouragement.

At once Mickey understood. Marie, now deadly calm, reached down and pulled hard. Triumphantly, her eyes victorious, she held up the man's heart for all to see and then threw it as as far as she could. The children rushed to her, their voices soft yet excited at what she had managed to do. They were busy then, cleaning the blood from her hands and her face. Anna stripped off Marie's gloves and handed her her own. Sophie hugged her around the knees, tears streaming down her cheeks. Bruno wiggled closer into the knot of children. The others separated, allowing the little boy to move to the front. He opened his coat and gently withdrew the little dog, his most precious possession, his *only* possession.

"He is getting heavy; would you hold him for a while?" he said.

Marie reached for the dog, her glazed eyes normal once again. She nodded as the little dog nuzzled her cheek. Her pinched little face began to relax as the children led her to a small copse of trees out of the driving snow.

"*Mon Dieu*, now I have seen everything," Yvette said, blessing herself reverently. "If my life depended on it, I don't know if I could do what she did. Where did she get the strength, how did she know to do that? God in heaven, she's just a child!"

"From God," said Anna. "He gave her the strength. He took the terrible look out of her eyes. See, she doesn't cry anymore. She did it for all of us! They butchered her father and hung him on a meat hook and left him to die. They raped her mother and stuck her head into a blazing stove. They killed her two sisters and brothers and did unspeakable things. Marie ran away when the soldiers got drunk on her father's wine.

Only God could help her do what she just did." Anna stared at the two women for a moment, then turned and walked back to the children.

Mickey's tongue felt thick and swollen in her mouth. "I don't ever want to talk about this again. It will be enough that I remember every second of this till the day I die. Not a word, Yvette; swear to me that we will never speak of this."

"Yes, Michelene," Yvette said in a subdued voice. She turned then, her eyes narrowed as she searched for Kort. Gut-wrenching sounds came from behind her.

"You should puke your guts out, you slimy bastard," she snarled. "Be a man and come out here before I set these children on you. I am a pussycat and they are the tigers, as you have seen. You shall have the pleasure of disposing of your countrymen. I don't care if you saved our lives or not, and they don't care, either." She jerked her head in the children's direction. "You're still one of them. You will be in my sight every step of the way. Now, be quick!"

Mickey sat down on a log covered with snow and crooked her finger at Yvette. "I hate to say this, but I think we should go on. The children are warmed with their . . . their exertion. We can cover several miles. The more distance we put between us and the command post, the better. At best we have an hour, possibly less. It's not so windy now, and the snow is thicker; it will cover our tracks. We're up so high now that the air is much thinner. We'll have to rest more often, and our progress will be very slow. Do you agree?"

"Yes," Yvette said, and approached the children. As she explained the situation, they banded together as one. Marie opened her coat to hand the little dog back to Bruno, who said he was very tired and asked her to carry him for just a bit longer. The little girl smiled and buttoned her coat.

"That was a very kind, wonderful thing you just did, Bruno," Mickey said gently. "Kinder perhaps than you will ever know."

"Will he love her more than he loves me?" the little boy asked fretfully.

"You are his master and he will always love you and be loyal to you. But he can love Marie, too. He's our protector. He's going to watch over all of us. I think he deserves a bit more food when we stop to eat next."

"He *was* getting heavy," Bruno confessed.

Mickey chuckled as she reached for the little boy's hand. "Step lively now, we have a long way to go."

"Will there be more Germans? Will they catch us again?"

"I hope not, Bruno, but none of us knows what is in store for us. Together we'll worry about it when the time comes."

"Together means all of us," Bruno said happily as he trudged through the snow with Mickey at his side.

Mickey had never in the whole of her life questioned the Almighty. What had happened was meant to happen, and Anna was right. God had directed Marie and given her the strength to do what she'd done, and He'd looked out for the rest of them. It had happened and she couldn't change it, nor could she wish it away.

At the bottom of the steep incline Mickey stopped for a moment and looked around at her charges. "Forward, march!" she cried.

At the crest of the incline and half a kilometer to the east was a German command post that had not been on Kort's map. It had been erected just twelve hours earlier.

Chapter Thirty

REUBEN'S EYES BLAZED WITH HATRED AS HE STARED through the blinding whiteness of the snow at the tight line of German soldiers above him. His head started to pound. Where was that son of a bitch Marcel? He waited, smelling his own fear, for the Germans to either gun him down or force him up and out of the ravine. When the rifles jerked upward, he felt himself go rigid and looked around frantically for his own rifle and the handgun that had been at his side. They were gone, along with Marcel. All he had was a razor-sharp knife stuck in the back of his trousers under his bulky coat.

Reuben crawled to the top of the ravine, then allowed himself to be dragged forward without resisting. When asked for his papers he affected a Gallic shrug, pretending not to understand the motions or the words. The Germans formed a circle around him, making escape impossible. They poked and prodded him with the butts of their rifles, making crude remarks and laughing as he stumbled around the circle.

There were six of them, young boys mostly, with one older man, a sergeant. Reuben was taller than all of them, more muscular, but he was also older, weary, cold, and tired. Only a fool would try something, and he was no fool, but he'd certainly fight to prevent his own death.

The soldiers drove him to his knees as the circle around him spread out. Out of the corner of his eye he noticed a motion that came from somewhere beyond the water-spotted German boots. He wanted to stare, to turn his head, but he didn't dare. Instead, he voiced his thoughts in sound, swearing viciously. The Germans laughed. He sensed now that the motion was coming from the ravine he'd climbed out of, but farther down the flat, snow-covered plain. It had to be Marcel. Perhaps he'd heard something, or else sensed it the way all the Frenchmen did, and gone for help. Even if the boy was a crack marksman, as he had boasted, he wouldn't be foolish enough to take on the entire patrol himself. Which could mean only one thing: he had help. But how much?

They were tiring of him now, their jabs stronger, their laughter more obscene. From his position on the ground, Reuben felt like a dwarf who was about to be cut down any second by a gang of giants. When were Marcel and his men going to make a move? After he was shot, he thought grimly. Well, by God, he had no intention of waiting around for *that*.

The snow had been packed down by the heavy boots and all the scrambling he'd done in the past few minutes. If he used every ounce of energy, he *might* be able to break through the circle and roll to the edge of the ravine, at which point Marcel—if it were Marcel—could open fire. He could then join the attack and do what he could with his knife.

Without giving himself time to think about possible consequences, Reuben put his plan into action a moment later, taking the Germans off guard. Thrusting his body through the ring of soldiers, he rolled crazily downhill and tumbled off the edge of the ravine in a whirl of snow. Sure enough, as he scrabbled for purchase on the rocky ledge below the lip of the canyon gorge, he heard gunfire. The moment he stopped rolling he was on his feet, his head reeling, scrambling to the top of the ravine for the second time.

He'd been right, there were two men with Marcel, their weapons belching fire. "We got two of them," Marcel grunted. He laughed, "I stand corrected, three. Here is your gun, monsieur, make yourself useful."

His weapon in hand, Reuben vaulted through a row of dead hedges filled with snow. A bullet whizzed past his shoulder, splattering the bark off a nearby tree. He crawled on his belly, a crab inching upward. A shot roared past, followed by a second and a third, splintering an entire row of young saplings that would never see green leaves again.

There was no way he could blend in with the snow and winterized trees and shrubs in the ravine. Boldly, he leapt over the rim of the ravine and rolled sideways, coming to a stop at the same time he fired his weapon in an angry burst. No Hollywood stuntman could have done it better, he thought grimly. "One more down," he shouted.

His ears were ringing as bullets sailed past and around him. Slipping into a crouch, he poised his weapon on his knee and fired blindly in every direction. Then he flattened himself in the snow, confident that he'd gained at least ten yards and was that much closer to the German who'd been raining bullets past him since he'd left the ravine.

The others were close behind him now, he could feel them scrambling over the brush. He felt better immediately—until he heard the silence. When he looked toward the rim of the ravine, Marcel held up two fingers. So, one of them had shot the fourth man. Four against two. He liked the odds.

Suddenly Reuben leapt to his feet and zigzagged to the other side of the ravine, landing in time to point his rifle between the eyes of the German soldier, the one who'd jabbed him the hardest with his gun. Smiling coldly, he knocked the man's weapon to the side and watched it slide all the way down to the floor of the ravine.

"Tell your friend to surrender," he said slowly and clearly. He jabbed the end of his gun under the man's armpit so that his arm shot in the air, then smiled again when he heard the harsh guttural words that he hoped meant surrender.

By the time Marcel's friends escorted the last German to the top of the ravine, Reuben was panting like a racehorse at the finish line. There was a hurried whispered conversation that was actually an argument; did they kill the Germans or take them prisoner? He himself didn't give a damn one way or the other. But if he had to make a choice, he'd vote for killing— which was exactly what the partisans did, on the spot, with fixed bayonets. They toppled the bodies into the ravine.

"They'll be found soon. Signs of your activity are prevalent, monsieur," Marcel said, pointing to the packed-down snow. "We'll stay with you for three more kilometers and then we must leave you. We're needed elsewhere. You will be headed in the right direction at that point. It is all we can do."

"It's enough," Reuben said.

"Monsieur, these friends have news of the woman you seek. I will draw you a map in the snow. See, here and here. This is the village and the church where the children were brought. Your friend is already on her way up the mountains with the little ones. We have word that the Germans have increased their patrols. You need to know this, monsieur. The devils are everywhere. This trail is the one we think they took. A parade such as the one your friend leads will leave prints in the snow. Follow them and pray for snow to be at your back. Go slowly as you climb, for the air is thin and it is difficult to breathe. You are not used to our mountains."

Two days later Reuben walked into the village church late at night. He was so exhausted he lay down on the hard wooden church pew and was asleep instantly. Had Germans been banging at the door with rifle butts, he would still have closed his eyes. His body craved sleep, needed it before he could continue. For four hours he slept deeply and dreamlessly. When he woke, he took a look around the church, lighting matches as he went along, hoping for some sign that would tell him Mickey had been here. But there were only cold ashes from the fireplace in the back of the church. Praying in the winter, he decided, had to be a cold business. When people were cold and hungry, how could they concentrate on their prayers?

He raised his eyes to the figure on the cross which seemed to be watching him. "I am a Jew," he whispered. "The Bible says we are Your chosen people. Why are You allowing this to happen? Children and women have no place in this war, yet they are dying. Hours ago I killed men who wanted to kill me. I defended myself to be free to find a band of children and two women who believe in You with all their hearts. They were here, this building offered them sanctuary for a little while. How can women and little children scale the Pyrenees? I don't know if *I* could do it. Are You keeping them safe? Will You help me to find them?"

Reuben dropped to his knees and folded his hands. "I ask nothing for myself. I ask only that You keep Mickey, Yvette, and the children safe until I can find them." Was it a prayer or a request? Both, he decided. He made an attempt at blessing himself. "Amen," he said spiritedly.

It was still dark when he set out in the direction Marcel had indicated. It seemed warmer to him somehow, the snow wetter and harder to wade through. The snowshoes he'd been promised had never materialized, but they wouldn't have worked in this kind of snow anyway. With many miles ahead of him, Reuben determined to walk until he dropped, simply putting one foot in front of the other until his legs gave way beneath him. When he reached the rocky slopes the going would be easier but steeper.

When daylight broke, Reuben was pleased with the progress he'd made. He reached into his knapsack for what he thought of as his most precious possession, his lifeline to survival: a pair of binoculars.

"You will need these more than me," Marcel had said when he'd handed them over. "If you reach safety, turn them over to the Resistance member you meet next. They'll find their way back to me."

Reuben had taken the boy's hand and shaken it gratefully, swallowing past the lump in his throat. "You're a fine son, Marcel, your father has reason to be proud of you."

"My father is dead," the boy had replied flatly. "It is the other way around, monsieur; I am proud of my father, for he died for our cause."

The binoculars revealed nothing but an endless expanse of white below and thick, gray clouds above, swollen with more snow that would shower down shortly. Two more hours should see him entering the mountains. How far behind Mickey and the children was he? He no longer knew what day it was or how much time had passed since Christmas. He knew only night and day.

Reuben trudged on, seeking a temporary place of shelter to rest his legs and time to gnaw on his last piece of dry meat. He had three cigarettes left, and when he stopped to rest, if the area was safe, he was going to smoke one. In the breast pocket of his coarse shirt was his second luxury, three of the rose petals from the jar on Mickey's mantel, wrapped carefully in a grimy handkerchief. From time to time he took them out and looked at them. They were his incentive to keep going, to find Mickey.

It was late in the afternoon, but still light, when Reuben reached the spot where Mickey had stood to view the awesome specter in front of her. The air seemed sharper somehow, the scent of evergreens strong and pungent. All above him were rocky bluffs and dense forest. His heart thudded and then quieted. Mickey and the children had climbed this, and so would he.

A straggly row of hedge bushes was his first obstacle to the narrow path that snaked upward. In the waning light he was sure it was the same path Mickey had taken; the deep footprints were almost filled. Eyes glued to the ground, he strode forward through the thicket, watching as the trail angled off to the right and then back to the left. It was an up-and-down course with huge, monstrous boulders to be scaled. Winded, the resin from the pines sharp in his nostrils, Reuben literally slid down the boulders, exhausted from his upward climb. How in the name of God had Mickey and the children managed this? Perhaps they hadn't, he thought miserably. Yet he had to believe that the instinct for survival would give them the strength to scale mountains.

Eventually he reached higher ground, where the trees were denser and the trail almost indiscernible. Reuben weaved his way left and right, past mountains of boulders that were taller than he, through thickets and deadfalls. Once, he lost his footing and slid down the last slope to land in an ice-cold stream. Cursing his clumsiness, he retraced his steps, crawling back up the slope and scaling the huge rocks—only this time he was freezing in his wet clothes and the thin air was singeing his lungs. At the top of the slope he gazed with widening eyes at a plateau that stretched perhaps for half a mile. The mountain loomed majestic in the night, black and ominous.

Some instinct warned him not to move, to wait and watch. There was too much open ground here, with no cover except the blinding snow. Even if he crawled on his belly, he'd be exposed to observation and would leave a trail that would be easy to follow in the daylight hours.

There were command posts and patrols all through the mountains, Marcel had said. And the locations were changed often to thwart those trying to get over the mountains into Spain.

The will to live, to survive, to find Mickey, made him cautious as he contemplated his options in the last remaining hours of darkness. Did he take the plateau, or did he walk along the line of trees and hope for a better place to cross? If he left this particular trail, he might become hopelessly lost and never find Mickey. The fine hairs on the back of his neck pricked a warning. Without allowing himself further speculation, he was on his feet and running through the line of trees.

He heard the sound before he risked a glance to the flatland through the trees: a military vehicle, a jeep probably, its tires crunching and crackling in the snow. The early dawn patrols Marcel had spoken of. Reuben moved farther back into a thick nest of evergreens, their fragrance so strong and so pungent he thought he would choke. It was getting lighter by the second. He pulled out his pocket watch and clocked the patrol. His breathing was shallow now, the air too thin for all the exertion he'd put forth. Wait. Wait . . . It was all he could do.

Twenty minutes later he heard the vehicle return, creating a new set of tire tracks. Thirty minutes, possibly forty, which meant the command post to the east was a mere ten minutes away, the one to the west, twenty. Twenty minutes of safety, twenty minutes to cross the plateau and leave no tracks.

In an instant he was up and running, back the way he'd come. Marcel had warned him several times to go in a straight line. He found his first resting place with no trouble, then leapt from his position at the tree line and landed dead center in the hard-packed snow left by the German vehicle. Panting with the effort, he stepped over the wheel line and poised a moment before leaping once again. This time he fell flat in the snow, disturbing the even coating to his left. There was no time to smooth out the snow, and sharp eyes would spot the indentation immediately. For one set of tracks they'd probably send a two-man patrol, possibly three. Fast as he could, he headed for the trees, knowing he had less than twenty minutes to make time and hide himself. And then what? Kill or be killed? If he killed, the whole damn army would be after him.

Now he was toiling higher and higher, his strength leaving him rapidly. But he kept going. It was cold, so cold . . . his body heat was leaving him, and his wet clothes had frozen to his body. Twice he had to blink his eyes to clear his vision. He stumbled and fell, picked himself up, and stumbled again.

Snow! He looked overhead through a break in the dense pines. Black clouds scudded over the treetops. He stumbled again and was down on all fours, his hands touching something hard and cold. A log, a dead animal. When his hands brushed the snow from a once-human face, he toppled back in horror. Fearfully, he forced his hands to continue their frenzied brushing. When he saw the gaping hole in the man's chest, he turned pale. At least the man was German, thank God.

His tired eyes swept around to take stock of his position. Others had been here, many others. Mickey and the children, perhaps. It hadn't snowed for a while now, so he couldn't be that far behind them. Within seconds strength returned tenfold. Quickly he scooped snow over the corpse, then broke off a branch from the nearest tree and did his best to feather the powder around.

Satisfied at last, Reuben rose and continued on his way. If he moved quickly, the threatening snow would be at his back, just as Marcel had hoped. Someone must be praying for him. He tried to relax then, his breathing quick and deep. Despite momentary bouts of dizziness, he forced himself to climb, to put one foot in front of the other, his movements automatic, robotic.

The snow hit him like a torrent, slapping and stinging him in the face. He hunkered down into his heavy coat and kept going. Ahead lay the steepest part of the mountain, with nothing but granite rocks and boulders and snow-capped peaks in the distance.

Up, up, up, the snow thicker, the wind stronger, and still he toiled. His lungs about to burst with his exertion, he flattened himself against a solid wall of granite and tried to figure a way over the top. Close . . . he was so close! Somehow he *had* to scale this huge mountain of rock. A desperate plan began to form itself in his mind. He climbed a tree, slipping and sliding as he searched for footholds in the bark. Forcing his mind to blankness, he climbed out on a limb, gingerly testing the branch's sturdiness. For a moment he swayed there sickeningly, his arms and legs gripping the thick branch. Then, swallowing hard, he inched toward the end of the branch to give himself momentum—and let go, sailing gracefully through the air to land with a thump in a pile of snow that covered him from head to toe.

Gasping and cursing, he was on his feet and moving within seconds. When he glanced up another slope stared him in the face. He wanted to die in frustration, to lash out first and storm the rise like an avenging maniac with superhuman strength. How was he, a mere mortal, to climb still higher into thinner air and more snow? How had Mickey and the children done it?

How would the Germans get over it? Would they take the trouble to climb the tree, or would they think one man wasn't worth the bother? He didn't know and he didn't care.

At that moment he was no more than five hours behind Mickey and the children.

Chapter Thirty-one

A GENTLE CALIFORNIA RAIN HAD STARTED IN THE MIDDLE of the night, then increased by early morning to a steady downpour, dampening Daniel's already dismal spirits. However, it would be good for the orange trees, he thought. Reuben's feathered friends would receive a good soaking, and so would their birdseed. As always when he thought of the birds and Reuben's past care of them, he felt puzzled. In his opinion, Reuben was the last person in the world to care about nature's winged friends. Of late, though, because of his life on the East Coast, he'd come to realize that there were many things about Reuben that surprised him.

Twice he'd gone up to bed and twice he'd come back downstairs. Earlier he'd unrolled the awning on the terrace, and now he watched the heavy rain, feeling miserable enough to cry or, at the very least, throw a temper tantrum.

Draining his sixth—or was it his seventh?—cup of coffee, he lit a Chesterfield from the half-empty pack and inhaled deeply. Coffee and cigarettes . . . he probably wouldn't be drinking so much coffee or smoking if he hadn't stopped by Nellie's room on his way downstairs at twenty minutes past four. Nellie was gone. The note she'd left said only that she'd gone home to Philippe's house because he might call in the

early morning hours. Besides, she'd added, she didn't want to
stay and be a burden to him with all her problems. She loved
him too much for that. Then, thanking him for being a patient,
wonderful father, she'd signed it, "Love always, Nellie." Un-
accountably irritated, he'd crumpled up the note and thrown it
on the glass-topped table.

His thoughts turned to Jane and how upset with him she'd
been. He loved her and she loved him, but here they were,
fighting each other over his daughter. Yet even though he hated
what he was feeling and thinking, the lawyer in him demanded
proof, proof of everything that had been said.

Suddenly Daniel jumped up from his chair and ran through
the house to the front door. He'd be damned if he was going
to stew one more minute about all of this. Pulling on a trench
coat and grabbing an umbrella, he strode to his car. He was
going to Jane's house to straighten this out right now.

Instead of ringing the front doorbell or using his key, he
walked around to the back of the house and peered through the
kitchen door. Jane was at the stove, her back to him, frying
bacon. Like him, she was in the same clothes she'd worn to
his house yesterday, which meant she, too, hadn't slept. Daniel
felt sick when he tapped on the pane of glass. Jane whirled, a
warm smile on her lips that faded instantly when she saw who
it was. Reluctantly she motioned for him to come in.

"Would you like some breakfast, Daniel?" she asked politely. "I just made coffee."

"I'd love some." Ill at ease, he watched her bustle about
the compact kitchen. The silence between them was strained,
awkward. Gone was the easy comaraderie they'd shared in the
past. When he could stand it no longer, Daniel cleared his
throat and began to speak.

"I . . . I had to come, Jane. This is too important for either
of us to try to sweep under the rug. I want to know, I need to
know if there is some kind of misunderstanding, something
that we can all rectify without . . ."

"Without hurting Nellie," she broke in, and turned to look
at him. "But what about me, Daniel? Do you have any idea
how I feel? Do you have any idea what you did to Bebe yesterday with . . . with your defense of Nellie? Good Lord, do
you think we wanted to hurt you like that? The old Bebe, the
Bebe you used to know, deserved those remarks, but not the
Bebe of today. She was trying to do what her son wanted
the only way she knew how. Daniel, I talked to that young

man. I listened to him and I *heard* what he said. Neither Bebe nor I lied to you. Your daughter is doing the lying. And you know me well enough to realize I wouldn't lie to you about something this important.''

''That's why I'm here,'' Daniel said carefully. ''You said the option contract on *Ambrosia* is in the files and the date had been tampered with. You also said your letter of resignation was in your desk. After breakfast, I'd like to go to the studio and see them both.''

''No, Daniel,'' Jane said, ladling fluffy scrambled eggs onto his plate. ''My word should be all the proof you need. I won't allow you to attack my credibility. I haven't lied to you. Either you believe me or you don't.''

''My daughter . . .''

''Yes, I know how terrible this must be for you, but I have to do what's right for the studio, for Bebe, and for Philippe. I can't worry about Nellie.'' She put the pan in the sink and sat down opposite him, her eyes troubled. ''I have this feeling, Daniel, that if you go to the studio, you won't find my letter in my desk, nor will you find the original *Ambrosia* option contract. Nellie is too smart for that.''

Daniel pushed his plate away. ''So what you're saying is that Nellie is a thief and a . . . a forger? My God, Jane, I . . . she's my daughter . . . surely you can understand why I'd go to the mat for her.''

''Yes, I do understand, and you must understand that I will do the same thing for the studio and Reuben.''

''Reuben has always loved Nellie,'' Daniel said.

''Reuben loved the girl Nellie allowed him to know, just the way she allowed you to see only one side of her. She's devious and manipulative, she lies and covers it all up with her wide-eyed innocence. Bebe told me there was something, something she couldn't put her finger on the day they had their first meeting. I think Philippe realized it, too, but only after it was too late. Daniel, open your eyes. What young man would get married and leave his bride two days later when it wasn't necessary?''

Daniel shook his head. ''That wasn't the reason he left. He felt guilty—conscience-stricken because his father had gone to France to find Mickey and fight the Germans while he remained here. He wanted desperately to do his part.''

''Perhaps,'' Jane conceded. ''But then there's the power of attorney. When Philippe realized the ramifications of giving

Nellie free rein to his inheritance, he changed his mind—and because the marriage was never consummated, he doesn't owe her anything except an annulment.''

She leaned across the table. ''Daniel, Philippe's fortunes . . . your friend Mickey secured his future, *his*, Daniel. I think she would take a dim view of Nellie helping herself at Philippe's expense. But there's no point in hashing this over again, is there? Would you like to see my letter of resignation? I brought a copy of the original home with me.'' She was out of the room before Daniel could reply. When she returned she handed it to him.

Daniel read the letter and gave it back to Jane. ''You could have typed this yesterday when you came home. Unless I can examine the original . . .''

''Damn you, Daniel, this isn't a court of law! I thought you loved me. I'm telling you the truth. I think,'' she said sadly, ''it would be best for all of us if you left now. I'm sorry you've been placed in a position where you have to choose sides. I just want you to know one thing: I was prepared to walk away from it all so I could keep you. I was going to let Nellie win, but I know now she would have done something, something to turn you against me, and you would have believed her. I'm glad Bebe called me, and I'm glad I had the chance to talk to Philippe. When Reuben returns I can face him with a clear conscience. . . . You can see yourself out now, and before you leave I'd appreciate it if you would give me back my key.''

Daniel unhooked the key from his key ring and laid it carefully on the table. He tried to see past the burning in his eyes and the lump in his throat. As he closed the door behind him, he heard Jane say, ''I love you.''

He was alone again. Reuben was gone, his one true friend in the whole world. Mickey was in France trying to stay alive. Bebe had turned her back on him, and Jane . . . Jane was abandoning him. All he had was Nellie. The thought gave him no comfort at all.

It was eight o'clock when Daniel returned home. He showered and changed his clothes, his thoughts in a turmoil. Promptly at nine o'clock, he started making long-distance phone calls back east, confident that he would reach the two people he wanted to talk with.

The first call he placed was to St. Margaret's, where Nellie had gone to school as a child. The Mother Superior there remembered Cornelia well, and when Daniel explained that he was calling for background and information on his daughter, she did her best to comply.

"Your daughter was an exemplary student scholastically, straight A's, if I remember correctly. We don't have all that many students who excel consistently. However, Cornelia never quite fit in; she had no real friendships, and on more than one occasion we had to call your wife in for conferences." To Daniel's growing horror, she went on to relate a series of instances where Nellie had been accused of theft, lying, and malicious mischief.

"I made a notation myself on Cornelia's records that I thought she was emotionally disturbed. On several occasions I suggested that Mrs. Bishop seek outside help for the child, but she refused." There was a slight pause, then the Mother Superior said gently, "I thought you were aware of all this, Mr. Bishop."

After he'd hung up, Daniel sat with his head in his hands, his chest heaving. Childhood misdemeanors . . . or incipient pathology?

The next call he placed was to the commanding officer at Fort Dix. When he finally got through fifteen minutes later, he was informed that there was no recruit named Philip Tarz or Philippe Bouchet at Fort Dix. Daniel swore, ripe, four-letter gutter words he'd learned in the Great War.

In a frenzy of frustration he ran up the steps and threw on whatever clothes fell into his hands. He was out of the house and in his car within fifteen minutes. But he realized then that he didn't know where he was going, if indeed he was going to drive somewhere. To Nellie's, to confront her? Back to Jane to share his information? To Bebe, perhaps? Well, Jesus Christ, he could sit here all day and play word games, he thought nastily.

At last he yanked the car into gear and drove to the studio, roaring past Eddie Savery without so much as a look. His destination—Jane's office.

A long time later Daniel decided that he would never make a detective. In his hands was the option agreement for *Ambrosia*, which he'd inspected carefully and thoroughly several times. The dates were typed cleanly, with no trace of an erasure. He didn't know whether he felt relieved or depressed. The clean copy proved that the dates hadn't been changed and the signatures on the last page hadn't been tampered with. Jane must have made a mistake or lied to him, it was that simple.

Nellie was in the clear. Next, he picked the lock on Jane's desk, careful not to disturb her possessions. There was no sign of her resignation letter. Again, that made Jane a liar and Nellie innocent. Perhaps Jane had simply overreacted to Nellie's intelligence, her youth, and her prettiness. But it was too late now for explanations; too much damage had been done. Nellie would always be between them.

There was still the matter of Philippe and Fort Dix. If the boy wasn't at Fort Dix, where the hell was he? Had he simply pretended to enlist to escape his marriage to Nellie? If so, why go to Bebe? Maybe she'd misunderstood—maybe he'd gone somewhere else.

Philippe's bankers in New York might know where he was. Certainly he would have notified them; he was that kind of young man. Within minutes Daniel was speaking with Silas Goodwin, who informed him that the Morgan bank no longer handled Philippe Bouchet's business.

"What!" Daniel roared. Immediately he lowered his voice. "I don't understand, Mr. Goodwin. If you aren't handling Philippe's business, who is?"

"His wife, Mr. Bishop. Your daughter, I believe. I would have thought you understood and perhaps encouraged the transfer." There was a coolness and a snideness that smacked of . . . Obviously the man was thinking . . . collusion. Daniel found himself sputtering and defending his position, trying to explain that he needed to reach Philippe.

"I hope you have more luck than I did. I tried all morning to reach the young man and couldn't. I had no other choice but to follow his wife's directive. She sent their banker here, and everything has been removed from our hands. The power of attorney was in order. I spoke to the lawyer who drew it up. Is there anything else, Mr. Bishop?"

"No. Yes! Yes, wait just a damn minute here. Are you telling me that *all* of Philippe's holdings have been transferred just today?"

"Several hours ago, as a matter of fact," Goodwin replied. "I don't mind telling you all of us here in the trust department think there is something . . . irregular going on, but we're powerless to do anything about it. It's impossible to reach Madame Fonsard. Your daughter is an incredibly wealthy woman, Mr. Bishop. Now, if there's nothing else, I'm due at a meeting."

Daniel's eyes were wild as he stared around Jane's office.

This was all happening too fast. One minute he was absolving Nellie and the next he felt like crucifying her. One moment he was sure Jane was an out-and-out liar and the next he knew that was impossible, because she loved him. And now this!

Daniel shook his head to clear his thoughts. What to do next, he wondered. See Nellie, confront her with everything? No, he decided, not everything. *Trap her, trick your own daughter?* His conscience pricked. "If that's the only way to get to the truth of the matter, then, yes, that's exactly what I'll do."

Nellie was curled up in a chair by the front window. On the table next to her chair was a writing pad and pencil. Her banker had just called, telling her that all the transfers from Morgan had been taken care of and he was on his way back to California. She'd agreed to a meeting in his office first thing Monday morning. For over an hour she'd delighted herself with all the different numbers in Philippe's accounts, holding off on totaling them until she couldn't stand the suspense another second. When she had the grand total in front of her, she'd squealed in delight, hugging her knees.

She was as rich as Croesus. She laughed, the sound rippling all about her. And it had been so easy!

The sound of her father's car in the drive startled her. Immediately she picked up her pad and pen and started to write a letter to Philippe. On the hall table were two other envelopes with blank paper inside addressed to "Mr. Philippe Bouchet." For show, of course.

A moment later Nellie opened the door to her father, dabbing at her tear-filled eyes. "Hi, Daddy," she said listlessly. "I was just writing to Philippe. It's silly, I know, because I don't have his address yet, but it makes me feel better."

Even though Daniel's heart swelled at his daughter's words and the woebegone look on her face, he took a deep breath and proceeded, using his courtroom voice. It was a front, but it was the only way he could get through the ordeal ahead of him.

"Why, Nellie, why did you do it? I spoke to Silas Goodwin today and he told me you had all of Philippe's funds transferred out here, everyone of his holdings! You're going to have to transfer it all back."

Nellie gasped.

"You called Mr. Goodwin! Why? Didn't you believe me? . . . Oh, I get it, Jane finally got to you. That's it, isn't it? Oh,

Daddy," she wailed, "I knew this was going to happen! I just knew it! I did only what Philippe told me to do."

"I'm ordering a freeze on all Philippe's holdings until I reach him. I can do it, Nellie. You see, I have a letter from Mickey that gives me power of attorney over Philippe's assets."

"Daddy, Philippe is twenty-one now. Everything is so legal, it's unshakable." She watched her father out of the corner of her eye.

Daniel attacked her verbally then, telling her about his phone call to St. Margaret's and his discussion with the Mother Superior. Nellie's eyes narrowed as she listened. When she spoke, her voice was that of a wistful little girl.

"I can't believe you did all that, Daddy. You're making me sound like a . . . deranged person, like . . . oh, God, like Mother. Why are you doing this to me? All I did . . . am doing, is what Philippe wants."

Daniel hardened his heart against his daughter's tears. "We'll find out if that's the case as soon as we hear from Philippe," he said in a flat voice.

"In the meantime, I have to have all of this hanging over my head," Nellie said reproachfully. "You believe everyone but me; you've been checking up on me. So what if I was a jealous child? That certainly doesn't make me evil and conniving. Why won't you believe me?"

"None of this is going to do you one bit of good, Nellie," Daniel said miserably. "The power of attorney Bebe has supersedes the one you have."

"That's just too bad about Bebe! Everything is in my name now, just the way Philippe wanted."

Daniel rubbed his temples. "That's what I thought. It's still illegal, Nellie. The courts will make you give it back."

"Not until Philippe returns. He's off serving his country, and no court is going to strip away a wife's holdings," Nellie cried. "I don't care what Bebe has. It's a forgery; she and Jane cooked it up between the two of them. I can't believe you're falling for their story. I'm your daughter, why would I lie to you about something so important?"

"They said exactly the same thing to me. Why? For Philippe's money, that's why. You want it all and the studio, too. That's it, isn't it?" Daniel demanded.

"No! It's what Philippe wanted. Call Fort Dix and ask him yourself."

"I already did. He isn't there."

Nellie's eyes widened. "What do you mean, he isn't there? He said in his note he was going to Fort Dix."

"Obviously he changed his mind because there is no new recruit at Fort Dix by the name of Philip Tarz or Philippe Bouchet. I'm having it checked out right now," Daniel said grimly.

Suddenly Nellie burst into fresh tears, and Daniel's heart went out to her despite his reservations. She was so alone, so defenseless. If he turned on her, she would have no one.

"Honey, let's go into the kitchen and have some coffee and really talk," he said, his voice gentler now. "I think I can help you if you'll cooperate. Nellie, I don't want us to have friction, there's got to be a way to straighten all of this out."

Nellie stood up and towered over her father, her eyes dark with anger. "No, there isn't a way to settle this. You believe *them*. I won't ever be able to forgive you for turning against me, my own father! I think you should leave before we say more hateful things to each other. I would never hurt you the way you've just hurt me. If Philippe were here, he'd never let you talk to me like this. And for your information, Daddy, I'm going to the office on Monday and I'm going to sit in Philippe's chair in his office just the way he wanted me to. I'm going to run my half. I don't care what Bebe does with her half. And you just try to take his money away from me, just try! If you do, I'll . . . I'll . . ."

"You'll what, Nellie?" Daniel demanded softly.

Nellie stared at her father with tears streaming down her cheeks. "Never forgive you," she said, picking up the pad and running from the room.

Daniel watched her go, tears rolling down *his* cheeks.

While Nellie plotted and schemed behind her bedroom door and Daniel stewed and fretted in Reuben's house, Bebe spent the entire weekend trying to understand the report Philippe had given her on the wave of the future—television.

It was so comprehensive, so detailed, Bebe felt as if she were reading a foreign language. The thing that struck her most in the entire seventy-six-page document was Philippe's conviction that television was a technological breakthrough guaranteed to revolutionize the entertainment industry. In his summary he recommended that Fairmont research and develop an electron tube and electronic scanning method to make the marketing of television systems practical. The words *licensing* and *patents* were underlined.

Bebe finished the report at three o'clock on New Year's Day. By six o'clock the dining room table was covered with sheets of papers full of numbers. At six-thirty she called Jane, who arrived an hour later. Together they added and subtracted on Sol's ancient adding machine.

By eight-fifteen Bebe was trembling badly. "I'd kill for a drink right now," she muttered.

Jane grinned. "What'll it be, cherry pop or ginger ale?"

"Coffee, strong and black." Bebe sighed. "Will it work, Jane?"

"What's the worst that can happen if it doesn't?" Jane said, eyes twinkling mischievously. "We get jobs in a defense plant and move into an apartment together with Willie."

Bebe swallowed hard. "I have a list of every single Fairmont employee and their phone numbers. You use Pop's phone in his study and I'll use the one in the kitchen. Tell them I'm calling a special meeting for seven-thirty tomorrow morning. That way I can be at the bank by nine."

Twenty minutes later Jane walked into the kitchen and clapped her hands together. "Done!" she cried.

Bebe smiled. "Reuben would say we're on a roll. Let's go over it one more time to be sure we have everything right. We're asking for basically all of Fairmont's reserve to develop Philippe's idea. And we're doing this now because once my lawyer presents Philippe's power of attorney to a judge, the studio's assets will be frozen. Right?" Jane nodded. "Okay. In a few minutes I'm going to call Simon and Dillon and ask their permission to tap their trust funds. That money will go toward paying everyone at the studio half wages. And we're going to promise all personnel a percentage of the television profits—if they materialize. Reuben would approve of that, wouldn't he, Jane?" Bebe asked anxiously.

Jane nodded. "You bet. Reuben's always been fair," she said loyally.

"Onward and upward. Next I'm going to petition the courts to allow us to make Reuben's film using our own funds, funds we will secure by mortgaging my house, your house, and the trust fund Reuben set up for me. If that works, we'll be in clover, as the saying goes. If not, we'll live with it."

Bebe cleared her throat nervously. "Now, at the meeting tomorrow morning I'll present all this as a package deal. And the whole thing has to be arranged by the close of business tomorrow. I'll turn over Philippe's power of attorney late tomorrow afternoon, but it may take a week before the judge renders his decision.''

Bebe met Jane's eyes over the rim of her coffee cup. "There's something else, isn't there?" Jane asked, concerned.

"Yes . . . My divorce from Reuben is far from final. I . . . I'm going to . . . withdraw my petition, which will place me in a position to mortgage the house in Laurel Canyon.''

Jane's jaw dropped. "Bebe, that house is joint property! You can't forge Reuben's name. All of this has to be legal!''

"I know. I wasn't planning on doing any forging," Bebe assured her. "I thought we'd go to Max and see if he can sway Reuben's banker in my favor. Look, it's something to think about; we *don't* have to do it.''

"Daniel and Nellie?" Jane said in a choked voice.

"I'll call them now," Bebe said quietly. "As Philippe's wife, Nellie has a right to be at the meeting. She'll be voting in his place, and we both know the way her vote will go. Daniel, of course . . . I believe Daniel will do whatever he thinks is right, regardless of Nellie.''

Sighing, she picked up the receiver and dialed Daniel's number. He answered on the first ring, his voice gentle and expectant. Bebe almost apologized for not being Jane. She explained about the meeting and apologized for disturbing him on New Year's Day. Then she broke the connection almost immediately and turned to Jane with a thoughtful expression.

"That's one troubled man, Jane. I feel sorry for him." Jane dabbed at her eyes. "But I think it will all work out in the end," Bebe added comfortingly. "Daniel is a kind, wonderful man full of principle, and he won't cast that aside when it comes to the final test. If he does, his whole life will have been a sham like mine. No, he'll come through, I feel it here." She held a hand over her heart. "And now for our final call.''

Nellie answered the phone sounding forlorn and wistful. She must have assumed it was her father calling, Bebe thought as she identified herself and explained about the early morning meeting. Instantly Nellie's voice hardened, taking on an edge of coolness when she replied that she would be there. This time it was Nellie who broke the connection. Bebe's eyebrows shot upward in surprise as she cradled the receiver. "I think our little Nellie has had a setback of some sort. I don't know what kind, but . . .''

"Let's hope you're right. Have you notified Tillie?"

"Lord, no. I'd better call her before I turn in. Tillie always stays up till the wee hours reading." Bebe stood up and stretched. "I could use some fresh air, how about you?"

Willie came on the run when he heard his leash rattling. He licked at Bebe's shoes and then Jane's as he waited for his ears to be scratched and the leash to be hooked to his collar. Two women meant a long walk, maybe a long run without the leash. He woofed happily, clawing at Bebe's legs to make her hurry.

"I feel so loved." Bebe giggled as she allowed Willie to pull her toward the front door.

Fairmont's conference room was fragrant with the aroma of freshly brewed coffee, thanks to Tillie's early arrival. Commissary personnel had sent over a huge tray with assorted pastries and several decanters of orange juice, which had been set up in the middle of the conference table. Cups and saucers, silver spoons, crystal goblets, and linen napkins were arranged at each place setting, again thanks to Tillie, who presided over the early morning continental breakfast. Identical pads and pencils were placed strategically in front of each cup and saucer. Only Daniel Bishop's pad was different: paper-clipped to the top sheet was an old, creased square of paper.

There was no small talk, only worries and frowns as seats were taken and coffee stirred. Bebe waited a full five minutes before she called the meeting to order. The picture of elegance and confidence, she folded her hands and leaned forward. "Ladies and gentlemen, enjoy your breakfast while I tell you a story . . ."

When she'd finished, she stood up and walked slowly around the conference table, her coffee cup held in both hands. "I imagine my . . . story, confession, if you will, has startled all of you," she said. "I'm going to ask for a show of hands in a few minutes. If any of you want to leave the room to discuss our decision, feel free. But before you leave I want you all to remember one thing. I'm doing this for Reuben. It's what he wants. I realize I'm asking a tremendous sacrifice from all of you, but I have no other choice. Please return in ten minutes."

The room emptied immediately. Nellie, in a little-girl dress that she'd outgrown years before, was the last to leave. Bebe's eyes flew to the paper clipped to Daniel's pad. Either he hadn't noticed it, or he'd replaced it exactly the way he'd found it.

Jane stayed behind, as did Tillie. No one spoke as they waited for the others to return.

To the minute Fairmont's hierarchy filed into the room and took their places at the conference table. It was clear now of cups and crumbs, the pads lined up neatly with the chairs. Bebe took her seat and tried to read the faces at the table. Just as she was about to ask for a show of hands, Nellie spoke, her voice wan and weak. Tears brimmed her eyes.

"This isn't what my husband wanted. Philippe Bouchet wouldn't approve of any of this. And I can't reach him to have him say so because he's at boot camp." The tears spilled over and ran down her cheeks.

Bebe risked a glance at Daniel who was unfolding the paper on his pad. Would he—*dare* he—renege on the agreement he'd drawn up years earlier? Drawing a deep breath, she turned to Nellie.

"Do you have anything to say, *Mrs*. Tarz?" she asked coldly.

Nellie shook her head. "Just that Philippe wouldn't go along with this. And I can't go along, either." She sobbed then into a dainty handkerchief.

"Obviously, your vote is a no. All right, let's get on with it," Bebe announced to the table at large. "I want to remind you one last time, this is what Reuben wants. Now, let's see a show of hands for Reuben's side. Your vote represents me."

Jane walked behind each chair, calling out a yes or no vote, which Tillie recorded in her dictation notebook. "One abstaining vote, Daniel Bishop," she said with a catch in her voice.

Both Bebe and Nellie stared at Daniel. "You must vote, Daniel," Bebe said coolly.

Daniel could feel his daughter's tear-filled eyes boring into him. As if in a trance, he stared at Bebe, recalling her singsong words years before after he'd signed his name to the hateful contract in front of him. "You owe me, Daniel. I'll call this in sometime in the future, and you have to honor it. You owe me, Daniel, and don't you ever forget it!"

"We're waiting, Daniel," Bebe said again. After a moment he inclined his head slightly.

"Is that a yes or a no, Daniel?" Bebe demanded.

"It's a goddamn yes, all right?"

Bebe smiled and reached for the old contract. "Thank you, Daniel."

"Fifty-one percent in our favor," Jane said happily.

Nellie scrambled from the table and ran to her father. Sobbing and choking, she lashed out at him. "How could you, my very own father! You know this isn't what Philippe wanted. I hate you for this, Daddy, and I will never forgive you! Never! You just pretended to be my father all these years. You never really cared about me. My father would never do what you just did! You betrayed me! I hate you!" she shouted as she ran from the office.

Bebe kept her eyes averted during Nellie's outburst, as did the others. Jane busied herself at the coffee table stacking cups and saucers. Once things had quieted down, she looked up and around the table, smiling her appreciation at them all.

"This meeting is adjourned," she said. "Thank you all for your vote of confidence. When Reuben returns he will thank you himself. Now, if you'll excuse me . . ." With a brief nod to Jane, she was out of the room and headed for her car.

In the parking lot Nellie blocked her way. "That was a bitchy thing you did in there," Nellie shrilled. "Somehow you tricked my father, I know you did. You haven't heard the last of this."

"I think I have," Bebe said calmly. "There are no more tricks in your bag, Nellie. This is the way things are until Philippe and Reuben return. Now, get out of my way!"

"You're wrong," Nellie called after her, and then headed for her car. From behind her she heard Daniel calling her name, but she didn't turn around.

"Nellie, wait, we have to talk. Nellie, please wait."

Nellie turned then, her eyes cold and hard. "I don't have a father. You had your chance back there to act like one and you didn't. I don't ever want to see you again." At the last moment, before she pulled away, she said, "I'm glad my name is Bouchet. I'd be ashamed to call myself Nellie Bishop." With that, she yanked open her car door, got in, and drove off in a spurt of gravel.

"I'm so sorry, Daniel. I wish there were something I could do or say," Jane said, coming up behind him. "I think you know now that what we're doing is the right thing. Bebe and I both want you to be a part of the project for Reuben's sake. He will return, Daniel, I know he will. And if he doesn't . . . for whatever his reasons, it will still be right. Look, come with me back to my office. We have to get our ball rolling here. We don't have to talk about Nellie or even about you. . . . I've missed you, Daniel—No, don't say anything," she broke in as he opened his mouth to speak. "You're raw and bleeding right now. Just let me be your friend. Later, if there is a later, we'll deal with it. No confidences, Daniel, I can't handle them now. Come along, Counselor, we have work to do.'' Her smile was so genuine, so warm and inviting, Daniel found himself falling into step with her.

"Yes, work," he said numbly. "Everyone's answer to problems they can't handle."

He'd failed, first with Rajean and now with Nellie. But he couldn't fail Reuben, never Reuben. Doing what Reuben wanted would mean his mental survival. His stride firmed and quickened until he was walking just as purposefully as Jane. Thank God, he hadn't been wrong about her. He'd trusted his instincts the way Reuben had taught him to do.

"We'll make it work, Reuben," he muttered.

"Did you say something, Daniel?"

"I was just telling Reuben we'd make it work," Daniel said sheepishly.

Jane smiled again. "He already knows that. He trusts us, and that says it all." She reached her hand down for Daniel's. It took a moment for him to grasp it in his own. Peace flooded through him.

"Yes, that says it all," he said quietly.

Chapter Thirty-two

MIRAMAR AIR STATION! FINALLY. PHILIPPE WAS ALMOST delirious with joy that things had gone so smoothly. It had been nerve-racking to stand by, sweating silently, while his papers were examined. Finally, after what seemed an eternity of waiting, the captain rose, shook his hand, and said, ''Welcome aboard, Reuben.'' Philippe knew in his gut that although his grades were topnotch, it was the creative letter from Rear Admiral William F. Halsey that had gotten him into flight school.

He was safe. Everyone thought he was at Fort Dix in New Jersey. It would be hard as hell to track him down, and who among those he'd left behind would even think he'd join the navy, much less become an aviator under an assumed name.

For the first time since arriving in the United States, he was actually happy, he decided. There was no longer any pressure to live up to his father's name and reputation. He was his own man now, and would be judged on his own merit. Nellie was already a dim, distant memory, the nightmare of their marriage shelved far back into the recesses of his mind. His mother was going to take care of things, but that didn't include the annulment he planned to file as soon as he could. There was no room in this new life of his for Nellie Bishop, his biological parents, or any of the people who'd been part of his life during his short stay in Hollywood.

Philippe turned in time to see fellow trainee Mike Almeda bearing down on him. Mike was as tall as Philippe and just as broad-shouldered. But there the resemblance ended. Mike had sandy hair, greenish-blue eyes, and ten million freckles splattered over his entire body. He had a pug nose that he hated and the whitest teeth Philippe had ever seen, and he saw them a lot because Mike wore a perpetual grin. The young recruit hailed from Sacramento, where he lived in a white-shingled bungalow with his parents and twin sister named Elizabeth. "I'm the only one she lets call her Lizzie," Mike had told Philippe when they'd first met. "She prefers Beth or Elizabeth. She's going to Berkeley. She thinks she's smart enough to be a vet—you know what, Phil? She is," he'd added proudly.

"Jesus, I can't believe we're really here," Mike called in a voice loud enough to be heard all over the field. "It's awesome, do you agree?"

"Hell, yes. Look at those trainers," Philippe said gleefully. "It's hard to believe we're going to be sitting in them, and did you see the *real* ones on the runway?"

"I not only saw them, I *touched* them! When we get our own planes we get to name them." His freckled face scrunched up into a solid mass. "I gotta give it a lot of thought. It's like naming a baby, you have to make the right choice. By the way," he said slyly, "I found that picture of my sister I was telling you about. Wanna see it?"

"You're dying to show it to me, so hand it over." Philippe laughed. "She can't look any worse than you do."

Mike handed over the black-and-white photo. "I don't know how the hell it happened, but she doesn't have one freckle," he grumbled.

Philippe stared at the small snapshot. The girl in the picture looked as if she had the same laughing eyes as Mike and the same infectious grin. Her hair was long, curling around her shoulders, and she was tussling on the front lawn with two collies.

"The dogs are hers," Mike explained. "She loves all kinds of animals. Those are called Frick and Frack. When we were kids she was always dragging some stray home and wrapping it in bandages whether they needed it or not. One time she put this cat in a sling and he almost scratched her eyes out. Another time she had two hamsters she thought were males. Two months later she had sixty-seven of the little buggers, and boy did they smell!''

Philippe smiled. ''You love her, don't you.''

Mike looked embarrassed, but only for a second. ''You have to love your twin, you dumb shit. We're a close family,'' he said defensively. ''You want to carry it next to your heart. And if you ever meet her and tell her I said that, I'll deny it.'' He laughed.

''Naturally. What's wrong with her?'' Philippe asked suspiciously, staring at the photo.

''Not a damn thing,'' Mike sputtered. ''She's a dreamboat and can get any guy she wants just by crooking her finger.''

''I'll bet,'' Philippe said. ''Most guys don't go around trying to palm off their sisters on unsuspecting guys. What's she got, a club foot or something?''

''Actually, she's about as perfect as I am. Sometimes she talks too much and she's kind of bossy. But you should see her smack a ball and take three bases, and she's as pretty as my mom. You don't want the damn picture, give it back!''

''Ah, shit, you'd just wrinkle it up.'' Philippe grinned. ''I've known you for only two days, but I can see you're a slob,'' he added, eyeing Mike's wrinkled pants and shirt.

''Enough of this bullshit, let's go see those planes again. I felt like I was touching a naked woman,'' Mike confessed.

Philippe decided that he could love planes and flying and Mike Almeda's twin sister, Lizzie. Carefully he buttoned the flap on his shirt pocket, the picture safe inside.

Chapter Thirty-three

IT WAS SNOWING HARDER NOW, THICK, FAT FLAKES THAT covered Reuben in minutes. Every so often he stopped to shake snow from his body, and he was constantly brushing at his eyelashes. Trudging up the steep incline was hard enough without adding to his burden. As it was, he had to stop every five minutes to catch his breath. The wind, vicious now, howled and roared in his ears. Christ, he was tired. If he could just sleep for a few minutes . . . But he couldn't, he'd freeze to death in the high altitude. He had to keep going. One step, another, three, atta boy, now two more. Keep going, don't look down, don't think, just keep moving. Don't stop. One time he fell, sliding backward and losing all the ground he'd gained in the past thirty minutes. He rested a moment, struggling to take deep gasping breaths. When at last he was on his feet, ready to move again, he heard voices. Adrenaline coursed through his veins, giving his tired legs the impetus they needed to reach the thin row of pines.

"Gut! . . . Schon! . . . Um so besser! . . . Abfahren . . . des Alter . . . er Apparat . . . beeilen . . . der Berg . . . bergauf! Beeilen! . . . Beeilen! . . . Der Bericht! . . . Die Bewegung . . . Beeilen! . . . Beeilen! Gut! Gut!"

Reuben struggled with the smattering of German he'd learned

years earlier under Mickey's tutelage. These were German
soldiers, and they were in a hurry because they suspected . . .
something . . . the mountain and going uphill . . . One of them
wanted a report because they had . . . what? What the hell did
die Bewegung mean? Reuben fought to remember. . . . Jesus
Christ, movement! That's what it meant. They suspect movement . . . Mickey and the children up the mountain. They didn't
know about him, were unaware that he was on the incline right
below them. Thank God he'd slipped and fallen when he had.
The voices were closer now, and crystal clear, carrying down
the mountain. Would Mickey and the children hear them?
Would these same voices carry *up* the mountain?

  *"Erloschen . . . Fahrplan . . . Fehler . . . Feind . . . Feind
. . . Fliehen . . . Beeilen . . . Gleichgültig . . . Gewehr . . . Kinder
. . . Gräbe . . . gehen zu Fuss."*

Reuben's blood ran cold. They knew about the children, and
the climbers had rifles. . . . Someone had been careless . . . and
they were . . . were . . . going to dig graves . . . or one grave . . .
something about a timetable and the enemy . . .

  "Jagd . . . Jagd . . . Frau . . . Kinder . . ."

The soldier in command was ordering his men to hunt for
the women and children. Reuben's heart lurched in his chest.
Exhausted or not, he had to climb after the soldiers. If only
he knew how many there were, he might feel a little braver.
His fear almost overpowered him as he started his climb. He
estimated he was no more than a tenth of a mile behind the
Germans and thanked God for the snow.

At least he had the advantage now; he knew about them,
but they were unaware of him. Everything that was happening
to him was happening to the soldiers. Snow squalled at his
eyes, blinding him. His footing was unsure, his legs shaking
with exhaustion. Snow stung harder, beating at him like a
thousand whips, and still he kept going, the German words *das
Grab* ringing in his ears.

By now he was shivering . . . in fear. Ahead he could still
hear the Germans moving, their feet stomping into the thick
snow. With grim determination he forced himself to move more
rapidly, hoping the exertion would warm him. Suddenly his
knee struck a huge rock and he barreled over it. Stifling a curse
of pain, he bit down on his lip and tasted his own blood. His
eyes smarted as he forced his numb hands to massage his knee,
and then he hurried on. Moments later he halted under a feathery, snow-laden pine branch when he became aware of the

silence around him. The Germans had stopped, and he saw a wink of light through the pines. He must have made a sound! Although he tried to breathe normally, the thin air and his fear forced him to take deep gulps of air. Quickly he covered his mouth with his hand, but he couldn't take in enough air through his nose. Suddenly he felt a cough in his throat about to erupt, and without thinking he buried his head in the snow. When he came up for air he was forced to struggle even harder for breath. His vision clouded as he strained to listen for a sound from the Germans above him. The winking light was to the right now. At last he heard them talking again:

"Darf ich rauchen, Kapitan?"

Reuben almost fainted with relief. They wanted permission to smoke! Fighting his light-headedness, he skittered to the left, a crab in flight, his numb hands and feet moving on his mind's command. The smoke carried on the wind to his nostrils, and a wave of dizziness attacked him. He, too, would give anything for a cigarette, but he knew his tortured lungs wouldn't be able to absorb the smoke. He'd probably die of asphyxiation. Desperately he forced the desire from his mind and concentrated on making his exhausted limbs move. It was better on all fours; he could feel for the jutting boulders and rocks and not slip and slide. The bastards to his right must be part mountain goat.

Now that he was hunkered down into the snow, his movements grew even more frenzied. If he could get ahead of the soldiers, he might somehow be able to divert them from their objective. Instantly he realized that it was a ridiculous idea; staying behind them or at least even with them would give him a greater advantage. Mickey and Yvette would have weapons.

Eventually Reuben heard other sounds, the slight shuffles and whispers of children being hushed into silence. The Germans stopped, as did he. His heart pumping madly in his chest, Reuben sidled to the right, his eyes strained upward. The Germans were concentrating on the voices from above. One of them muttered, *"Schlachten."* Slaughter . . . They were going to ramrod their way upward and gun the women and children down without a second thought!

He could see their boots now, perhaps thirty yards ahead of him. There were four of them. Certainly he could take out two of them, but the other two . . . If he shouted, gave a warning, Mickey and Yvette would be alerted and have the advantage of shooting downward.

Now. He had to decide now. This instant. Her name birthed

in his belly, raged through his chest, and roared out his mouth. "Mickeeeeee!" Instantly he fired two shots in rapid succession; the first struck one soldier in the neck, the second in the center of his back. The third shot missed its mark by a foot. Moving instinctively, Reuben dropped to his knees and rolled to the left, then fired off a fourth, this one blind. He hit something, he knew by the sound of the grunt. From above he heard wild, ricocheting shots. Jesus, what if they hit *him*!

"*Mickeeeeee!*" he bellowed a second time as he rolled to the right. A branch fell over him, pelting him with wet snow. Furious with himself, he moved on, this time scrambling upward.

The goose-stepping son of a bitch in his knee-high boots would never march again. He heard Yvette curse as she smashed the barrel of her gun onto the man's head again and again. Pulpy flesh splattered the ground all about him.

"What took you so long, Monsieur Reuben?" Yvette chuckled. "Did we get them all?"

"Four . . . there were four of them," Reuben gasped.

Yvette chuckled again. "All accounted for. It's good to see you again, Reuben," she said, throwing her arms around him.

His breathing was easier now. "I guess I am a little late, twenty-one years to be exact, but I made it. Jesus, you don't know what I've been through. . . ."

"Yes, Reuben, I do know. We have been through the same thing. I've lost track of the Germans I've killed. Go, straight up. I'll cover these swine and try to feather our trail. There will be more, many more. You will have only time for a hello and we must move again. Reuben . . ."

"Yes?"

"Be kind. Like any woman, in a moment like this, she is thinking of her appearance and remembering how you last saw her. We have been through so much, endured . . . more than you know. In her heart she is the same person she was back then."

"You are a foolish woman, Yvette," Reuben said, not unkindly. "Do you think I look any better? I'm still the man who walked away. I'm hoping she will forgive me."

"She forgave you the moment you walked away. She's loved you all these years. Go now, don't keep her waiting."

Reuben grinned. "Still as bossy as ever."

"We have a German prisoner. Actually, he's our pack horse. So be alert."

"Jesus. Is there anything else I should know?"

"There are seven children, . . . and one dog." Yvette smiled.
"It figures."

Reuben grinned as he made his way through the thick stand of evergreens. He was here at last. He would see her in another minute. Sixty seconds. The years were wiped away as he straightened his shoulders.

"Mickeeeeee! . . ."

Chapter Thirty-four

NELLIE STOMPED ABOUT THE MANICURED GARDEN SEETHING with anger. Outdone! She'd been outdone, outmaneuvered, and outfoxed. Her stepfather had betrayed her. Philippe had betrayed her. Bebe and Jane . . . well, they were fighting for survival, so they didn't count. Technically, she was out in the cold, and it could either be temporary or permanent, depending on what she chose to do.

Right now her options were pretty dim, she decided. She didn't have a job, not that she needed one. Of course she could still go to the studio and sit in Philippe's office. No one could stop her from doing that. But to what end? No one would listen to her.

On the other hand, she could . . . Her mind flashed to the calendar on her vanity and the red X that alerted her to the day her menstrual flow would start. She was in what her mother would have called her "dangerous days," when she could conceivably get pregnant if she wanted to. But . . . a baby? The very thought repulsed her. Still *they* would have to view her differently. A baby would be an heir and a gilt-edged guarantee of comfort and security. Judges were always favorable to mothers and children. Lawyers, too, as well as bankers.

Her mind whirling, Nellie strode back into the house. The

housekeeper was in the kitchen preparing lunch. Nellie looked at her out of the corner of her eye, then quietly made her way to her bedroom.

Upstairs, she checked the vanity calendar. Then, apparently satisfied with the feasibility of her plan, she sat down at her desk and addressed several envelopes with blank pieces of paper inside. The first was to her old home in Washington, D.C. The second bore the name of St. Margaret's Convent, also in Washington. When she'd finished, she carried the envelopes downstairs and into the kitchen.

"Minnie, I'd like you to go to the post office and mail these," she said casually. "And I feel in the mood for some fresh fish. Will you go to the wharf and get some? And stop by the farmer's market and pick up some fresh fruit."

"But, miss, I just went to the market yesterday," the old woman complained. "We have plenty of fresh fruit."

"Miss? *Mrs.*, Minnie. Always call me Mrs. Tarz. Yesterday the fruit was fresh, today it isn't. It's a beautiful day, I should think you'd be happy to get out of this stuffy house. Of course, if you don't want to go . . ."

Sighing, Minnie pulled off her apron. "Very well, Mrs. Tarz, but it will take some time. I'll have to take two different buses."

"Take all the time you need, Minnie," Nellie said with a wave of her hand. "I'm sorry I'm being so . . . so . . . poopish, but I think—mind you, this is just . . . intuition—I think I might be pregnant."

The old woman, a grandmother of six, warmed immediately. "Mrs. Tarz, how wonderful! Of course I understand these little cravings. Sometimes they come on at the very onset."

The moment the housekeeper was out the door, Nellie rushed upstairs and stripped off her clothes. First she rubbed her entire body with baby oil, all the while admiring her lithe body in the long mirror on the door. Then she slipped into a belted cover-up and walked back downstairs and out to the pool, her long hair rippling behind her. She knew she was a picture of loveliness, a mermaid about to slither into the water—but not until the pool boy arrived. Smiling, she stretched out on a chaise longue to wait.

She didn't have to wait long. Five minutes later she sensed rather than saw him as he came up behind her. "I have to clean the pool," he muttered.

"Oh, that's right, I forgot today is the day. You come every two weeks, don't you?"

He nodded, his ears pink. A big stumbling boy, tall for seventeen, he wore faded khaki shorts and a sleeveless shirt that displayed his muscular legs and arms to advantage. Nellie rose lazily to her feet. He wasn't bad looking, she decided. Blond and blue-eyed, possibly Polish.

"It's so beastly hot," she said, smiling. "Would you mind terribly if I just took a quick swim? Better yet, why don't you join me. You're all sweaty, and the water will feel sooo good."

"It's against the rules," the boy mumbled.

"Oh, phooey. Rules are meant to be broken. You don't see your boss out here sweating. He'll never know. Besides, your clothes will dry in an hour."

The boy hung back, clearly uncomfortable. After a moment Nellie shrugged. "Well, I'm certainly not going to beg you," she said, and let the pool wrap slither down her oiled body. She heard him gasp as she dove into the pool. When she surfaced she laughed and crooked her finger, then swam quickly to the opposite side of the pool when the boy dived into the water.

She was a playful porpoise, he an attacking shark. Twice he almost had her in his grasp, but Nellie heaved herself backward into the water, swimming through his kicking legs. Suddenly she reached up and loosened his shorts, tugging until she had them in her hand. Then she swam to the top, the shorts clutched in her hands. "Come and get them!" she called as she crawled over the side of the pool. She stood there tall and slim, the water beading on her oiled body.

The pool boy's eyes blazed with desire as he swam across the pool. There was no sign of embarrassment when he too climbed from the pool, his penis ramrod straight. True, he'd never touched a girl before, but his older brother had told him what to do and how to do it. When he reached out for his shorts, Nellie relinquished them and he tossed them to the side. He was on her in a second, his hands caressing the oiled skin. Several times he tried to kiss her, but she kept turning away. She wouldn't let him kiss her, but she allowed him to touch her *all over*. Different girls liked different things, his brother had told him.

They were sprawled together on the spiky grass, a shapeless tangle of arms and legs. He took a second to register the fact that the girl's eyes were closed tightly as he pried her legs apart with his knee. And she was shivering, too—but no more than he was. When he thrust hard within her, she squealed once, and he realized with a shock that she was a virgin. But it was too late—he was powerless now to stop himself. He pumped his body in a frenzy, and when it was over he rolled onto the grass, his breathing harsh and labored.

Nellie grimaced. If *that* was all there was to it, she didn't care if she never had sex again. Rising, she slipped into her pool wrap and walked to the kitchen door, calling over her shoulder, "Don't forget to clean the pool." The screen door slammed behind her. A moment later she was back outside. "What's your name?" she called.

"Stanley," he replied.

The boy's name was not Stanley, it was Frank—Frank Wojesky. After Nellie left, he dressed, cleaned the pool, and drove straight downtown to enlist in the army. Lying about his age, he gave the enlistment officer his brother's name—Harry Wojesky—and was relieved when no one questioned him. One week later he left for boot camp.

Frank Wojesky left behind a legacy, a pregnant woman who gave birth nine months later. He died in Bataan, never knowing he'd fathered a child.

Chapter Thirty-five

IT WAS AN AUSTERE ROOM BEFITTING THE JUDGE, WHO'D had no time to remove his long black robe. He settled himself behind his desk, which was covered with manila folders, a box of Havana cigars, and a telephone. The room reeked of jurisprudence, rich leather, furniture wax, aromatic cigar smoke, and the faint scent of Aqua Velva.

The open folder on Judge Malcolm Taylor's desk wasn't thick at all, in fact it held fewer than a dozen legal papers on which he'd based the decision he was about to render to the assembled lawyers and their clients.

Judge Taylor was a go-by-the-book, eye-for-an-eye judge on the brink of retirement. His colleagues and the attorneys who appeared before him referred to him as "Tight-Ass" Taylor, and that was the only halfway complimentary name among scores of others that had been given him. His sense of humor had long since surrendered to a resigned pragmatism, which only recently had degenerated to a resentful, caustic fatalism. For some time now he'd found himself hating all smart-aleck lawyers and their smart-aleck clients. He hated the fact that these same smart-aleck lawyers made twice as much money as he did and could retire anytime they wanted on the spoils of other people's misery.

In appearance Judge Taylor was as austere as the chamber in which he was now presiding. He was tall, well over six feet, with thick speckled gray hair that he wore cropped close to his head. His eyes were blue, faded now to the color of washed-out denim, and they never sparkled; they penetrated. His nose was exceptionally long, a beak actually, that sloped down and then curled under. Once, his clerk who was perturbed about something muttered under his breath that the judge's nose was like that of a chicken hawk. That clerk was still a member of his court, and every time he came within a foot of the man he sniffed and blew his nose. The clerk thought he had an allergy. The judge did—to him. He had no lips to speak of, perhaps because he sat for seven hours a day with his cheeks puffed out and his teeth clenched as silver-tongued lawyers defended the guilty and prosecuting attorneys damned the innocent.

All Malcom Taylor wanted, had ever wanted, was to retire to Baja and fish from morning to night. He sighed now, wearily and indignantly, at the injustice of having had this particular case assigned to his court. Reuben Tarz was an acquaintance of his; he'd played poker with the man once or twice. And he'd even been on hand one time as a consultant when Tarz had filmed a courtroom scene in these very chambers.

Taylor cleared his throat and leaned forward. He hoped there wouldn't be any hysterics; he hated bawling women. "Ladies, Counselors, it is the verdict of this court that Mrs. Philip Tarz is in the right. This"— he waved Philippe's second power of attorney in the air disdainfully—"is not worth the paper it's written on. I'm basing this opinion on the fact that it has not been notarized and that young Mr. Tarz has gone off to fight for our country. However, I should point out that for the past three days I've had my clerk checking with the army as well as the navy, Air Force and Marine Corp. and we have not been able to affirm that Mr. Tarz *has* joined up. All of this leads me to believe there is some sort of hanky-panky going on. Therefore, in the best interests of Fairmont Studios, and in the absence of Philip Tarz, I must find for the studio. The studio will therefore be closed and all revenues placed in escrow until Philip Tarz returns. There will be no movies made at the studio, and only a skeleton crew is to be maintained." With a loud bang, Judge Taylor brought his stamp down on his decree. "Good day, ladies, Counselors."

"Your Honor," Bebe's lawyer interjected, "what about the money the board voted for Mr. Tarz's television research?"

"Frozen, in escrow!" Taylor boomed. "You're dismissed, Counselor. That means all of you!" The court clerk scurried to open the door and usher everyone out into the corridor.

Bebe looked at Daniel with tears in her eyes. Jane took her arm. "It's not the end of the world, Bebe," she said. "In a way I can't blame the judge. He's protecting the studio, and while he's doing that, Philippe—and Reuben—are automatically protected. We'll just go on as we planned, rent space and lease equipment elsewhere. Now we go to the banks and see what we can come up with."

Daniel spoke up for the first time. "I have some money, quite a bit, as a matter of fact. Consider it yours. I just thought of something. I'm unemployed!"

"Aren't we all." Bebe smiled tremulously.

"I had the feeling it was going to go like this, so I put the bite on Max," Daniel went on. "He gave me enough to cover Philippe's research project and to take care of putting all studio personnel on half salary. If we need more, all we have to do is ask." He chuckled. "It boggles my mind when people can write out a check for five or ten million dollars and not even blink."

"It's a drop in the bucket, Daniel," Jane said quietly. She tried for a cheerful note. "Well, we're going to need some kind of an office, a headquarters, so to speak. That's your job, Daniel. You are now officially employed with no salary. For now let's use Bebe's house as our office. Agreed?"

"Fine with me." Bebe smiled. "I want to personally thank Max for his contribution. Daniel, did you explain what Philippe's research is about?"

"That was the clincher, not that I needed one. He told me if that was the kid's dream, he'd work his ass off to make it a reality, and said he wants one of those little boxes in his living room."

By now they were at the courthouse door. Nellie's lawyer was holding the door open for her. She turned to face Bebe, her eyes sad, her lips trembling. "I'm pregnant," she said. "You probably don't care, but I . . . I thought you had the right to know." To Daniel she said, "I guess you'll be sort of a grandfather, too."

She was through the door and halfway down the steps before the others could close their mouths.

"This has to be the quickest pregnancy in history." Jane counted on her fingers, then grudgingly admitted that it was possible. "Never having been in that condition, I suppose one knows about these things almost immediately."

Bebe didn't hear her; she was too busy trying to digest the fact that she was going to be a grandmother. Reuben would be a grandfather. Lord! "This . . . Nellie's news . . . it changes nothing. Daniel, if the court can't find Philippe . . . what does it mean? Where is he?"

Daniel shook his head. "I don't know. I called Fort Dix myself and got nowhere. If I had to guess, I'd say he enlisted under another name. But if that's the case, we may never find him."

"Why would he do that?" Bebe demanded.

"To get away from the mistake he made with Nellie," Jane said boldly.

"He said his marriage was never consummated," Bebe mused, frowning. "We spoke of an annulment. Now Nellie is saying . . . Dammit, Daniel, he wasn't lying! I was there, I heard him."

"With all due respect, Bebe, you hardly know the boy," Daniel reminded her. "Look, I'm not taking sides here. I know you believe what you just said. But Nellie just announced her pregnancy, so that should tell us something."

"Ever-loyal Daniel," Bebe snapped. "Have you given any thought to the possibility that Nellie could have been pregnant before she tricked Philippe into marrying her? I for one plan to keep that foremost in my mind. You can think whatever you want. In the end the truth will win out."

"Jane?" Daniel said quietly.

Jane sighed. "I'm afraid I agree with Bebe. Philippe wasn't lying. If Nellie is pregnant, she was that way before she married the boy. I'm sorry, Daniel, but I'm not going to budge one inch in my opinion of your daughter."

"It's Nellie's intention to put us all into a flap, and we're doing just that," Bebe said suddenly. "I suggest we forget Nellie and get on with the business of the day. Nellie has nothing to do with our project, so, speaking strictly for myself, I don't want to hear her name mentioned in my presence again,"

"Or mine," said Jane.

"All right, ladies, I read you loud and clear," Daniel said grimly.

Bebe smacked her hands together. "It's time to go to work."

* * *

Nellie wandered around the house in a frenzy. She'd anticipated winning, but she hadn't been prepared to have the studio closed down. Now what was she supposed to do? Shop? Spend Philippe's money? Eat? Get fatter and fatter until the baby was born? She *was* pregnant, she could tell in subtle little ways. And if she needed hard-core proof, her calendar supplied it. She was now *late*. If she hadn't missed her period, she would never have had the nerve to make her announcement at the courthouse.

Somehow she'd been disappointed in everyone's reaction, especially Bebe's. If it hadn't been for Bebe's bland reaction to her news, she'd never have spoken directly to her stepfather; that had been a mistake. But Bebe's indifference had irritated her enough to court Daniel's reaction. Even there she'd seen nothing—no love, no joy, not even surprise. Jane, on the other hand, looked surprised enough for the three of them. But it wasn't your typical surprise, it was more like horror, or a shocked revulsion. Jane would immediately assume she'd become pregnant before marrying Philippe and would try to convince the others. Nellie laughed then, an unholy sound.

It was after, Jane. Afterafterafterafter.

Chapter Thirty-six

NOW. IN SECONDS, HE WAS GOING TO SEE HER AGAIN. WHAT a fool he'd been to shout her name like that. Even now he could hear it echoing about him. But it didn't matter—nothing mattered except seeing Mickey again. How would she see him? As he was now, exhausted, weary, filthy . . . older? So much older. The gray in his hair, the lined face that was wind-burned and raw from constant exposure to the icy snow? The anticipation was excruciating; he was trembling so badly he could hardly make his feet move. Yes, he could see her now, her dark form silhouetted against the white snow! He whispered her name, hearing it carried away on the wind. She was moving now, so slowly, or was he the one moving slowly? The moment. His heart raced, threatened to leap from his chest. Desperately he tried to clear his vision, to wipe the crusted ice from his lashes; his thick-lensed eyeglasses had long since vanished, casualty to one skirmish or another. But even without them he could see—see his past, the present, coming toward him, arms outstretched.

How quiet it was suddenly, his thundering heart the only sound in the stillness. He heard his name carried on the wind, knowing her name would meet with his and echo down the mountain.

A waist-high boulder stood between them. It seemed insurmountable to his exhausted body, and in his overanxiousness it never occurred to him to walk around it. He gave birth to an anguished cry at nature's injustice and stretched out his arms beseechingly. His hands touched other hands, hands he never thought he would feel in his own . . . ever again.

He could see her now, his eyes drinking in the sight. His arms yearned to hold her, his body hungered to feel her next to him. She was smiling, the warm, gentle smile that was just for him, just as he remembered it.

All his stored-up memories engulfed him, the past years forgotten as time stood still. A sob tore from his throat—or was it hers? It didn't matter, he was finally here, touching the woman he'd vowed to love unto eternity.

He could feel his feet moving, feel his arms arms sliding across ice and stones, as Mickey guided him around the boulder. Then she fell into his arms, her sobs matching his own. "Mickey, Mickey . . ." Her name on his lips was a benediction, an offering of profound gratitude and a promise of infinite peace.

"Reuben, my darling Reuben, I cannot believe you're here. How I dreamed and prayed for this moment, and now that you're here I cannot think of a thing to say."

"Shhh, there's no need for words. I'm here and I'm never going to leave you again. Don't cry, Mickey, please don't cry. We're together, we must be happy," he said in a choked voice. He held her tight to enforce his words, to give substance to his feelings.

"I'm remembering everything, every single moment we spent together," Mickey said softly against his coarse coat. "I kept every memory alive by thinking of you each day."

"And I did the same. I don't suppose this is the time for me to recite the litany from the winemaker's calendar," he murmured.

She chuckled. "No, my darling, it is not the time. We have no time at all for our feelings. Our voices carry about the mountain. We must go on, the children must be taken to safety. There is a German with us, and he says we have only perhaps six or seven kilometers to go to reach free soil. From here on in the littlest have to be carried. Reuben . . . I want nothing more than to stay here in your arms and never move again. When I first saw you, time stood still for me. Nothing mattered but you. But that moment is gone, and we must—"

"I know," Reuben said hoarsely. He kissed her eyes, her cheeks, and then her mouth, a lingering kiss filled with twenty years of longing. When he released her he was giddy with feeling, his head full of . . .

"There's no time for more," Yvette hissed, coming up behind them. "Now, Michelene, we have no more time. I can hear them, the whole damn German Army is after us. Quickly! I'll carry Sophie, Kort will take Stephan, and you, Reuben, will carry Bruno. Mickey will lead the way. Now move!"

The children were on their feet, staggering with exhaustion. At Mickey's motion, Bruno raised his arms for Reuben to pick him up. The little dog under his coat gave a soft yip.

"The German is . . . he's okay, Reuben, he's helped us," Mickey said. "Without him we'd all be dead. Reuben, if anything . . . I love you. I've always loved you. When I go on to my other life, as we all will someday, I will carry that love with me. I wish we had more time, but I cannot ask more of Him. He has already sent me you. Pray now for the little ones, for these German swine will rip them from their necks to their groins if they catch us."

She smiled at the little boy in Reuben's arms. "Bruno, this is my friend from America. He has come a very long way to help us. You must be quiet, and you must keep your friend quiet."

"*Oui, mademoiselle,*" he said, snuggling closer against Reuben's chest.

With a catch in her voice, Mickey said, "He is just like Philippe was at that age. Later you will tell me of Philippe." Reuben nodded.

They walked and climbed, stopping only a few minutes each hour to rest. It was a tortuous climb. Reuben's lungs felt seared, his back one mass of pain as he struggled up one incline after the other. At one point he looked to Yvette, who seemed to be having no trouble at all with the little girl in her arms. The German was making good time, too. Clenching his teeth in determination, he kept on climbing. When the boy slipped out of his grasp, he tightened his hold and boosted him to his shoulders.

Bruno patted Reuben's shoulder to show he approved of his new position.

Suddenly Mickey's hand shot up and she turned calling a halt. "We've reached the plateau. We can rest now. We have less than a mile to go to Spain. A ten-minute rest and then, my little friends, I will tell you a story," she whispered.

Bruno sighed with happiness. "Mademoiselle Mickey tells wonderful stories, monsieur. There is a red wagon and a blue bicycle at her château. She promised us a pony cart and a sailboat. It will be so wonderful. Did you ever have a red wagon, monsieur?" he asked wistfully.

Reuben's throat constricted. "No, I never had one, but I did see the red wagon and the blue bicycle at Mademoiselle Mickey's château. There are all kinds of wonderful things in . . . in Philippe's room. I saw roller skates, too." Bruno sighed again; he was so relieved to hear Mademoiselle's American friend confirm all the wonderful things at the château.

They were sitting in a half circle in a copse of pungent evergreens, taking fast, shallow breaths in the thin air. For the first time in hours they were truly relaxed with the knowledge that freedom was less than a mile away. Suddenly, German soldiers came out of nowhere, their guns pointed, their heels clicking at attention. The order was simple. All weapons tossed to the ground. Mickey and the rest of them obeyed the guttural command, one by one. They were powerless, helpless in the enemy's hands. Reuben's stomach heaved, his eyes murderous. He took in the children with one glance. They were too young to die; they hadn't even tasted life yet.

Mickey rose up on her knees and addressed herself to one of the Germans, pleading for them to let the children go. In desperation she pulled out the small sack of diamonds Daniel had given her and held them out. The German snatched them from her hand and then knocked her backward with the butt of his gun. An animal cry escaped Reuben as he made a move to go to Mickey's aid. He felt a rifle ram into his neck.

"No, Reuben, I am all right!" Mickey gasped. "Do nothing. Nothing, Reuben!"

The children moved then, in unison, their small bodies hurtling forward toward the German boots. They were devils driven by their hatred of the Boche. It happened so quickly, the others were caught off guard. Yvette was the first to pounce on her rifle; screaming and cursing, she swung the gun butt this way and that. Kort was behind her doing the same thing. Mickey rolled to her feet with lightning speed and tossed Reuben his rifle.

The children were shrieking now, either with glee or hatred, Reuben couldn't be sure. Anna, the oldest girl, brought her

foot up into one soldier's groin and crunched it downward.
Marc kicked out with his foot and caught the man square on
the side of his face. The sound of bone splintering made him
laugh, so he kicked out again, this time toppling to the ground
when the German's hand snaked out and caught his leg. Bernard
dived for the man's arm and yanked it backward. The children
showed no mercy as they kicked and kicked, their small arms
yanking and pulling. The little dog, free of Bruno's warm coat,
was busily tugging at a German's ear. Reuben knew the sharp
little teeth would rip it from the man's head. He made no move
to interfere.

There were so many of them. All around him was a frenzy
as he jabbed down, then up, swinging the gun this way and
that. Yvette was a dynamo as she fired round after round from
her gun.

When it was over, the snow was scarlet with German blood.
Bodies, a dozen of them, lay in various states of mutilation.
Reuben felt sick as he stared at the children back in their pine
nest. He heard Mickey say, "You are a brave little army, the
finest warriors France has ever known. We are not prisoners,
we are . . . almost free."

"Michelene, Michelene, you've been shot!" Yvette cried.
"Reuben, she's been shot!"

"It . . . it is . . . it is nothing . . ."

Reuben was at her side in a second, ripping at her heavy
coat. The children surrounded her, their faces fearful for the
first time. Reuben examined the gaping hole in Mickey's chest.

"It is not . . . *nothing*, Mickey, it is . . . *something*. Something I . . . Hold still, don't move. Mickey, don't move and
don't talk." He looked around wildly. "Bandages . . . anything?" he asked helplessly. Yvette shook her head, tears
streaming down her cheeks. Reuben's mind raced back to the
Great War, when comrades' wounds were packed with snow
until medical help arrived. With clumsy hands he ladled snow
onto Mickey's bare chest. "It's all I can do," he whispered,
and closed her coat. He knew it wouldn't help. She was going
to die, and he was powerless to stop it.

"Reuben . . . come closer," Mickey whispered. "Take them
over the border, leave me here. You must, chéri. I have never
asked anything of you, but this . . . you must. We have come
too . . . far, they have gone through too much . . . you saw what
they did . . . go, Reuben, go now." She began to cough blood
trickling from the corner of her mouth.

"No, mademoiselle, either we go together or we stay," Anna said firmly. "I speak for all of us."

"No . . . it isn't safe."

"I'll help you carry her," Kort said to Reuben. Yvette wrung her hands, sobs racking her body, all hatred driven from her body. Kort prodded her, none too gently.

Reuben gathered Mickey into his arms, and Kort helped him to his feet. He walked alongside, bracing one arm while Yvette braced the other. An hour later they were at the border, where willing hands led the tired band of Frenchmen to free soil.

There were no shouts of happiness, no tears shed for their freedom. The promise of hot food and warm beds was ignored as the tight little group stood at attention waiting . . . waiting for Mickey to give them their new orders.

But she was in a bed now, her wound receiving attention.

Reuben ushered the children into the warm kitchen, where bowls of thick soup and warm, crusty bread awaited them. A jug of milk stood in the center of the rough table next to thick slabs of yellow cake.

"Sit down and eat," he ordered. When the children remained where they were, he said, "Mademoiselle Mickey said you are to eat. So you will eat, that is an order!"

The moment the door opened, Reuben shouldered his way past the old woman with her basin of warm water. She pulled him back out with a firm hand. "I could do nothing but try to make her comfortable. She will die in a bed on free soil. The bullet is too deep. Even if we had a doctor, a surgeon, it is too late."

Death circled the room . . . waiting. *Not yet, please, not yet*, Reuben pleaded.

The cabin they were in was coarse, erected quickly and none too substantially for those crossing the border. There were cracks between the pine boards in the ceiling as well as in the walls. It was cold, but then, death was always cold, Reuben thought as he dropped to his knees by the side of the bed. There was so much he wanted to say, needed to say, to this wonderful woman.

"Reuben, the children, they are safe?" Mickey asked weakly.

He nodded. "They're all safe. They're eating now, thanks to you. Mickey, I . . . I want to tell you so many things . . . to try to explain . . ."

"There is no time, Reuben. I know . . . I've always known.

What is in my heart is in yours ... I must ... I must ... Philippe ..."

"He told me to tell you he loves you," Reuben said gently. "And he does. As much as I do."

"I need your promise ... Will you—"

"Mickey, save your strength, don't talk. Let me talk. I need to tell you everything. I'll do whatever you want, you know you have my promise ..."

"Yvette ... will go back to the Resistance ... I promised the children ... after the war ... my promise, Reuben ... especially Bruno. At the time I told them all the ... stories ... it was to insure their silence. They weren't really lies ... When the war is over you will take them all to the château, and Yvette will join you ... You can find someone to ... look after them ... I need to hear your promise, Reuben. ..."

"I promise," Reuben said, biting down on his lip.

"In ... in my backpack there is ... the wineries, the château, they are yours. I ... knew you would come back someday ... You will hang the calendar and do all the things I ... couldn't allow you to do years ago—" She coughed, blood trickling from her mouth and nose. Reuben wiped it away with the edge of the blanket.

"Rest now," he murmured. "It is my turn to talk." He held on to her hand and stroked her hair. Through his tears he saw her as she was when he'd first left her. Once again time stood still as he spoke of his life after leaving her.

Now she was leaving him; he could feel her life slipping away. Desperately he clutched her hand tighter, willing her to live. Her fingers slipped from his. "No," he moaned, "no, Mickey, hold on. Please don't leave me. Mickceeee!"

He thought he'd whispered her name, but the children scurrying to her bedside told him otherwise. Rage swelled in his heart when the children murmured their love. This last moment was his, he would never have it again! His last good-bye ... yet everyone was talking at once. Little Bruno was on the bed on his hands and knees.

"*Au revoir*, Mademoiselle Mickey," he sobbed. "I will take care of Philippe's wagon. You can trust me, Madamoiselle." The little dog bounded onto the bed. He looked around uncertainly at these new soft surroundings. His small head inched closer to Mickey, his pink tongue licking tentatively at her cheek, his tail wagging furiously.

Kort lifted the boy and dog to the floor. "*Auf Wiedersehen*, mademoiselle,'' he said quietly. ''I am proud to have known you and served alongside of you to guide these little ones to safety.'' He saluted smartly, an American salute, before he ushered the weeping children from the room.

Yvette was next. Dropping to her knees, she reached for Mickey's hand as she howled her grief. ''*Au revoir*, old friend, I will never forget you. You have my promise that one day France will be free again.'' With infinite tenderness, she pressed Mickey's hand to her lips, then fled from the room, leaving Reuben to say his final good-byes.

''Can you hear me, Mickey?'' he asked stroking her hair.

She smiled and struggled to speak. ''You . . . mustn't let them grieve . . . Life is . . . for the . . . the living.''

Reuben shook his head. ''There is no life without you, my love.''

''Ah, *chéri*, but there is . . . now . . .'' A fit of coughing racked her body, and still she struggled to speak. ''Now you . . . are . . . free . . . to love . . . Bebe. Free . . . Reuben . . . my last . . . my last . . . gift to you . . .''

Reuben raised his eyes, tears blurring his vision. ''Why?'' He watched as a snowflake fell between the cracks and floated down to caress Mickey's cheek. Tenderly he leaned over and kissed it away. ''Good-bye, my love.''

Within the hour Mickey's body was placed on a sled and taken to the bottom of the mountain and into the nearest town for burial the following day.

The children were taken on another sled to a convent school with Reuben's promise that he would come for them the moment the war was over. Bruno looked skeptical as he stared up at the tall man. ''How do we know, Monsieur Reuben, that you will keep your promise?''

Reuben scooped the little boy into his arms. ''Because I promised Mademoiselle Mickey I would take you to the château. You must trust me. And I want your promise to take care of that four-legged creature and to give him a name.''

Bruno digested this. ''Very well, monsieur, I will trust you because Mademoiselle Mickey trusted you. I have one little question. Will I be too big for the red wagon when you come for us?''

Reuben swallowed past the lump in his throat. ''A boy is never too big for a red wagon, but if you are, I will make you a new one, bigger and redder than the one in Philippe's room. That's my promise to you.'' The boy nodded happily as he climbed onto the sled. The children waved and shouted until they were out of sight.

"I leave you now, too," Kort said, coming up behind Reuben.

"I suppose you expect a rousing send-off," Yvette said gruffly. She would never admit it, but she was going to miss the German.

"A simple good-bye will suffice," he replied.

She hesitated a moment, then nodded. "*Auf Wiedersehen*, Kort. Thank you for helping the children. Don't you dare kiss me, you stinking German!" she cried. Kort laughed as he started off down the mountain.

Yvette's eyes brimmed. "We're all that's left, Reuben. What are you going to do?"

"I'm going to stay here for a few days and write." He explained about his journal. "I told Mickey about it, but I don't know if she really understood; it was toward . . . the end. It's what I want to do. When I'm finished, I thought I would join up with the Resistance. If you don't mind waiting, we can travel back down the mountain together. After the war I'm going to stay on." He showed her the papers from Mickey's backpack. "I made a promise to Mickey and the children that I will honor. I won't be going back to America. France is my home now."

"Did you happen to notice the deed to our farm among the papers?"

"Yes, I did. Do you want me to do something in particular with it?" Reuben asked, puzzled.

"Keep it for the children. We . . . both of us promised them cows and chickens and ponies. I know I won't be going back there. I feel it in here," she said, placing a hand over her heart. "Do not be sad for me, Reuben. I am prepared to meet my Maker, and Henri is getting impatient waiting for me. I'm tired, as tired as Mickey was. But to answer your question—yes, I will wait for you, but only if you promise to carry hot water for me to take a bath."

Reuben smiled. "I think that's fair. And in return I would appreciate some hot food. Now!"

"Arrogant American!"

"Obedient Frenchwoman!"

"So, we start out even, eh?"

"It's as good a place as any. I'm thinking of it as a new beginning."

"And the past?" Yvette queried.

"Dead and buried, as it should be. That doesn't mean it's forgotten. It will live in us all for the rest of our lives, but we won't dwell on it. Time will heal all our wounds."

"Yes, in time." Yvette smiled.

Chapter Thirty-seven

AS THE WAR YEARS PASSED ON, AMERICA FOUND itself saying good-bye to its sons and then waiting to say hello. . . . Life moved on as did the buses and trains that traveled from one end of the country to the other carrying civilians and servicemen on a horde of war missions. And young women who still lived with their parents suddenly moved from home and hearth, some to enlist in the WAVES, WACS or Coast Guard SPARS, thousands of others to work in defense plants, their way of helping their brothers, cousins, and boyfriends. Store shelves went bare as goods once taken for granted suddenly disappeared. Packaged cigarettes became a memory, and people took to rolling their own. Americans groused and complained, but accepted food rationing, standing in lines for butter, sugar, coffee, and shoes. These same Americans hunkered down, driving less to conserve precious gasoline and willingly turning in their old toothpaste tube when buying a new one. Bond rallies, tin-can drives and wastepaper drives were a weekly occurrence. Housewives salvaged grease from cooking, collected clothing and anything else that could be used for the war effort on the home front. For once in collective agreement, Americans despised the Japanese, loathed all that the Nazi system stood for and felt only contempt for Mussolini.

War was hell.

Philippe Bouchet agreed. By now he was a full-fledged navy aviator fighting a war in the Pacific. Although certain he'd be sent immediately to the European theater, he had been assigned first to the *Yorktown*, then to the *Lexington*, and finally to the *Enterprise*. With Mike Almeda he'd started out flying F4F Wildcats, later transferring to the F6F Wildcats designed specifically to fight Japanese Zeroes. The F6F was a tougher plane and a better high-altitude fighter than the lighter Japanese Zeke, and Philippe preferred it, as did Mike.

Philippe knew he'd done well these past years and was proud of his contribution to the war—a war that was rapidly coming to an end.

Talk was of D-Day and a massive invasion.

"Jesus Christ, Phil, do you ever feel homeless?" Mike Almeda demanded. "We should be planted somewhere, piloting the same plane day after day. I don't mind telling you, I'm not real crazy about Corsairs."

Philippe shook his head. "Don't worry about it, we're back on our Hellcats. A plane is a plane; you either fly it or you don't. We got it off the *Intrepid* and they said it couldn't be done. All I want is to be part of this invasion and get this fucking war over with." His voice was so vehement, so intense, Mike's eyes widened.

The two young pilots were assigned to Task Force 58 and headed toward the southern Marianas. Theirs was a massive array of sea-air power, the greatest armada ever assembled. As far as the eye could see and beyond, great warlike ships churned through the Pacific. There were seven heavy carriers: the *Hornet, Yorktown, Bunker Hill, Wasp, Enterprise, Lexington*, and *Essex*, along with eight light carriers and seven new battleships, eight heavy cruisers, thirteen light cruisers, and sixty-nine destroyers.

The ward room was buzzing with questions from jittery pilots. The invasion was set for the fifteenth, yet here it was only the eleventh. Philippe's stomach roiled. Three days ahead of schedule. He looked toward Mike, who shrugged as if to say, This is the navy, pal, we just fly 'em, we don't make the decisions.

"Listen up, men," their flight commander called, rapping sharply on the table in front of him. "Right now we're two hundred miles east of the Marianas. You're doing the first sweep. The way I look at it, the Japs will be expecting a dawn attack or an early evening one. We're gonna fool 'em, you're going up at high noon!''

The date was June 1, 1944, five days before the Normandy landings in Europe.

While Philippe flew his Wildcat over Saipan, Tinian, and Guam, destroying all the planes on the ground and in the air, his father, along with other Resistance members, was destroying the submarine pens in Brest that the bombers overhead couldn't seem to target.

Having successfully completed their mission, the Resistance members moved north, into Paris itself, where they took to fighting in the streets, openly and savagely killing German soldiers. They fought valiantly, rejoicing when the skies filled with Allied parachutes, part of the Seventh Army's amphibious assault from the Mediterranean.

On August 25, Paris once again became a free city. Reuben waved wildly as he watched the French Second Armored Division sweep through the city, followed by an American marine division. If only there were someone with him to share his joy. But Mickey was dead, and he'd lost track of Yvette a year before.

It was dusk and the streets were quiet, the German garrison gone forever. The war was almost over. For Reuben, it was completely over. The damn armies could do anything they wanted from this point on. He'd done his share, perhaps more . . . he was through with war and death and killing.

Reuben found his feet walking down familiar streets, streets he thought he had forgotten. He hungered for the sight of the flower stall where he'd once bought violets for Mickey. Everything was so achingly familiar, so heart-wrenching. It was truly over.

Suddenly he found himself in front of Mickey's Paris town house, a place he'd visited with her, a place where he'd made love to her. It looked the same, but Germans had lived in it over the past few years. How Mickey must have hated that. He walked on; this was one memory he didn't want to tackle now.

Reuben jammed his hands into his pockets and started to whistle as he walked away. He had things to do and places to go. First he would finish his writing and see about getting it mailed off or on a plane with a newsman. Then he was going back up the mountain to a convent school in Spain.

* * *

Ten days later Reuben strode into the walled yard of the school, whistling and shouting the children's names. He was met with silence. A nun appeared, a frown on her face, her hands tucked inside the long sleeves of her dark habit. "May I help you?" she asked cautiously.

"I've come for the children from the mountain. Where are they, Sister?"

"From the mountain, you say?"

"Yes. Anna, Marie, Marc, Bernard, Sophie, Stephan, and Bruno. What's happened to them?" Reuben demanded.

"They are gone, monsieur, for many weeks now. People came for them. I could not stop them."

"Who? What people?"

"French people, a priest. I could not ask questions of a priest. He said it was necessary for the children to . . . to be taken. We have prayed daily for the little ones."

"The dog? Bruno's dog, what happened to it?"

"He took it with him, monsieur. They were happy to go. All of them were happy."

"And you have no idea, no clue as to where they went?" he asked.

The sister shook her head. "A journey is all I know. I heard the good Father say something about a splendid journey. I am so very sorry, monsieur. Each day they waited for you, at night they prayed for you to come, and now you are too late."

Reuben's mind grappled for words. "The priest, surely you know where he is from and how I can reach him."

"He is from Madrid, and I never saw him before. If only you had come sooner."

"You shouldn't have let them go, they were to stay here and be safe." Reuben said reproachfully.

"They are with a man of God, they are safe with him," the Sister replied, and began to turn away. "I'm sorry I cannot help you anymore. It is time for prayers. I will pray for you, monsieur."

"Wait a minute, what about the other children from the mountain, the ones who came to you first. Where are they?"

"They left also, monsieur. All of them. There are no children here now." Inclining her head slightly in farewell, the nun turned and walked back into the shadows of the chapel.

This was a hell of a mess. He'd been so eager, so determined, to return for the children, and now he wouldn't be able to honor his last commitment to Mickey. Sixteen children, all gone. . . . In this war-torn country he knew he would never find them. Most likely he'd never see them again. It was like everything in his life—too much, too little, too late.

"I tried, Mickey," he whispered. "I kept my promise. Perhaps one day they will find me. As soon as the government starts to function again, I'll write letters, I'll initiate searches. Whatever it takes, I'll do it. I gave you my word, and I'll honor it."

Reuben's destination now was the château in Marseilles. His job, to repaint the red wagon and blue bicycle and oil the roller bearings on the skates. He'd find the children or die in the attempt.

Chapter Thirty-eight

GLOBAL PICTURES, THE MAKESHIFT STUDIO ESTABLISHED BY
Bebe Tarz and Jane Perkins, crackled with electricity. This was
the last day of shooting on *The Sands of Time*, Reuben's film.

Three long years in the making in less than desirable conditions. Unknown actors and actresses fighting to give extraor-
dinary performances so their careers would escalate. The
polished director, demanding perfection from every scene; the
producer hovering like a mother hen to be sure the director
was following *her* orders. Three long years of concentrated,
unified effort on everyone's part. Minimum wages, long hours,
treks to location, sleeping in tents and eating from a cook wagon
. . . the perfect setup for the advertising blitz Bebe planned.

One more scene and it was all over. This was the longest,
the most difficult, and had deliberately been left until last.

Bebe took her seat next to Jane, whose eyes were shining.
"Jane, do you feel as . . . as proud as I do?" she asked. "Maybe
proud isn't the right word. Fulfilled. You did one hell of a job,
you know. Carlyle, well, his direction is absolutely flawless."

Jane squeezed her hand and nodded. "*We* did it, Bebe.
Reuben would be so proud, so very proud." She tried to swallow past the lump in her throat. "He's not coming back, is
he? For a while I thought he would, I expected . . . hoped my

phone would ring . . . but it was all wishful thinking on my part. This is his grand finale. It's so sad, yet it's so fitting, so . . . so right. I've cried so much, I have no tears left in me. And I can't even begin to imagine how you feel.''

''Much as you. This last scene . . . I'm not sure I can handle it. Seeing Mickey die . . . feeling Reuben's grief . . . I . . . Death scenes are tearful enough . . . I guess I wasn't . . . I'm not prepared to see Mickey die and to remember my part in all of it. So many years. How devastated he must have been to go all that way, endure tortures daily, then finally find her . . . and lose her forever. To die so tragically and be buried hastily, without ceremony or acknowledgment . . .'' Bebe gazed off into the distance, her eyes misted with tears. ''I think that's the hardest part,'' she murmured.

''Yes, but look at her legacy,'' Jane argued. ''Millions of people will see this film and mourn her, thanks to you and me and everyone else who helped make this movie. I think we should be happy.''

''Quiet on the set!'' shouted John Carlyle. ''Bruno, take your place. Make your dog sit! Now! Okay, roll 'em!''

Bebe watched, hardly daring to breathe as Bruno marched on sturdy legs to the set, his dog trailing behind at just the right pace. It was so real, she clamped a hand over her mouth to stifle her gasp. Real because it *was* real; Bruno was reliving the moment. His tears were real as he paid final tribute to the gallant woman who gave her life for his. Bebe fled from the set when she saw the little dog's pink tongue flick out to touch the cold cheek. She ran straight into Daniel's arms and through her tears she saw his own.

''This is one hell of a goddamn movie,'' he muttered.

Bebe nodded as she blew her nose lustily. ''The goddamn best, and it's going to take every award the Academy has to offer. Ten bucks, Daniel,'' she said, blowing her nose again.

''I'd be a fool to take you on. I don't know what you call a film like this in the business, but I'd call it a masterpiece.''

''That's good enough for me.'' She turned away, hiding the pain in her eyes. ''Oh, Daniel, where is he? Why hasn't he sent word? I was so sure, I hoped that he would come back. Surely he wants to know how . . . why, Daniel, why?''

''This part of Reuben's life is over. I don't think he'll ever come back.'' He shook his head. ''I'm sorry, Bebe, it's what I feel. He trusted Jane to make this film knowing she would do just what he wanted. In my heart I believe he knew you would be part of it all. He was so proud of you, Bebe. He's in love with you, you know. If you want him, you're going to have to go over there. Not right away. He needs time for his wounds to heal, and they will heal. Mickey set him free with her last breath, at long last.''

Bebe threw herself into Daniel's arms and wept for the gallant Frenchwoman known as Marchioness Michelene Fonsard.

"That's it! It's a wrap!" they heard John Carlyle shout. "Ladies and gentlemen, we turned out the best movie this town has ever seen! The drinks are on me! Soda pop for the kids. Let's party!"

"You heard the man," Bebe said, giving Daniel a tremulous smile. "Let's go!"

John Carlyle swooped down on Bebe and Daniel like an avenging bird, his arms flapping, his face one wide grin. "If you ever pay me for this, I'm going to have to give the money back. This wasn't work, it was pure joy. I can't wait to see that Oscar! I'm going to hold it in my hand, sleep with it, kiss it good night, and . . . and . . ."

"Yes?" Bebe chortled.

"Hell, I don't know. Take pictures of it, wallpaper my office with the pictures . . ." He shook his head in patent admiration. "Jesus, I had to blow my nose so bad when that kid was on the bed, I thought I would choke. One take, that's all it needed. They were so perfect, Bebe. Hell, there wasn't a dry eye on the set. This is it! My only regret is that we didn't make it at Fairmont. I hope Reuben understands.''

"He'll understand," Bebe said confidently.

Carlyle shrugged. "I suppose. It's just that Reuben *was* Fairmont; it should have been made there. A fitting tribute, that kind of thing.''

"When do we see the rushes?" Bebe asked excitedly.

"Tonight if you think you can handle it. I'm going to get soused so I won't shame all of you and cry over my best work.''

Bebe walked to the long table, where the children, all sixteen of them, were sitting, their faces solemn. She bent down to pick up Bruno's dog. "You were wonderful, all of you. I'm terribly sorry that you had . . . to go back into your memories. Mademoiselle Mickey would be so proud of you, so very, very proud.''

"Will Monsieur Tarz be proud of us, too?" Bruno asked wistfully.

"Yes, very," Bebe replied, smiling. "I'm sure he's thinking

of all of you right now. I will bet each of you one licorice stick that Monsieur Tarz is getting the château ready for you. He hasn't forgotten any of you. I know this because I am his wife, and . . . I know these things."

Sophie took her thumb out of her mouth long enough to ask, "When are we going home?"

Home. What a wonderful word, thought Bebe. But these children didn't have a home anymore. Bebe handed the squirming dog to Bruno and dropped to her knees. "Where is home, Sophie?" she whispered.

"Mademoiselle Mickey's château. She said that would be our home when the war was over. Monsieur Tarz said so, too. It was not a lie, mademoiselle; they did not lie to us."

"No, they didn't, Sophie. I'm going to take you back myself when it is time." She stroked the little girl's hair and added softly, "I know you don't understand all of this, but I'll try to explain. We just finished filming the movie that is a tribute to . . . Mickey. You all played a part in it. Now the film will be distributed all over the country, and it will be nominated for an award. I know this in my heart. I want all of you here so you can share in that award. Mickey would want this. Mr. Tarz, too. The very next day I will take you all back to France. I promise you.

"Now," she continued, clapping her hands for attention, "we are all going back to my house, where you will tidy up your rooms before we go swimming. After we swim and have our dinner, I'm going to introduce you to your tutor, who will give you English lessons. When you return to France you will be able to greet Monsieur Tarz in English. There will be other lessons, too." Bruno made a face, and she laughed.

"Tell me, Bruno," she said, "have you given your dog a name yet?"

He nodded. "Dog. That's a name, mademoiselle."

"Yes, but . . . well, I couldn't help but notice that . . . Dog is a . . . a girl dog." Bebe giggled.

"That is so, mademoiselle, a girl dog."

"And Willie is a boy dog." Bebe giggled again, and the rest of the children laughed.

"That means puppies," Sophie said, wide-eyed.

"That's exactly what it means," Bebe replied with a sigh. "Well, we'll deal with that when the time comes. It's time to go ho—to my house. I have a surprise for all of you!"

As one they chorused, "What?"

"If I told you, it wouldn't be a surprise. You'll just have to wait and see." Earlier that day she'd virtually bought out the children's department at Bullock's. New dresses and hair ribbons for the girls. Shiny black shoes and white socks. For the boys, pants and shirts, suits and ties, belts and suspenders, new underwear, and sturdy shoes. It had cost a fortune, and she'd had to sell the pearl earrings Reuben had given her, her most treasured possession to manage it. But it seemed right and fitting. She'd also sold the pearl necklace Mickey had given her that same Christmas. The money would be used to care for the children until after the Academy Awards.

"Well done, Bebe, well done indeed," she muttered under her breath.

Hollywood, land of milk and honey, glamour and sparkle, closed its ranks for the second time in order to protect Reuben Tarz. None of them knew *exactly* what went on with Fairmont Studios, but when word filtered out that Bebe Tarz and Jane Perkins had rented an empty warehouse and leased movie equipment, they knew something was in the air. Spies sent to ferret out the inside scoop could report only that most of the filming was being done on location, and that the budget was practically nonexistent.

A meeting was called by the major studio heads to discuss what they *didn't* know. They spent days hashing over what little they *did* know and concluded that the movie being filmed had something to do with Reuben Tarz's life. In tandem they agreed to aid and abet Jane and Bebe in ways that could never be traced back to any of them. The very secrecy surrounding the film made them certain that Jane Perkins had a winner, and they recognized that by aiding and abetting, they were putting their own projects in jeopardy. But they didn't care. As one they voted to nominate the movie for an Academy Award even though they knew nothing about it. They owed Reuben Tarz, all of them.

"Done!" shouted Sam Goldwyn. "Gentlemen, we just slit our own throats, so let's get the hell out of here before we bleed all over the rug."

"What are we supposed to do—*bribe* the Academy into these nominations?" David Selznick snapped.

"Are you crazy?" Goldwyn demanded. "Doesn't your gut tell you those broads have a winner? We talk it up, all of us. We can doctor up the numbers, pay off box office. We simply hype it like it was one of our own. It'll be a first for this fucking town. You know what? I feel good about this!"

"I'm gonna remind you of this conversation at the Awards when we're sitting there with our thumbs in our mouths," Selznick grumbled. But it was a happy sound.

Exactly one month after the release of *The Sands of Time*, all Hollywood sat back and clapped their hands for Reuben Tarz. *Sands*, as it was called in the industry, outsold and outplayed every other movie released that year. Newspapers ran stories about it, with pictures shot from all angles showing the long lines, grumbling patrons, and harried theater owners. One theater manager was quoted as saying, "It wouldn't be so bad if people didn't keep coming back to see the film over and over." Another owner announced that he was selling tissues and making a fortune. Box office receipts were nothing short of phenomenal, even topping those of *Gone With the Wind* in the first thirty days.

The media, hoping to arouse some friction among the other studios, took to camping outside the gates, waiting for the moguls themselves to appear and give a quote. Sam Goldwyn tipped his gray homburg and said, "It's a hell of a picture, and I wish I'd made it. My wife wants to see it again." David Selznick grinned and said, "It's not the picture of the decade; it's going to prove to be the picture of the century. Simply put, gentlemen, I'm jealous as hell that my studio didn't turn it out." Cecil B. De Mille pursed his lips and said, "As much as it pains me to say this, I think *Sands* is the finest picture I've ever seen, and I've seen them all. Every detail was perfect."

Accolades continued to pour in, each one better than the one before. Global Pictures, Jane and Bebe's brainchild, raked in millions of dollars daily, and the movie seemed destined to run forever.

Bebe started a scrapbook, conscientiously pasting each article, each headline, in chronological order. She planned to take it with her when she escorted the children back to France. After dinner each evening she read the write-ups to the children, first in French and then in English.

For once, Hollywood's immortals sat back so as not to dim Reuben Tarz's light. He was one of them and deserved every shining moment that glowed for him and him alone.

As generous and complimentary as the moguls were, they weren't stupid. They knew *Sands* was a one-shot deal and that

Reuben Tarz was not going to return to Hollywood. The slices of the Hollywood pie would be thicker without him.

Nellie Bishop Tarz-Bouchet walked out of the theater, her eyes dry, wondering what all the hullabaloo was about. As far as she was concerned, she'd just seen three hours of sappy, sentimental garbage. Driving home from the movie house, she replayed various scenes in her mind and tried to figure out what it was that had turned *The Sands of Time* into such a hit. It was romantic and sad. Death scenes were traumatic, to say the least. Women obviously like to cry, to identify with a loss. The children of course, were an asset in more ways than one; even the stupid dog had performed on cue. It all added up to . . . what? Shrugging, Nellie decided to catalog all the separate elements in the journal she kept.

The journal was thick, almost filled, with ideas and plans for Fairmont Studios, plans she'd expected to implement long before and because of the judges ruling had never even been introduced.

These last few years hadn't been easy. The estrangement from her father really didn't bother her, but what *did* bother her was the fact that she couldn't go to the studio every day as she'd planned. Everything was in a holding pattern, awaiting an appearance by her husband. Apparently, Reuben had no intention of returning to America, so Bebe was still in control of half the studio. But as long as Philippe was an absentee husband, the studio would remain closed.

Next week her attorney would petition the courts again. This time he assured her she would win thanks to Philippe Tarz.

Nellie smiled to herself as she walked along, her stride loose and carefree as she hummed the lyrics to a popular song. This time around she was going to win, and half the studio would be hers. If Philippe did come back someday, she'd fight him to the death for what he'd put her through. Let him dispute the child, no one would believe him. No one!

Philippe Tarz was a pretty child with curly blond hair and dark gray eyes, taking after her. He was a contented little boy with a doting nanny who saw to his needs twenty-four hours a day. Nellie called him Little Philly when she spoke to her attorneys or to anyone who inquired about the child, and her tone was always that of a mother in love with her child. But the true extent of her mothering consisted of a kiss in the morning and one at night. Of course, she bought him the best clothes and the finest toys, but it was the nanny who fed him, bathed him, read him stories, and tucked him into his crib. It was the nanny who sang him lullabies and stroked his brow when he developed a cold or fever.

She'd given birth to Little Philly alone, with only her housekeeper visiting her in the hospital. That was how she'd wanted it, and it would aid her now when she petitioned the court. No grandmother in attendance, no father peeking into the nursery for a glimpse of the tiny pink bundle wrapped in his blue blanket. With consummate skill she'd played the part of a suffering, lonely wife. The nurses and her doctor had held whispered conversations about her, saying how brave and noble she was. And although she'd cooed and fussed over the little bundle the way she was supposed to, she never undid the snug little blanket to check out the baby the way other mothers did.

Everything was on schedule according to her plan. She was even a volunteer at the local Red Cross chapter where she made a few friends and confided just enough personal details to make everyone feel sorry for her. Like all patriotic wives and mothers, she worked on paper drives and collected tin cans, bought war bonds in her son's name, and entertained her fellow volunteers once a month with a dinner or a picnic in the backyard. Most of her guests mistook the blank look in her eyes for worry, never thinking they bored her to tears or that they were all part of her plan to control her husband's share of the studio.

Tonight before she went to bed she was going to write a note to Jane and Bebe and compliment them on *Sands*. All during the picture she'd written the note in her mind. She'd say she was moved to tears, that the film was so very realistic and Philippe was going to be so proud when he came home. And she'd sign off with the wish that they could all work together someday.

Nellie continued to hum as she danced her way into the house. Her plan was working.

Walking to the mailbox at the end of Mademoiselle's driveway proved to be one of the more exciting events of the day for the children. Even the dogs sat at attention by the front door where the leashes hung on a peg. Sophie opened the door, and Bruno went first with his dog, who detested his leash. The others followed in single file until they reached the mailbox, where Bebe went through a ritual initiated by Bernard. The question was always the same—would there be a letter from

Monsieur Tarz? Each child voiced his opinion. Bruno, the eternal optimist, always said yes, and when proved wrong said, "Tomorrow there will be one, maybe two," at which point they would all turn and walk back to the house—slowly, because lessons would start on their return.

Today Bebe lagged behind with a letter in her hand that had set her heart to pounding. It was from Nellie's attorney. Only the presence of the children kept her from ripping it open immediately. Above all, Bebe strove for a relaxed, calm environment for the children, doing nothing that would cause them even a moment's anxiety. No, she would go upstairs to her room and read the letter in private.

"Licorice sticks for everyone if you do well today," she called gaily as the children trekked out to the terrace to begin the afternoon's lessons. Impishly, Bruno held up two fingers, which meant an extra licorice for his dog and Willie. Bebe smiled and nodded.

Don't dilly-dally, just rip it open, she told herself as she transferred the letter from one hand to the other. She held the envelope up to the light and squinted. The letter inside was short, no more than three lines. Bebe slit the envelope with her thumbnail, inadvertently ripping the letter inside. She read it through twice before she tore it to shreds. Ordered—ordered, by God, to appear in the judge's chambers, a week from today for the final resolution of Philippe's holdings. Obviously Nellie had petitioned the courts a second time.

Bebe's foot lashed out at the end of the bed, and yelped as pain shot up her leg. "Oh Philippe, you've been so foolish, and now you're going to lose it all to that little . . . that bitch! There's nothing I can do . . . son." How nice the word sounded. Son . . . She had three sons, she reminded herself, two of whom she was going to call right now.

As usual, Simon responded to her queries in a cool, practical voice. "Business is great, Mother. I have more work than I can handle. Now, if you had let me handle the advertising for *The Sands of Time*, I could retire to Carmel with Uncle Eli. Everyone is talking about that movie. Have you heard from Dad?"

"Not a word. Nothing on Philippe, either. That's why I called. I got this letter today from Nellie's lawyers. There's a hearing a week from today for a final resolution to Philippe's holdings. There's nothing I can do. I feel so helpless."

"It will all right itself in the end, Mother. Think positive, that's what you always told me."

"Simon . . . I hope to be able to repay your trust fund in another six weeks or so. It was so kind and generous of you and Dillon to come through for me."

Simon chuckled. "Mother, I'm not worried, I never was. The way I look at it, it's Dad's money anyway. There's no hurry. In fact, I don't care if you ever pay it back. I mean that, Mother."

Bebe swallowed hard. "I know you do, Simon, and it's more than I deserve. So, tell me, what are you advertising? Do you have your own accounts now?"

"More than I can handle. Right now I'm doing one for Lucky Strike cigarettes. I'm doing a presentation tomorrow, so I'd better get back to my desk. Just remember: take it one day at a time. Philippe will just have to accept whatever happens when he comes home. Nice talking to you, Mother."

"Good-bye, Simon." Bebe said, smiling. Simon the philosopher.

Next she dialed the Forestry Service Dillon worked out of and asked for Ranger Tarz. Moments later Dillon's voice, so like Reuben's, boomed over the wire. "Ma! What's up?"

Bebe blinked. As always, she was taken aback by Dillon's upbeat cheerfulness. Her youngest son was a rogue, handsome and so like his father at that age, and lived each minute of the day with zest and verve. She loved it when he called her Ma.

"All kinds of things, some good, some not so good. I need . . . to talk to you," she said tentatively.

"Shoot!"

Bebe went through her spiel a second time, and Dillon's reaction was much the same as Simon's.

"Look, Ma, you struck it lucky with Simon and me, so it stands to reason Philippe has to be the jackass. He'll come back when he's damn good and ready, and probably be some kind of war hero in the bargain. Fifty bucks says I'm right. You a gambling woman, Ma?" he chortled.

Bebe smiled in spite of herself. "No, I'm not. I feel as if I let him down. It wasn't easy for him coming here and learning . . . you know. I should have tried harder, done more. I failed him."

"Ma, you're wrong. *He failed you.* He comes crying to you at the eleventh hour and gets you all steamed up, then takes a powder. He lied to you, goddammit! Stop feeling sorry for him. Don't sweat that trust fund, either. There's not a whole lot a guy can do out here in the woods with money.''

"Thank you, Dillon. How are things going? Catching any poachers?''

Dillon's voice softened immediately. "Ma, yesterday this doe gave birth to the most incredible fawn. I wish Uncle Eli were here so he could paint her. She is so beautiful! The doe ate out of my hand. The little one is knock-kneed and skittish, but curious as hell. You wouldn't believe how protective that doe is. Yet they trust me,'' he said proudly.

"And well they should,'' Bebe replied warmly. "You are the kindest, most gentle human being I've ever met. I can't imagine who you take after.''

"Pop, of course. He's the kindest, most gentle man I know. Speaking of kind and gentle, how are you doing with your little army?''

"Not bad, all things considered. They want to go home so badly. I alternate between wanting to take them back now and waiting till after the awards. I know *Sands* is going to make a clean sweep, and I want the children to accept for Reuben. I think they understand, and then I hear them crying at night.''

"It's tough to grow up, Ma. Bribe them with licorice sticks like you used to do with me.'' Dillon laughed uproariously.

"I do. Look, thanks for listening, Dillon. I'll call you next week.''

"Right. Bye, Ma.''

Bebe's next phone call was to Jane. "Did Daniel say anything to you about Nellie petitioning the courts again?'' she asked.

"We don't talk about Nellie,'' Jane told her. "To tell you the truth, Bebe, I don't know if he even sees her anymore. Since he started up his own law offices here, he doesn't have much spare time. Most evenings he's with me or working late. What's she want this time?''

"To wind things up, I guess. It has been a long time, Jane, three years and ten months. All this time with no word from Philippe does not look good. The judge will find for Nellie and give her his half of the studio. Then we can open for business, if there is any business. It was inevitable. I guess what I dread most is having to see her again. I actually hate her, Jane, and I won't make any apologies about it, either. If Reuben were here, she wouldn't have gotten off the ground with this thing. I know she's lying, but I can't prove it. I know that child is not Philippe's, and I can't prove that, either. When the judge asks me if I've heard from my son, I have to say no. That's a plus for Nellie."

"You could lie," Jane said morosely.

"Under oath? Oh, Jane, I couldn't!"

"Nellie's lying under oath, so why should you be different? . . . Sorry, I didn't mean that. Of course you can't lie." She sighed. "You know, one of these days that little witch will get what's coming to her, and I hope I'm around to see it. She's *evil*, Bebe!"

"I know."

"Lord, I almost forgot. Daniel asked me to call you and find out if the children would like to play some baseball. He said there's a sand lot somewhere close by. He'll get the bats and balls, and you and I are going to be the umpires. I think it might be fun. I can pack a picnic lunch. Sunday afternoon. What do you say?"

"That's a great idea!" Bebe said enthusiastically. "The kids are getting bored. I hope he plans to hire a bus."

Jane giggled. "He is, how did you know?"

"Sixteen children, three adults, and two dogs. Call it an educated guess. I'll see you Sunday, then."

Alone with her thoughts, Bebe lit a cigarette as she stared out over the gardens. *Reuben, where are you? Where is our son? You were never here when I needed you. Physically yes, emotionally no. I need you now, so badly. What can I do?*

"Not a damn thing," she muttered, answering herself.

It was precisely 9:55 A.M. one week later when Bebe walked into the courthouse. The first person she saw and recognized was Daniel, and her eyes narrowed angrily. He hadn't said a word on Sunday about coming, she thought. What made her angrier still was the little boy he was holding in his arms. Without a word she turned and walked toward the judge's chambers.

"Bebe, wait," he called after her. "Please. This child is innocent, don't take out your feelings on him. Regardless of what you believe, he is *my* grandson. At least look at him, and then tell me you don't believe he's Philippe's son."

Jaw clenched and shoulders rigid, Bebe turned and walked back to her old friend. "He might be your grandchild, Daniel, *but he isn't mine or Reuben's*," she said. Impassively, she studied the boy for a few moments. "He is a handsome little boy," she conceded at last.

"Nellie is teaching him French so he can speak to Philippe in his own language when he comes home," Daniel said evenly.

Bebe shook her head. "You are a dreamer, Daniel. This makes me . . . sick. I don't even know why I have to be here. I'm not in the mood for more lies or your daughter's version of the truth. I thought she hated you, disowned you? What did you do? What did you promise her?"

"My support," Daniel replied. "That's all. I can't turn my back on this child the way you did. Nellie has no one. So, we . . . we came to terms. I'm the first to admit it isn't like it was, but in time all wounds heal."

"Not all wounds, Daniel. Some never heal," Bebe said coldly as she walked away. *Oh, Philippe, how could you be so foolish? Now everything is lost. One phone call, one letter, that's all it would have taken to stop her. Now it's too late.*

It took the judge thirty-three minutes to award Nellie Philippe's share of Fairmont Studios and unlock the freeze he'd previously imposed. Bebe sat with her back ramrod stiff as the judge examined three years worth of letters lovingly written from Nellie Tarz to her husband—letters that had been duly sealed, awaiting a mailing address that had never been sent her. Now he ripped them open, glancing at the baby pictures contained within and perusing a few of the letters themselves, his jaw tightening as he did so.

"It is the opinion of this court that Philip Tarz is an irresponsible young man and does not deserve one iota of consideration from this court," he announced. "He has been gone for three years and ten months, in which time his wife has given birth to their son. I find that she has acted in an exemplary manner in caring for her son while this young man is off doing God only knows what. It is the opinion of this court that Cornelia Bishop Tarz be awarded her husband's share of Fairmont Studios. Mrs. Tarz, Mrs. Cornelia Tarz, has petitioned this court to have all her husband's holdings placed in trust for her son. This court sees no reason to deny this request. Therefore, I am granting this request and appointing Cornelia Tarz sole custodian of that trust. This court is adjourned!"

Eyes straight ahead, Bebe marched from the judge's chambers seething with anger. From behind her a tiny voice called, "Grandmama." She fought to suppress the scream of rage building in her throat. Her feet sprouted wings as she raced from the building.

Grandmama . . . . The child was a puppet, obediently mouthing the words Nellie prompted him to say. At his age he neither knew nor cared about a grandmother.

"Damn you, Nellie, damn you to hell!"

Chapter Thirty-nine

AS THE JUDGE WAS DECIDING HIS FINANCIAL FATE, PHILIPPE was starting thirty days of R and R with his buddy, Mike Almeda. Thirty days of rest and relaxation and then three days of paperwork, and he would be an ex-navy aviator with reserve status. Counting their accumulated leave, they were leaving the navy six weeks ahead of schedule.

Dressed in navy whites, their aviator wings pinned securely to their dress blouses, the two flyers saluted each other smartly. Battle fatigue, not uncommon among flyers with twenty-two zeros apiece, deserved special consideration, the C.O. had told them.

Mike snapped a second smart salute. "Lieutenant, after you," he said with a wide, sweeping bow, a wicked grin on his face.

Philippe snapped off his own salute. "Mike, if I don't say this now, I might never say it. Aside from being the best goddamn wingman a pilot could want, you're a hell of a guy. Do you realize we've been through a war together and are still alive to talk about it?"

"Hell, yes, and I don't want to talk anymore. I don't want to think about all those Nips and that fucking flak and those carriers. We're home free, buddy."

Philippe's face clouded. Home. He was going to Sacramento with Mike to spend his R and R and to finally meet Lizzie, Mike's sister. "I guess I can give this back to you now," he said, handing Mike the picture of Lizzie.

Mike squinted at it. "It's a little wrinkled, Phil. I seem to recall your telling me I was a slob and would wrinkle it all up and that's why you were keeping it. Shit, I can't even see Lizzie's face for all the wrinkles. What'ja do with it? It looks like it's been through a war!" He laughed at his own joke, but he didn't reach for the picture.

"You know, Phil, I bunked with you, flew with you for almost four years," he continued. "There are times when I think I know you better than you know yourself, and then I realize I don't know you at all. I feel that way right now. Look, I never wanted to stick my nose into your business, and I never asked questions because you . . . hell, this is going to sound corny, but there were times when I thought you looked haunted . . . with memories. Jesus, you have the saddest eyes. I *know* you have a family. In my gut I know, yet you went through this whole goddamn war without a phone call or a piece of mail. You're not just an ordinary fly-bird like me—you come from high up, and I can smell the money that's behind you. Anytime you want to open up, you know you can talk to me. Contrary to belief, I do not have a loose lip. End of speech." He laughed. "What do you say we break a few hearts on the way to Sacramento!"

"Yeah, you break 'em and I have to mend them," Philippe grumbled good-naturedly. "You son of a bitch, you left a trail of broken hearts halfway around the world. I bet you have nightmares that they're all going to show up on your doorstep at the same time."

Mike grinned. "Can I help it if I'm irresistible? Women throw themselves at me. Only a fool would back away, and my mother didn't raise any fools. C'mon, we've kept Lizzie waiting long enough. I better warn you now, that girl drives like a bandit."

"Must run in the family," Philippe snorted. "You fly like a bandit."

"I saved your ass more than once," Mike countered laughingly.

"I know, Mike," Philippe said, his eyes softening, "and I'll never forget it."

Mike stopped in his tracks and turned Philippe around until

their eyes were locked. "How come you didn't remind me of the time you wet-nursed me back to the *Hornet*? Without you sweet-talking me in and flying under my belly, I would have hit the drink and Uncle Sam would have taken that plane out of my hide."

"Part of my job, Lieutenant. I'm the shy type, not like some guys I know."

"Yeah, well, I owe you for that."

"You don't owe me anything," Philippe said, embarrassed. "Both of us did what we had to do. Knock it off."

"Nah, I owe you and I'm gonna pay up in about . . . oh, three minutes from now. I'm giving you Lizzie!" He doubled over laughing as he raced through the gates, Philippe on his heels. Both pilots came to a grinding halt when a tall, willowy blonde stretched out her arms to welcome them.

Philippe sucked in his breath, his hand poised on the visor of his cap. An angel with a wide, warm smile stood before them, laughing now as her twin hugged her, her dress hiking up over long, slim legs. She was dressed in cornflower blue with matching shoes and a wide-brimmed white straw hat that was being carried off in the light breeze. Philippe ran for it and caught it just as it was about to land in the dust. He carried it back, his ears and neck warm as he waited to be introduced.

"This guy," Mike said, his arms around his sister's waist, "is the best goddamn flyer the navy has turned out, next to me. Lizzie, this is Philip Reuben, the guy I wrote you about."

Greenish-blue eyes full of tiny little yellow flecks stared into dark brown eyes. "Welcome to Sacramento, Philip. Thanks for taking care of this dodo. You probably know by now he doesn't have sense enough to come in out of the rain."

"I noticed," Philippe said huskily as he extended his hand. Lizzie ignored it, reaching forward instead to kiss him lightly on the cheek. How soft and pink her lips were, Philippe thought. Christ, she wasn't just pretty, she was downright beautiful. Mike hadn't lied; the picture he'd carried all during the war hadn't done her justice.

In the time it took the three of them to walk from the gates of the base to Lizzie's car, Philippe Bouchet fell totally and hopelessly in love with Lizzie Almeda, and Lizzie Almeda, doctor of veterinary medicine, fell totally and hopelessly in love with Philippe Bouchet.

"Ah, now, hold on a minute, Lizzie," Mike said, opening

the car door. "You don't expect me . . . us, to sit in there with that . . . that menagerie!"

Philippe bent down to peek through the car window and burst out laughing. Inside, a speckled hunting dog and a taffy-colored spaniel sat upright in the backseat with a hissing cat in a cage between them. On the floor a bright green-and-red parrot was squawking his disapproval. Six puppies of unde-termined origin slept in a box on the front seat.

Lizzie laughed, her eyes sparkling with merriment. "Tough, little brother. You called at the last minute, what do you expect? Get in and shut up!"

"I told you she was nuts; now do you believe me?" Mike grumbled to Philippe, who was grinning from ear to ear. "The least you could have done was . . . Hell, I thought you'd want to impress my friend here. Now what's he gonna think?"

Lizzie looked straight at Philippe over the top of her car. Her voice, he thought, was like a melody. "This," she said, waving her hands about the car, "is who I am, it's what I do. I operate a free clinic."

Philippe smiled. "I'm impressed."

"See!" Lizzie said, pounding her brother on the chest.

"Free! You mean you don't charge! You went to school to do this for nothing! Nobody's going to be dumb enough to marry you if you . . . Free! For God's sake! Get in, Phil," he muttered.

Lizzie turned to Philippe. "Would you like me to put the top down?"

"Jesus, no! Somebody might see us!" Mike snarled.

"It would be nice," Philippe said quietly as he settled him-self between the cat's cage and the hunting dog. Yes, it would be nice to see her long blond hair swirling in the breeze. How capable her hands looked on the steering wheel. Hands that could gentle an animal . . . or a man.

Lizzie pulled the car to a halt at a stop sign. Both dogs slid off the seat. The cat hissed and the parrot squawked. But the puppies in the box on Mike's lap continued to sleep. "I think I should tell you that Mom has a party going on. They roped off the street. Some kid is going to play 'Anchors Aweigh' on his trombone, and everyone is bringing food. They even put up a sign. Some guy from the local paper is going to take your picture. You're gonna love it. Pop took off work." Her eyes held all the warmth and merriment of a sunny day. How perfect she was, Philippe thought as he met her gaze in the rearview mirror.

"You better be properly grateful, too, Mike. Mom went to a lot of trouble," she continued. "Everyone is . . . well, you know, you're a flyer and all. They think you're important."

"Aviator, and I am important, so is Phil. Between us we shot down forty-four Nips. That's goddamn important! Oh, shit, these dogs just peed through the box! For Christ's sake, Lizzie, you could have put some straw or something in it!"

"If you don't shut up, I'm booting you out of this car," Lizzie retaliated. "Why can't you be as . . . nice as your friend?"

Philippe loved every second of the verbal give and take. He loved the idea of a neighborhood party to honor Mike, and he loved it that Mike's father had taken off work to welcome him home. He loved every animal in the car, and he loved the young girl with the flyaway golden hair.

Nellie Bishop Tarz did not exist as far as he was concerned.

Philippe almost expected Mike's parents to snap to attention when he leapt from the car to run to them. No peacock was ever more proud. Philippe watched shamelessly as Mike's mother wiped her eyes with the hem of her apron. Mike Almeda, Sr., was clapping his son on the back, his face proud, tears glistening in his eyes. Their son was home safe and sound.

"He's a very lucky guy to have all of this," Philippe said quietly.

Lizzie touched Philippe's arm. "We share. And whatever we have is yours. It's not a lot, but . . ."

Philippe offered his arm, and Lizzie took it. It was his turn now to be welcomed by the family. He was never happier.

The Almeda family, and there were dozens of them, welcomed him as if he were one of their own. Mrs. Almeda whispered in his ear, "Thank you for taking care of my son." Mr. Almeda's rough, callused hands clapped him on the back. "My boy don't think they come any better than you," he said heartily.

"Yes, they do, Mr. Almeda. Mike's one of a kind."

The older Almeda beamed proudly. Philippe found a bottle of beer shoved into one hand and a thick ham sandwich in the other. He smiled at aunts and uncles and neighbors and marveled at the number of cousins milling about. Scads of children laughed and played, all calling Mike by name. And all the while his eyes kept searching for Lizzie. An hour or so later she finally rescued him and took him into the cool house to show him his room.

In the upstairs hallway she suddenly turned shy. "Mom won't be cooking dinner tonight because of all the food everyone brought, so you better eat hearty. We have just the one bathroom, and you'll share this room with Mike. I hope that's okay."

"It's fine." Damn, why was his tongue so thick in his mouth? "You're very pretty," he blurted out.

"Why . . . thank you. You're rather handsome yourself," Lizzie said self-consciously. "Do you mind if I ask you something? It's personal, and Mike is such a—" She wrinkled her nose to show she was searching for a word or phrase that would describe her brother.

"Great guy, is that what you were going to say?"

"Yes . . . no . . . he can be a real joker sometimes, a dodo, if you know what I mean. That doesn't mean I don't love him heart and soul, but he's such a joker sometimes . . . He said you carried my picture all through . . . the bombing raids. Is that true?"

It was Philippe's turn to become self-conscious. He lifted the flap of his blouse pocket and withdrew Lizzie's picture. His face was red as he held it out. "It's been through a lot. I kind of tricked Mike into giving it to me back in flight school. Does it bother you that I . . . you gave it to Mike . . ."

Lizzie laughed. "He said he tricked you into taking it. No, it doesn't bother me. As a matter of fact, I was flattered. I don't know if you know this or not, but his letters were full of you, every one of them. That's why we all feel we know you. He'd start out with the weather, what he was doing, what he'd just done, and how he missed us. That usually took two paragraphs. The rest of the letters were about you and what a great guy you were and how he was lucky to have such a good friend. He said you were the better pilot."

"I feel the same way about Mike."

Their eyes locked for a few heart-stopping moments, and then Lizzie broke the contact and turned away. "Well, I guess I better get back to the clinic. Later, if the party gets too boisterous or you want to crash out of here, have Mike bring you by. I board dogs, too, so I have to be there all the time." She made a little face. "I can't afford an assistant."

Philippe smiled. "I'd like that."

"Good, I'll see you later, then. Have fun."

Mike caught up to his sister as she was getting into her car. "So, sis, what do you think of Phil?"

"Very, very nice," she said judiciously. "He thinks a lot of you, Mike."

"Yeah, yeah, nice, sure, but what did you *think* of him? Did'ja like him? You know, *like* him?"

Lizzie knew her brother wouldn't let her drive off until she gave him the answer he wanted to hear. "I think it will take me a few days to fall in love with him. Happy now?"

He grinned. "Sure. He's already in love with you. I could see it the minute he tricked me into giving him your picture. He's an okay guy, Lizzie."

"You said *you* tricked *him*!" she reminded her brother. "You're playing matchmaker, Mike. Stop it, I'm too old for such nonsense."

Mike grimaced. He hated it when Lizzie caught him at something. Ever since he could remember, she'd been quicker and brighter than he was, probably because she'd been born two minutes ahead of him. "You better get going to that free zoo you operate. I'll see you later."

"Why don't you bring Phil by later," Lizzie called over her shoulder.

"Yeah, I might do that." Eyes glinting devilishly, he shouted, "I didn't hear you telling old Phil not to call you Lizzie. That must mean something!"

"You wait, I'm going to sic my Great Dane on you." Lizzie laughed as she drove away. It was true, she hadn't asked Philip to call her Beth instead of Lizzie. When he said her name, it was as though music played in the background. Lizzie sounded like Lee-zay.

Yes, she liked Philip Reuben. Very much.

The following days were wonderful for Philippe. He slept late, as did Mike. Mrs. Almeda cooked up enormous breakfasts of waffles and eggs and ham and kissed both of them good-bye at the door when they drove off to the clinic to help Lizzie. They laughed and kidded, kibitzed and joked, and enjoyed each other's company. They sat on the lawn out by the dog runs, and ate the picnic lunches Mrs. Almeda packed in a wicker hamper. It wasn't until the fifth day that Mike tactfully absented himself, but only after Philippe threatened to throttle him if he didn't make himself scarce.

"I heard that!" Lizzie laughed as she taped a splint on a

dog's leg. Philippe faced her across the stainless-steel table, holding on to the dog in a firm grip.

"I was hoping you did," he said. "I wanted to be alone with you."

"We're hardly alone." Lizzie gestured to the long, double-tiered row of animal cages.

"They don't count," Philippe said huskily.

Lizzie's cheeks flushed, and she lifted her head to meet Philippe's eyes. She knew where this was going. "Would you like to go to the movies this evening? Mike said he'd stay here. He's not much for the pictures, but I love them."

Philippe sighed. "I thought you would never ask."

"I'm asking, but you're doing the paying," she teased.

"Fair enough." A vision of Nellie flashed before his eyes as he recalled the number of times he'd taken her to the movies. Resolutely he pushed her far back into his mind, but he knew she wouldn't stay there.

"The early show, okay. I want to get to bed before eleven. I've scheduled some surgery tomorrow morning. There's this wonderful movie that's playing," she continued, focusing now on her work. "Everyone is talking about it. My parents saw it, and Mom said she cried all the way through. Dad said it was so real, he couldn't believe it. The papers say it's going to win all the awards on Oscar night."

Instantly Philippe grew alert and oddly apprehensive. "Who made it?"

"What?" Lizzie asked, glancing up.

"Which studio filmed the movie? Do you know?"

She shrugged. "I have no idea. Is it important? Mom might know since she already saw it. Wait a minute—yes, I do know, I read about it in the paper last week. A new company . . . Global Pictures. Yes, I'm sure that's the one. It's the story of one of the big guys in Hollywood. I think he owned one of the studios and left to go to Europe in the middle of the war to find his old love. Anyway, the paper said they closed his studio down, something to do with the courts, so this man's wife and someone else made the film at Global Pictures. For very little money, apparently, and all the actors and actresses are unknowns, which is supposed to make it all the more believable. It's called *The Sands of Time*. If you'd rather see something else, I don't mind," she said uneasily, watching Philippe struggle to conceal his agitation.

"No, no, that's fine," he said, his voice strained. "Listen, do you mind if I skip on out of here and head back to the house? I'll see you for supper."

"Sure . . . Philip, is anything wrong?" she asked.

Philippe walked around the stainless-steel table. "I'm not sure," he said quietly. He leaned over and kissed her, a gentle, sweet kiss full of longing. Lizzie clung to him, wanting the kiss to go on, but he drew away, his eyes clouded with worry he couldn't disguise. "I think I love you, Lizzie," he said.

"I know I love you," Lizzie whispered. "I fell in love with you through Mike's letters."

"When I saw your picture . . . I fell in love. Seeing you and getting to know you . . . my whole world has changed. I wasn't prepared to fall in love. Loving a picture is one thing . . . Look, I don't know what I'm trying to say. Later, we'll talk later, all right?" Without waiting for her reply, he kissed her again and ran from the clinic.

Philippe ran, the hounds of hell at his heels, to the movie house in Lizzie's neighborhood. His eyes drank in the big letters on the marquee and the huge poster next to the cashier's cage. His trembling finger traced the line of credits. Filmed by Global Pictures, produced by Barbara Rosen Tarz and Jane Perkins. They'd done it! What had been only a possibility was now a reality; the proof was in front of him.

He couldn't go to this movie with Lizzie. He had to go alone. Even worse, he had no right to go *anywhere* with Lizzie, no right to tell her he loved her. He had no damn rights at all! Once again Nellie's face flashed before his eyes, and like a sleepwalker he shook his head to clear it.

What had happened to Fairmont? He had to know. Stopping a nearby pedestrian, Philippe asked where the town newspaper had its office. Then, his hands jammed into his pockets, he ran all the way to the brick building the man had indicated.

Inside the office he demanded several back issues of the newspaper from a startled receptionist. An hour and a half later he left the building, disturbed and sick at heart. He walked aimlessly, up one street and down another. When he saw children playing in a park, he stopped and lit a cigarette. He didn't want to think about what he'd just read. Think only about the moment, he told himself, not the past, not the future, just the moment.

The beginning, the middle, the end. Think about the moment, the present, not the beginning, not the end, and don't ever think about Nellie. Think about how good you felt when you kissed Lizzie Almeda. Think about all the hurt and helpless animals she's helped. Think about how gentle her hands are. Think about Mike and the grin that's always plastered all over his face. Not Nellie, not Bebe, not Jane. Her lips were so pink and soft, and she smelled like sunshine and apples. Be glad you're alive and don't worry about anyone else.

Fairmont Studios . . . closed on the court's order. Had been closed for over three years, ever since he'd left. Oh, Jesus, all because of me. He groaned. Her hair was like cornsilk, soft and curly, wispy bangs on her forehead. Kind eyes, warm eyes, gentle eyes. Was his father dead? The end meant the end. His mother, Mickey Fonsard . . . was she dead, too? His fist pounded down on the park bench. He had to leave, return to Los Angeles. He couldn't go back to the Almeda house, couldn't let them love him the way he wanted to be loved. He didn't deserve them, didn't deserve Lizzie. He hadn't been honest with any of them, not even Mike.

Come on, argued an inner voice, *you didn't deceive any of them, you simply didn't confide in them. There's a big difference. It's not written anywhere that you have to confide in people.*

Again Philippe pounded the bench. "You are as bad as you said your old man was. You gotta make this right, and soon." Hands shaking, he lit another cigarette from the one in his mouth, and started to walk again, to retrace his steps to the movie house. Standing in line waiting to buy his ticket, he was oblivious to those around and behind him. Otherwise he would have seen Mike staring at the back of his head.

Inside the cool, musty-smelling theater, Mike waited until Philippe was seated and then sat down two rows behind him. Finally, he thought grimly, he was going to find out who Philip Reuben was.

Mike watched the movie, mesmerized, almost forgetting why he was sitting alone with Philip's head in clear view. It wasn't until he saw a tall, dark-haired young man step out of a Red Cross plane that he put two and two together. When the film rolled to a close, he was fighting tears; navy aviators didn't cry, at least not this one. But the one in front of him was so choked with emotion, he *couldn't* cry.

He waited for the last stragglers to leave the theater before he made his way down the center aisle to where Philippe was still sitting. For a moment he thought his friend was in a trance. Touching his shoulder lightly he said, "It's time to go, Phil. I'll ask Pop to loan me his car and drive you to L.A. Up and at 'em, guy, they're going to close the theater."

Philippe bit down on his lower lip, his eyes still on the now-blank screen. "She's dead and I didn't even know. I should have felt something, known somehow. It's not right."

"No, it isn't, but there's nothing you can do now," Mike said sympathetically.

"Man, did I fuck up," he murmured, shaking his head. "No wonder it's coming down around me now."

"A temporary condition. You can fix a lot of this if you make the effort. To do nothing . . . then I'm going to have to take a second look at you, pal."

"I have to go back."

"I know. I'm ready right now. We could go home and pack some duds, but if you're in a hurry, I can sprint home and get Pop's car. It's up to you."

"I never touched her; that kid isn't mine," Philippe said miserably.

"Hell, I know that," Mike said with a dismissive wave of his hand. "I know you, buddy, I went through a war with you."

"I should have been bombing the hell out of Europe, and where the hell was I? In the fucking Pacific, that's where," Philippe said bitterly. "I could have made a difference. I put in for a transfer fifty times, and all fifty times they said I was needed in the Pacific. I should have joined the army. Oh, Jesus, how am I ever going to fix all this?"

"C'mon, pal, they're closing up, and I don't want to get thrown out on my ear."

Philippe turned to his friend with pleading eyes. "I can't go back to your house. I can't face your parents . . . and Lizzie."

"It would be kind of tough, I guess," Mike murmured thoughtfully. "But, my family . . . especially Lizzie, we believe in people. My parents . . . they aren't real, you know, book smart. That's why they made sure Lizzie and I went to college. But they do have what we call street smarts, good old common sense. They reflect, Phil, they don't react or overreact. Look, old buddy, we both know you cut out, ran out when things got tough. You can do that again if you want, but that isn't going to solve anything. I kind of thought you and Lizzie

. . . I thought . . . something is . . . was developing. I'd hate to see that cut off just as it was getting off the ground. Another thing—I'd hate like hell to see you go back with your tail between your legs. No sir, you're going to step into your spiffy dress whites, the ones that girls drool all over, and march in there, wherever *there* is, and be the conquering hero, and if you're bashful about your record, I'll run it up the flagpole.''

After a moment Philippe gave a short, decisive nod of his head and stood up. ''You're right, let's go. You sure you want to do this, Mike? I'll be glad of the company, but who's going to help Lizzie?''

''The same person who helped her before we got here: my mom,'' Mike said, rising. ''It'll work out, don't worry.''

But he did worry. His face clouded with shame when he sat down at the Almedas' kitchen table. But they didn't condemn his actions or pass judgment upon him. There was not one word of reproach. Instead, the elder Almeda put a callused hand around Philippe's shoulder and said, ''It's never too late to fix things if you want to.'' Mrs. Almeda hugged him, tears in her eyes as she cut him a huge slice of her apple pie and set down a glass of milk, her answer to all life's problems. ''Be proud of your family, son,'' she said. ''No one is perfect, not you, not me, not anyone. Your mother is going to be very happy to see you. I'm a mother, and I know this, so take my word for it.''

Eyes glistening, Lizzie leaned across the table and spoke softly. ''I liked you when you just had your navy pay and were Mike's friend. Nothing is changed. So what if you come from big bucks? We come from little bucks, or no bucks, right, Dad? As for Nellie and the baby . . . go back and fix it, make things right for yourself. I'll be here when it's all settled.''

Philippe felt so light-headed with her words, he started to tremble. Mike's steady hand on his shoulder quieted him almost immediately. She hadn't said, if what you say is true about Nellie and the baby . . . she believed him, they all believed him. His eyes burned with their belief in him. It was too much; he didn't deserve it. Pushing back his chair, he addressed Mike in a croaky voice: ''Dress whites, you said.''

''I took them to the dry cleaners,'' Mrs. Almeda said briskly. ''They're hanging in the hall closet. Go on, both of you. Make your mother proud of you, Philip, and you, Mike, be a good boy and see that things don't get fouled up.''

''Mom, I'm twenty-seven years old. Don't you think I'm a

little old for you to be telling me to be a good boy?" he grumbled good-naturedly.

"If your mother says be a good boy, she means be a good boy," the elder Almeda interjected in a stern voice, his eyes twinkling.

"Okay, Pop." Mike grinned as he took a playful swipe at his father's broad shoulder.

Thirty minutes later both young men stood in the open doorway resplendent in navy whites. Mrs. Almeda kissed them both and Mr. Almeda looked straight into Philippe's eyes and said, "Son, you do whatever you have to do, and don't be shy about it. I know you can handle it. Mike, don't you go driving my car the way you fly them airplanes."

"You call and let us know how things are. Do you have enough money?" Mrs. Almeda asked worriedly.

Philippe felt his throat constrict as he heard echoes of his mother's voice calling after him on his way to school. Impulsively, he hugged her ample frame.

"I'll walk you to the car," Lizzie said, and gave her brother a meaningful glance. Tactfully Mike hurried on ahead, leaving Philippe and Lizzie to linger on the porch steps.

"I hope everything works out the way you want it to, Philip," she said when the front door had closed behind them.

Philippe reached for her hand. "I'm younger than you." It was such an inane thing to say that he laughed, and so did Lizzie.

"I never did pay attention to numbers," Lizzie said softly.

"I'll be back," Philippe promised.

She nodded. "I'll be here. You better hurry, you have a long drive ahead of you. I'll be thinking of you. Good luck, Philip."

By now they'd reached the car, where Mike waited impatiently. Philippe turned to Lizzie, searching her eyes with an intensity of emotion. "I want to kiss you so badly, but I can't. When this is . . . settled . . ."

Lizzie reached up and kissed him warmly on the cheek. "Whatever you do, Philip, don't let Mike get the acting bug. He's a big enough ham as it is," she said lightly.

Philippe grinned. "Can't you just see his puss on the big screen?"

"Yeah, yeah, yeah, let's go," Mike blustered. Damn, how did she do it, he wondered. How did she always know exactly what he was thinking? Hell, acting was just a simple matter of make-believe, and he had as much charisma as any of those stars in Hollywood. He glowered at his sister, who was laughing as she waved them off.

"It's a long ride, Phil," Mike said as they neared the highway. "What say we talk. You talk so I stay awake. Everything, all of it from the earliest time you can remember. Suddenly I need to know who you are. I think you might get serious about my sister, and I . . . dammit, I want to know. I'll have you in the City of Angels for breakfast. That's a lot of hours away."

So Philippe talked nonstop as Mike drove, grunting from time to time to show he was awake. When they reached the outskirts of Los Angeles the sun was starting to rise. Mike pulled into a gas station to get the tank filled, then leaned back in his seat with a weary sigh and stretched. When at last he turned to Philippe, his eyes were soft and filled with understanding. "You'll do, Tarz," he said. Philippe's heart lightened.

When Mike had paid the gas station attendant and pocketed his change, he said, "Okay, let's get this show on the road. How much farther?"

"Thirty minutes, give or take," Philippe said uneasily.

"Nervous?"

"Hell, yes, I've been gone for almost four years."

"My best advice is be yourself. You do owe an explanation, but don't drag it out, for God's sake. Your mother will understand."

The sun was an hour into the sky when Philippe told Mike to turn left. "My mother usually walks her dog about now. Maybe we should wait here. No, let's leave the car here and walk up to the house."

Mike shrugged. "Fine with me. This is your show. I can wait here if you like."

"I don't like. Come with me."

Inside the mansion the children were trooping into the dining room for breakfast when both dogs suddenly went wild. Bebe raised her head in alarm. Someone was out there. Her first thought was that Reuben had returned. She ran to the door and opened it in time to see two incredibly tall young men dressed in white, walking up the driveway. Her hand flew to her mouth. Dear God, it was Philippe! She turned to the children and cried, "It's Philippe, he's come home!" And then she ran, her robe flying out behind her, her slippers flopping beneath her feet, the dogs ahead of her, sixteen children running behind her. She felt herself being lifted high in the air.

"The prodigal returns," Philippe said loudly enough to be heard over the clamoring around him.

"Jesus, and you said *my* family was loud," Mike shouted as he backed up several steps.

"Oh, Philippe, I was so worried! We tried to find you for so long. We didn't know what to do," Bebe said, her voice trembling with tears. "And—oh, you look so handsome, just like your father. . . ."

Philippe scooped Bruno up with one arm, keeping the other around his mother's shoulder. "Mother, this is Mike Almeda, we flew together. Mike, this is my mother."

Bebe glanced from Philippe to Mike and back again, her mouth open. "Flew? . . . Dear God, you flew airplanes! It's nice to meet you, Mike. Where?"

"Pacific. I thought for sure I'd get assigned to the European front, but"—he shrugged—"no such luck. Did . . . has . . . ?"

"No, Philippe, we haven't had a single word from your father," Bebe replied. "We do know he's safe, though. The children . . . but that was so long ago. When we got his last installment we knew he was safe then . . . but . . . I don't think he's going to come back. There's so much to talk about . . . so many things. . . . Listen, have you had breakfast? Let's go inside, I have to feed the children. Afterward you'll want to talk to them. They were the last ones to be with your mother."

"I saw *The Sands of Time*," Philippe told her. "Last night. If I hadn't seen it, I don't know if I would ever have come back. I don't know if I'm going to stay now. I still have to be mustered out and put on reserve status."

Bebe nodded. "I understand. Tell me, what did you think of the movie?" She stopped then, her face full of horror. "That's how you found out about . . . about Mickey. Oh, I'm so sorry, Philippe. When we received the last installment we had practically everyone in the world looking for you. I wanted you to hear it from me, but I guess it wasn't meant to be."

Philippe was silent for a moment, his eyes dark and far away. "The movie was . . . it was . . ."

"Sensational," Mike supplied as he extricated himself from the two dogs bent on climbing up his leg.

"It was superb. I think my father will be very proud. Novice that I am, I could see that is was a masterpiece of direction."

Philippe hesitated. "How authentic . . . what I mean is, did . . . you add . . ."

"No, Philippe, we didn't gild anything," Bebe assured him. "What you saw is what happened. When you speak with the children they'll tell you. I don't think they'll ever forget it."

"How did you get the children here?" Philippe asked several minutes later as he slipped a piece of sausage to Willie under the table.

"Daniel's friends," Bebe replied. "The Red Cross got hold of a priest in Madrid who was willing to undertake the pilgrimage. Once your father and Mickey and Yvette got them over the Pyrenees, they were taken to a convent school. Reuben told them he would come back for them, but . . . that's the part we don't know about. Only the end was fabricated, the part where I take them back, and actually that isn't a fabrication at all. I am taking them back after the awards ceremony."

Suddenly Bruno let loose with a long string of French punctuated every so often with the words *red wagon*. Bebe smiled indulgently. "Bruno, speak English. You must practice. Philippe will be happy to discuss anything with you provided you speak English."

Bruno sighed. Philippe's eyes grew moist when the little boy looked up and pleaded, "I must know, Monsieur Philippe, if the red wagon is truly mine. Mademoiselle Mickey and Monsieur Tarz said this is so, but they are not here."

"It is totally and completely yours, my little friend. Will you pull your dog in it like I used to do?"

"Egg-zackerly." Bruno beamed. Such a little thing to mean so much to a child, such a marvelous promise his mother made.

"Come along, let's go outside in the sunshine and talk," Philippe said quietly.

"Run along, no lessons today. Remember, you must speak to Philippe in English," Bebe ordered.

"More coffee, Mike?" she asked when Philippe had gone outside with the children.

He nodded, and she poured him a refill. As they stared across the table at each other warily, Mike made a pretense of drinking the coffee he didn't want. "How bad is it?" he asked finally.

Bebe sighed. "Pretty bad. Nellie has everything, all his holdings and his half of the studio. The television experiment is starting to roll. Technically, he has nothing. I don't know if the courts will intervene. Nellie is claiming the child she has is Philippe's. I don't believe it is. However, we can't prove it. I have a feeling Nellie would contest a divorce. She'll say the war changed him, damaged him somehow, and she'll come across as a sympathetic young mother who kept the home fires burning.''

"Philippe is in love with my sister," Mike said quietly.

Bebe stared at him. "And your sister?" she asked at last.

"I think she feels the same way." He told her about his family's part in Philippe's decision to return. "He's hurting, Mrs. Tarz, real bad."

"I know that. But there's nothing I can do. I'm . . . for him to find out his mother is dead by watching a movie, that's so terrible. My heart is bleeding for him. If there were anything I could do, I'd do it."

"He knows that, Mrs. Tarz. He's not negating his share of the blame in all of this. He can petition the courts, for whatever good it will do him." Mike shrugged. "At least it's a place to start."

"I'm so glad he had someone like you these past years. When he left here, he—" Bebe's voice broke, and she had to clear her throat to continue. "The studio is . . . it's like it was when Philippe's father took it over years ago. I don't know if it can be built up again. We've lost so much time, it would take so much work."

"In the navy we say it's time to batten down the hatches," Mike told her. "You just plant both feet on the ground and start to move forward, and you don't look back."

Bebe nodded. "Is Philippe planning on going to see Nellie today?"

"I think so. There's no sense in putting it off. I think he wants to get it over with as soon as possible."

"If that's the case, then I'd better call Nellie's father and have him there. I'd like him to hear what Philippe has to say."

Mike sighed. "It's a hell of a mess, and Phil doesn't deserve this."

"I agree. Look, you've been driving all night. Why don't you go upstairs and get some sleep," Bebe suggested. "Take any bedroom."

"You'll call me if you need me?" Mike said, rising.

"Yes, I will. And I'll try to keep the children quiet."

"Don't do that. I love to hear kids laughing and playing." He grinned. "I must have a hundred cousins. They won't bother me. I like that little guy Bruno and the way he's holding on to that red wagon. I bet if it you'd gone out and bought him one, he wouldn't touch it.''

"You're right, that's why I didn't do it," Bebe said. "It's all part of going home, and by home I mean the château where the wagon is. He's so little, so lost. The others are his family. It's so sad it breaks my heart."

"Mine, too," Mike muttered as he made his way upstairs.

It was midmorning when Philippe walked into the kitchen. Bebe noticed immediately that the tension seemed to have gone out of him. His eyes were dry, but then, she knew they would be. There was a sense of peace and a calmness about her son that she'd never seen before. The children had done that for him. Smiling, he poured himself a cup of coffee.

"Great bunch of kids," he said. "There are things I want to say to you, apologies I want to make . . . things I want to ask . . . but somehow none of those things seem important now except maybe the apology. I wish my father were here."

"I wish he were, too," Bebe said quietly. "But you don't have to apologize to me for anything. I did what I had to do just as you did. As long as both of us understand that, we're okay. Someday your father will know. I rather think he knows now."

Philippe set his cup in the sink. "Time to beard the . . . lioness. Any advice?"

"I've been thinking, Philippe. I'll give you an hour, and then I'll call Daniel and tell him to go to Nellie's." She frowned, fingering her coffee cup thoughtfully. "He needs to hear what you have to say. He's stood by Nellie. In my heart I don't think he believes her, but I can't be absolutely sure. Tell the truth, and if you want to make demands, then you make them. You do whatever you feel you have to do. I am behind you one hundred percent."

Philippe smiled. "Mike's father said exactly the same thing. I guess I'll wing it."

"Wait here a minute. Don't leave till I get back." Bebe ran to her room and rummaged through her desk until she found the stock certificates Reuben had returned to her. Flipping them over, she scribbled her name and then ran back down the stairs into the kitchen.

"Here," she said, holding out the certificates, suddenly shy. "They belong to you. I never did want them, not really. So, you see, you aren't exactly penniless. Nellie needs to know that. You'll be starting off even. What you do from there on in is up to you."

Philippe was stunned. "I can't . . . you don't have to . . ."

"I want to. I've never been able to give you anything. I can give you this, and I know I speak for Reuben when I tell you it's what he would want. Please, Philippe, accept it," Bebe pleaded.

He stared at the papers in his hand, then looked up into her eyes. "I don't know what to say."

" 'Thank you' will do nicely," Bebe said, smiling. "Go along now and stay there till Daniel arrives."

The moment the door closed behind her son, Bebe ran up the stairs a second time. Once again she rummaged through her desk, papers flying in every direction. When she found what she was looking for, she jammed it into her purse, then ripped at her clothes and dressed quickly.

Three minutes later she was careening down the driveway, headed for Daniel Bishop's offices. She arrived just in time to meet Daniel getting off the elevator. Eyeing her warily, he invited her into his office.

"What's wrong?" he asked, offering her a chair.

Bebe pulled out the old agreement he'd signed, the one she'd used in the conference room three and a half years earlier. "I'm calling this in now," she declared. "Three and a half years ago, when you voted the way I wanted you to, it was all rescinded by the judge's order. That means you still owe me, Daniel, and I want to collect *now*. I don't want to hear any of your legal bullshit, and I don't want any ifs, ands, or buts. All I want is for you to go over to your safe and give me your two shares of voting stock. . . . Look, Mickey's dead," she hurried on when she saw the look of utter astonishment on Daniel's face. "Your daughter wiped out Philippe's fortune, the fortune Mickey secured for him because she thought of him as her son, and he is . . . was her son, more her son than he ever will be to me. So I want those shares for Philippe, Daniel, and I want them now!"

"For God's sake, Bebe, Mickey entrusted them to me!" he gasped. "Why are you doing this?"

"Because you owe me!" she cried. "You owe Reuben! And you owe *my son*!"

For several long moments Daniel merely stared at her, weighing the justice of her words. At last he rose and walked to his office wall safe. Without a word he unlocked the safe and withdrew the certificates, then returned to his desk and endorsed them.

When he inched the stock certificates across the desk, Bebe snatched them up and stuffed them into her purse. "We're square now, Daniel," she said, rising. "You don't owe me anything. If Mickey were here, I'm sure she'd applaud this generous gesture on your part. If I didn't believe in my heart that she would have approved, I wouldn't be standing here like this. On behalf of my husband and my son, I thank you."

At the door she turned. "I think you should know that Philippe is back. He's at Nellie's right now. If I were you, I'd go there as soon as possible."

Daniel was on his feet. "Philippe's back!" he cried, incredulous.

Bebe grinned wryly. "Oh, yes, he's back, and I can't wait for you to see him and hear what he has to say. Good-bye, Daniel."

In her rickety car with the doors locked, Bebe collapsed. She was shaking so badly, she could barely put the car into gear. Cracking open the window, she struggled to take great gulping breaths. She had it! The two certificates necessary to control Fairmont Studios. Once Philippe signed his name to the back, he would be in control of the entire studio. "I did it for you, Mickey," she whispered as she drove back to her house in the canyon, "to try to make up for all the nasty things I've done. I know it's what you would have wanted."

It suddenly occurred to Bebe that Daniel had barely said two words; she'd done all the talking, all the maneuvering. She laughed then until the tears flowed. Poor Daniel. He never had a chance.

She'd finally beaten Nellie Bishop at her own game.

Chapter Forty

NELLIE HEAVED HERSELF OVER THE EDGE OF THE POOL. AFTER fifty laps, she was barely winded. The regimen was second nature to her now; she'd followed it faithfully every day since she'd given birth. The doctor's nurse had told her it was the best way to regain her figure, and she'd been right: she was now exactly the same weight and size as she was before she decided to get pregnant. The only problem was that swimming gave her a ferocious appetite, she thought sourly.

These days she spent a lot of time in the sun, and her skin glowed a golden bronze, her hair bleached almost white. She was the perfect picture of health and happiness. Well, she might be healthy, Nellie conceded, but she definitely wasn't happy. Although in control of Philippe's fortune, she still ranked a mean second at the studio, and it was the studio she really wanted. Bebe wouldn't give an inch; every decision, every little thing, had to meet with her approval. It was an intolerable situation, and she'd have to do something about it—soon. It was obvious to her, as well as to everyone else, that Philippe wasn't coming back. Most likely he was dead somewhere in Europe. In seven years if he didn't come back she'd be legally a widow. A widow at the age of twenty-five! . . .

A shadow fell across her line of vision, blocking out the

un. Damn, she thought, they weren't supposed to clean the
ool till tomorrow. She'd wanted to sun a while longer. An
ngry accusation on her lips, she looked up—and her eyes
lmost popped from her head. "Phi—Phi—"

"Say it, Nellie, say my name," Philippe said quietly. "Did
ou think I was dead, that I wasn't coming back? Well, I'm
ere now." Lord, he thought, she was just as pretty—almost
s pretty—as Lizzie. Where Lizzie was tall, Nellie was petite.
Iellie was more rounded, Lizzie more muscular. He tried to
emember what it was that he'd ever seen in Nellie.

"When . . . how long . . . I'm so glad you're home," Nellie
lurted out as she struggled to her feet. She drew in her breath.
'How handsome you look! Are those aviator wings? That
xplains it! We all thought you'd joined the army. Lieutenant,
et. How ever did you manage it? You must know some very
mportant people in high places." What was he doing here?
he thought wildly. Calm—she had to remain calm, not let
im upset her, no matter what he said. Everything was taken
are of, she'd done it all legally. What could he do?

"I've been here awhile," Philippe said, watching her with
arrowed eyes. "You might say I've been getting the lay of
he land. I understand you've been guarding"—he waited a
noment before he dragged out the words—"my fortune."

"Yes, I've made some excellent investments," she replied
ervously. "I think you'll be . . . satisfied."

"In both our names?" he asked with a grim smile.

"No, yes . . . well, not exactly. Actually, they're in Little
'hilly's trust."

He nodded. "Little Philly. Your son?"

"Our son, Philippe Reuben Tarz. Not just mine, *ours*," she
mphasized. "My attorney said it was the right thing to do
ince none of us had heard from you. Oh, Philippe, I wrote
ou every day, twelve thousand letters, and had nowhere to
nail them. Why didn't you write or call?" she asked tearfully.

He ignored her. "I don't have a son. You have a son. I
ever touched you, so let's not have any lies. I'm back now,
nd this is all going to get straightened out."

"Philippe, you weren't yourself then," Nellie said desper-
tely. "How could you forget something so important? How
an you say you never touched me? Little Philly is the living
roof. He even has your nose and chin. Ask anyone.

"You drank too much that second night, that's why you
lon't remember," she continued when he didn't respond. "We

have a son, and you don't even remember making love to me. I remember, I remember every little detail, and what do you do? You run off like a little boy and join the navy and lie about everything. You're lying about Little Philly now because you don't want the responsibility of being a husband and father. How could you do this to me?'' she wailed. "How?''

"I never touched you,'' Philippe said stonily. "I'm going to petition the courts and have all that crap you took care of rescinded. You're not going to get away with this. I'm having the marriage annulled.''

Nellie shook her head, eyes glittering. "That's going to be hard to do with a baby in evidence and your past record. And I'm not giving you a divorce, either! When you come to your senses we can talk about your loss of memory. Your *convenient* loss of memory,'' she spat out. "You wait right here.'' She was gone in a flash of running legs, returning a minute later with a pink-cheeked toddler in her arms. "This, Philippe, is *our* son!''

Philippe stepped back and almost fell into the pool. He drew in his breath in a sharp hiss. "He's not mine, he's yours. I don't care what you say or how you say it, he isn't mine!''

"Let's hold on a minute,'' Daniel shouted from the terrace.

Philippe and Nellie turned in surprise. Daniel's heart hammered in his chest as he approached them. Lord, if Reuben could only see his son now.

"Sir,'' Philippe said respectfully.

Daniel grimaced. "How . . . Are those aviator wings you're wearing?'' he asked incredulously.

"Yes, sir.''

"How?''

Philippe allowed himself a small smile. "The same way you got to Harvard, sir. Mr. Sugar helped me.''

Daniel nodded. "I can see that you two young people are pretty hotheaded right now, so I'll mediate this. Philippe, I want to hear from you what the hell happened. I've already heard Nellie's version.''

"As you know, we got married. However, we never . . . consummated the marriage.'' Philippe looked Daniel straight in the eye. "It was my decision—I wanted it that way. And afterward . . . well, I knew I never should have done it, gone off like that, and I regretted it immediately. I just turned tail and ran, that's the beginning and end of it. I stopped by my mother's to say good-bye and gave her a new power of attorney.

Now I understand that all my money has been turned over to Nellie's son. But this is not my child. I never touched Nellie— not before we were married or after we were married. I swear to you, I did not touch her. I don't know whose baby this is, but it isn't mine!''

For the first time in his life Daniel was truly at a loss for words. Philippe sounded truthful. What was worse, he believed the boy. Finally he found his voice. ''Those are very serious statements, Philippe.''

''I know that, sir, and I'm not making them lightly. When I left here I was a fabulously wealthy man by American standards, thanks to my mother. I go off, fight for *your* country, and when I come back I find out that your daughter has used the time to misrepresent my wishes and then question my very existence—all in order to help herself to my fortune. I'm not proud of the way I went off, but I feel I redeemed myself and I want what's mine. I'm willing to make a settlement with Nellie for all the aggravation I've put her through. Whatever you think is fair, sir.''

''What?'' shrieked Nellie. ''How *dare* you! How dare you deny this is your child! You're insane! Settle with me? I already have it all—you can't settle with me!'' Little Philly started to cry, his chin trembling at the harsh, strident words.

''Now look what you've done, you've made him cry!'' Nellie ran into the house, gave him over to the nanny and was back at poolside in less than two minutes, her eyes shooting sparks.

''I can't believe you're doing this to me,'' she cried. ''This should be the happiest moment in our lives, and you're standing here in that handsome uniform lying to my face!

''You've fallen in love with someone else, haven't you?'' she continued, groping wildly for a plausible diversion. At her husband's startled expression she realized her shot in the dark had hit home. Daniel saw it, too. ''And now you don't want me anymore or Little Philly. You found someone else, and you think you can get rid of us. Well, it isn't going to work, Philippe. I don't care about myself, but we have a son to consider. I stayed home, was faithful, I wrote you every single day, and I had the baby alone while you were falling in love with someone else.''

She turned to her father. ''*Now* do you believe me?'' she demanded. At Daniel's obvious distress and uncertainty, she shrieked in frustration and flailed her fists in the air. ''All *right*! I don't care if you do or not! You can go to hell!'' She whirled

on Philippe. "Get out of here, husband *dear*, and don't come
back. Or I'll get a restraining order from the police!"

Daniel's stomach churned as he watched his daughter run
into the house. The vicious pounding in his head was making
him nauseated. He turned to Philippe. "Is it true? Have you
fallen in love with someone else?"

"Yes, sir, that's true," Philippe replied soberly, "but it just
happened. It has nothing to do with why I left Nellie. I am not
that child's father. I never touched your daughter!"

"I think we better leave. And I wouldn't come back here,
Philippe," Daniel advised. "Nellie will get a restraining order.
Everything is on her side, and I have to be honest, you don't
have a chance in court. The baby makes all the difference, and
if I'm called as a witness, I'll have to testify that you admitted
you're in love with someone else. Think very carefully, Philippe. Whoever it is you're in love with is innocent in all of
this, and you don't want to drag her through a mud-slinging
divorce. You don't want to ruin her name. This is what your
father would tell you."

Philippe seethed. "That's *not* what my father would tell me,
and you damn well know it. He'd tell me to fight for what's
right. I told you the truth—Nellie is the one who's lying. Jesus,
can't you see it? She's *sick*, Mr. Bishop!"

"I don't want to hear any more, Philippe," Daniel snapped.
"Believe it or not, I am not involved in all of this. However,
there is one thing you should know. Bebe came to my office
a little while ago and I gave her my two voting certificates. I
believe she intends to turn them over to you. I agreed to the
transfer only because I felt, as she did, that Mickey—and
Reuben—would have wanted it that way. But I absolutely
refuse to take sides between you and Nellie. You'll have to
straighten out this mess yourselves. I suggest you do it legally. . . ."

Philippe smarted over Daniel's words all the way back to
his mother's house. This couldn't be happening to him, it just
couldn't. How could a young woman so pretty and innocent-
looking be so evil? The baby was . . . whose? The fact that he
now held the controlling interest in Fairmont didn't fully register until he reached Bebe's house and saw the stock certificates
on the table, where his mother sat waiting for him.

He was angrier than he'd ever been in his life. He was also
scared. "More than anything," he told his mother, "I feel
guilty. All those years when my . . . other mother tried to safe-

guard her fortune for me, I took it for granted. Now it's gone, in trust for a child I don't even know.''

"But Nellie has control of that trust," she pointed out. "She made sure of that. You're going to have to see an attorney first thing tomorrow. If nothing else, the wheels will be in motion. How did Daniel take it?"

Philippe grinned wryly. "He talked more like a lawyer than a father. I had the feeling there was a lot of strain between him and Nellie. Also, I think those two certificates were a thousand-pound weight on his shoulders. If you want my opinion, I think he was relieved to part with them."

Philippe's gaze was far away as he idly stirred a fresh cup of coffee. "I won't win any court contest. Nellie . . . Nellie homed in on the fact that I'm in love with someone else. She said I wanted to be rid of her and the baby so I could be with my new love . . . made a big deal about being loyal and waiting, having the baby alone and writing me all these letters. . . . Mr. Bishop asked me how I got into flight school, and I told him about Mr. Sugar. Nellie will probably use that, too. I'll be painted as a bogus war hero trying to steal a child's trust fund so I can go off with my girlfriend."

Mother and son stared across the table at each other. From outside came the happy sounds of the children frolicking in the pool. "Cut my losses and go on from here, right?" Philippe said at last. Bebe nodded. "I never wanted the studio. I still don't want it. I made no plans for the future, and I don't know why. I guess I didn't want to think that I might eventually end up here. Mike knows what he wants to do. He was born to fly, and that's what he does best. He's going to take out a loan and open up a flying school. I was going to surprise him and give him the money. Now I can't do that. It looks like I have no other choice but to come back to the studio. There's nothing I can do about Lizzie, either. If I file for divorce, Nellie will contest it, and I know they'll paint Lizzie as some kind of . . . I can't do that to her," he said miserably.

"You're standing on a very rocky road, Philippe. It's a terrible feeling, I know because I've been over that road." Bebe sighed. "It's definite, then, you aren't going to fight Nellie?"

"I'll talk to a lawyer, but for every reason I can come up with to fight her, there are three more why I shouldn't." He shook his head. "I don't want to hurt Lizzie or have her family dragged into something because of my stupidity. The baby . . .

that's her ace in the hole and she knows it. Whoever would have thought she'd be that devious, that evil?''

Bebe grimaced. "Jane knew. She saw it first. In my heart I know Daniel agrees, but unless he sees Nellie take an ax and kill someone, he isn't going to do anything. He is so incredibly loyal. In the end, if it comes down to the wire and he has to choose, really has to choose between what you say and what Nellie says, he'd go with you. At least the old Daniel would. What strange paths we've all taken," she said sadly.

"Well, you're on the right road now," Philippe said, reaching across the table to squeeze her hand.

"All I can tell you, Philippe, is if I can do it so can you. Believe in yourself and you can do anything." She rose and began to pace the kitchen floor. "Look, why don't you go to Jane and ask her to come back to the studio. Listen to her. You'll be starting out fresh, from the bottom, just the way your father did when he began working at the studio. Fairmont was a low-grade sleaze operation when my father had it. He was no businessman, but Reuben was. And you're your father's son, Philippe. This is just a suggestion, but while you were gone I've been thinking. Your friend, Mike, you said, loves to fly. How about some pictures with stunt flying? War hero turned stunt pilot . . . publicity could get a lot of mileage out of that. It's worth a thought if you seriously plan on taking over the studio."

He shrugged. "I don't have any other choice. There's no way I'm going to let Nellie get her money-grubbing hands on it."

"Good for you! The studio is open for business. You should take Mike down and show him around when he wakes up." Bebe smiled at her son. "I have the impression—correct me if I'm wrong—that you two are friends, the way Daniel and your father are friends."

"I'd say so." Philippe finished his coffee, his eyes on the children through the kitchen window. "Great bunch of kids. Jesus, what they've been through, and they can still laugh."

"At night they cry," Bebe said softly. "All of them."

"I've learned that each of us has to make our own happiness. My mother used to tell me that, but I didn't understand. *She* made me happy. I wanted to cry, to grieve, but I can't. Maybe I never will." He turned to Bebe, his eyes deep with memory. "She's still with me. In my mind I can see her, see her so clearly. My mother and cantankerous Yvette."

"Life goes on, Philippe," Bebe said, leading him to the stairway. "Get some sleep and we'll talk later. I . . . I'm very proud of you, as proud as your mother would be if she were here. You're going to make it, even if you think things are . . . at their lowest ebb. You're my son, mine and Reuben's, and if there's one thing both of us learned, each in our own way, it's how to survive. Someday Nellie will be nothing but a bad memory." She patted his hand. "If you aren't up by dinnertime, I'll wake you."

Philippe leaned over and kissed his mother lightly on the cheek. He grinned then, his eyes sparkling with sudden confidence. Bebe's hand flew to her mouth. "You look so much like your father," she said, "it's uncanny. If only he could see you now. When you first arrived you were a young boy, and now you're a young man. You bring back so many memories. . . ."

At the top of the stairs Philippe turned, smiled Reuben's smile, and saluted his mother smartly. She smiled back and nodded.

After all this time she had another son, she thought, a bittersweet ache in her heart. *Oh, Reuben, if only you were here. If only you could see him now the way I see him. But do fathers ever view their sons the way mothers do?*

This was her time now, hers and the little ones'.

She walked out into the sunshine that filled her life and waved to the children. "I'm coming," she called. "I'm coming."

Nellie raced through the kitchen, stopping only when the swinging door into the dining room closed behind her. Dropping to her haunches, she took huge, gut-wrenching breaths to ward off her dizziness.

He was back. All the praying, all the wishing, had been in vain. He should be dead, she wanted him to be dead. Why wasn't he dead? Everything was ruined now. She choked back a sob of anger.

Get up, she urged herself. Get up and go upstairs, where you can close the door and think. Plan.

Her legs were rubbery as she planted one foot in front of the other up the stairs. He was in love with someone else. That she hadn't counted on; how could she, when she'd been so sure he was dead and never coming back? Men in love did stupid things, unpredictable things. Besides that, Philippe was too emotional, and emotional people often acted irrationally.

Bebe would orchestrate his actions, she was sure of it, just as she was sure that in the end her father would side with Philippe against her.

Nellie paced the frilly bedroom, smacking one clenched fist into the other. How, she asked herself. How could she best them at their own game? As it stood now, she had all of Philippe's money and 49 percent of Fairmont Studios—and in case of a legal contest, she had Little Philly, who had already influenced the courts to her advantage. Philippe, on the other hand, had little more than a story that could never be proved . . . and the combined wiles of Bebe, Jane Perkins, and—perhaps—her own father.

She was pacing faster and faster now, her movements frenzied, her eyes narrow and mean. The scales might be weighted on her side, she conceded, but that wasn't enough. She wanted to be *sure* that nothing of hers could be taken away—and she wanted more.

Full, 100 percent control of Fairmont Studios. Nobody was going to destroy her dream of sweeping down that circular stairway in her sparkling gown with all of Hollywood at her feet. Least of all, a husband she despised.

The phone on her nightstand buzzed to life. Philippe, she wondered. Or her father? Although she didn't want to talk to either of them, she knew she couldn't hide. Her hands were shaking as she picked up the receiver and pressed it to her ear.

It was Bebe.

"Good afternoon, Nellie," she said in a polite, noncommittal tone. "I called to say there will be a board meeting tomorrow morning. I wanted to give you the courtesy of hearing what I have to say in private, so you don't repeat the performance you gave the last time. I signed over my shares of stock to Philippe this morning."

Nellie digested the information. "Then that makes us equal partners, doesn't it?" she said. When she heard Bebe chuckle, her heart began to pound.

"Not quite. Your father signed over his two shares to me this morning, and I am transferring those two shares to Philippe. By the close of business today, he will have controlling interest in Fairmont. Have a nice day, Nellie, and I'll see you tomorrow at the board meeting."

"You're lying!" Nellie snapped. "My father would never give *you* his shares." But she knew Bebe was telling the truth. Sold out by her own father!

Seething with anger, she slammed down the receiver and hurled the phone across the room. *Dammit!* There had to be something she could do, some action she could take, to get what she wanted, and she wanted the studio. Perhaps . . .

It was a calculated risk; she might be underestimating Philippe or her father, but it was worth a try. Retrieving the phone, she called Daniel and schooled her voice to calmness as she told him about her conversation with Bebe, gently chastising him for turning over his two shares to her. "But I understand why you did it, Daddy," she added sweetly. "I'm just so sorry that it's come to all this. I certainly never expected . . . what I mean is, Philippe is so . . . so different. I guess he feels guilty. I even understand what he's feeling, but what he's done is unforgivable. He's forcing me into a fight, a legal fight that I never expected or wanted. I just want you to know that when I'm forced to expose him, you yourself will come under scrutiny, and I'm apologizing now for what will happen. Daddy, they'll disbar you! How can you allow Philippe to put both of us through this . . . this scandal? It's going to be an absolute disaster. I never wanted this. Just because Philippe found some . . . someone else . . . he can't do this to . . . to our son."

Daniel's heart leapt into his mouth. Nellie—his own beloved Nellie—was actually threatening him! And he knew she was speaking the truth; he would be disbarred. Certainly Philippe would be dishonorably discharged, and it would be all over the papers. Al Sugar, well-meaning Al, would spend the rest of his years in shame for his part in all of it. He might even go to prison for fraud or forgery.

When he could finally speak he choked out the words. "What is it you want, Nellie? Exactly what do you want from me?"

"Make Philippe go away," she said. Her voice was strong now, in command, as she pressed her advantage. "He's shamed me once too often. I don't want our son to hear about this someday and know his father rejected him and his mother for some . . . some bimbo he met while he was in the navy."

"I can't make Philippe do anything, Nellie," Daniel protested weakly.

"Oh, yes, you can. Bebe listens to you, she's your friend. Tell them Reuben wouldn't approve. Everyone is always singing about Reuben and his old love. Sing again, Daddy. Sing loud, or I will fight both of you. Do it for Little Philly," she added as an afterthought. "And when you call Bebe, tell her I won't be able to attend the board meeting tomorrow. I promised to take Little Philly to the zoo. Good-bye, Daddy, see you soon.''

On her way downstairs, Nellie walked past the open door of the nursery. She didn't look in, she never did. Little Philly didn't need her, she needed him—but only on paper. To her Little Philly wasn't a person; he was a thing to be used as leverage, her ace in the hole, her trump card. And like any good player, she knew how and when to expose him, to use him to win the game.

That night she slept deeply and dreamlessly.

It was a little past midnight when Daniel Bishop knocked on the screen door of Bebe's kitchen. About to retire, Bebe was clearing the table and chatting with Philippe and Mike. His mouth set grimly, Daniel joined them at the table and began to recount his telephone conversation with Nellie.

Thirty minutes later Bebe snapped, ''I don't believe this! You can't let her do it! She's sick, she should be institutionalized!''

''I can't stop her,'' Daniel said glumly. ''I don't think anyone can.''

''I can,'' Philippe said.

Daniel shook his head. ''I'm sorry, Philippe, but you can't. You can go to court, you can fight, but in the end your reputation will be in shreds, as will mine, and she'll still win. And don't think for one minute that she won't make good on her threat to smear Mike and his family. She'll leave no stone unturned.''

Philippe slammed his fist on the tabletop, his eyes wild. ''Then what the hell am I supposed to do?''

''Sell her the studio,'' Bebe suggested forcefully. ''Global Pictures is still operational. We have all the leased equipment and the building. Start from scratch. The company already has one movie under its belt. Sell out, Philippe, and cut your losses. Don't let her destroy you!''

''But my father . . . Mr. Bishop, what do you think?'' Philippe asked in an anguished voice.

''I agree with Bebe,'' Daniel said thoughtfully. ''It's one way of getting your fortune back. Anything is worth a try at this point. If you like, I'll speak to her attorney tomorrow.''

''Phil,'' Mike interjected, ''don't base your decision on me and my family; we can handle it. Whatever you decide will be okay with us.''

Philippe clapped his friend on the back, gazing at him with love and affection. "Thanks, Mike. I think my father would understand if I let the studio go. Do you agree, Mother?" Bebe nodded, a smile on her face. "Okay, Mr. Bishop, run it up the flagpole and let's see what happens."

Five days later Daniel reported back to the house in Benedict Canyon. Bebe ushered him out to the terrace, where she, Philippe, Mike, and Jane Perkins were having dinner.

"Nellie accepts your offer, Philippe," he announced. "It'll take a week or so to transfer the funds back to your name. Once I convinced her lawyer that you would make your offer only once and that you wouldn't back down, Nellie began to see the light. There's a possibility that a different judge might not be as lenient as the last one, which also helped to sway her. You walk away with what was yours and Nellie walks with full control of Fairmont Studios. The accrued revenues are to be divided evenly. She has working capital and so do you." He paused, gazing around at all the expectant faces. "It was the best I could do, Philippe, and I want to apologize now, in front of everyone, for what my stepdaughter has put you through."

Philippe drew a sigh of relief. "It was more than I hoped for, and I accept your apology."

"I do, too," Bebe said, coming around to give him a quick hug.

"Me, too." Jane grinned. "You did real good, Daniel."

"There's one more thing, Philippe," he added. "One of the conditions of the transfer was that Nellie agree in writing not to expose either one of us. To do so would mean giving up the studio. Naturally she agreed. There's going to be at least a ton of papers to sign, so don't leave until that's all been taken care of."

Philippe heaved another sigh. "What about the divorce?" he asked.

"No, she wouldn't budge. There is no divorce for either of you in the immediate future. I'm sorry, she dug in her heels on that one."

"So you live in sin," Mike quipped. He sobered instantly when no one laughed. "I didn't exactly mean that the way it sounded," he said lamely.

"What will *that* cost me?" Philippe asked, tight-lipped.

Daniel shook his head. "God only knows. She said no and

refused to discuss it further. She's asking the courts for five hundred dollars a week support for . . . for her son.''

"Like hell!" Philippe cried. "That boy is not mine. If I pay, that's an admission he is. No, I absolutely refuse. I won't even discuss it.''

"You have to discuss it. It was one of *her* terms. We gave one, she gave one. If you don't agree, it's back to the beginning.'' When Philippe remained silent, Daniel sighed and drew his chair closer to the table. "Look, you don't have to decide today; tomorrow will be soon enough.''

Bebe grimaced. "So in the end she beat us after all.''

"In a manner of speaking, yes,'' Daniel muttered.

"And the television . . . ?''

"Philippe will make a fortune on it, there's no doubt about it. Nellie is entitled to nothing since you did it all in your name, Bebe,'' Daniel reassured her. "The wave of the future is here, and sooner or later it will hurt this industry. That's when you'll get your pound of flesh, Philippe.''

Whatever was good, kind, and decent in Philippe died at that moment, replaced by vengeance, ruthlessness, and hatred. "What about my house?''

"Nellie's lawyer said the child needed a home atmosphere and suggested she keep the house. You can fight it if you want.''

"Philippe, why not move into your father's house,'' Bebe suggested. "I'm sure if he were here, he would offer it to you. Daniel isn't there anymore, not since he moved in with Jane. He only goes by to check on things every few days. Someone should live there. I think Reuben would want it to be you.''

"Where do you stand on all of this, Mr. Bishop?'' Philippe asked coolly.

Daniel reached over and took Jane's hand. "Well, first of all Jane and I are getting married.'' He grinned. "She's finally going to make an honest man of me. And as far as Nellie is concerned, once all the legal paperwork is done, I wash my hands of her. I told her so, and it didn't seem to matter to her one way or the other. One part of me believes I've failed her, and the other part, the legal part, knows I am no longer responsible for her because she's of age. Someday I guess I'll be able to forget all this.''

"I'll never forget it,'' Philippe snarled as he stomped from the room.

* * *

Ten days later, with the ink barely dry on all the legal documents, *Variety* broke the news. Hollywood raised its eyebrows and decided to take a backseat, wait-and-watch attitude. Two days after the announcement that Cornelia Tarz was taking over Fairmont Studios, a second story broke that Philip Bouchet Tarz, son of mogul Reuben Tarz, was starting up production at Global Studios, the film company that had turned out *The Sands of Time*. At this piece of information Hollywood lowered its brows, climbed onto the front seat, and started to buzz. Odds and bets were the order of the day.

The war was on.

While Hollywood flapped its wings, Philippe wrote a note to Mr. and Mrs. Almeda thanking them for their hospitality. Then he wrote a second note, this one stiff and formal, to "Elizabeth," as he referred to her now. In it he apologized for taking up so much of her time and said he wouldn't be returning to Sacramento in the near future. He closed by wishing her well in any and all future endeavors and signed the note Philip Tarz.

When Philippe said his good-bye to Mike outside his mother's house, he handed over a check for the down payment on a building for Mike to start his flight school. "It's a loan, nothing more," he insisted when Mike began to protest. "Look, buddy, I don't want you thinking I don't want you here. I do, but this is best for you and for me. I have to tackle this on my own and either fall on my face or make it big-time like my old man. And I'm asking you please not to make up any fairy tales for your sister. I want your promise." Mike nodded glumly. "Maybe someday I'll be free to . . . to . . . you know." He shrugged.

"Nellie sounds to me like someone who'll live to a ripe old age," Mike predicted, his voice tight with the effort at holding back tears. "Evil people usually do. Jesus, there must be a way. . . ."

"If there is, I'll find it. I don't have the right to ask Lizzie to wait for me. I would never ask that of her, and it wouldn't be fair. So, let's say good-bye here." Philippe forced a grin. "Hell, it's not really good-bye, I'll see you at March Field when we sign out for the last time. Good luck, buddy."

Mike wanted to shake his friend, to do something—anything—to make him change his mind, but he knew he couldn't. "Guess I'll see you around. Listen, if you decide to do anything with stunt pilots, you give me a call, okay? I'll be here in a minute.''

"Right. Now get out of here before we both start to blubber.''

"Lizzie isn't going to understand any of this," Mike muttered as he settled himself behind the wheel.

"I know." Philippe sighed. "I don't understand any of it myself."

"Think of it as a new beginning."

"Yeah, yeah, I'll do that. You drive carefully, you hear?"

In frustration, Mike threw the car in gear and roared down the drive, tires squealing. He didn't look back or blow the horn.

Philippe turned and walked back to the house. At the door he turned and waved . . . to nothing. Mike was out of sight. "Okay, Hollywood, it's my turn at bat," he muttered. "Only time will tell if I'm the man my father is."

Time. Time was the answer to everything.

Chapter Forty-one

HOLLYWOOD TURNED OUT EN MASSE TO HONOR ITS OWN on Academy Awards night. Elaborate hairstyles, designer gowns and furs, glittering jewelry, and handsome tuxedos were the order of the evening, as were the gleaming smiles and gracious handwaving to the public that lined the entrance to the theater.

There was a subdued excitement as filmmakers and actors took their assigned seats in the plush theater. There wasn't one among them who didn't covet the small golden statue, but they all knew, regardless of the nominations, who would walk away at the end of the evening with Hollywood's highest honor.

In the front row, sixteen children sat alongside Bebe, Jane, Daniel, and Philippe. The children were restless, uncertain of what to expect. All they wanted was for the evening to be over so they could return to France the following day. There had been one bad moment at the door when the usher wouldn't allow Bruno to bring his dog inside. As one, the children backstepped. Anna spoke for all of them: "If the dog doesn't go in, we don't go in. He was as valiant as all of us." Those lining the plush ropes jeered and booed the usher's decision. Photographers snapped pictures of Bruno sticking out his tongue at one of the royally clad emmisaries of the awards. It took ten minutes of negotiation on Bebe's part before they could enter—the dog in tow.

Two hours later, backstage, Jane and Bebe hugged each other ecstatically. *The Sands of Time* had won Oscars for Best Picture, Best Director, Best Original Screenplay, Best Actor, Best Actress, Best Supporting Actor, and Best Supporting Actress. Best *everything*! Each time an award was accepted, the entire theater surged to its feet, applauding to show its support for the academy's decision.

"And now, ladies and gentlemen, members of the Academy of Motion Picture Arts and Sciences, we have one last honor to bestow before we adjourn for another year," announced Clark Gable. "Tonight the academy wishes to honor sixteen courageous little soldiers from France. Ladies and gentlemen, I give you Marchioness Michelene Fonsard's little army. Come forward, children!"

The house rose and roared its approval as the children trooped up to the stage. Marie took her place before the microphone and in almost perfect English spoke.

"We wish to thank you for this honor. Mademoiselle Mickey and Monsieur Tarz saved our lives. We accept your honor on their behalf. We will always remember this wonderful time in your country. Tomorrow we return to France, where we will join Monsieur Tarz, who is waiting for us. We will tell him of this wonderful evening. Thank you."

One by one the children were handed their small statues. As Bruno reached for his award, his dog leapt from his arms and scampered across the stage. The bright lights and laughter of the audience confused the dog, and he immediately peed on Gable's leg, to the uproarious delight of the audience. Good sport that he was, Gable picked up the dog and announced, "It's a rented tux."

Backstage there was pandemonium. "You'll need a truck to carry all of these back to the house," Daniel said, laughing.

The children shyly posed for pictures and murmured their thanks over and over, their statues held aloft.

"I'm so tired I could go to sleep on my feet," Bebe whispered to Jane.

"Take them home, Bebe. Daniel and I will make an appearance at the party and join you in a little while," Jane promised. "The kids look absolutely exhausted. Daniel's bags are in the car. You're all packed and ready to go, right?"

Bebe grinned. "The children have been packed and ready

to go for the last two months. I'm ready to go, that's for sure. I've had enough of Hollywood to last me the rest of my life. I wish you were coming.''

"I will, but I have to help Philippe get Global off the ground. Eight, ten months, and I'll be knocking on the door of that château. I'm glad Daniel's going, though,'' Jane added. ''He has to get away from here, away from Nellie. It's best. I'm going to miss him terribly, but it'll give me something to look forward to. In the meantime, you be sure and tell Reuben we made a hell of a team.''

"I will. I'll see you later.'' Bebe glanced around. ''Have you seen Philippe? He came with all of us in the bus and said he would leave with us, but I haven't seen him since the children accepted their honors.''

"He left a few minutes ago in my car,'' Jane told her. ''Said he wanted to write a letter to his father. I think the young man has a lot to say at this point. He's going to be all right, Bebe. This thing with Nellie . . . it'll be resolved eventually. Philippe is starting a new life, and at this point Nellie is nothing more than a nuisance he has to deal with. Don't worry about him; I won't leave until I'm sure he's on the right road.''

"Bless you, Jane, what would any of us have done without you?'' Bebe said in a choked voice. Jane kissed her on the cheek before she linked her arm with Daniel's.

Bebe clapped her hands. ''Okay, listen up! We're going out to the bus in an orderly manner. We're going home to . . . to get ready for our trip tomorrow. All in favor, say aye!''

The mad scramble through the crowds with Bebe dashing behind her young charges had photographers clicking their cameras madly.

It was over. Tomorrow, Hollywood would be a memory.

Epilogue

"I FEEL LIKE I'VE JUST COME HOME FOR THE SECOND TIME IN my life," Daniel said softly to Bebe.

"I feel the same way. So many years, Daniel. . . . This is the right thing, isn't it?" she whispered.

"More right than you'll ever know. You go ahead, we'll all wait here. This is your moment and you've waited long enough. I don't know if those shoes are sturdy enough to tramp through a vineyard, though."

"My feet have wings." Bebe smiled as she started off toward the vineyard where Reuben was pruning the grapevines. She saw him first, her hand flying to her mouth to stifle an exclamation of joy. Quietly she waited at the end of the vines, willing her husband to turn and notice her. *Turn, Reuben, look at me*, she prayed.

He did turn then and noticed the slim young woman in a cornflower-blue dress, the same dress he'd seen once before in Paris. Bebe . . . Sucking in his breath, he started forward. When he got closer, but not within arm's reach, he heard her say, "I'm Barbara Tarz from California."

He wanted to say, I'm Reuben Tarz, but all he could manage was, "What took you so long?" She ran straight into his outstretched arms.

"I . . . I had a . . . couple of things to do. . . . But I made it," she said, kissing his eyes, his cheeks, his mouth. "I'm here, Reuben."

"I . . . I wasn't sure you'd come. . . . I hoped . . . I actually prayed . . ."

"Oh, Reuben, how I've missed you! I didn't get the . . . divorce . . ."

Reuben smiled. "I know."

"How do you know that?" Bebe asked, looking up in surprise.

He stroked her hair tenderly. "Because you love me and I love you. I could never divorce you back then any more than you could divorce me. . . . How are the boys, Simon and Dillon?"

"Fine, they send their love."

"Philippe? Is he with you?"

"No, he isn't, but he sent a letter to you." Bebe grinned suddenly, mischief dancing in her eyes. "I did bring . . . Come along and see who came with me."

His arm about her shoulder, Reuben walked with her to the château and stopped when all sixteen children ran to him, Daniel in their wake. "You arranged all this?" Reuben gasped as he lifted Bruno high on his shoulder. Amid the laughter, the squeals of joy, the hugs and kisses, Bebe watched tears stream down her husband's cheeks. "I've spent months looking for these children. I had no idea . . . I wrote letters, I did everything I could think of. . . . Thank you, Bebe, thank you from the bottom of my heart."

"Daniel deserves most of the thanks," Bebe replied, blushing. "His friends got the children out. Oh, Reuben, we have so much to tell you! It will take days."

"You son of a gun!" Reuben cried, clapping his friend on the back.

"Old times, old friend," Daniel said in a shaky voice.

"You here to stay, or . . . or just passing through?" Reuben asked gruffly as Bruno yanked at his hair, clamoring to see the red wagon.

"I thought I'd stay on. Someone has to look after you, you big galoot," Daniel said, grinning.

"I kind of feel that way myself," Bebe chirped. "Unless, of course, you don't want us." She held her breath expectantly.

In a voice tight with emotion, Reuben said, "This is where

we all belong. We're home now, and none of us is going to leave.''

Bebe positively glowed with happiness. Daniel beamed and said, ''We have one more coming in a little while: Jane. We're getting married, but that's a long story. I think we should get this kid his red wagon before he wets his pants.''

Reuben chuckled. ''I think you're right. I painted it and it's waiting; so is the bicycle. The barn is full of dogs and new pups. I've also got a goat and six chickens and two roosters. I'm trying to negotiate a cow, but it's tough. I did get a donkey for the pony cart, however.''

''Okay, single file now,'' Bebe called out, clapping her hands. ''March. Straight line, Bruno.''

The little boy did a fast double step and turned. ''I am glad to be here, monsieur. I counted the days. You are now our papa and Mademoiselle Bebe is our mama and Monsieur Daniel is our uncle,'' he said in English. ''You are proud of us, eh?''

''Damn right, kiddo,'' Reuben said huskily.

Bruno grinned. ''For you, monsieur, we learn the English to say thank you.''

''And you did a damn fine job. At the top of the stairs, down two doors, is the red wagon. Go!''

A short while later they found Bruno sitting in the wagon fast asleep, the dog curled up next to him.

''For this alone, it was worth it,'' Reuben whispered, his eyes misting. ''Mickey would be so happy.''

''Yvette . . . has there been any word?'' asked Bebe.

Reuben shook his head. ''I tried to find out, but things were so . . . there were no records. I think she's safe and will find her way here one of these days just the way you have. I've been trying to work at the farm a few days a week in case she returns. With the children here we can get it back into shape. Jesus, I've never been so glad to see anyone in my life as you two.''

''I love you, Reuben,'' Bebe said softly.

''And I love you,'' Reuben said, drawing her close.

Daniel stood quietly, watching them. ''The Three Musketeers,'' he said. ''Where is it, Reuben?''

''It no longer exists. It's a memory. *We* are the Three Musketeers.''

Bebe's eyes brimmed. At last she belonged.

''All our sins are forgiven,'' Reuben said quietly.

Bebe smiled.

Before there were
SINS OF THE FLESH,
there were
SINS OF OMISSION . . .

Fern Michaels's previous novel goes back to World War I: American soldiers Reuben Tarz and Daniel Bishop have been wounded while fighting in the French trenches. The beautiful and sensual Marchioness Michelene Fonsard whisks them away from the hospital to her lavish French château. She falls in love with Reuben and life is idyllic for the three friends—until the arrival of lovely and spoiled Bebe Rosen unleashes savage passions and desperate deceptions that are soon to explode.

Be sure to read this steamy introduction to Fern Michaels's thrilling new saga!

Have you read Fern Michaels's Texas trilogy?

TEXAS RICH

The Coleman saga begins: Moss Coleman meets beautiful Billie Ames in the Philadelphia Navy Yard and falls in love. He brings her home to Sunbridge, his 250,000-acre ranch near Austin. This is the riveting story of Billie's struggle to become her own person in a world dominated by Colemans.

TEXAS HEAT

The story of betrayal and deceit continues with Moss and Billie's daughter, Maggie, now in charge of Sunbridge. Maggie is divorcing Cranston Tanner and doing her best to raise their son, Cole. Cole and his cousin, Riley, are bitter rivals for the legacy left to only one of them by their grandfather, Seth Coleman.

TEXAS FURY

In the sizzling finale, Maggie's husband, Rand, discovers he might have a grown daughter. Cole is both betrayer of and betrayed by an old flame, while Riley is torn between Eastern traditions and western love. Maggie's daughter, Sawyer, finds success running Coleman Aviation in Tokyo, though her heart remains in Texas.

The saga as hot as the Lone Star State itself!

All of Fern Michaels's books are available in your local bookstore.

Title	SBN	Price
SINS OF OMISSION	34120-1	$5.95
TEXAS RICH	33540-6	$4.95
TEXAS HEAT	33100-1	$4.95
TEXAS FURY	31375-5	$5.95
ALL SHE CAN BE	34812-5	$3.50
CAPTIVE EMBRACES	31353-4	$4.95
CAPTIVE INNOCENCE	30804-2	$4.95
CAPTIVE PASSIONS	34683-1	$4.95
CAPTIVE SPLENDORS	31648-7	$4.95
CINDERS TO SATIN	33952-5	$4.95
FREE SPIRIT	30840-9	$3.95
TENDER WARRIOR	30358-X	$4.95
TO TASTE THE WINE	30360-1	$4.50
VALENTINA	31126-5	$4.95
VIXEN IN VELVET	34014-0	$3.95

To order by phone, call toll-free 1-800-733-3000 and use your major credit card. To expedite your order please mention interest code "MRM 19." Postage charges are $2 for the first book, 50¢ for each additional book.

To order by mail, send this page, with choices checked along with a check or money order (no cash or CODs please) to: Ballantine Mail Sales, 8–4, 201 E. 50th St., New York, NY 10022.

Prices and numbers subject to change without notice. Valid in U.S. only.